U.S.S.A.

BY DAVID MADSEN

*Black Plume: The Suppressed Memoirs of
Edgar Allan Poe*

U.S.S.A.

U.S.S.A.

DAVID MADSEN

William Morrow and Company, Inc.
New York

Library of Congress Cataloging-in-Publication Data

Madsen, David.
     U.S.S.A.
     I. Title.   II. Title: U.S.S.A.
PS3563.A344U17   1989   813'.54   88-34569
ISBN 0-688-07876-1

Printed in the United States of America

BOOK DESIGN BY BRIAN MOLLOY

To Christine

U.S.S.A.

America is like the Vatican and it sees Russia as the devil. When the devil is no longer the devil, you have a problem.

—ANONYMOUS FRENCH MILITARY OFFICER, 1988

Later the police would determine that several people had seen the body in room 1365 without reporting it.

The window washer, working his way across the sleek exterior facade of the thirteenth floor, must have seen the blood sprayed against the glass in a grotesque scarlet spider web. But he had kept quiet.

A suitcase belonging to a guest in the adjoining suite was found saturated with fresh blood, which had puddled under the door from room 1365. A bellman had answered the guest's complaint but hadn't filed a report on what he'd found.

Even the maid had been in the room. Fresh linen was squared off on the bathroom towel racks; sanitary-wrapped drinking glasses were stacked in a neat pyramid on the wet bar. She would have seen the man's body twisted on the bed, the tie stiffly knotted as though he were preparing for a business meeting. She would have been horrified by the condition of the victim—it was the raw material of nightmares—but she had kept it to herself.

The Russian police found the silence easy to explain. This may be the new Russia on paper, they patiently explained to the Americans, but it's still the old Russia inside people. In the old Russia you learned to live with fear. Paranoia was an overcoat you put on each morning, both a protective casing and a camouflage. You didn't ask needless questions. You didn't look into shuttered windows. You didn't try to pry open locked doors.

And you didn't want to know what went on on the thirteenth floor of public buildings. In Soviet mythology the thirteenth floor had been the KGB's province, the floor of shadows, of harassment and interrogation. A dead body discovered in a room on the thirteenth floor was something to be instantly forgotten.

So the body had gone unreported for an entire day. Knocks on the door to room 1365 were not answered. Phone calls were put through from the front desk, but no one picked up. Dusk dimmed to a long November night, but the lights in room 1365 didn't come on.

Later, when the shock faded, the hotel staff would joke that capitalism finally found the body. The night room service waiter, addicted to the generous tips doled out by the guest in 1365, grew concerned, when by eleven-thirty in the evening, there had been no order placed for dinner. The waiter rode the elevator to the thirteenth floor and, unnerved by the soundproofing in the French-built luxury hotel, padded down the corridor; though the rooms were fully booked, the hotel wore the scent of vacancy and isolation.

He knocked on the door to room 1365.

When there was no answer, he used his master floor key. He stepped into flickering darkness; his feet sank into blood-matted carpeting. An American Airlines billboard glittered across the Mira Prospekt, promising the world, streaking the room in red, white, and blue neon.

He saw a dark suit contorted on the bed. For some reason he looked at the feet first and saw spit-shined Italian shoes, tautly laced. Then he saw a pale Russian face and dead black eyes.

He turned on the light, then snapped it off immediately, the grisly picture impaled in his mind in that half second of illumination. Against his better judgment he called the police.

The Russians got to the body first. They'd seen death by stabbing, by strangulation, by gunshot, by vodka, by boredom. But this murder resonated with an eccentric brutality. There was too much blood; the wounds were too deep and ragged. This was overkill.

An unspoken verdict passed among the deadened Russian militiamen, as they called in their American superiors.

Somehow, they knew this crime was connected to the new Russia.

CHAPTER ONE

The last thing Moscow needed was another Gothic spire piercing the sky like a mocking exclamation point. Ringed by scaffolding, the tower of Sleeping Beauty's castle grew more grotesque day by day, as armies of construction workers sculpted it into the landscape of Izmailovo Park.

Dean Joplin cracked the car window an inch and exhaled cigar smoke into the dusk. The architect in Stalin might have approved, he thought—if not of the content, then certainly of the form. The crenellated castle tower was a perfect complement to the seven overbearing skyscrapers the "Strong Master" had erected after World War II in his symbolic attempt to establish the Soviet Union as a world power. America had built the suburbs; Russia had thrown up seven Empire State Buildings that could have been designed by Mad King Ludwig of Bavaria. Who could say what would last? You didn't see Levittown on any travel brochures. Still, Dean spent a good deal of his time staring out of car windows and would have preferred something a little more aesthetic as the city's newest landmark.

He stirred in the cracked vinyl seat of his 1975 Zhiguli-3,

flexing each muscle in deliberate sequence, a man accustomed to a cramped mannequin existence. He was a series 000 private investigator, chartered by the United States Military Occupation Police to operate in occupied Moscow and environs. He felt he spent half his time stuffed into his car on stakeouts, waiting for petty crimes and misdemeanors to unfold, but this was the first time he'd ever staked out a client he hadn't met.

He was parked on the Garaznaya Ulitsa, a side street which ran northwest toward Izmailovo Park and the Lefortovo train station. The neighborhood was better known for one of Moscow's most notorious institutions, the Lefortovo Prison. In one of the many ironies of occupation, Disneyland Russia was being constructed within easy walking distance of the prison. Dean speculated on the view from the top-floor cells. Would the prisoners be able to catch a glimpse of Tinker Bell's descent from the castle tower on opening night? As a matter of fact, since Tinker Bell's act was all done with wires, couldn't she shoot a grappling hook from Sleeping Beauty's castle into the prison and help stage an escape? Something new for the guards to worry about.

A slate gray sunset was spreading across the southwest horizon. The uncertain weather made him uneasy; the November sky promised snow but delivered only a chilling mist. The Moscow winter was well under way, and it would be months before Dean would feel warm again. Meeting an unknown client unsettled him as well. He liked to interview prospective clients in his office, where he could size them up on his home court. But the man he was to meet this evening had been calling him repeatedly, intent on hiring him for an assignment which he refused to discuss on the phone. Nor would he identify himself or provide a reference. The telephone hide-and-seek had continued for a week, until Dean had finally agreed to a meeting across the street from the Disneyland construction site. He'd given the caller a description of his car and been told to wait.

Most of Dean's cases were drab and routine. Industrial espionage primarily. Beer companies that didn't want the secret of their extra bubbles getting out. Fabric softeners stealing each other's fluffiness formulas. Moscow was a thieves' market for foreign sharks and hustlers, from multinational conglomerates to desperate insurance brokers from Sioux Falls. The Central Business Authority, formerly the Ministry of Foreign Trade, tried to regulate the privatizing of the Russian economy by handing out numerical ratings from 100 to 1,000, the lowest rating indicating complete government control, the top, most coveted rating signifying total private ownership. As yet only the Walt Disney Corporation had achieved 1,000 status; without it the company had refused to lay a single brick of its Moscow theme park. Dean's own business was so small that it fell outside the Central Business Authority's purview.

But the authority couldn't control every salesman who was out to make a buck in occupied Russia. Everyone knew about the hundred billion rubles Soviet citizens had accumulated in state savings banks at 2 percent because under the Soviet government there had been so little to spend money on, and they all wanted their chunk of it. Moscow was a salesman's paradise; its citizens' pent-up urge to consume made them ripe for the plucking. When the pluckers needed a detective, Dean was their man.

As the sky darkened, streetlights flared on, illuminating a neighborhood of closing shops and gas stations and homeward-bound pedestrians. Dean focused on every passerby, no matter how unlikely. If his prospective employer had chosen such an odd meeting point, then it was possible he'd come in an equally bizarre disguise.

The number 144 electric autobus fanned a spray of water onto Dean's windshield as it fishtailed to a stop in front of him. A construction worker stared at him from the back seat, through rain-dotted windows. He seemed to look Dean straight in the eyes, as though to ask, "What are you doing parked there like a parasite? It's quitting time. Don't you have a home to go to? Wife, kids, and TV?"

Dean squinted into the bus. Maybe his client was on board. But the only passenger to disembark was a blond woman, damp hair matted to an overworked face. She dodged through light traffic to the other side of the road and flagged a cab. A Chevy, piloted by a thickset Georgian, its interior trellised with roses and icons, snatched her up, seemingly without stopping. The bus, one taillight missing, slogged up the street and turned the corner, folded into the shadows. Dean was nearly alone now. Mist muffled the patter of distant footsteps and blurred the neon blush of a Coca-Cola billboard.

A man appeared at the corner of Zigulenkova Ulitsa, a broader avenue which paralleled the park. He was wrapped in a thick coat, much too heavy for the season. What would he do when it really got cold? His head was topped by a heavy fur hat, earflaps secured. He smoked a pipe and fiddled nervously with his tie knot with one hand, held a black briefcase in the other. He hovered at the corner, like a disoriented tourist.

A MOP car eased to a stop at the light. The two farm boy faces inside looked bilious in the light of their dashboard computer. Dean noticed the man stiffen and transfer the briefcase to his right hand, a telltale gesture. He smoked right-handed, but until now the briefcase had dangled lackadaisically in his left. It was obviously important to him.

Once the police car had proved its indifference, the man set off down the street toward Dean. He walked with a relaxed gait, his breath clouding so rhythmically Dean surmised he was whistling. Could be a new branch of police science, he mused. The analysis of speech through breath patterns, lipreading for cold climates.

The stranger made an amusing picture as he theatrically feigned nonchalance, strolling contentedly while everyone else hurried through the damp with a shivering determination to get indoors. He stopped at a glass case housing the day's *Pravda,* appeared to struggle with the Russian headlines, then stepped to the opposite side to examine the English translation.

He won't last long there, Dean thought. The day's front page dealt with dry economic matters: currency reform; bidding between Chevron and Texaco for the Leningrad gasoline franchise; the Vienna discussions, which had trudged along for

18

two years now, concerning the proposed merger of COM-ECON and the EEC. Nothing on the trial of Nadia Suslova, the teenage Kirov star accused of strangling her American lover with a pair of leg warmers. It was the only thing worth reading in the paper these days.

The man seemed unnaturally interested in the fine print. How would Dean have described the scene years ago? An operative, obviously studying a sophisticated code, in which the day's football scores could be transposed into letters, deciphered with a decoder book sewed into the lining of his overcoat.

If this was Dean's client, what the hell was he waiting for?

A loud patter, like applause at an outdoor concert, reverberated from the end of the block. Dean stared into the drizzle, which eddied in the wake of a mysterious funnel of wind. Five charcoal figures in a wedge formation, led by a squat, sweat-suited man, his face bursting with exertion, ran toward the *Pravda* case, pacing themselves like the trotters at the Moscow Hippodrome.

They were joggers. Blue handwriting scrolled across the lead man's sweatshirt—"Dodgers." Dean recognized him as a member of the Russian Occupation Secretariat, the governing body that was supposed to wither away following the elections in January. The man's paunch shuddered, and his barrel thighs jiggled together as he ran.

Dean considered his own physical condition and was grateful. At forty-three, he would not describe himself as taut and lean—his waistline expanded annually, largely because he could not bring himself to turn down a good restaurant meal—but he kept his extremities in shape, his legs with an exercise bicycle, and his arms with chin-ups and push-ups. They were the tools that mattered most. He'd never heard of anyone winning a fight merely because his stomach was flat and rippled with muscles

Reeboks slapping against the puddled cobblestones, the formation pounded past Dean's car, bodyguards bringing up the rear, radio transmitters poking from their pockets as they

looked furtively over their shoulders. An exercise of professional caution, or was Dean really that conspicuous?

His car was a modest tan box with Moscow plates. He always smoked cigars on a stakeout; they didn't burn as brightly
as cigarettes. Ensconced in the passenger seat, he could have
been taken for someone waiting for the driver to return. What
were the bodyguards staring at?

Then a Taiga van, one of the specialized new vehicles flowing from the Kama River truck plant—could a Russian Win-
nebago be far behind?—pulled even with the joggers. The
word "Vremya" was stenciled on its flanks in bold black letters.

Television news. A video camera stuck its scavenging nose
out the side window, following the runners, recording the
dedication of this government official, who, despite the hour
and the inhospitable weather, was honing his physical state to
the peak necessary to confront the country's massive problems. He'd probably hired an off-duty Vremya crew to film a
campaign commercial. With the water too cold for most
Americans to swim in, soccer season a memory, and ski season
an expectation, there weren't many photo ops for a candidate
to present himself as an up-and-at-'em hard charger. A rainy
jog through Moscow offered dramatic lighting and the opportunity to prove he wasn't afraid of pneumonia.

Dean mentally began to convert the scene into a coded cable, a habit left over from his days with the CIA: ATTN: SOVOP
COM: eyes only: "Candidate aggressive, but overweight. Recommend additional troops and crash diet." END

"Gavnoe," he spat. While he'd been dreaming up his telegram, the man with the briefcase had vanished. The television
crew must have scared him off. Even the most forthcoming of
Dean's clients wouldn't appreciate it if their meetings showed
up on the nine o'clock news. Now he'd have to repeat the
whole charade of cryptic phone calls.

Disgusted, he fitted himself into the driver's seat and cajoled
the engine to life. Radio Moscow crackled over the Zhiguli's
torn speakers, noting the time with seven hollow peals from
the chimes in the Spassky Tower. His debt to tradition paid,

the Russian disc jockey announced that beginning next week, commercials would be introduced, allowing Radio Moscow to "broadcast a wider spectrum of music." Shostakovich punctuated by Tampax ads. Dean snorted. *The conquest of Russia is complete.*

As Dean flipped off the radio, a black shape suddenly thumped against the passenger window. It was the man in the overcoat, his briefcase clutched in gloved hands. He peered in through the misted glass and motioned for Dean to roll down the window.

"Mr. Joplin?"

The face framed by the fur and earmuffs was so plain and businesslike it took Dean by surprise. Dean didn't speak, forcing the man to commit himself first.

"Mr. Joplin, we spoke on the phone yesterday morning?"

Dean recognized the voice. He nodded flatly and pushed open the squeaking passenger door.

"Richard Gardner," the man said. "I trust you'll forgive the delay?"

Gardner propped the briefcase primly on his lap and peeled off his gloves. He extended a friendly hand to Dean. Their shake was competitive. Gardner seemed to feel a viselike grip was called for but didn't really have the strength to back it up.

"Dean Joplin. Glad we finally established contact."

Gardner rubbed his hands together, as though he were warming up in front of a campfire.

"Do you mind if we drive while we talk?" Gardner asked.

So far almost every word out of his mouth had been a question.

"Well, carrying on a conversation in rush-hour traffic isn't the best way to begin a business relationship."

"It's just that I imagine you've been parked here for quite a while. Someone may have seen you."

"Plenty of people have seen me. But they wouldn't have noticed anything special. Blending in with the surroundings is part of what I get paid for."

"Well, someone may have seen me then. Please, I don't want to insist."

21

Dean shrugged. The point didn't seem worth contesting at this early stage. Make the client feel comfortable, isn't that what he was always telling Natalie, his secretary? If Richard Gardner wanted to drive, they'd drive.

"Again, let me apologize for dragging you out here like this, but really, it was the only convenient time and place for me today."

"Sure, why wouldn't a construction site in the middle of a rainstorm be convenient?"

As Dean drove toward the perimeter of the Disneyland to be, he caught brief glimpses of Gardner when they passed beneath streetlights. "Shipshape" was the word for this fastidiously dressed man in his late thirties. His clothes were not expensive, just thoughtful. His copper blond hair was neatly combed and trimmed. His eyes were gray and neutral. White, orderly teeth peeked from behind thin, determined lips. He came from what Dean's ex-wife would have called "good stock." As he unbuttoned his overcoat, he revealed a red silk handkerchief squared off in his pocket, a perfect match for the red silk tie that pierced his gray flannel suit like an artery.

This is a man who's never cut himself shaving, Dean thought.

"Not just any construction site," Gardner said. "I've lined it up so my family can take a behind-the-scenes tour. You're a father. You can imagine what a kick it is for a kid to peek inside the Matterhorn as it's being built, to see what makes a dinosaur work, to peel back the stars over Peter Pan's head and learn what makes them twinkle."

"Seems like it takes the mystery out of the place," Dean said.

"I have two children. Eight and five."

"Cute names," Dean joked.

He turned north along the Proletarskovo Vschoda, which edged along the western flank of the park. The construction site was hidden by a gaily painted plywood barrier, which opened only on the north to admit the armies of construction workers recruited from the unemployment ranks.

"Impressive as all get-out, isn't it?" Gardner said with genuine awe.

"In a depressing sort of way."

"The magic kingdom, depressing?"

"All those thousands of construction workers . . . they remind me of European peasants whose lives were spent building cathedrals, of Egyptian serfs who slaved for generations on a single pyramid."

Look what democracy is bringing you, Ivan, Dean thought. Job security and Mickey Mouse.

"You must be in the construction business if you can get your kids in here," Dean said. "They keep a tight lid on the place."

"Construction," Gardner said. "Good trade. You start with your blueprint, hire workers, order materials, and go to town. In a few months, easy as pie, you see the results. Unfortunately there are no blueprints in our business."

"Our business?"

Gardner produced an alligator billfold from his breast pocket and gingerly leafed through it, like a grandmother opening a Christmas gift to preserve the wrapping paper. A gold shield reddened in the glow of a traffic light.

"I'm with the Military Occupation Police, Mr. Joplin. Naval Division. I think that makes ours allied professions."

Much the way the four powers had carved up Berlin after World War II, the four branches of the American armed services shared police jurisdiction in Moscow. The city had been sliced into four geographic quarters governed by the military police forces of the Army, Navy, Air Force, and Marines. Gardner's attachment to the Naval Division meant he was responsible for law and order in Moscow's northeast quadrant.

"Excuse my stunned silence, Mr. Gardner. But a cop wants to hire a private investigator? It's not exactly in the daily routine, is it?"

"This isn't a routine case."

Gardner focused on Dean. The whites of his eyes were so pure they seemed never to have been bloodshot by drink or exhaustion.

"You really don't recognize me, do you?"

Dean didn't remember the face, but the demeanor and the mold in which Gardner had been cast were familiar. Prep schools. Ivy League colleges. State Department. Central Intelligence Agency. A world of men with first names like Blair and Montgomery and McGeorge.

"Nineteen seventy-seven?" Gardner hinted. "Camp Peary, Virginia? You taught a Soviet operations course. I was in section five. You were a little thinner, wore a neat little beard, made us memorize quaint little quotes you'd picked up from Soviet defectors."

Dean thought back on that distant summer of thunderstorms and weekend business picnics with mixed emotions. He'd just spent two years in obscurity, slaving in the Luxembourg section, and had been rewarded with a teaching position in the Central Intelligence Agency's training center at Camp Peary—the Farm, as it was known to the recruits who spent six sticky months there.

"You were in my class?"

"This is all a bit embarrassing, since I've never been much of a hero worshiper. But every once in a while we encounter a teacher whose insights fix in our brain; they turn us like a compass needle to a course that sets our future."

"Don't tell me. . . ."

"You don't appreciate the compliment?"

"It would have meant a lot more to me back then. I always felt like an asshole standing in front of that blackboard. It was like throwing baseballs in the dark. And call me Dean. If I revolutionized your thinking, we can be on a first-name basis."

"You don't really take me seriously, do you?"

"I can barely get the landlord to let me slide with my rent. It's a little shocking to realize I've been rattling around in somebody's brain for this long."

"Do you remember the surveillance course? The way you had us following each other all over suburban Virginia? And the final—that was a bear cat. Leave the camp; get to the drop point; make it back to class without being spotted. I sat up two straight nights working out the details of my plan. I'd been married only three months. It drove Emily crazy. I finally recruited her help. Three A.M. before the final she was helping me sketch out my route. My drop point was at National Airport, the United check-in counter. I was to leave a briefcase supposedly filled with cash, pick up a matching briefcase of Czech troop dispositions. I switched cars twice on my way to the airport, turned my coat inside out in the men's room. Snatched the briefcase, pushed my way through the crowds, fought off skycaps. Rushed to the gate like a harried commuter, nearly boarded the Eastern Shuttle, then pretended I'd forgotten my ticket and left the airport through the TWA terminal. Changed taxis twice, buses three times on my way back to the Farm. I huffed and puffed into the classroom, swollen with confidence. I snapped open the briefcase. It was the wrong one! Five minutes later you sauntered in with my briefcase, dressed in a skycap uniform! It was quite an education."

"I suppose I should be grateful for the flattery," Dean said.

"You can express your gratitude by helping me, Mr. Joplin."

"Dean."

Gardner shook his head, a skittish smile inching across his face. "That'll take some getting used to. I guess it starts in grammar school, but we never feel quite equal to our teachers. As it is, it's taken an incredible act of will to approach you like this."

"This isn't an audience; it's just a friendly chat. You don't approach me; you just ask away."

They reached the northwest corner of the park in silence and turned east on the Izmailovsky Prospekt. Dean could sense Gardner's mounting anxiety.

"The Romanovs used to unwind in Izmailovo Park. Their private little manor. You ever wonder what they'd think of all this? Can you picture Anastasia losing her breakfast on the teacups?"

Dean's stab at humor failed. Gardner's shoulders rose as if he were slowly inflating them with air. He exhaled heavily, nervously slapped the handle of his briefcase against his thigh. He turned a severe, almost painful expression on Dean, and when he spoke, his voice darkened with desperation.

"This may sound strange coming from a homicide detective, but I want you to solve a murder for me."

25

CHAPTER TWO

They were parked in the yawning mouth of an underground garage, across the street from the construction site. Though Dean had suggested they continue the interview in a nearby café, Gardner had insisted on the privacy of the car. But now he was having trouble getting to the point. His eyes wandered to an overalled mechanic who was topping a radiator with vodka, anticipating a freeze. Above the gas pumps, a sign in Russian and English proclaimed: CHAMPION SPARK PLUGS—GETTING RUSSIA STARTED AGAIN. In a country that was conducting a love affair with the automobile that matched America's car-crazed fifties, the availability of reliable foreign spark plugs was a bright spot on the dim landscape of occupation.

"Suppose you begin by telling me who was murdered," Dean prompted.

"Well, that's just the point. We're not exactly sure."

Gardner opened his briefcase and began to sort through ink-smudged notes and official documents. "Three weeks ago, on the fourth of November, a male Russian, approximate age forty-two to forty-five, was killed in his room at the Kosmos

Hotel, after registering under the name Zhores Borisovich Shukshin. The body was found by a room service waiter. Apparently several other people had seen the body but hadn't reported it, fear of the police being what it is in Russia. But there's no listing for his name and patronymic in Moscow. The name he provided the desk clerk turned out to be nonexistent. He had no ID on him, no driver's license, no Moscow residency permit, no perimeter pass if he was from out of town. Time of death was fixed between eleven P.M. and midnight, two days after his arrival at the hotel."

"Russian and American pathologists in agreement on that?"

Both were required to certify findings in a murder case. In the first year of the occupation, forensic scientists on both sides had been known to juggle the facts in politically sensitive crimes.

"That's the only thing they agree on," Gardner said. "The murder weapon is the subject of intense debate." Gardner shuddered and formed his next words gingerly. "It looks like he was killed with a saw. I was with the first squad of MOPs to view the body. . . . I'm still trying to cleanse it out of my mind." Gardner handed Dean the pathology reports. "Shukshin's throat was slit by a wide-toothed, sawlike implement. It severed the carotid artery. He bled to death."

Dean skimmed the reports with his penlight. "You think the choice of weapons is significant?"

"It's certainly quieter than a gun. But death would have been awfully slow and messy. You have no idea how much blood is contained in the human body until you see something like this."

"And it would have taken a certain finesse to wrap a saw around someone's neck. Any suspicious lumberjacks spotted in the area?"

Maybe the killer simply couldn't get hold of a gun. Under the Soviets, gun control had been strictly enforced, and it was even tougher under American occupation. Dean scoffed at the irony. For decades the National Rifle Association had warned Americans that the first thing to expect when the Commies landed was the abolition of firearms. Instead, it was the Yanks who'd junked the Russians' right to "keep and bear arms."

"I've got people who insist the murder weapon was a hand-saw. I've got a deputy coroner from Cape Cod who claims the wounds are consistent only with shark attack. I've ordered catalogs from every hardware store, every specialty tool company in Moscow. Haven't found a blessed thing."

"Was it robbery?"

"If it was, we don't know what was stolen."

"He have money?"

"The Kosmos isn't cheap."

"I mean, on him?"

"A couple hundred rubles in his wallet. A gold wedding ring, which at the current market would fetch about two thousand."

"If the killer didn't flinch from cutting a throat, he probably wouldn't have anything against sawing off a finger. No obvious suspects?"

"One very obvious one. The trouble is, no one's been able to identify him."

"That doesn't surprise me."

Gardner blushed defensively. "But we do know the suspect's occupation. He seems to have been some sort of sketch artist, you know, one of those guys who dash off your portrait for a couple of rubles. He was seen hanging around the lobby the day of the murder, trying to drum up business with the tourists. Later several guests reported seeing him arguing with Shukshin. Apparently it got quite heated. A couple of the bell-boys had to throw him out."

Gardner had rested his case. He retreated to his pipe, pressing in the tobacco with an intense screwlike motion of his index finger.

"Well, it's a fascinating story, I'll give you that. But there's one aspect of it that's bothering the hell out of me."

"And that is?"

"Why you've come to me. What makes this case so special? There's a murder a night in the squatters' camps, and nobody even blinks."

"The Kosmos is Moscow's showpiece hotel. The occupation government is trying to attract the serious investor to Moscow, you know. Multinationals lease suites there to conduct negotiations with the Business Authority. A secure, scandal-free environment is a necessity if we want our young business community to thrive. As you can imagine, a crime like this isn't the best publicity."

"Still, I've never heard of the MOPs admitting they need help with a case. Especially an important one."

"Didn't I make myself clear on that point? I've always remembered you as competent, careful. And you know Moscow inside out, I'm told. I simply need the best man for the job."

"There are those who would argue a duly appointed homicide inspector is the best man for the job."

Gardner's face slackened. His manicured facade was peeling, like old paint in the sun.

"Why have I turned to you? Simple, really. This case seems insoluble—correction: For me it's insoluble. Every line of investigation I develop dies. Every hunch I play backfires. Every guess, theory—nothing."

"When is it ever different? The answers to a case like this don't come gift-wrapped," Dean said.

"Maybe if I fill you in on my background, it might help your decision."

"It couldn't hurt."

"I was transferred here from Berlin about a year ago. I'd been waiting for an opening in the occupation police forever. Since the Company was reorganized, it's a road without a future. . . . I don't need to tell you that. Anyway, I was biding my time in this grimy little office on Alexanderplatz, grinding out organizational papers. I'd been pressuring my superiors to move me into operations, so I could get some visibility, do what I'd been trained to do.

"I finally quit the Company, just like that. Moved back into Naval Intelligence, begged, borrowed, and stole my way into the deputy chief of homicide's office here in Moscow. I'm not an abrupt person by nature, so it was quite a step for me. Sold the house in Wedding we were renovating. I pulled the kids

29

out of the American school, pulled Emily away from her friends, and moved us. The kids were just beginning to get a grip on German, and now they've got to deal with Russian."

"In that respect, you're unique. Most occupation employees spend their two years here without learning a word of it."

"I believe in assimilation. I believe in what we're trying to accomplish here. I believe in setting an example for my employees. I've even instituted a Thursday night Russian cultural evening in my department."

Gardner sneezed violently. Rather than disturb the silk handkerchief in his jacket, he blew his nose into a rumpled ball of Kleenex he pulled from his pants pocket. "I don't know how people ever get used to this weather. I've had a cold since I got to Moscow."

"And you'll probably have it when you leave. Americans never get rid of their Russian colds. 'Uncle Lenin's revenge.'"

"You see, everyone's waiting for me to fail, Mr. Joplin. I've mortgaged my future, my family's future to Russia. I foul up here, it's back to Berlin. You know the Company. If they take you back at all, they like to see you climb the ladder all over again. I've been climbing it for ten years. I can't start over. I can't put my family through that."

Dean surveyed Gardner's face as he turned his profile toward the street. Dean hunted for the twitch, the blink that would help him decide if Gardner's pain was genuine. But there was nothing, just an empty chalkboard.

"Listen, Richard. The occupation cops are run by people who don't exactly see eye to eye with me. They cleaned house after the war, and I got tossed out with the trash. I waltz in there and punch a time clock, and you'll hear one hell of an explosion. You know what that'd be? Every goddamn door in the place slamming in my nose all at once."

"That won't be a problem," Gardner said. "They won't even know you're on the case."

Dean shook his head groggily. This was getting surreal. He'd spent the last year of his life rifling mailboxes and peeping through corporate keyholes, leading what he called a career of insignificance, and suddenly a murder investigation dropped into his lap. And now he was supposed to conduct it in secret.

"That'll never work, Richard. I need access to information. Physical evidence. I'll need to interview suspects. How will I—"

"Get paid? Directly from me. Cash, any currency you name. No checks or wires. I hope that's all right. Information? You can have everything I have. It's my case after all."

"They count every doughnut and cup of coffee over there. Balancing the books is a religious experience. How will you mask your payments to me?"

"I'll pay you out of my own pocket. I'll just be another one of your clients. I may have to concoct some explanation for my wife. . . ."

"I guess you could tell her you were squandering the money on a mistress."

"She'd never believe me."

"Not the philandering type, huh? Good. Makes you less susceptible to blackmail. Did I teach you that?"

"You know what you taught me, Mr. Joplin? Possibilities. You taught me that change can happen anytime, to any institution. Look at the work that's going on across the street. There are still possibilities, and for me I think they're here in Moscow. But I need your help to keep me afloat temporarily. If you knew how difficult it is for me to speak my mind like this . . . Look, I've been sitting here gushing a load of sentimental nonsense. I know I was just another white shirt and tie to you back at Camp Peary, so don't help me for old times' sake. Look on it as a simple business transaction. You can use the money; I can use the help."

Dean usually didn't trust men who were so flawlessly groomed as Gardner; they were so busy with details they never saw the big picture. But Gardner was so uncomfortable, so apologetic that Dean felt he couldn't possibly be talking him into some bizarre trap.

"Ah, here they are," said Gardner, disrupting Dean's thoughts.

At the entrance to the garage appeared three figures, an adult woman and two children, backlit by the headlights of passing traffic. Gardner's family, fresh from their tour of Disneyland.

A darkly beautiful woman with shoulder-length black, curly hair bent over a pale boy with freckles, jeans, and a build other kids would call skinny, and a girl, cute but sticklike, laminated in red plastic boots, slicker, and rain cap.

Dean and Gardner got out of the car to greet them.

"It's hopeless," the woman called to Gardner. "They want us to take them out for vodka, or they say they'll stay outside all night and catch pneumonia."

Gardner grinned, rekindled by the sight of his family. "Tell them if they guzzle too much vodka, it'll rot their stomachs and they'll have to have them removed," he called, his voice booming in the cold garage.

"I have stubborn kids," Gardner explained to Dean. "I'm New England; Emily's Latin. You can imagine the genes."

"Jack says he's read they can feed you through your veins. He thinks that sounds neat and wants to try it," Emily said.

Emily and her children huddled again amid more hushed inducements. Eventually the two kids snapped open their umbrellas and disappeared around the corner.

"They want to test their new umbrellas," Emily said as she approached. "We'll pick them up on the way out."

There was something undeniably erotic about Emily Gardner as she shook the water from her hair, toweled her face with her husband's silk handkerchief, and smoothed the rumples from her raincoat, gliding her hands along her thighs. Perhaps it was her movements, which recalled those a woman makes stepping from the water after a swim, always a compelling image in sun-starved November. Dean found himself wishing he were on the receiving end of the healthy kiss she bestowed on her husband. He was envious of their comfortable passion.

Gardner introduced them, his arm entwined around Emily's waist.

"Emily, you'll never guess who I just ran into as I was coming from the car. Dean Joplin, remember?"

Her piercing bronze eyes examined Dean quickly, and she shook hands politely. Dean found it difficult not to stare. Her features were boyish yet brittle, her skin a sunny duck egg brown. She seemed a mix of southern hemispheres—Latin American, Asian—perhaps a trace of Mediterranean added for spice. She reminded Dean of the type of exotic woman he'd often pursued in the past, with little success.

But when she spoke, it was in wide-open spaces American phrasing, suggesting that sometime in her family's history her ethnic past had been consciously buried.

"I'm sorry I don't recall you, Mr. Joplin. Did you work with Richard in Berlin?"

Dean was a little miffed at Gardner. He hadn't agreed to take the case, and here he was, already forced into inventing a cover story.

"No, I'm with the disarmament team. Swords into plowshares, you know?"

"Interesting work?"

"Not really. You've seen one warhead, you've seen them all."

"You're not radioactive, are you?"

"Just to be on the safe side, I'd have Richard go over you with a Geiger counter tonight."

"Emily, Mr. Joplin was an instructor back at Camp Peary." An edge had slipped into Gardner's voice. It was obvious he didn't enjoy his wife's ability to banter sarcastically when he didn't seem capable of it himself.

"How could I forget Camp Peary?" She pointed sharply at Dean. "You very nearly caused our premature divorce. We'd just gotten married, and instead of spending my time in bed, I spent it in training exercises, running around Washington, trying to give my husband the slip. Come to think of it, I did pick up a couple of valuable pointers if I should ever decide to have an affair." She suddenly focused an intense gaze on Dean's chest. "I love your tie clasp, Mr. Joplin."

There was an uncomfortable pause.

"Emily collects them," Gardner explained.

"Among other things," Emily said.

Dean handed the clasp to Emily. "It's all yours."

She protested meekly, then dropped it into her purse. She lit up a cigarette and blew a fragrant cloud into the cold air.

"Cloves. She's trying to quit the real thing," Gardner said.

"I'm not an exhibit, Richard; you don't need to explain me."

Gardner coughed. He gave Emily a demonstrative kiss, in an obvious effort to allay the growing tension. "Shall we be going?" he said. "I don't want Jack to be late for Russian."

Gardner plucked his briefcase from Dean's car.

"You'll think over the offer then?" he asked.

"On the basis of what I've heard so far, we might as well go ahead."

"Good. I'll call you with the details."

"What offer is that, Rich?"

"Mr. Joplin's agreed to buy my golf clubs. Not much you can do with them in winter."

"Thank God. Rich only took up the damn game to win a promotion, if you ask me. Well, we're getting along quite well now without those ridiculous social rituals. Come to dinner next week, Mr. Joplin. Who knows what else you might find worth buying in Rich's closet?"

The Gardners excused themselves and walked to a cream-colored, four-door Moskvich with MOP license plates. The car spouted a hot blue burst of exhaust as it lumbered out of the garage. The two kids and their rainbow-colored umbrellas met the car at the garage entrance and tumbled in. Through the rear window Dean saw Gardner trade fisticuffs with his children, who were delighted as he swung wildly above their heads in a flurry of deliberate misses.

Gardner's cover story about meeting Dean while getting his car was puzzling. He could understand Gardner's need to keep his request for help a secret from the police. But why go to the trouble of deceiving his wife as well?

"All happy families are alike. Every unhappy family is unhappy in its own way," said Tolstoy. Which were the Gardners? Dean wondered.

CHAPTER THREE

T he Kalinin Prospekt was the future as imagined by a 1950's comic book artist. Flying cars would have been at home in its spacious canyons. Businessmen, with jet packs strapped to their backs, could have happily rocketed from its glass apartments to its glass offices. Under the Soviet regime, offices kept their lights on all night, spelling out the abbreviation CCCP in twinkling twenty-story-high letters. Because its massive audacity was still impressive, many young high-profile enterprises were headquartered there. Joplin Investigations was there, too, its dark, cramped cubicle waiting to capitalize on its proximity to big, glamorous, and aggressive. But so far Dean's rented furniture hadn't accommodated either the famous or the notorious, his rented fax machine hadn't brought him any urgent international dispatches, and his rented copy machine hadn't duplicated any important documents or life-and-death legal briefs.

Dean had just gone through the mail, which he gathered daily from the PO boxes and drop sites he still maintained around Moscow. Four years ago the drop sites had bulged with coded messages and agent payments; now they fed him junk mail and bills.

He stared out his one smudged window at the Kalinin Prospekt, where a campaign poster was being unfurled from the roof of a twenty-five story office building. Like a giant window shade, it would eventually cover ten stories with its Mount Rushmore-size portrait of a politician and his glib slogan. Russians were used to being served their politics larger than life, and the Election Authority felt that by preserving the physical trappings of prewar politics, the transition to democracy would be less traumatic.

"What do you see out there that I don't, Mr. Joplin? The future? The past? A woman undressing in a window?"

Natalie Yurchenko, his Ukrainian secretary, had edged through the door from the outer office. She was a short, diligent woman in her sixties, loyal to Dean, gifted with a bright sense of humor and a quirky formality which permitted her to tease him but not to address him by his first name. She also had the advantage of being married to Gennady Yurchenko, the owner of the White Palm, Dean's favorite bar. She cradled a pot of tea and a stack of information Dean had asked her to obtain.

"I was just empathizing with those poor bastards across the street," Dean said. "They fight for years to get a corner office with a view, then poof, they're buried beneath a six-foot mustache."

"It has its advantages. I spent six years in the accounting section at GUM. Every May and November, when Red Square was decorated for the parades, they'd slap a placard of Vladimir Ilyich across the facade of the store, completely covering our window. As the sun set, our office would be bathed in the most flattering red light. If it weren't for that light, I'm convinced Gennady would never have asked me to marry him."

"Don't tell me your marriage was based on something as superficial as looks," Dean said.

"It was based on something as superficial as lust." She dropped a pile of manila envelopes on his desk. "*Russian Law Review*, 'Law Enforcement in Moscow Today,' 'Roster of Occupation Forces and Officers,' 'Trends in Occupation Policy.' You private investigators do some awfully exciting reading."

Dean had sent Natalie to the Leninka, the Lenin Library, to dig up information on Richard Gardner in the law enforcement journals. His first order of business was the same on every case: Learn everything about the employer. She'd been waiting in line there since 8:00 A.M., and it was now 2:00 in the afternoon. The explanation for the crowds was not a sudden upswing in Soviet literacy—the Russians had always been voracious readers—but a dramatic explosion in the quantity of material that was now available to the public. The Leninka had been infamous for its system of double cataloging. Those books approved for the average citizen were found in one section; those books deemed *spetskhrany*—the special holdings restricted to party members and the scientific elite— were housed in a closed wing of the library, filed according to a secret alphabetizing system. Now the library's entire stock was available to everyone, and Russians began lining up at 6:00 A.M. to catch up on what they'd missed.

"I should confess I spent my lunch hour going through scientific treatises on antisatellite weaponry, criticism from foreign Communist parties, and novels by someone named Judith Krantz. I can't see why this was all top secret."

Dean began to sift through the information on Richard Gardner. The picture that emerged was of a man whose career had proceeded in a straight line, a constant upward grind, never spectacular, but free from severe setbacks.

He was born in Concord, Massachusetts. News clippings traced his patriotism to childhood games played on the Lexington green and other Revolutionary War battlefields. His father was a career naval officer and Vietnam War hero, who used his influence to rent *Old Ironsides* for his son's tenth birthday party. Richard had graduated from Annapolis and joined Naval Intelligence, assigned to an intergovernmental office liaisoned to the CIA. Married in 1970 to Amelia Benes, the daughter of an émigré Cuban intelligence officer and an American translator employed at the American Embassy in Havana before the revolution. Marrying into a staunchly anti-Castro family couldn't have hurt Gardner's career, Dean thought. The only deviation from this wholesome norm was a brief hospitalization in Moscow last year for "exhaustion," a common enough occurrence in the postwar chaos.

Dean stared at a news clipping of Gardner accepting his Moscow post, all confidence and patriotism and boyish enthusiasm. "What really brought you to me?" Dean asked the picture. He looked at the gorgeous figure of Emily. Consigned to the wifely background, she nevertheless dominated the photograph.

He knew he would take the case.

That evening Dean ate at the Yakimauka, an Uzbek restaurant, gorging himself on its famous "lagman," a meat and noodle soup which he swore was skimpier now that Pillsbury was marketing the dish as a frozen dinner.

He compensated for the heavy dinner by pushing himself through twenty laps at the Moskva swimming pool. He suffocated in the prerevolutionary decadence of the Sundonovsky baths, where he endured a torturous massage for the reward of a cold shower and a pitcher of beer. Dean sat in a private booth, listening to the hiss of steam and the crackle of dried branches slapping against flushed skin, as old-line Russians tried to banish the poisons of city living from their pores.

A picture formed in his mind: the chart of his career superimposed on that of Richard Gardner. Where Gardner's was a straight, gradually ascending arrow, Dean's was a choppy series of ups and downs, like the graph of a volatile stock.

Russian studies degree from Berkeley. The realization that it was a useless scrap of paper outside academia. Travel. Searching. Failed novels begun at European sidewalk cafés. Recruitment by the Central Intelligence Agency, which'd promised him RUSSIA. By then he didn't care how he got there. A scholarship to the Defense Language Institute in Monterey, California, and then the drama of his first posting, the Luxembourg desk at Langley headquarters. Initial exposure to the government's uncanny ability to employ you where you were needed least. Firings. Attitude problems. The summer teaching at Camp Peary. Finally the realization of a dream: He was transferred to the Clandestine Services of the Soviet/East European (SE) division, the crème de la CIA crème, and was assigned to Moscow. Along the way he'd acquired and lost a family.

When Dean first arrived in Russia, the Moscow station had been evenly divided between hawks and doves. As war began to appear inevitable, the sides polarized even further. By the time American and Russian soldiers met on the battlefields of East Germany and Syria, in the waters of the North Atlantic and the Mediterranean, the postwar jurisdictional spoils were already being carved up. The hawks had long argued that a nuclear war with the Soviet Union could be won. Unexpected twists of history—a coup in the Kremlin and the stubborn refusal of the Soviet's solid-fuel missiles to fire—had proved them right. The doves, of which Dean had been one, were booted from the nest.

In theory the CIA was no more, absorbed into the bureaucracy of the Occupation Military Authority. The enemy had been defeated. Who was there left to spy on?

Dean's decision to open his own detective agency had been made much easier by the grim career choices that faced a retired spy.

The first option was guard duty.

Depending on which government agency's glossy report you believed, the Soviet Union had, at the time hostilities with the United States broke out, 1,298 land-based missiles, 300 launch control centers, 5 airfields capable of supporting fighters and bombers, 1,200 air defense missile sites, 3 submarine bases, 5 naval fleet headquarters, and a still-undetermined number of factories and research facilities developing or producing chemical and biological weapons. Since the primary goal of the American occupation had been security through total disarmament, thus preventing another, more devastating war, all that hardware had to be guarded, down to the last bullet. A job for accountants and retirement-age clerks.

The second choice was data processing.

Before the war there had been approximately a hundred thousand KGB agents, not counting border guards and customs officials, and an unpublished number of GRU, military intelligence, operatives. They had generated thousands of volumes of information, thousands of miles of encoded telemetry, millions of anecdotes, observations, and insights, all tenaciously recorded over two years of debriefing sessions conducted in cold concrete basements of KGB buildings across the Soviet Union.

It all had to wind up somewhere. It had to be cross-referenced and collated, the lies separated from the half lies. It was like using a flour sifter on a grain elevator.

Firms in the Silicon Valley were growing rich developing computer programs which would help the occupation's data processors organize the blizzard of information their satellites and fiber optic phone lines were collecting every day. So, if you were willing to sit at a computer screen as Cyrillic nonsense paraded across your forehead, turning pasty white in a room without windows under fluorescent, scalpellike light, they'd retrain you and increase your pension contributions 17 percent retroactively. There was only one condition: They didn't appreciate it if you asked why. What would they do with all this information now that the enemy had lost the war?

Why, analyze it, of course.

And then?

Get back to work, coffee break's over.

CHAPTER FOUR

"'**B**ut I reckon I got to light out for the territory ahead of the rest, because Aunt Sally, she's going to adopt me and civilize me, and I can't stand it. I been there before.'"

Dean closed the book and set his empty tea glass on its back cover, already darkly ringed from a hundred cups. Vera Polivanova's eyes were closed. She was wound into the corner of the couch as though she were asleep in a cold bed, drawing into herself for warmth, but he could tell from the irregularity of her breathing that she was awake.

"So what do you think? All American literature is supposed to stem from this one book."

"I have already read it. In Russian, in the school."

"What? Why the hell didn't you tell me? For two weeks I've been talking myself hoarse. I could have saved what was left of my voice."

"I wanted to hear it in English. My literature tutor was not as gifted as you with the southern dialects."

"My southern accent wouldn't get me a mile past the Virginia state line, honeychile. You've just never been exposed to the real thing."

"There is one thing I don't understand, though."

"One thing? That's pretty impressive. Entire careers have been devoted to this one book."

"I told you. I've read it before. My question is as follows: If Jim is a fleeing slave and Huckleberry Finn is aiding him in his escape, why do they continue to follow the river, which leads them deeper into the South, deeper into the slave country?"

She sat up, rotated her shoulders to clear a cramped muscle, and turned to face him, smiling in satisfaction, her eyes still closed.

"You ever try to paddle *up* the Mississippi? Look, the river's just a metaphor."

"Yes, quite possibly. For America, always so convinced it's leading the world downriver to freedom."

Dean laughed. "I guess you can take the girl out of the party, but you can't take the party out of the girl. A Marxist interpretation of Huck Finn? Sam Clemens had critics shot for less."

Vera opened her startling green eyes, eyes that always seemed afraid of missing the slightest detail.

"The old habits are difficult to annul. When I was preparing for the entrance exams to Moscow State University, my parents engaged a literature tutor." She smirked. "He turned out to be somewhat of a sex educator as well, but he was hired because his political interpretations of American writing had been approved at the highest levels of the Ministry of Culture. Take Superman, for example," she said, without a trace of irony.

She turned her angular face toward him, the gray tracings of dawn backlighting her dusty hair. There was something iconlike about her face, in the lacquered smoothness of her skin, and the seeming absence of perspective; she always appeared to be staring at him straight on.

"The Man of Steel is midway along the dialectical path toward the finalization of the new Soviet man. Caught between identities, on one hand, he's Superman, a triumphant, selfless, hardworking leader, totally divorced from private property, able to ignore class distinctions—"

"And leap over tall buildings in a single bound," he reminded her.

"On the other hand, he's Clark Kent, an exploited worker without even a smattering of trade union consciousness, a lackey of Perry White and the bourgeois class that owns the *Daily Planet.* Eventually these twin identities will merge, and the worker and the leader will be fused . . . communism!"

"Where does that leave poor Lois Lane?"

"Lois is on her way toward total emancipation. She's engaged in common productive labor. But she must be on her guard. Her infatuation with Superman is dangerous. Wantonness in sexual matters is bourgeois. As Lenin reminded us, 'Self-control is not slavery, not even in love.'"

Vera punctuated her remarks by draining a pewter vodka tumbler filled with the mix of Coca-Cola and vodka that she loved and strolled through the living room, stretching the drowsiness from her body.

Dean's apartment was in a chestnut brown eight-story shoebox on the Sadovoya Koltso, the Garden Ring Road. Because Soviet construction had emphasized assembly-line speed and uniformity, high rises grew out of the Moscow soil like weeds after a rainstorm. Addresses were an alphabet soup of Building X, Entry B, Block H, Apartment V. Apocryphal stories spoke of men returning from work to the wrong apartment and not noticing the difference for years, spawning entire duplicate families, their mistakes only uncovered at their deaths when city officials were called to cart away the bodies, and the dental work did not match official records.

His apartment had three bedrooms, but two were vacant, still waiting for the wife and son who had once intended to join him. The rooms sat there, like white scars, still stacked with paint cans and wallpaper.

Because Dean's building had been designed to house foreign journalists and minor diplomats, his apartment was more spacious than the nine square meters of living space Lenin ordained were the birthright of every Soviet citizen.

So Vera was able to stake out a lengthier course as she

43

paced, laying out the party line on everyone from Faulkner to John Updike.

There were hundreds of thousands of physically displaced people in the occupied Soviet Union. There were millions of mentally displaced, of whom Vera was one.

Most Russians were bored with politics. They ignored the blitz of propaganda, the lurid red banners, the exhortations to work, fulfill the plan, surpass their quotas. They were indifferent to the party bureaucracy, concerned only when it failed to deliver a promised shipment of lamb cutlets or bumped them back down the waiting list for an apartment in favor of some party apparatchik.

But Vera had been a true believer. From her first days with the Young Pioneers she'd clung to Uncle Lenin's words: The party is the mind, honor, and conscience of our epoch.

For many, party membership was a ticket to a snazzier car, higher salaries, a trip abroad, but to Vera it had been gospel.

Through loyalty, diligence, and her father's influence, she had finagled her way into the lower echelons of the Moscow city party hierarchy. It was a privileged position. Because of Moscow's importance, one could occasionally advance directly to the republican apparatus, detouring around the regional committees.

Then, in the fifteen days between the declaration and the cessation of hostilities, the armies of Lenin stopped their forward march. Imagine a devoted priest, serving his church for years, without doubt or hypocrisy, confronted with the incontrovertible proof that there is no God, an unsubstantiated myth that had now been disproved. The day after the armistice Vera faced a featureless horizon, a world with no borders, no signs to warn her when she approached the edge.

The Communist party machinery was absorbed by the occupation and grudgingly handed limited powers. Busywork. The same way the Communist party had presided over the facade of the Soviet government, so the occupation now dominated the party. It was renamed Shadowland by those who chose to remain and carry out its uninspired, harmless tasks.

Vera was not one of them. She became an ideological vagabond. She wandered, searching for a myth to hang her life on. Religion. Travel. In three years she visited all fifteen republics, meandered through eight different jobs. She'd dyed her hair, lost weight, gained weight. Conducted affairs with a series of men of different nationalities. Dean had dubbed her "Womanhood's Ambassador to the United Nations."

Finally she'd found the ideal job to match her unsettled personality. She landed a position with Mostours as a guide, escorting foreign tour groups through the occupied Soviet Union.

Dean had met her on a bus tour of Moscow. Vera had been attempting to explain what irony of history had planted Detsky Mir, Moscow's largest toy store, next door to the Lubyanka, the KGB's infamous headquarters. Dean had been tracking an adulterous couple who masked their indiscretions by riding the tour bus to a different hotel every afternoon.

Dean and Vera became part-time lovers.

They tried to conduct their affair in a vacuum. Vera knew Dean had been married, had a teenage son, but knew only that the dissolution of his marriage had something to do with career and thwarted ambition. Dean knew Vera had never married, placing party above personal considerations. He knew her father was dying an intellectual death with the collapse of Leninism; that her mother had reacted to war and occupation by turning to mediums and a belief in reincarnation. On one occasion Vera had had to restrain her mother when she decided that a setting of eighteenth century gold tableware on display in the Kremlin's Arsenal Museum belonged to her family and had insisted on "liberating" it.

Otherwise, their lives were left blank to each other. Instead of recalling incidents from their pasts, as new lovers do in bed, they read aloud to each other classics from Russian and American literature.

"Dean, I must discuss something with you," Vera said.

"I don't think I can endure more pronouncements from the Ministry of Culture."

"It's about my job. I am being considered for a promotion."

"It's about time. I sat through a lot of tour guides when I

was working that divorce case. None of them had a tenth of your . . . imagination."

Dean folded his arms around Vera's waist, joining his palms in the warm dab of sweat in the small of her back. The white cotton blouse with the oversize pockets which arched across her breasts; the navy blue tie unknotted around her white neck; the severe black skirt designed to discourage male advances—for some reason he found her dour uniform unbelievably arousing.

"You can congratulate me without fondling me, can't you?"

"Who's fondling? I'm embracing."

"That sort of embracing usually leads to me undressing."

"We've got time. It's barely light out. Even the Japanese aren't dedicated enough to sightsee at this hour. Besides, I was hoping you could show me some of the techniques your tutor imparted to you back in your student days."

"You wouldn't find them very interesting. He followed a strict party line, even in bed."

Vera pulled away. She was making a point. They'd made love earlier in the week, an unexpected, spectacular session in her Rossiya Hotel room. A repeat performance so soon might signal the beginnings of a schedule.

"I suppose we met our quota for the week already. Fulfilled the plan?" He kissed her cheek. "For someone with good news, you're awfully edgy."

"That is my point. Is it good news?"

"Is it more money?"

"I presume so."

"Then how can it be bad news?"

Vera walked the edges of the living room, dragging a knuckle across the bare white walls. "Did I ever tell you my father's theory of progress?"

"I can imagine. Feudalism leads to capitalism, leads to socialism, leads to communism. The unswerving path of mankind."

"It was more personal than that. Party membership was a tradition in my family. Much the way your West Point dominated American military families. My grandfather was in the

46

secretariat of the local party committee. My father was a middle-level functionary in the Moscow oblast, the regional party apparatus. One notch higher. With the help of a historical mathematician, my father mapped out the career paths of his descendants. He dreamed that I would rise to the *rezpublika* level, that I would climb one step higher up the mountain than he had. My children would progress to the Central Committee, and at the current rate of advancement my grandchildren—his great-grandchildren—would occupy seats in the Politburo; maybe one of them would even be elected general secretary. As you can see, it was all according to plan, and it has all vanished now. Do I wish to begin climbing a different ladder all over again, only to have the ladder snatched away? Today communism is abolished. Tomorrow it might be tourism."

Her dilemma hit home. He'd been wondering about his decision that morning to take the Gardner case. Was it really time to climb out of his comfortable, unrewarding routine? Time to start challenging himself again? Did he miss it that much?

A Russian pessimist is convinced life will get much worse. A Russian optimist knows life can't get any worse. In a country that loved to describe itself in metaphors, as though its grotesque, unknowable size could be pared down to a few choice words, it was the single most revealing description of the Russian soul Dean had ever encountered.

They debated the future inconclusively for another hour. But the future had become a meaningless concept. They had seen how it could flip-flop at the push of a button. Human nature urged them to make plans, but logic told them to live for the present.

Vera knotted her tie and stepped into her low-heeled walking shoes. Dean turned off the overhead light, which the glare of dawn, reflecting off new-fallen snow, made unnecessary.

"Will you choose another book for me next time?" she asked.

"Any requests?"

"Nothing western. No dust. Something romantic."

Dean led Vera to the bookshelf, the one concession he'd made to giving his apartment that lived-in look. He'd crafted the shelves himself, designing them asymmetrically to fit the apartment's sloppily framed corners, none of which managed ninety degrees. His collection was an orange wave of British Penguins, broken only by Russian classics, their spines a rainbow of whatever dye the Soviet bookbinder had in surplus. Lately the Book-of-the-Month Club had become available, but Dean couldn't bring himself to subscribe. Another old habit he was sentimentally attached to: Don't give your address to anybody you don't have to.

"How about *The Great Gatsby*? You can't get much more romantic than that. It's about an ex-bootlegger who destroys his life and those around him to win a girl who exists only in his memory."

"Is there a girl like that in your life?"

"Nothing like that. I'm just one of those guys like Gatsby with an unhealthy attachment to the past. I tend to think last year was better than this year, yesterday was better than today, that I was happier a half hour ago than I am now."

Dean kissed Vera, tasting vodka and sleep on her lips.

"You would have made a terrible Communist," she said.

She laughed and opened the door. From the stone-cold corridor came the rumble of water pipes and the smell of freshly ground coffee. Vera inhaled with appreciation.

"Well, our coffee's gotten better under the occupation. Even you have to admit that."

"Think what it would have been like if the Italians had marched in."

"Before the war you couldn't even get a decent cup in the Politburo dining room . . . or so I've heard."

"So that's why Brezhnev always looked so tired. And our intelligence reports said he'd been up all night fretting over the harvest."

Vera stepped into the corridor and blew Dean a kiss.

"Thank you for the book, Dean. It was a lovely time. I'm sorry that Huck Finn didn't make me feel any sexier."

"The Mississippi isn't a very sexy river."

She flounced down the hall, and as Dean shut the door, he heard her exchange good mornings with the elevator operator who'd just come on duty. It was 5:30 A.M., the hour Moscow struggled to life.

A twin-rotor Swidnik police helicopter whopped overhead, perhaps chasing illegals back to the squatters' camps, maybe beginning the day's patrols of the Moscow perimeter, but most likely, at this hour, on its way to one of the country restaurants outside town which offered discount breakfasts to police chopper crews.

Dean walked to the window, which was curtained in smoke-stained yellow fabric. It reminded him suddenly of the color goldenrod, from the sixty-four-piece crayon collection with sharpener which had been his prized possession as a boy. That goldenrod crayon represented his first real attempt to recolor the world to his liking. During summer, the days artificially stretched by daylight savings time, he'd been forced to go to bed before dark. To conjure up a more exotic vista than the one presented by his suburban backyard, he'd colored his window goldenrod, working several crayons to stubs, attempting to duplicate the light of a sunset on the west coast of Africa, as he remembered it from the latest issue of *National Geographic.*

He chuckled. How had his mother ever cleaned it off?

He drew back the curtains and looked down at Zubovsky Boulevard. Snow, the season's first, had fallen during the night. Vera emerged from the building. With an over-the-shoulder wave she joined a jumble of gray coats and pushed into a bus.

Giant, hand-painted snowflakes ornamented the bus, the Transportation Authority's effort to spread a little postwar cheer. The Moscow city buses now operated in four seasonal coatings: There was the white snow on blue sky, which had been rushed into service this morning to commemorate the arrival of winter; silver birch on green grass was the spring motif; in summer the buses were painted with a huge greeting card sun; and in autumn, falling leaves were stenciled onto their rusting steel sides. The buses still spumed brown, unfiltered exhaust, which eventually settled on these pastoral settings, creating rolling murals of a polluted countryside, hardly the intended effect. But a few hundred gallons of paint were less bother than a couple of thousand catalytic converters. It was classic *pokazukha,* the type of cosmetic improvement the Americans felt they could afford, and the Russians had long been used to.

Mist rose from the Tschaika swimming pool a few blocks away. It resembled a simmering cement bowl of soup in which three pink overweight men were about to immerse themselves.

This is the key to Russia's survival, Dean thought. In the bleakest of circumstances, their country overrun by invaders, there were still Russians willing to rise at 5:00 A.M. and pad barefoot across icy cement for a swim. Undoubtedly, back in the desperate winter of 1812, Napoleon had awakened from a warm bed to see three similar hardy souls carve a swimming hole in the Moskva River, had turned to his troops, and said, "*Allez, vite* . . . we're packing it in. We'll never whip these fanatics."

Would the Americans ever say the same?

CHAPTER FIVE

D ean had spent the night in the bed of a murder victim before. It was a morbid father-and-son outing he'd tried to keep secret from his wife, Molly.

His son, Patrick, had been fifteen at the time, his life circumscribed by secret six-packs and television cop shows. He was becoming lazy and uninquisitive. Molly, a proud, hardworking New Englander, had not grown up lazy or difficult and had trouble dealing with these traits in her son.

Patrick began to show an interest in Dean's job, but only in its tactical aspect. He was bored by politics but fascinated by the lurking potential for violence. Dean tried to explain to Patrick that he had never fired a gun in a nontraining situation, had never dropped out of a plane in a parachute, had never slit a Communist throat, but his son didn't want to hear it.

He'd tried to divert Patrick's growing fascination with mayhem by inviting an occasional dinner guest from the Company, from the worlds of criminology, psychiatry, and law. But he sadly realized that Patrick's interest was not in the psychology of criminality but in the bloodletting itself, in weaponry and technique.

So, when Patrick developed an unhealthy obsession with a grisly motel shoot-out in McLean, Virginia, Dean told Molly he was taking his son camping. Instead, they checked into the actual room where the crime took place. He hoped to impress on his son the squalor and desperation that accompany the average murder, to separate it from the palm-lined streets and parquet floors of television death.

They'd told Molly they were going camping. It was a move that symbolized the split in their marriage. Molly believed in steadiness in life and in raising children. Dean voted for shock treatment; he felt that dramatic gestures were required to fix dramatic problems. Only later did he admit to himself that he was too busy to influence his son gradually. Emergency measures were all he had time for.

The Wagon Wheel Motel faced on a scrapyard. The rooms faintly stank of vomit and Formula 409; the television sets were hospital castoffs with nightmare colors.

He talked Patrick through the crime: the shots fired through the dirty window by the jealous husband; the crippled path across the carpet followed by the bleeding lovers, who, attempting to escape, crawled to the bathroom, where they both were shot again. Dean and Patrick examined the fading bloodstains in the carpet, inspected the headboard, chipped by gunfire. He told Patrick about the bits of skin and hair the police would have had to scrape from the blood-slick imitation-cedar paneling, tried to describe how the room would smell when the bodies were discovered, how the victims would be buried and conveniently forgotten by shamed relatives, how the thick-witted killer, who hadn't bothered with a disguise and had barely bothered to run, had been found in a neighborhood bar, playing his usual game of darts, and how he'd blown his brains out beneath the Miller High Life sign, as four scared cops tried to arrest him.

The experiment seemed successful at first. Patrick awakened Dean at 4:30 A.M. He couldn't sleep; he was grossed out; the place gave him the creeps. They'd gone camping the next morning after all. They had a trunkful of sleeping bags and fishing gear they'd loaded up in front of Molly as part of their cover story. Dean couldn't recall a single detail of the camping trip: where they'd pitched their tent; whether they'd caught any fish or just poison ivy; how the burned steaks and bitter coffee had tasted. What remained from the whole sick episode was the unexpected fear on Patrick's face and the clammy grip of his son's hands on his shoulders, as he'd been shaken awake in the motel.

The Kosmos Hotel on the Mira Prospekt was certainly not the Wagon Wheel. Discos, saunas, several bars and restaurants, twenty-six stories of "luxury" which overlooked the Permanent Exhibition of Economic Achievements. But the Soviets had not trusted those same workers whose accomplishments were so massively glorified in the exhibit with the creature comforts of a four-star hotel. That task had been turned over to the French, who'd poured the concrete, raised the girders, and designed everything, down to the bellhops' brass buttons.

Three days after accepting the case from Gardner, Dean checked into the Kosmos Hotel and registered as A. Hidell. Aliases had long been second nature to him, and it was only last year that he'd applied for a driver's license in his own name. But his choice of aliases was becoming sick, perhaps a sign of his growing boredom with his job. A. Hidell was the name Lee Harvey Oswald had used to mail-order the Mannlicher-Carcano carbine that had killed JFK.

In keeping with the cover story he'd improvised for Emily, he listed his occupation as assistant deputy inspector with the Disarmament Authority.

The desk clerk, a surly Leningrader, was unimpressed. "Do you intend to impound the dining room's forks and knives? In the right hands they could be weapons of resistance."

"Son, I understand how you're pissed off. If the Russians had marched into Texas, they'd have had to confiscate every last needle off every last cactus. But I'm just doin' a job." He broke into a loud Texas guffaw. Dean was an expert laugher, able to chuckle, snicker, snigger, and chortle in as many inflections as there were American accents and gifted enough in foreign languages to be able to color his French with a Belgian titter or an Alsatian giggle. It was his humble addition to the literature of deep cover.

Dean palmed the key to room 1365. Russians were not superstitious when it came to the number thirteen, and it was one of the issues facing the Office of Cultural Continuity: Should the floors in occupation government buildings be renumbered?

Dean let a teenage bellhop carry his suitcase up to the room, which lay at the end of a long wallpapered corridor. A balalaika tune stirred softly from Muzak speakers tucked into the ceiling. Dean tipped the bellboy and entered the room alone.

Pictures of Patrick and the Wagon Wheel Motel snapped through his mind like static on a phone line. He drank a glass of ice water from a plastic pitcher to steady himself.

The room was actually a small suite. A sitting room adjoined the bedroom and could be closed off by a set of double doors. Everything had been designed for businessmen, not tourists. The emphasis was on technical refinements: two phones, one local, the other long distance; hookups for personal computers, a telex, and a fax. Television offered standard Russian and American programming but also listed channels for news, weather, and worldwide stock quotations. An exercise bicycle stood next to the bathroom door, with digital readouts for kilometers, speed, heart rate, and blood pressure. The room did not invite relaxation; it urged work. Dean felt as if he'd checked into the executive suite of a Fortune 500 company.

He looked into the bathroom: another phone, a portable Quotron machine. He couldn't find any soap, and the room was low on towels. Perhaps the class of businessman who put up here never got dirty.

He parted the curtains. A bleak sunset. Bare trees which cast no shadows flanked the Mira Prospekt, thirteen floors below. A protest march paraded glumly up the center of the street, demanding the release of relatives held in the squatters' camps. They were weekly parades for progress that would not be made in the foreseeable future. The Americans had learned the art of safety valving; fine-tuned expressions of dissent were necessary to prevent a wider explosion of rebellion.

To the west rose the obelisk comemmorating the launch of the first sputnik, a concrete spire which resembled an Art Deco brooch crowned by a Buck Rogers rocket. Beyond that lay Dzerzhinsky Park, home to the thousands of squatters, presided over by the headquarters of Soviet television.

Dean collapsed on the bed and laid out the reports Gardner had dropped at his apartment two nights ago, once they'd settled on Dean's fee. There had been one snag. Gardner would not permit Dean to bring Natalie into his confidence. So Dean had intructed her to tie up any loose paper work ends and take two weeks' paid vacation. She was grateful for the uninterrupted paycheck but disappointed at being left in the dark.

The situation was curious. Dean had become Richard Gardner's shadow, a ghost cop. All the work and none of the fame. And now, thanks to Gardner's string pulling, he was putting his feet up on a dead man's bed.

He always tried to read crime reports at the scene, whether it was a murder or a stolen soft-drink formula. Surrounded by the scene he was studying, he found it easier to inhabit the crime itself.

According to the report, the mysterious Mr. Shukshin had listed his occupation as sales manager. The night clerk had asked him what he sold, but Shukshin had been evasive. The clerk didn't find this curious; everyone who stayed at the Kosmos these days was secretive and selling something.

Shukshin had been stylishly dressed. A maid noticed his overcoat was foreign, not one of the new Yves Saint Laurents manufactured in Kiev under French license, but a prewar import that would have cost a fortune on the black market. The same maid had commented on the high-quality colognes and shaving paraphernalia Shukshin had arranged neatly in the medicine cabinet.

The bellboys remembered him as a generous tipper and had

formed the impression he was wealthy. He had kept to himself, a late riser who usually missed breakfast and ordered room service. He had been quiet, and apart from one complaint about late-night typing, not an unusual occurrence in a business hotel, he'd been an ideal guest.

But ideal guests did not get murdered. Still, in keeping with the Kosmos's grand hotel image, Shukshin had at least been killed in grand style.

To judge from the position of the body and the pattern of bloodstains, which had geysered up the walls and onto the ceiling and windows, Shukshin had been killed while sitting in bed relaxing, shoes off, back propped against a pillow, much as Dean lay now. Gardner concluded that Shukshin had either known or been expecting his killer.

The spray of blood was so widespread that according to the management, the whole room had to be repainted. A tumbler of expensive scotch had been found on the far side of the room, perched on the television, an oil slick of blood floating on the rocks. Dean noted that a few stray flecks of blood still dotted the window.

As Dean read through the evidence lists, cross-checking the Russian with the English, the hours drifted by. He soon realized he was squinting and turned on the light. As always in a murder case, there were too many clues, too many leads. Every item in Shukshin's suitcase, every bar of soap and dull razor blade could be significant—or absolutely worthless.

The most intriguing discovery Gardner and his squad of investigators had made was two envelopes found on Shukshin's nightstand, one standard business, the other airmail, neither one stamped or addressed. Inside each envelope was a piece of paper on which was written a single number, 50,000 and 75,000 respectively, each in a different handwriting. MOP computers were working overtime trying to establish some link between the numbers. Still stranger, each envelope had been wiped clean of fingerprints.

Dean was also struck by several items conspicuously absent from Shukshin's belongings. According to the hotel staff, Shukshin had presented himself as a businessman on a selling trip to the capital. His choice of the Kosmos coincided with that claim. Yet where was his permit to cross the Moscow perimeter? Where were his business cards, his sales records? The evidence listed no appointment book, along with an ingratiating smile and a talent for stretching the truth, a must for a traveling salesman. There were no product samples, no brochures detailing his company and its operations.

Maybe he wasn't a businessman at all and was staying at the Kosmos to pamper himself during a vacation to Moscow. Then why wasn't he ever spotted at the pool, or throwing back shots of vodka at one of the hotel bars, or trying to pick up Air France stewardesses in the disco?

Maybe he wasn't the social type, preferring to hole up in his room with a good book. Then why did he spend his nights typing? Was he a would-be Tolstoy, who'd run away from life to work on a novel in seclusion? Dean stood, stretched the knots from his legs, and stamped his foot, which had fallen asleep. He looked over the well-stocked bar. A writer could get along quite nicely here.

Dean had reached a plateau of frustration, which came from reading dry, tiresome information in bad light. He had a headache, and the overhead heating, which had choked to life while he'd been reading, added to his discomfort, with its doglike moans and narrow shaft of heat, which pinpointed the foot of the bed like a spotlight.

But it wasn't only the heat that was nagging him. There was something else very obvious missing from the evidence list, something that would belong to a man like Zhores Shukshin, something that was a part of him.

What the hell was it?

He couldn't dredge it up.

So he went down to the bar, where he circulated some Texas slang and a few twenty-dollar bills. For the most part Russians love the Lone Star State. The Texan obsession with bigness stirs a Russian's heart. An authentic Texan, who also spoke Russian, was a real showpiece, and Dean won a few friends over drinks.

As he steered the conversation toward the subject of the unidentified sketch artist, there was a blur of movement at the end of the bar. A young man with a chic slash of blond hair and a goatee got up abruptly and hurried into the lobby.

"You know him?" Dean asked the bartender.

"Anton Semyonov, the hotel pool boy. A health food fanatic. Never orders more than a Perrier with a twist. Inspects the lime first."

"He a nervous fella?"

"Only when he weighs himself."

His suspicion aroused, Dean paid for his drink and followed Semyonov into the lobby. The pool boy knifed through the crowd, tossing glances over his shoulder at Dean. A subdued group of Russian tourists waited at the front desk for a sallow tour guide to hand out their room assignments. They're still waiting in line, Dean thought. He realized the tourists were from Moscow, stealing away from their dim, loud apartments for dinner, dancing, and a night in a luxury hotel room. Under Soviet law, spending the night in a hotel in one's own city had been forbidden. Now Moscow's first-class hotels, once strictly off limits to its own citizens, did a brisk business in overnight package "tours."

Shielded by a gray flannel wall of business suits, Semyonov disappeared into an elevator, and the doors closed behind him. Dean followed the blinking destination lights. The car was stopping at every floor.

Dean figured Semyonov would head for familiar ground. He consulted the hotel directory and ran to the pool level.

The pool was small, its waterline stylishly level with the tiled floor. An elderly woman pulled dutifully through a painful breaststroke; a yawning waiter collected empty glasses from empty tables.

"You seen Anton?" Dean asked.

The waiter shrugged and tapped his watch. "He's off duty. Try the health club, one floor up." The waiter walked off, banging the glasses against each other, amused by their echoing music.

Dean was left alone with the grimacing breaststroker. He

bent over to talk to her, but her eyes were shut in concentration, her ears buried beneath a bathing cap.

He listened to the lapping water, the chug of an elevator motor engaging far away. He felt as if he were the only person in the entire hotel.

Then he heard creaking bedsprings, a scrape of metal, and a burst of exhaled breath. It came from an open doorway near the diving board.

He squished across the wet tiles, beneath a portrait gallery of Soviet Olympic swimming stars. Metal creaked again, then slammed. Dean angled through the open doorway and found himself in a drab cubicle furnished with a narrow bed and a fractured sink, the walls decorated with cheap art prints.

Anton sat among coiled sheets, a padlocked box propped in his lap. His meek blue eyes shifted to the ceiling, where a plaster panel was slightly askew.

"What do you want with me?" the young man asked.

"I've just got a couple questions. Relax."

Anton gallantly tried to broaden his shoulders. His coat flared open, revealing a scrolled-up sheet of canvas tucked into his pocket.

"I've answered the police's questions already."

"Well, I'm not the police. Were you expecting the police?"

"No."

"Meaning yes. Look, son, I'm from Texas. And we don't like the police nosing into our business any more than you do." Dean thumbed over his shoulder. "You keep a nice clean pool here, you know that. Nice little job for a young man."

"Thank you." His voice was thin, reticent. He nervously pulled at his goatee.

"Nice little beard you got going there. It new?"

Anton nodded. Dean approached him, trying to be wide open and friendly. "Look, I didn't mean to chase you around the whole hotel here. It's just that my wife was a guest here last week. She paid some guy she met down in the lobby to do her portrait, gave him a down payment and everything, and now the sucker's taken off. No phone call, no letters, no picture. I figured I better get into this deal myself, so I started

59

asking a few questions down in the bar. The minute I bring the subject up, I see you take off like sixty. Well, you can guess what I thought. . . ."

Anton's eyes darted to the paper rolled in his pocket. "You are actually not the police?"

"Swear on a stack of Chagalls. See, not all Texans are uncultured."

"I am an art student," Anton said, the words rounded with pride. "I attend the Surikov Institute. The pool work—"

"It's just a hobby, I know."

"The police have been asking about an artist who was here the day of the killing. I thought you had been sent to continue their inquiries."

Dean sat on a bench in front of the lockers. "That I've got to tell the wife. That someone thought I was a cop. What do you got to hide from them anyway?"

"I know this artist. Rather, I am familiar with his work."

"That something of his?" Dean nodded toward Anton's pocket.

"I was afraid they would take it as evidence."

"How'd you get hold of it?"

Anton shifted edgily.

"C'mon, son, give your nerves the night off. No one's calling nine-one-one here. You buy it at a gallery or somewhere?"

"I saw him in the lobby. I thought my eyes were performing magic tricks. He was once a promising painter; we even studied one of his works at the institute. There he was, doing five-ruble sketches of tourists. I approached him somewhat in awe. Before I could even express my admiration, he'd done this."

Anton reverently unfurled the sheet of paper. It was a charcoal sketch, a collision of wedges and arcs that somehow fought their way into a human face.

"It's you."

Anton nodded enthusiastically. "The triangles are somewhat reminiscent of Lissitzky, in a figurative sense, of course."

Dean reached for the painting, but Anton snatched it away.

"It's OK, son, I'm no art thief."

Anton's eyes beaded in suspicion. "I cannot allow you to touch it. You will disturb the charcoal."

"I just want to check out the signature. That's it, I promise." Dean drew an imaginary line across the floor with his toe. "I won't move an inch."

Gingerly, like a mother showing off her newborn, Anton held the portrait up. Dean squinted to read the slashing Cyrillic signature: Anatoly Mintz.

The prime suspect now had a name.

Dean thanked Anton and left him alone, admiring his treasure in the ultramarine light reflecting off the pool.

Dean had difficulty falling asleep in Zhores Shukshin's deathbed. He tangled for hours with the case's unanswered questions until, having worked himself into a knot of frustration, he turned on the television.

CBS Moscow was trumpeting the impending arrival of Dan Rather, who would anchor the evening news from Moscow during historic election week, now barely two months away. Dean turned to a local station in time to see Mary Tyler Moore dueling with the Ted Baxter character in Russian. He shut his eyes. Mary dissolved into Vera, their voices a flawless blend, their irritated tones identical.

Vera, attempting to unwind in her compartment on the Trans-Siberian Express, toasting the sunset, fending off the complaints of her tour group: Their compartments were too cold; the dining car was suffocating; their breakfast was late; the Russian steward was rude.

Then she smiled as Dean joined her in the compartment, changing into pajamas, the Russian habit on a long train trip. He brought her tea, purchased from a dour old woman at the end of the sleeping car, who kept the samovar on the boil around the clock. He read a paperback mystery aloud to her. They made love in the upper berth while the cream and red express train drilled through the taiga. In the middle of the night he pulled back the curtains and spotted the fiery eyes of a Siberian tiger staring back at him. . . .

. . . It was stifling. Was that his own sweat misting the compartment window? He grappled with the heat, but the lever snapped off in his hand. . . .

When he awoke, he was bathed in sweat, the sheets twisted at his feet. He'd thrown the pillows onto the floor during the night. Like most Russian hotels, the Kosmos was painfully overheated. Curiously, five minutes later the manager phoned him to apologize for the fact that the heater was not working and promised to repair it right away.

It took Dean two days to realize that this seemingly minor misunderstanding was a significant clue to Zhores Shukshin's indentity.

CHAPTER SIX

Dean checked out the next day. He had reinterviewed the waiter who found the body but hadn't learned anything new. Dean returned to his apartment, to the raised eyebrows of the *dezhurnaya,* the concierge who always assumed that whenever Dean spent the night on the job, it was with female company. He did dishes. Paid bills. Threw away mail, except for a bleached color postcard of Akademgorodok, a scientific community near Novosibirsk, that Vera had sent. "Love from your Daisy." She must have asked one of her American tourists about *The Great Gatsby.* She was leading a three-week tour of Siberia, which featured stops at many of the gulags, which were now operating as museums and were popular destinations for returning émigrés and former prisoners.

Dean ate breakfast at a cafeteria near the Park Kultury metro station and argued with the owner about the television, until he switched from preelection commentary to a baseball game in Yakutsk. The nine-hour time difference between Moscow and Siberia meant that one could enjoy a live doubleheader with one's breakfast eggs—minor-league Russian baseball to be sure, but it was a simple pleasure that U.S. baseball, with all its network revenue, had never managed to provide.

He called Gardner at MOP headquarters, identifying himself as Mr. Hidell.

"I'll call you right back, Mr. Hidell," said Gardner, his voice harried and breathless.

Ten minutes later Gardner called, presumably from a secure phone outside the office. He was instantly impressed by the progress Dean had made in identifying Anatoly Mintz.

"Good grief, that was fast. Mintz, Mintz . . . the name rings a bell. I took a night class in Soviet painting; maybe I ran across it there. I'll put together a file on him today. Oh, and Dean. Come to dinner tomorrow night. Emily and I would love to have you. If you're free, that is."

"You could say I'm free."

"Perfect. And you won't say anything about our arrangement?"

"What arrangement?"

"That's what I like to hear. Well, I'll get right on this. Like my father used to say, 'The ship can't sail till you pull up the anchor.'"

A note of sadness entered Gardner's voice when he mentioned his father, and it hung there for the rest of the conversation.

Dean began his search for Anatoly Mintz in Red Square.

It is impossible to overestimate the prominence of Red Square in the Russian mind. If Moscow is the country's center, then Red Square is the center's center. The Americans had wisely decided to leave Red Square free from the physical reminders of occupation. Lenin's tomb still drew crowds, though sparser and less reverent than in the past. The honor guards, stiff and unflustered in their starched green uniforms and bright yellow belts, still goose-stepped through their rounds, though a seasoned Kremlin watcher could detect a certain weariness in their pace. The eight onion domes of St. Basil's Cathedral still attracted throngs of oohers and aahers, and Russians still bunched together on the cobblestones to argue politics, sip vodka, and compare purchases from the GUM department store.

In the past Red Square had cleared at dusk. At night it had become a deserted heartland, echoing with goose-stepping bootheels and church bells. But now it was packed, often until past midnight. People—Russians, not tourists—simply did not want to go home. They huddled in clumps, breath clouds turning blue in the glare of the streetlights, carrying on conversations that used to unfold at the dinner table. It was as though they were plugged into a mysterious source of Russianness which still lived under the cobblestones.

As darkness hovered, Dean threaded through the crowds toward the red-bricked Kremlin walls, behind which were buried the icons of Soviet politics: Stalin, Andropov, Suslov. The men who had presided over the most recent war, and those killed engineering the coup which ended it, were buried elsewhere, in neutral surroundings, while historians debated who had been the villains and who the heroes. Presumably, when the verdict was reached, the heroes would join their compatriots behind the Kremlin walls. And the villains . . . only their relatives would know where to find them.

"Portrait, sir? Have done Gorbachev and others before the war. Very flattering."

A pouchy man in a smock confronted Dean. He stood next to an easel, which held a sheaf of charcoal drawings. He was a portrait artist, one of dozens who now congregated outside the Kremlin, offering their services to tourists.

"Actually, my brother had his portrait done here recently. I'd like to find the same artist to do me. Maybe with the Kremlin in the background?"

"Perhaps I did your brother myself?"

"Are you Anatoly Mintz?"

"Well . . ." The expression on the man's face told Dean he could be Anatoly Mintz or Rembrandt if the price was right.

Dean moved off. The artist turned his attention to a Japanese couple. Dean marched down the ranks of painters, many of whom were supplementing the fading light with gas lamps.

"I know Mintz." Dean was prodded from behind by a thin

young man with arched, skeptical eyebrows and shoulder-length brown hair. He wore a paint-spattered overcoat and fashionably tattered blue jeans and sucked hungrily on a Lucky Strike, as though it were pumping life into him, rather than the other way around. In short, he knew how tourists expected their artists to look.

"Great. Is he here tonight?"

"His was the easel next to mine. We even shared paper. But he is missing now for a week . . . and with a convention of stockbrokers staying at the Rossiya . . . all good customers—"

"Listen, do you mind if I ask you a couple questions?"

The artist's face folded into a mask of suspicion, the inevitable Russian reaction to a stranger's questions.

"I represent a prominent collector who's after a particular work of Mintz's."

The artist surveyed the crowd of tourists, many of whom were comparison shopping and pulling out their wallets.

"I may have a customer in a minute."

"You've got a customer now." Dean sat in a stool and elevated his chin haughtily. "Profile, please. My right side's the best."

The artist looked dubious. "I must warn you, a Valentin Orlov portrait will be brutally honest. I leave in the wrinkles, the blemishes. Not like these other hacks. Like Klimov there." He pointed out a brisk, gap-toothed man in black fur, working on an acrylic portrait of an elderly woman in a wheelchair. "He was known for his flattering pictures of Brezhnev. They made him look thirty when he was so dottering he could barely prop himself up to review the May Day parade. He'll turn that woman into an Olympic high jumper, just wait."

"About Mintz?" Dean prodded.

"Yes, Mintz," replied Orlov as he readied his charcoal. "A graphicist in the Leningrad Union of Artists before the war. He designed political posters. He once drew an abstract catalog for the GUM department store. He became quite controversial."

"A rebel, huh?"

"He was arrested, yes. For organizing an exhibition of the

Futurists. The exhibit was destroyed by bulldozers, and Mintz was sent to a labor camp."

Mintz was starting to sound interesting. Motives were starting to suggest themselves.

"Were you a friend of his?"

"He had no friends. No relatives either, it seemed. None of us knew where he lived. He would pack up his easel at sunset and disappear into the metro. Turn your head."

"Would you call him the violent type?"

"What artist is not? When his work is attacked?"

"And his was?"

"Yes. The authorities often confiscated it."

"Maybe he felt the need for revenge. You know, against the KGB. Or the Ministry of Culture?"

"Strange questions for someone representing an art collector," said Orlov.

"He's a strange collector. He keeps reminding me that an artist's background is inseparable from his work. Did Mintz ever mention the name Shukshin to you?"

Orlov tilted his head quizzically. Dean thought he had struck a nerve, but it was merely the artist, evaluating the thin light as it played across Dean's forehead.

"I told you, he had no friends."

"Enemies then. A dissident had enemies."

"Perhaps there is a file on him in some basement. Perhaps there are names in that file."

It wasn't likely. Any citizen who had an active KGB file at the time of the war, as a dissident painter like Mintz would certainly have had, was nearly impossible to investigate. Days before the armistice the KGB, in a final explosion of paranoia, had shredded its files and burned its computer records. Hitler had met with the scorched-earth policy when he invaded Russia because at that time grain had been the Soviet Union's most valuable commodity and it wished to deny sustenance to the encroaching Nazi armies. In the years since World War II, information had replaced grain as the country's most precious asset, and the Americans had been forced to deal with "scorched software."

"No friends, no readily identifiable enemies. No known relatives. This man seems to have been erased from life."

"It's not the first time it's happened in Russia. There, your opinion, please."

Orlov held the sketch up to the white-hot glow of his gas lamp. It was rough but impressive. He'd accurately caught the bruised cynicism in Dean's features, the spider web of anger lines which angled toward the eyes.

"Are you insulted?"

"Not at all."

Orlov seemed disappointed. Dean handed him a twenty-ruble note. "As a matter of fact, here's a tip. I think brutal honesty should be rewarded." Dean wrote his home phone number in charcoal on a sheet of Orlov's sketchpad. "Call me day or night if you think of anything that could lead me to Mintz."

Dean examined his portrait again before he rolled it up and tucked it in his overcoat.

"Are my ears really that large?"

Orlov laughed as Dean walked off into the crowd. Then, when he was nearly out of range, he heard Orlov shout after him: "One more thing about Mintz. His work was mediocre . . . extremely mediocre."

Emily Gardner didn't cook the night Dean came to dinner. At Richard's insistence, Wednesday night was devoted to experiments with Russian cuisine, part of the total cultural immersion program he'd designed for his family. He himself cooked.

"It's good, Rich, really," Emily said.

"Ochen korroshow," announced Jack, practicing his Russian.

"Very *korrowhow,*" seconded Bryn, their daughter.

"I certainly didn't teach you this at Camp Peary," said Dean. He spoke with a full mouth, pretending he was so overcome with gusto that he couldn't pause to comment. "I find a recipe that asks for sauce, I throw away the recipe."

Thank God he'd loaded up on the packaged hors d'oeuvres

Emily had served: cold sturgeon in aspic; liver pâté, kulebiaka. The Stroganoff Gardner had created was bland; the fried potatoes overcooked, little black lava dots in a sea of sour cream. The meat was . .

"Tough. Stringy. This is inedible, damn it," Gardner said.

He slapped his wrists on the table on either side of his plate, knife and fork gripped tightly in his hands. Tension spread through the room, like a guest who doesn't know when to leave.

The kids traded ominous looks and picked at the potatoes.

"Don't make it an issue, Rich. I'm sure Stroganoff himself burned a potato or two."

"Was there a Stroganoff?" asked Jack.

"Maybe a couple hundred years ago," answered Gardner. He lifted a forkful of meat, examined it with abhorrence. "I think he made this."

Throughout the rest of the meal Dean and Emily traded eye contact, at first innocently, then with a shade of embarrassment, finally with a subtle overlay of flirtation. Her hair dangled down her forehead, shading her eyes as she lowered her face. Her cheekbones drew the light; their curve guided Dean's eye to the opening of her blouse and the pearl that dangled there.

Gardner insisted on doing the dishes. "At least I can do something right tonight."

To the sound of cursing and chattering china, Emily took Dean on a tour of the apartment, her narration punctuated by the kids' comments. Gardner's voice followed them, fighting through the Russian-language tape he was listening to on his Walkman as he cleaned the kitchen.

Their apartment was spacious and high-ceilinged, the former residence of court nobility before the revolution, later occupied by a succession of anonymous but influential Soviet artists. The Gardners lived on a small side street between Kropotkin Street and Metrostroyevskaya, in a district under historical conservancy.

"What's in there?" Dean asked as they brushed by an ornately filigreed door that seemed narrower than the others.

"Used to be a servant's quarters. I guess in the old days, they didn't feed them very well, so they could get away with skinny doors."

"Mom's collection room," Jack said. "She won't let anyone in there without permission. It's weird, huh?"

"Come on, Jack, you collect rocks. I don't call you weird."

"Yeah, but you collect everything. And you never used to—"

"Jack!" Her stern tone and flashing eyes forced Jack to retreat from what seemed to be a taboo area.

"Don't think I'm being secretive, Mr. Joplin. But I'm married to a policeman. I have to work a little harder to preserve my privacy, that's all."

"We all need our privacy," Gardner shouted as they passed a second door into the kitchen. "That's one of the things we're trying to teach these people, isn't it? Respect for private property. Well, if I don't respect it at home, I certainly can't respect it on the job."

They passed a room that was exaggeratedly masculine. Framed diplomas shared wall space with photographs of Gardner's naval career. Nautilus equipment crouched ominously in the corner. One wall was given over to an elaborate homemade chart titled "Timetable of Russian History."

Jack darted to an Exercycle and began to work out. Bryn, losing interest in the tour, collapsed in her dad's easy chair.

Emily nodded toward the timetable. "Rich is a great believer in context. Whenever something happens, something uniquely Russian that he doesn't understand, he comes home, pours a vodka, and attempts to fix it in history. 'Nothing in Russia exists in a vacuum,' says Rich . . . except me, perhaps."

"What was that?"

"Nothing. You didn't hear a thing. If you tell Richard I said anything like that, I'll deny it. Plausible deniability, right?"

There was a definite cry for help in her sarcasm. But help with what? And why would she feel pressed to open up to him, a brushing acquaintance?

Gardner entered with ice cream for Bryn and Jack, brandies for himself and Dean, alcohol-free beer for Emily.

"Trying to give up alcohol, too," Emily said, taking a sip

70

from her ersatz beer and lighting up one of her clove ciga-rettes. "I drink decaf when coffee time rolls around."

They sat on the couch, Emily between the two men.

"You remember *glasnost,* Dean? Well, we believe in it around here. We drink in front of the kids, discuss work in front of them, argue in front of them."

"A lot," observed Jack, digging into the ice cream while pedaling at a furious clip.

"I assure you, we don't do everything in front of the kids," Emily said.

"Who are going to bed now, anyway," Gardner said.

"C'mon, Dad. We have guests," Jack protested. "Let's play flutter."

"Jack, it's late."

"One game."

"Is that what I think it is?" Dean asked.

"Afraid so. It's a little family game I dreamed up a couple years ago. Jack loves it, but—"

Emily nodded to her husband, and they both turned con-cerned gazes on Bryn, who, shrunken morosely into the over-stuffed chair, was staring at her ice cream.

"Bryn's like her mother," Emily said. "She doesn't like to have her innermost secrets revealed."

"She can go to bed," said Jack.

"Don't want to. I want you to watch me dance."

"We're gonna play flutter. *Dobre vecher,*" declared Jack.

Bryn tangled her mouth in confusion.

"That means 'good night.'" Jack hopped off the exercycle and walked to Gardner's desk. He withdrew a scarred tan leather attaché case, set it on the coffee table, and began to work the combination lock. They were going to play flutter, and Gardner didn't seem able or inclined to dissuade his son.

Bryn was made to kiss her parents good-night, offer a sticky handshake to the guest, and sent to bed with the promise that they'd watch her latest homemade ballet tomorrow.

"I don't understand that girl," Gardner said. "She keeps ev-erything bottled up, won't talk to me sometimes. The minute we have guests, boom, it's show time."

"Bryn," Dean said. "Was she named after the school?"

"I plead guilty," Emily said. "I believed education was the most important thing in life. But Rich went to Annapolis, so . . ."

"Jack was named after Kennedy."

"Ich bin ein Berliner," pronounced Jack in perfect German. He slowly lifted the lid off the briefcase, attempting to stir up an aura of mystery, and took out a polygraph.

"OK, here's how it works. The interrogator—that'll be me—can only ask questions he thinks are true. The guys being fluttered—that's you guys—can answer any way they want, but the object is to beat the machine with a real lie. You get ten questions and a point for each that makes it. But you gotta be careful. If you tell a lie and the machine catches it, you lose a point."

The polygraph was an early seventies model, a portable that Gardner had bought, at Jack's insistence, at a government auction. All CIA officials had been periodically fluttered, subject to lie detector tests, as had all the agents they recruited. Polygraphs were transported by diplomatic pouch, and the tests were always administered by teams of two, a unique breed who were thick-skinned enough to deal with the universal scorn in which they were held. They traveled the world with their clumsy little machines, their arrivals dreaded and their departures cheered, keeping to themselves, as friendless as baseball umpires.

Emily seemed stiff. This was clearly not a game she enjoyed, but she volunteered to go first, maybe trying to deprive the game of its significance.

"You ever feel like a conquerer, Dean?" asked Gardner.

Dean was concentrating on Emily's sleeve, which Jack was slowly rolling up in an unconscious striptease. Inch by inch an olive brown arm was unveiled. The fringe of hair on her wrist bristled. Dean noticed his breath was clouding the glass.

"A conquerer? Sure. Of course. Especially on the street. You see it in people's eyes. The resentment. What's worse, the acceptance. They've been invaded before—the Mongols, the Poles, the French, the Nazis. We're not the first, probably not the last."

"I never feel like that. You know how I feel?"

Dean wasn't listening. He watched Jack wrap the blood pressure cuff around his mother's arm and turn on the lie detector. As though responding to the warmth of his gaze, Emily loosened the second button on her blouse. Jack planted an electrode pad against Emily's palm, securing it across the back of her hand with a spring. Already one of the three pens on the lie detector console registered an increase in Emily's perspiration.

"Like a scientist, and Russia is my laboratory."

"What does that make the Russians, Rich? Mice?" asked Emily.

"It makes them fellow scientists. Experimenters in the laboratory of democracy. The societal structures, the institutions, those are the guinea pigs. We're prodding them, pushing them, seeing how they'll respond. Crossbreeding them to see if they'll reproduce as an entirely new species. I've never doubted that the new breed will be free and democratic."

Gardner's words were corny, but the intensity was naively genuine.

Dean, who'd been staring at Emily's crossed legs, determined to pay closer attention to Gardner's commentary.

"Come on, you guys, stop talking," Jack complained. "This is getting boring. Is your name Emily Gardner?"

"Yes." The machine indicated she was telling the truth.

"Do you live in Moscow with your husband and two lovely children?"

"Yes." Again the truth.

"Do you have a dead body hidden in your collection room?"

"Jack, I've told you that's not fair. You've been in there; you know it's just a hobby." She looked at Dean. "I collect things. Coins, subway tokens, first editions, whatever. I become easily addicted, I guess."

Dean answered with a live-and-let-live shrug. What kind of comment did she expect him to offer?

"Are you happy with your life here?"

Emily hesitated. She answered with a weak yes, which the polygraph recorded as a weak lie.

73

"Whoa! Mom hates her life! Dad, did you know that? Mom hates her life?"

"I do not hate it! I'm perfectly satisfied with it!"

"Not according to the machine."

"I'm sure it's exaggerating her response, Jack. We did get it at a government garage sale, don't forget. And that was a loaded question. No one's ever perfectly happy."

"I do not hate my goddamn life!" Emily shouted. "You're blowing this way out of proportion."

"Emily, come on, it's just a game," Gardner said, his voice trembling. "Talk about proportion."

"What does that machine know? Government surplus. It's full of shit, like everything connected with the government. See, Mr. Joplin, we swear in front of our kids, too."

Dean shifted uncomfortably.

"Emily, if you'd rather call it quits here—"

"I'm sorry, Rich. I guess it's the weather. The prospect of another long winter, you know. It's making me tense up." Emily downed her near beer. "OK, Jack, next question. Anything goes. Fire away."

Jack thought, anxious to exploit his sudden freedom.

"Am I getting a new bike for Christmas?"

Everybody broke into laughter, and Emily tousled her son's hair affectionately.

"Jack, you are the best antidote for tension. Are you sure you weren't born in a Valium bottle?"

"Just answer the questions, ma'am."

Emily looked at her husband. They attempted some facial shorthand, in a valiant effort to keep their son's present a secret.

"Yes," Emily finally answered.

The machine went wild, recording the biggest lie of the night. Jack's face sank with disappointment.

"I'm not?"

"Maybe you're getting something better," said Gardner.

Jack tore into action, reading off a barrage of questions. "A car? A rifle? A radio-controlled airplane? A VCR? A helicopter?" The machine seemed to smoke as it absorbed a volley of nos

74

from Emily. Finally she unwrapped the cuff from her arm in triumph.

"You just blew it, honey. Your ten questions are up."

Jack slowly floated back to earth, shaking his head as he realized his mistake. "That's not fair—counting each of those as a question."

The phone rang, and Gardner got up to take it in the foyer.

"OK, Mr. Joplin. You're next, OK?" asked Jack.

Dean paused. This could get tricky.

"Well, I don't think so, Jack. I'm a little tired. I probably wouldn't make a very intriguing subject."

"But you promised!"

Jack's lower lip shot out in a plaintive pout.

"Oh, come on, Mr. Joplin," said Emily. "Indulge my son. I'm sure you have a few skeletons dangling in your closet that we'd all find interesting."

He could refuse Jack, but not Emily. He looked to Gardner for guidance. He stood shadowed in the living-room door, watching them as he nodded soberly into the phone. Jack brandished the blood pressure cuff in one hand, the electrode pad in the other, coiled, ready to pounce.

"Go ahead, Jack," Gardner said. "But don't ask him about his job. He's here to leave the office behind."

Jack agreed to the conditions and fitted a fresh sheet of graph paper into the console.

As Dean turned up his sleeve, Emily was rolling down hers, and for a flushed second, their bare arms touched. Was it Dean's imagination, or did she deliberately prolong the moment? Was she telling him something by helping Jack with the pressure cuff, fitting it snugly onto his bicep, her nails grazing his skin?

"OK, here we go. Is your name . . ." Jack looked to his mother, who helped him out.

"Dean Joplin?"

Truth.

"Do you live in Moscow?"

Truth again.

"Are you having a good time tonight?"

"Yes." Again the truth. Emily smiled in agreement.

"Do I drive you crazy?" Jack asked.

"No." Again the lie detector indicated Dean was telling the truth. This time Jack smiled in satisfaction.

"Congratulations, Dean." Emily laughed. "You're the first person who's ever beaten the machine."

"Mom!" Jack stuck out his tongue, then continued the interrogation. A devilish gleam entered his eyes. "Do you think my mom's pretty?"

"Jack!" Emily burst out.

She tried to defuse the growing sexuality of the moment by adopting a cartoonish modeling pose, but her eyes were serious; they didn't leave Dean's for an instant.

"Yes."

Jack recorded the truthful answer.

"OK, do you think you would have married her, like my dad did?"

"That's enough, Jack, damn it."

"Mom, it's for the game. It's a fair question. You don't need to get all embarrassed."

"I don't? Well, how'd you like it if the next time I flutter you, I ask a lot of prying questions about your girl friends at school?"

"I don't have any girl friends. They don't like me."

"Right. That's why little Natasha, or whatever her name is, is always after you to sharpen her ice skates."

"That's 'cause she knows we're from where it's cold, too. Every other American in the class is from California. All they can fix is a surfboard. What do Russians care about surfing? Now, do you or don't you, Mr. Joplin?"

"Well, since your mother is married, that sort of takes me out of the running."

"But if she weren't?"

Dean glanced at Emily, whose mischievous gaze was no help at all, then over at Gardner, who appeared to be concluding his call. Dean liked the way he fitted into this picture. Sharing the couch and a few drinks with Emily, speculating on what really filled her thoughts, flirting, letting the heat build between them, trading jokes with Jack, who at eight, was still susceptible to the influence Dean had lost over his own son long ago.

What's wrong with this picture? He was wrong with this picture.

"Well?"

"No, no, probably not. I wouldn't've—"

The needle jumped as if it were registering the San Francisco earthquake.

"God, that'll cost you. And adults always think they're such great liars. God, this is great. I can't believe it!"

Gardner returned, and as he bent over to retrieve his drink, his eye fell on the graph paper, which was nearly black with the ink traces of Dean's answer.

"Good grief. And to think you once taught an interrogation seminar, Dean."

"Interrogators don't always make the best subjects."

"By the way, what was the sixty-four-thousand-dollar question?"

Emily winked at Jack, then crisply ripped the graph paper from the machine and crumpled it in her fist.

"That, I'm afraid, is classified. Strictly on a need-to-know basis."

Gardner drove Dean home. Though it was barely past midnight and the metro was still running, Gardner had insisted. Perhaps public transportation didn't fit in with the Hooverian democracy he imagined for Russia. But before they got a car in every garage, they'd have to do better on getting a chicken in every pot.

Before they'd left, Emily had let Dean look in on Bryn, who had fallen asleep with the TV on. She lay splayed across the bed, one ballet slipper still clinging to her foot, a Mickey Mouse night-light throwing a big-eared shadow over a portrait of Lenin; a Russian variation of a scene out of Norman Rockwell.

Emily chuckled. "She found dozens of Lenin portraits in the attic. She says he helps her sleep. She also wondered if he'd made any records." Fondly remembered fragments of Dean's past tried to reassemble themselves, like a shattered windowpane attempting to jump back in its frame. With Emily at his side, staring down at the bed, the soft textures of her body inadvertently caressing him, it was nearly possible.

He'd kissed Emily good-night on the cheek, a kiss he could still taste. It seemed natural. New friends kissed good-night after dinner parties. A somber handshake would have seemed suspicious, as if they were trying to cover something up. Cover up? How was that for jumping to conclusions? This was not an affair; this was everyday, innocent compatibility. She was a beautiful woman; he was a handsome—he assessed himself in the rearview mirror—make that passable, man. As he retraced the evening, trying to recall a word or gesture that would help clarify Emily's feeling toward him, he realized Gardener had been talking to him for several moments.

"That was the office that phoned while Jack was giving you the third degree. They've found a studio that Anatoly Mintz rented. My men have been through it already, but I thought you might like to have a look-see."

Gardner's quaint language was beginning to amuse Dean. He used phrases like "look-see" and "easy as pie" and "good grief." Was his speech consciously developed, or had he inherited it from his father?

They moved through sparse traffic, edging around dark corners in a neighborhood near the zoo. A sign caught Dean's eye: BEST TEXAS CHILI FOR 10,000 MILES. It announced the northwestern barracks of the Air Force Security Police. They were troops assigned to guard duty at missile sites around the country and were periodically recycled through Moscow as the sites were destroyed or redesigned.

Gardner stopped at the gates to the Vangankovsky Cemetery.

"Here?" Dean asked incredulously.

"A shack out back. An artist will do anything for inspiration, I guess."

Dean climbed out of the Moskvich and, slapping his shoulders for warmth, followed Gardner into the graveyard.

They passed a small concrete bunker marked *tsvety* (flowers) and crunched over hard-packed snow, following the day's footprints along the well-traveled paths between the graves. Bare locust trees extended spidery branches above them; stars glittered beyond.

Gardner stopped, and Dean nearly collided with him in the darkness. He flipped on a penlight and consulted a notepad.

"They said to turn left at Sergei Yesinin's grave." Gardner darted his penlight around the headstones. Now that Dean's eyes had adjusted to the dark, he realized theirs was not the only light. Candles flickered in the night, casting smoky shadows across the headstones they decorated, backlighting the glasses of vodka left as offerings.

They walked slowly forward. Just being in the graveyard made them hesitate in their stride, made them lower their voices.

Gardner continued to hunt for Yesinin's headstone. An illustrious poet and Isadora Duncan's lover, he summarized the qualities Russians love most in their literary heroes: a melancholy temperament that drove him to suicide, an inability to conquer his drinking, and a rough, volatile emotional style.

The night carried sound. A siren screamed. A man and a woman argued in Russian from a nearby apartment building. Dishes shattered. A door slammed.

Suddenly Gardner stopped short. He motioned for Dean to be quiet and cupped a hand around his ear.

Then Dean heard it. A dull murmur, like a priest reciting a liturgy under his breath.

Gardner's hand went to the gun hidden beneath his overcoat, Dean's to his pocket, where they closed around his house keys, the only makeshift weapon that came to mind. Together they crept toward the sound.

Gardner's penlight jabbed the darkness. Its slender beam highlighted a detail here and there, but broad outlines remained obscure. Suddenly it struck a reflection—glasses!

An owlish face spun toward them, eyes wide in shock. A muscular middle-aged man wrapped in a heavy overcoat, backed away from the light, swearing in Russian.

He dropped something in the snow, but before he could bend to retrieve it, Gardner had roughly pinned the man's arms behind his back.

"What the devil are you doing here?" Gardner asked.

The man seemed terrified, perhaps fearing he was going to be robbed. "Nothing. Nothing. Only reading. Please, I have no money."

"What do you mean, reading? It's darker than a coal mine out here."

Dean brushed through the snow and picked up the mysterious object the man had dropped. It was a paperback book.

"This is not a robbery," Gardner barked. "I'm with the police, and this is the scene of a murder investigation."

"Relax, Richard. He may be telling the truth."

Gardner shone the penlight on the book: *Collected Poems of Sergei Yesinin*. Then he pointed the light at the headstone that faced them not three feet away: Sergei Yesinin.

"I read poems and bring flowers." The grave was adorned with several glasses of vodka and a bouquet of flowers, glazed with frost.

"It's too dark to read," Gardner insisted.

"Poems in memory. But I bring book in case. During day it's very crowded here. People remembering Yesinin. I come at night to be alone with him."

Russians were profoundly sentimental about their writers, an attachment that seemed strengthened in death. Dean had been to Pasternak's grave in Peredelkino; it was the focus of a steady pilgrimage, a site which drew factory workers and party officials alike.

Gardner let the man go after noting his name and address. As the man wound his way along the tangled paths he'd long ago memorized, he hissed a parting shot at Gardner.

"What was that?" Gardner asked.

"*Eb tvoi mat* . . . literally, 'I fuck your mother.' You don't want to come between a Russian and his poetry."

They continued through the cemetery, toward a fat wooden shack, the shadow of which they could now discern against the low gray walls. They passed a new section of cemetery, a chilling procession of identical headstones. Gardner played the light across the row nearest the path and read a few of the inscriptions aloud: "Boris Tvardovsky, Born 1965, died 1990. Klim Inozemtsev, Born 1967, died 1990; Vladimir Ulm, Born 1966, died 1990." The inscriptions did not mention the war, only that they had died "fulfiling their internationalist duty," a euphemism that had entered the language after the Red Army's first defeat in Afghanistan. They moved on without comment, trying to forget the enormity symbolized by the graveyard, preferring to concentrate their energies on a single death.

Gardner clicked through the police combination lock on the shack and pushed open the door, which was swollen from the evening damp.

Gardner flipped a broken porcelain light switch, and they entered the cluttered room. Twin bars of fluorescent light, encased in a metal frame, provided an irritating glare.

"Odd choice of light," Dean commented. "Most painters hate fluorescent."

The shack was also used by the cemetery caretaker. Among the chaos of Mintz's art supplies were open sacks of fertilizer, artificial flowers, votive candles, and a jumble of shovels and hoes. A mattress, a hot plate, and a pyramid of canned goods suggested Mintz lived where he painted.

A large window extended the length of the back wall, its frosted panes looking out on the Minsk rail line and, farther north, the Greco-Roman facade of the Moscow racetrack. Dean noticed scraps of paper lying everywhere, stiff with frozen oil paint. Evidently Mintz had used old betting slips to mix or apply the paint.

Gardner began unscrewing the plastic containers of powdered paint, inspecting them one by one. His hands were soon rainbow-colored. Dean sorted through several paint-spattered smocks, searching their pockets.

"You know, I want to thank you for coming to dinner tonight. For being such a good sport."

"I enjoyed it."

"It did Emily a world of good. Being around someone who

81

doesn't talk shop, I mean. This whole move has been rather rough on her. There've been some tense moments. . . ."

Dean thought of the hospitalization mentioned in Gardner's dossier, wondered if that fitted his definition of "tense moments." Gardner seemed to be angling for a male buddy, but Dean didn't want to become allies. It was selfish and totally presumptuous, but he didn't want to be railroaded into taking sides against Emily.

"But things are fine now," Richard added, a bit too exuberantly.

The two investigators worked silently for a moment, in separate corners. Dean thought he saw a flicker of motion beyond the tracks, but when he looked closer, there was nothing, just a black, freezing landscape.

They each grabbed an end of one of Mintz's many large canvases, which were rolled up and stacked like bolts of cloth. They unfurled it across the floor, like rug merchants displaying their wares.

The canvas was a rough sketch, just streaks of black paint, but the effect was chilling. The setting was a Moscow street. The onion domes of a cathedral were contorted so far out of proportion that they looked like wax gargoyles, leaning over to spit on a flock of pedestrians. A man—Mintz?—seen from the rear, naked, drawn perfectly to proportion, stood at the center of the sidewalk, facing a wave of onrushing people, compressed like those telescopic views of New York that are meant to convey hustle and bustle. But what caused Dean to shiver unconsciously were the other people in the street scene, easily a hundred or more. They all were shrouded in straitjackets, all screaming in agony, as though all of Moscow had been released from an insane asylum on a single day.

They moved wordlessly on to the next canvas. With slight variations it was the same picture. The third canvas was nearly identical, as were the fourth and the fifth. All together, eleven canvases were devoted to the same scene. None was finished; none featured the slightest trace of color.

Dean realized his pulse had quickened; his breathing was clipped. Gardner showed the same symptoms.

They rushed through Mintz's sketchbooks. They contained still rougher drawings of the same scene, breaking it down into fragments. Every doodle in the studio was identical.

"I'm no art critic," Gardner said.

"But I know obsession when I see it," answered Dean. "Orlov called his stuff mediocre."

"Artistic jealousy," scoffed Gardner.

"When did Mintz rent this shack?"

Gardner consulted his notes. "Detective Malenkov, he's one of my senior men, tracked down the caretaker. About five months ago Mintz just wandered in and asked if he could use the shack. Said the cemetery inspired him. Paid ten rubles a month."

"He have any visitors?"

"According to the caretaker, he was gone all day. Only painted at night. Said the light was better then."

Dean looked around the shed in frustration. "What light? This fluorescent shit is giving me a headache."

"What are you driving at? You think he was up to something else in here?"

"We know he painted. The same damn thing over and over. But when did he paint them? Maybe he'd had those canvases for years; maybe he'd bring in a new one every week to make the caretaker think he was working."

Gardner rolled up one of the canvases and tucked it under his arm. "If they can date a Da Vinci, it shouldn't be beyond the reach of police science to tell us when these were painted."

"Get me the fingerprint reports, too. Maybe our dead Mr. Shukshin was one of Mintz's art patrons. Maybe they got up to something together here all those nights."

"That won't tell us much until we know who our Mr. Shukshin really is."

The shack began to rumble as the headlights from an approaching train swept across the window. The noise was appalling; the flimsy structure rattled and heaved.

The din shook up Dean's mind. Somewhere in the shack there was a familiar image. He'd noted it when they first en-

tered, then discarded it because it blended in with the surroundings somehow. He retraced his steps around the shed,
passing hands over paint bottles, brushes, and stacks of wood,
like a desperate nightclub magician.

The train clatter faded. The walls stopped vibrating. Silence
returned.

"How he could even think in here is beyond me," Gardner
said.

Dean held up an impatient hand. Suddenly he marched to
the caretaker's workbench and pulled several paint smocks off
a mildewed shelf. When he found a particular smock, gray,
missing several buttons, its pocket ripped off, he tossed it to
Gardner.

"Have this examined, too."

"For what?"

"I need to know where it was made. Bloodstains, fingerprints, microscopic bits of human hair—that you can keep
to yourself."

"It's just an old rag, isn't it?"

"We'll see."

A car engine started nearby. They opened the front door.
The cemetery was still deserted. A streetlight by the main gate
had burned out. If a car was pulling away from the curb, they
couldn't see it. Across the street the brilliant neon of a new
Michelob sign winked out.

The engine growled again, nearly as loud as the train that
had passed.

"Soviet car," Dean observed. They pressed their faces to the
back window.

"A Volga?" asked Gardner.

"Bigger."

The view was unchanged: the racetrack; the desolate train
yard; a low black fence.

Then the fence moved.

"Jesus Christ, a ZIL!" Dean said.

Before they could react, it was gone, a black streak wiped
off the landscape.

The ZIL was a block-long eight-cylinder luxury suite on

wheels, used by Soviet premiers and Politburo members and still favored by high-ranking occupation officials, though Cadillac was negotiating with the Lenin military plant in Moscow for the manufacture of a more fuel-efficient limousine. Handmade, each costing more than seventy-five thousand dollars, ZIL was Russian for Rolls-Royce.

Dean and Gardner looked at each other. They knew what it meant. Someone checking up on them. Someone looking down godlike from above. But who?

Gardner drove Dean home, and they barely exchanged a word.

Once upstairs, as Dean tinkered with his temperamental thermostat, he drew back the curtains on a whim to watch Gardner's car pull away. It didn't surprise him to see the ZIL cruise slowly past his apartment a moment later. He grabbed his binoculars. Curtained windows, no rear license plate.

Ominous. Or was it? Plates from official vehicles had always made good souvenirs.

CHAPTER SEVEN

The exterior of the Central Employment Authority on Gorky Street was commanding, an architectural style befitting a former governor's palace. Its interior was a pulsing, deafening human flea market, as hundreds of typewriters clacked, phones chimed, and voices quarreled in Russian and English.

Dean took a cardboard number from an old man dozing behind a steel desk: 657. According to a digital display, which had been rudely strapped to one of the lobby's marble pillars, they had reached 589.

"Four to five hours," the old man barked behind closed eyes. A line for numbers was already forming behind Dean. At least that guy has a secure job, Dean thought as he joined the ranks of job seekers cooling their heels in row after row of metal chairs. The chairs had been screwed into the parquet floor to prevent theft. Perfect. To save a few flimsy, torturously uncomfortable chairs, the Employment Authority had permanently scarred a beautiful building.

Dean snared an aisle seat. He scanned the crowd. It was easy to distinguish the Russians from the Americans. The Americans were poorly equipped. They had brought nothing to read but the morning papers, which now littered the floor, soaking up wet footprints and cigarette ash. They sat in restless agony, yawning, smoking, stretching, constantly synchronizing their watches with the wall clock as it dragged through the hours.

The Russians, on the other hand, were quite chipper. They had knitting, model airplanes for their children, box lunches. They'd brought bulging classics, Russian translations of Solzhenitsyn's *Gulag Archipelago,* now freely available. One couple shared a Pizza Hut sturgeon pizza; another enterprising woman had set up a samovar and was selling tea. You couldn't teach a Russian much about waiting in line. The velvet ropes which American businesses installed for their "customers' convenience" were insulting to Russians. As if they couldn't be counted on to organize themselves into a line.

By the time Dean's number was called, the sun was setting, throwing weak yellow light into the cavernous hall. The room seemed to generate its own atmosphere; a dense stratus cloud of cigarette smoke hugged the ceiling.

Custodians began working their way up the aisles, lifting sleeping legs, brooming away the day's debris. But the crowd had not thinned. The flow was continuous. The long march through the day's numbers would simply begin again tomorrow, wherever they left off.

Dean's counselor was a thin, icy Russian woman whose one stroke of defiance in her conveyor-belt existence was her hammer-and-sickle earrings. She waited impatiently for Dean to make the first move as she cleaned her fingernails on the spine of a small cactus which decorated her desk. Dean cleared his throat.

"Aren't you supposed to ask me something?"

"If you like."

"My name, for example. What kind of work I'm looking for."

"I don't have anything right now."

Dean pointed to her alphabetized filing cabinet.

"You've got four drawers of jobs there."

"All filled."

Dean sighed and lit a cigarette. A coded message appeared

87

in his mind: "ATTN: Langley. Subject recommended for Termination."

He tried another approach. He coolly slid the pack across the desk, and she just as coolly pushed it back.

"No bribes here, please."

"That wasn't a bribe." Dean produced his wallet and fanned through a wad of rubles. "This isn't a bribe either." A stern black-suited man strolled into view, hands clasped behind his back. He warily appraised the situation. Dean casually dropped the wallet back into his jacket pocket. The man's sour expression reminded Dean of a Las Vegas pit boss; he felt as if he were about to be nabbed for card counting.

"Where you from?" the black suit asked. Despite three years of occupation, Americans were still interested in where other Americans were from.

"Washington, D.C. What about you?"

"New York. Staten Island. But I used to get down to D.C. every now and then. You'll excuse me, but it's a marble shithole. Boring as hell. Capitals usually are. Bonn? Forget it. Bern? Wake me up when it's open. Moscow? You'll excuse me again, but it's D.C. with good vodka. What kind of work you after?"

"Heating technician."

"Why don't you take a look at the unit in my Moskvich? Might be a couple rubles in it."

"I do industrial stuff. Factories, airports, hotels."

"You picked a good town for it. I guess if you're in heating, you must think you'd died and gone to hell when you saw Moscow." He turned to the employment counselor. "You fix him up, Natasha?"

"Miss Collective Farm here says she can't help me."

"She's full of it. She hates Americans, that's all." He hissed at Natasha in Russian. "You let this guy see the listings, or tomorrow you'll be sitting where he is!" The pit boss said, "Have a nice day," and went off to ruin someone else's.

"Just why do you hate Americans? We didn't bomb Moscow after all."

Natasha, presenting the curve of her back as she dug

through the H file, had a one-word answer: "Chaos." She spread out a computer tearsheet, printed in Russian with handwritten notations in English. As Dean scanned the list, he realized this was going to take more legwork than he'd anticipated. There were at least ten openings for heating technicians or repairmen in the Moscow area, some at tiny local businesses, others at giant factories outside the city.

His own heater, which had died a loud, gurgling death an hour before dawn, had given Dean his brainstorm. As Dean watched the repairman, he'd pestered him with questions. His building's system was similar to that in the Kosmos Hotel, so complex it could be dealt with only by a professional.

He'd rushed back to the Kosmos and checked the hotel's maintenance log. He was convinced that only Shukshin could have fixed the heater in his room—the heater management thought was broken. Shukshin was the only one with the opportunity and the means—the room had been sealed and guarded since the murder.

Shukshin had been putting on an act. The cosmopolitan wardrobe and foreign colognes had been a disguise of sorts. If Shukshin had been working as a heating technician at the time of his death, there'd be a job opening somewhere. To prevent corruption, all openings for skilled labor were required to be listed by the Employment Authority.

"Do you let them know I'm coming? Do I call first? What's the procedure?"

"No procedure."

"That offends you, does it?"

Anxious to be rid of this rude mosquito of a woman, Dean quickly copied the list.

"Listen, mister, before, everyone had a job."

"Oh, sure, the workers' paradise."

"Maybe not paradise. But not confusion either. Now no one knows how long the job will last. Have to argue pay, negotiate. People are crazy thanks to you."

"If you're looking for an argument, you won't get it from me."

She wiggled her fingers, then waved toward the tired people in the metal chairs. "People have to wait in line before, but never for work. Maybe you should take my job, and I'll join the resistance."

"The resistance is a myth."

"We Russians can still be proud, though. The largest country in the world. Has largest unemployment office in the world. Get out of here and go to work, *podonki.*"

Dean dodged the brooming janitors as he gratefully zeroed in on the exit. *Podonki.* He pronounced the word aloud a couple times. *Podonki* (scum).

At least she hadn't threatened to fuck his mother.

Two long, dreary days behind the wheel of the Zhiguli, the weather getting colder, the light getting thinner. Two days trying to drive the image of Emily Gardner out of his mind.

By his third or fourth stop he had his moves down pat. He posed as an American tourist. An insurance man from Cincinnati—here was his card. His wife, Raisa, was Russian, an émigrée who was trying to reestablish contact with her long-lost brother. He was a heating repairman, he'd been in trouble with the authorities before the war—nothing that reflected on his work, of course—but he'd had to change his name, you understand. Now we don't know what name he's using, but here's his picture, maybe he works for you?

Oh, that. Well, the picture was taken on vacation a few years ago. Sochi, on the Black Sea. He worked so hard during the year, all he wanted to do was loaf. That's why his eyes are shut; he's napping.

Two days of shrugged shoulders, blank stares, and *ne znayus.* Russian managers, helpful as always. Toward late afternoon of the second day Dean faced the inevitable: a long drive outside town. He hoped Gardner would reimburse him for mileage.

He drove north on Leningradskoye Chaussee, crossing the Moscow perimeter behind a coughing throng of trucks carrying freight to Sheremetyevo Airport.

He hated crossing the perimeter, which was formed by the Outer Ring Road, a sixty-eight mile superhighway which enclosed the city limits. The checkpoints, shadowed by boxy apartment buildings which clustered in the suburbs, reminded Dean of prison, of paranoia, of the war.

Before the occupation the perimeter had been a paranoid formality. Now it was a true border. It existed to keep foreigners and Russians alike *out* of the capital. Moscow, undamaged by the war, was still a magnet, the focus of culture, government, and jobs. In the anarchy of war thousands had swarmed to Moscow, hoping to carve a niche for themselves when the dust settled. The city could not absorb them. The perimeter was now guarded by several police forces, all squabbling for jurisdiction: United States occupation forces; Russian militia; traffic police. Hundreds of *druzhinki* (vigilantes), public-spirited citizens who used to help direct traffic on holidays, or maybe keep an eye on that outspoken professor on the fourth floor, now ranged through the forests around Moscow, throwing up chain-link fences and reporting trespassers to the authorities.

They were trying to prevent another squatters' camp from developing, like the makeshift city which filled Dzerzhinsky Park. As he slowed at the checkpoint, Dean smelled the cooking fires of the camp rising on the northwest wind, mingling with factory smoke and truck exhaust.

A Russian face peered in the passenger's window, an American from the other side, each trying to appear more severe and officious than the other. They passed Dean's documents back and forth over the car roof, shoulder holsters scraping the door. The drab green uniforms of the Occupation Forces Guard Division were a warning flag to Dean, who knew the rules of their postings. For many, a Moscow assignment was a reward for six months of hazardous duty guarding the quarantined NUCDET sites in Siberia. Who knew if they hadn't been inadvertently contaminated somehow? Just how low were the radiation levels out there? Chernobyl low? Hiroshima low?

As the American turned Dean's identity card between his fingers, he could almost feel the radiation settling onto his black-and-white portrait.

Formalities cleared, Dean was waved through. He sank into

his seat, hands clammy, yet relieved, and followed the truck convoy into the darkening forest.

The Lenin Rolled Steel Mill No. 5 was a washout. But the gate guard at the Dawn of the First of May Scrap and Salvage Plant thought he recognized Shukshin's picture, and he directed Dean to the personnel office.

The American disarmament officer called a meeting of his foremen, who passed the photograph among their workers. Dean waited in the disarmament officer's glass-enclosed office, eavesdropping on his frenzied existence. Above him hung the banner of the Disarmament Authority, an SS-20 missile wrapped in an olive branch; below him was the factory floor. The missiles, now just hollow tubes, their warheads and guidance systems stripped and cannibalized, their solid-fuel cylinders turned into noxious gases far enough from Moscow where the pollution wouldn't produce an outcry, lumbered along the assembly lines as workers tore them apart with blowtorches and pneumatic hammers. The end result of a week's work was a square of sheet metal, its origin betrayed only by an occasional stenciled "CCCP." A wide door swung open at the end of the assembly line, admitting the cold light of dusk, and the finished product was loaded onto railroad cars, where they'd be shipped to every corner of occupied Russia and turned into refrigerators, mailboxes, or golden arches.

An hour later the officer took a phone call from the floor, and even though walled in by six inches of allegedly soundproof glass, he was forced to shout.

"That was my sheet metal foreman," he told Dean. "There's a man in his section who recognized the picture. He'll be up in a minute."

Dean waited in the deserted employee lounge. Rimsky-Korsakov played quietly, the din of the factory somewhat lessened.

A man in scorched green overalls entered and wiped his hand on his knee before offering it to Dean. He was stocky and out of breath, his face swept back from a flat nose, reminding Dean of a football.

"Boris Gelb. Bad timing this visit of yours. I'm off in ten minutes. You came an hour earlier, I could have stalled off work for the rest of the day."

Gelb dumped his heavy frame into a plastic chair. Dean poured them each a cup of tea from an electric samovar.

"So, the boss says you're Bukharin's cousin," Gelb said.

At last we're fulfilling the plan, Dean thought. The body has a name: Bukharin.

"Brother-in-law actually. Bill Gregory."

"Andrei Pavlovich never mentioned any American relatives."

"I wouldn't think so. His sister—my wife, Raisa—was in a good deal of trouble before leaving the USSR. He wouldn't have mentioned it. You could have been First Department."

Gelb laughed through steely teeth. "Me? KGB? Three letters on a typewriter, that's all it means to me."

"May I have the picture back, Mr. Gelb?"

Gelb slid the picture of Shukshin, now known as Bukharin, across the table. Five minutes in Gelb's pocket had torn it to shreds.

"When was the last time you saw my brother-in-law? I hope you'll help us. My wife's rather frantic."

"Must've been a couple months ago. Our usual Friday night barhopping. Tried to pick up a couple of girls."

"You didn't succeed, I take it?"

"A disaster." He pointed an accusing finger at Dean. "You disarmed my prick as well, you son of a bitch. The girls know what we do for a living here. Grinding up the same rockets that were supposed to defend us. It's humiliating, a work of betrayal."

Dean looked into his tea. "So you don't think he ran off with some girl?"

"What girl would have him? He always dressed like hell, never had any money."

Just enough to wear imported cologne and rent expensive hotel rooms.

"Did he have any enemies here at the factory? You know, people he owed money, that sort of thing?"

"He owed me ten rubles he lost playing *zhelka.* So what the

93

hell, I killed the bastard. Cut him up with my blowtorch and now he's been turned into Volga hubcaps."

"I'll ignore that remark for my wife's sake, Mr. Gelb. This next question is rather delicate, I hope you'll forgive me. Did he ever take narcotics?"

"I knew Andrei for ten years. Right before the war I slept in the bunk above him for six weeks at the evacuation center. You get to know a man when you expect the end of the world with every toast. He wouldn't know an opium poppy from a chrysanthemum."

Dean refilled their tea glasses. Gelb was watching the clock, probably anxious to have another go at the local girls.

"I don't suppose you remember Andrei's address?"

Gelb was instantly suspicious. "You don't know your own brother-in-law's address?"

"Half the housing records in Moscow were destroyed. If I knew his address, I wouldn't need to drive out here and deal with characters like you."

Dean pulled out a hundred-ruble note. He'd known by Gelb's face that bribery would be involved sooner or later.

"Here's the ten rubles Andrei Pavlovich owes you . . . with interest. I hope it'll make up for the overtime you're putting in with me tonight."

Gelb pocketed the money and downed his tea.

The disarmament officer entered with a box labeled "Bukharin" and set it in front of Dean. "The life and work of one Bukharin, Andrei Pavlovich. This is all that was left in his locker. Maybe it'll help you find him. Although if it were my brother-in-law, I doubt if I'd make the effort. And by the way, his job won't be waiting for him." The officer slammed the door, and Dean began to sift through Bukharin's effects.

"You know who you ought to talk to? Viktor Gerasimov," Gelb said.

"Gerasimov?"

"He was our factory *tolkach*. Andrei Pavlovich hero-worshiped him."

Dean closed the box against Gelb's prying eyes. "Would he still be on duty?"

"Somewhere in the motherland Viktor Gerasimov is on duty, squeezing something valuable out of somebody in exchange for something worthless. But he's not doing it here. He quit a few months before the war."

To a Soviet factory operating under the narrow dictates of the plan, a *tolkach* (pusher) had been more important than the chief manager. A factory received a yearly quota of supplies: raw materials; machinery; toilet paper. Flexibility was not built into the system. Supply and demand were nonexistent. Moscow called the shots. What if a section of train track rusted, a boxcar of rivets derailed and was plundered by the locals, who were experiencing a rivet shortage? The factory that had originally ordered the rivets couldn't simply buy more; it wasn't in the plan. Enter the *tolkach,* part traveling salesman, part liar, part master of ceremonies, part mafioso. It was his job to scare up new rivets. A few bribes, a few shots of vodka, and a few girls later, the factory had its rivets. No one asked where they came from. What mattered was that the plan was fulfilled and the bosses were content. According to Gelb, Viktor Gerasimov was the best *tolkach* he'd ever seen.

"Viktor could get his hands on anything. Maybe he can get his hands on your brother-in-law."

As Dean left, tucking the box of Bukharin's possessions under his arm, Gelb snagged him with a lurid smile. "Feel this."

Gelb produced a slim, deadly-looking knife blade from a tool pocket in his overalls. Its precision lines were frightening, surgical. He drew it slowly up the back of Dean's thigh. Dean could feel the steely touch; any more pressure, and the knife would slit his pants.

"Some of us down there on the assembly line get a little bored. We have a few drinks when the foreman's taking a nap. I made this out of sheet metal. Most of the guys have a couple; this is my smallest."

Dean thanked Gelb for his time and squeezed out the door. The *1812 Overture* boomed from hidden speakers.

Dean called Gardner from a phone booth in the parking lot, filling him in on what he'd learned. As before, Gardner's enthusiasm was boyish and voluble.

"That's terrific, Dean. How the heck did you— No, I'm not going to ask how. Listen, we've got a couple old Moscow directories here. Maybe I can track down Bukharin's address. If we're lucky, we might dig up a few relatives. I'll pay them a visit and—"

"No. Absolutely not. Let me make the first approach."

"Dean, we at least have to pretend to follow the rules. We'll have to send an officer to notify the next of kin."

"After I've talked to them. This whole thing feels off center. Why would his relatives wait two months for him to come home from work? Why didn't they come looking for him at the factory? Why didn't they file a missing persons report? You won't learn anything if you go crashing in there like a cop."

"Well . . ."

"Believe me."

"I can't delay it too long."

"Tomorrow night. Let me handle it my way. You came to me, remember?"

"The teacher's pulling rank on the student?"

Dean was getting annoyed. He began a game of ticktacktoe on the frosted glass of the phone booth. They hung there at opposite ends of the line, wordlessly.

"Silence from the lectern, huh?" Gardner said at last. "That was always one of your most effective strategies. You'd just let us talk ourselves into a corner. Listen, Dean, I'm sorry. I'm starting to get a little pressure to make some progress on this thing."

"I call identifying a corpse progress, don't you?"

"Yes, yes, of course. I'll, ah—I'll get Bukharin's address and phone you tonight. Oh, and one other thing—"

"I'll be discreet."

"I don't mean that. I'm through giving advice for the moment. We identified that smock of Mintz's. You know what a *telogreika* is?"

"A prisoner's coat. They were issued to all arrivals at Soviet labor camps. They usually fit you when you entered, were too big by the time you were released. That could explain the missing pocket. Mintz's name would have been stitched on it, a constant reminder of his ordeal. He probably ripped it off."

"You knew it all the time."

"I suspected it. But I didn't want the lab to have any pre-conceived notions. Most of the camps sewed their own clothes. They tell you which camp it was from?"

"It was made in Mordovia, camp number seven, section three. I'll get our computers on it. Maybe we can find some of his fellow inmates."

Something inside Dean tightened. He looked at the tick-tacktoe game. Cat's game. He rubbed it off with his sleeve.

"Richard?"

"I'm here."

Dean was silent for a moment, attempting to focus his energy on the earpiece. No electronic whistles, no mysterious buzzes. No click of an extension being replaced. Then why did he feel someone was listening to their conversation?

"Dean? What is it?"

"I just wanted to say good job on identifying that coat. Talk to you tonight."

Dean hung up, forcing the receiver out of his hands as though it were contaminated.

CHAPTER EIGHT

The checkpoint was closed for an hour when Dean returned to Moscow. A truckload of perimeter crashers had been discovered. The driver had been arrested, and several of the refugees had fled into the woods. Occupation forces were hunting them down now with rifle and flashlight, while traffic backed up for several kilometers.

With a frost coming on, no one trusted the battery enough to turn off the engine, so Dean sat in his rumbling Zhiguli as exhaust from a hundred other cars smudged his windshield.

He passed the time by examining Bukharin/Shukshin's effects. Wrenches, screwdrivers, an extra fuel tank for his acetylene torch. Ration cards, change, a set of house keys, and a pint of American bourbon. Prewar, Dean noticed, since it did not bear the seal of the Liquor Authority. But nothing connecting him to the Kosmos Hotel.

Dean spent half an hour at home. He answered a call from Vera. She was in Sverdlovsk and would be flying home in two weeks. He opened a beer, took two grateful sips, answered a call from Gardner, and jotted down Bukharin's address. He nailed down a piece of molding that fell when a door was slammed down the hall, finished his beer, and hurried out.

98

It was better to catch people in the evening, when they were off work, relaxed in comfortable surroundings, their guards down.

Bukharin's building was prerevolutionary, but austere, in a quiet neighborhood not far from Red Square. Bukharin lived on the first floor, across from a wrought-iron elevator cage which lent a bit of decoration to the building's dusky interior. Bukharin's name was one of five listed for a single apartment.

When the door was opened by an elderly woman in a black dress and black bandanna, three men looked up from three different dining-room tables, three women turned hostile over-the-shoulder glances from three side-by-side stoves. A communal apartment. Once the spacious quarters of a single aristocrat, it was now the claustrophobic home of three families.

"Mrs. Bukharina?" Dean guessed.

The old black-clad woman replied with a stony, hate-filled gaze.

"I'm from the factory social committee?" This was Dean's timid mode, every sentence lilted into a question.

She scowled and slammed the door in his face. Dean stood there in consternation. Was he losing his touch? Or did this woman, dressed entirely in black, already know the truth about Bukharin?

He rang the doorbell again. He heard a young woman's voice arguing with an elderly voice. Then the door was roughly thrown open. A wispy blond woman in her late twenties faced him. She may even have been beautiful, but time and experience had bruised her features and taken the light out of her eyes. She brushed hair out of her face in exasperation and draped chafed hands, lightly foamed with dish soap, over her very pregnant stomach.

"Sorry about Mrs. Bukharina. I'm Nina Zinovieva, a friend of the family."

"Well, as I was saying," Dean began, in English, "some of Andrei Pavlovich's friends down at the factory are organizing a party for him, and the job's sort of fallen in my lap."

"A party? For what?"

Dean consulted some imaginary notes. "Well, I guess to celebrate ten years with the factory. I haven't been there that long myself, of course."

"But what do you want with his mother?"

"If it's not too much of an imposition, I was hoping she could get together a list of his friends. So I'd know who else to invite. We want a well-rounded crowd, not just a bunch of us jawing about work."

Nina's expression shifted from surprise to impatience. "Mrs. Bukharina's on her way to work. Ludmilla, you'll be late!"

"Like I said, I don't want to impose. Perhaps she could get together a list in her spare time."

Mrs. Bukharina, bundled into a thick black overcoat, slogged through the door, assisted by Nina. They shut the door and made their way to the elevator.

"For another thing, as you might have noticed, she's in mourning."

"I'm sorry. If I've come at a bad time . . ."

"For Russia." Mrs. Bukharina whispered in Nina's ear. "She says the mourning clothes come off when the Americans are crushed by the Soviet resistance."

A glimmer of pleasure crept into Mrs. Bukharina's expression as she anticipated the mass destruction and torture of a despised enemy.

As they waited for the elevator car, Nina added: "She says it took twenty million deaths to whip the fascist Nazi invaders. Now this is a direct quote: She says it should only take a fraction of that to erase the spineless imperialist Americans from the map of the motherland."

The elevator thudded to the ground floor, cables whining. Mrs. Bukharina whispered another message to Nina.

"Mrs. Bukharina will allow you to accompany her to work. Ordinarily she despises Americans. You must appeal to her on some primitive level."

"No problem. I'm parked right outside."

"We'll walk."

"You sure she can manage?"

"We're standing in her office."

Nina lowered a wooden seat from the rusting wall of the

elevator, and Mrs. Bukharina took her post: She was the elevator operator. With a fluid, muscular motion, she reached for the grating, and Dean hopped briskly into the car as the door slammed behind him. Mrs. Bukharina's hands whirled over a series of levers and buttons, like a crewman in the engine room of a steamship, and with a shudder, the car began its ascent.

Mrs. Bukharina didn't say a word, her attention nailed to the arrow indicating the floors.

"Why the sudden change of heart?" asked Dean.

"I would say she's decided she hates her son almost as much as the Americans. She hasn't heard from him in months. She hopes you may have."

"I don't run into him too much at work, Mrs. Bukharina. It's a big factory, you know."

Still not a word from the rigid old lady. Dean looked at Nina for clues.

Nina shrugged. "She still hates you enough not to talk to you directly. I'll interpret."

"Well, I guess that'll have to do. Ask her if there are any friends or neighbors I should invite."

Mrs. Bukharina muttered an answer, of which Dean caught only fragments.

"My son has abandoned his friends in the same way he has abandoned his family" was the translation.

"What does she mean by 'abandoned'?"

"Andrei Pavlovich moved out several months ago," Nina said. "She says he's changed. He never calls or stops by. She feels deserted."

"Does she have any idea what caused the change?"

Nina hesitated. She seemed afraid to ask the question, afraid of what Mrs. Bukharina would say. Did she suspect Dean spoke Russian?

In Russian she asked Mrs. Bukharina an innocent question about the weather and translated the answer into English: "She has no idea why a son would so callously decide to break a mother's heart. Such behavior was not common before the occupation."

Dean mentally filed away Nina's evasive tactic. "And she doesn't know where he's moved? She doesn't have his number?"

Mrs. Bukharina answered with a disgusted shake of her head as the elevator groaned to a stop on the fifth floor. A bulky man entered, leading a bulkier child. After a formal exchange with Mrs. Bukharina, the man secured her permission to tape a campaign poster to the wall of the elevator. It showed a bald man with a reluctant smile presiding over a bilingual slogan: "Occupied but still Russian." An anti-American candidate— the only sloganeering Mrs. Bukharina would allow in her elevator.

The descent through the floors was a curious sensation. From each floor came the babble of voices, some laughing, some fighting in intense dinner table conversations. Dean felt like a frantic eavesdropper, listening in on a succession of lives, all flashing past without impression, all dominated by the echoing assault of the TV news. By the time they reached the ground floor, Dean had absorbed the weather forecast and the "exciting rumor, now fact," that David Wolper would be staging the election day festivities in Red Square. He promised a "million goose bumps," an extravaganza that would put the May Day parades to shame.

They waited on the ground floor, the elevator doors open, ready to take on passengers.

"Perhaps I ought to speak to Anatoly Mintz or Viktor Gerasimov. They were your son's best friends before the war, I've heard."

"Don't know them," Nina replied quickly. "Neither does she." It was obvious by now that Nina wanted to be rid of Dean as quickly as possible. She took a hammered gold cigarette case from the pocket of her apron and lit up a *papirosi,* a stub of a Russian cigarette, fitted into a long cardboard holder. Dean was less interested in the cigarette than in the case, an expensive trinket for someone who lived in a communal apartment. She exhaled a gray parade of smoke rings and leaned against the grating.

Mrs. Bukharina erupted. She leaped to her feet with startling agility and snatched the *papirosi* from Nina's hand. She furiously stamped it out with her boots. Then, as though it were a cockroach that she'd squashed but that was still breathing, she forced it down the slit between the elevator and the building floor.

A shouting match broke out, with Mrs. Bukharina lashing at Nina in biting obscenities, accusing her of killing the baby.

Nina fought Mrs. Bukharina word for word. "This baby is doomed, Ludmilla. Condemned. It has no life. Why not let it enjoy a smoke once in a while? As a matter of fact, I think it might like a few shots of vodka right now. Why not introduce it to the pleasures of opium while we're at it? I think I'll take a tram down to the Kursk train station and buy it a little package of *koknar*. Start them while they're young, don't you think? Just like the Young Pioneers. With little needles dangling from their bellies like a pine tree."

Mrs. Bukharina turned her back on Nina and began singing quietly to herself. But Nina was relentless, pushing her face into Mrs. Bukharina's. "I have the right to kill it, don't I? Didn't Khrushchev give me that right?" She turned her fury on Dean. "Do we still have that right? Will the Americans let us keep our five-ruble abortions?"

Suddenly ashamed and unsure of himself, Dean stepped out of the car. Mrs. Bukharina's son was dead, she still didn't know it, and here he was trying to cajole a few tidbits of information out of her. She was at least seventy and still reported to work every evening, riding up and down the building's six drafty floors, a job that would probably reward her with pneumonia if it didn't make her deaf first.

An image came to mind, an image that perfectly captured what he was: a mortician stripping the body of valuables before burial.

The old lady retreated into the elevator and threw the grating shut behind her. The car climbed slowly out of sight. The last glimpse Dean had of Bukharin's mother was her broad back, stubbornly turned toward him, her voice still humming melodically.

"Mrs. Zinovieva—"

"Miss, if it's not too embarrassing for you."

"Please, if there's anything I can do. The factory has a little emergency fund . . . if you're short of cash right now . . . if you need a medical referral—"

Nina stomped toward her apartment. Curious stares withdrew from the doorway.

"What you can do for me is get the hell out of here. I don't want to talk about Andrei Pavlovich. I don't have any idea where he is, and I certainly won't be attending your little party."

She disappeared into her communal dinginess, which now smelled of frying onions and raw fish. The light timer clicked, leaving Dean in half-darkness. Somewhere above him the elevator grated to a stop as Mrs. Bukharina continued her rounds. Television echoes filled the empty shaft. Dan Rather was interviewing David Wolper.

Dean walked for several blocks. He needed clean air and freezing weather. Cold was satisfying. You could beat it. You could just keep wrapping your body in layer after layer of clothing, until you felt warm again.

Even buses looked inviting, their interiors basking in a warm orange glow, as though the passengers had lit a campfire in the aisle.

He felt profoundly depressed. He'd appeared to these people under a silly pretext and had succeeded only in triggering their latent misery. And he'd accomplished nothing but to raise new questions. Shukshin/Bukharin was still an enigma. Why had he quit his factory job? Why had he moved out at about the same time? Why had he so jealously guarded the secret of his whereabouts? Was Nina's baby his? Had he left her to raise it herself? Was that why she seemed to despise him? Just what was her relationship to the family?

Bukharin, with his deadly grind of a factory job and his roots in a shabby apartment building, wore tailored foreign clothes and pampered himself in an expensive hotel room. Nina Zinovieva carried a cigarette case which would fetch thousands on the underground gold market. Everyone who seemed to have no money had lots of money.

104

Dean would tell Gardner to send his most sympathetic Russian officer to break the news to Mrs. Bukharina of her son's death. A limp gesture. But he felt that somehow tonight he'd aggravated old wounds that the two women were trying to heal.

He tried to kid himself that an unconscious decision led him onto a bus which passed by the Gardners' apartment. But he knew that a glimpse of Emily, her gorgeous body sheathed in a silk nightgown, tucking in the kids, maybe having a drop of cognac as she pulled the shades, would be instant therapy.

He lucked into a window seat on the right side of the bus and rubbed away the steam from the window as the bus trundled down Metrostroyevskaya.

He picked out the Gardners' building with its many porticoed windows. The lights were out. So much for therapy. There was always TV. Then a light blinked on in the living room. He recognized Emily, though her figure was blurred by lace curtains. Dean cupped his face to the window. As if to reward him, Emily drew back the curtains. So much for the silk nightgown, too. She was caked in a lumpy white bathrobe as she peered into the night. But he didn't care. Folded up in terry-cloth, her face nearly invisible in shadow, she was still enticing. He felt a hollowness between his ribs, a symptom he usually associated with insomnia, but tonight, he knew it was serious attraction.

When it hit him in the ribs, it usually meant trouble.

As the bus turned a corner, Dean's erotic musings were stopped cold. Parked behind Gardner's building was another ZIL limousine. Though this one had license plates, it could easily have been the same car he'd seen at the cemetery. Arguing heatedly at the rear passenger door was a prosperous-looking man in his fifties with an expensive haircut and an equally expensive full-length leather coat . . . and Richard Gardner.

Dean longed for the elaborate hardware he used to be able to draw from supply. A nice, ultrasensitive boom mike would be perfect now, the kind where you could hear fleas jump on a dog a mile away.

He watched Gardner retreat from the leather coat, clearly intimidated, seeming to shrink physically. The leather coat followed and spun Gardner by the collar. Gardner nodded in timid agreement to some final words from leather coat, who stalked back to the ZIL and disappeared into the back seat. Gardner looked small and alone as he trudged back to his apartment.

An unseen chauffeur propelled the stately limousine into the empty boulevard. Dean strained to read the license number, but it was hopeless. Dean looked over the bus driver's shoulder, watching the limousine shoot off into the darkness ahead. The traffic lights all turned green at the limo's approach, as though they sensed its power.

CHAPTER NINE

I t has never been easy to find someone in Moscow. Under the Soviet regime, street maps were nearly impossible to obtain. They were often artificially skewed to make interpretation difficult for foreigners. Sensitive ministries went unnamed; entire blocks were left blank. The situation outside the city was equally bizarre. Cities that were listed on some maps never existed; cities that did exist were left off other maps, all in the name of military secrecy. A geographical arm of the Occupation Economic Authority employed a staff of twenty who fanned out across Russia, correcting the deliberate mistakes of Soviet cartographers.

Telephone books were rarer than Bibles. They didn't come with the phones; you couldn't find them in phone booths, the post office, or the Central Telegraph Office on Gorky Street. A personal directory was a treasured possession, published only sporadically, and then only a few thousand at a time, to serve a metropolis of eight million.

All this made life difficult for people who wished to turn a flirtation into something more serious—you'd better get a detailed dossier on that secretary you were attempting to pick up on the metro if you ever expected to see her again—and for others, like private investigators, who relied on official sources of information to lighten their work loads. The situation was improving but, like everything in Russia, at a glacier's pace. The Communications Authority had contracted with NYNEX and Bell Atlantic to compile the first Moscow yellow pages, but after three years they were only on *G,* the fourth letter of the Russian alphabet. Russian paranoia and secrecy still ruled. A man in a perky yellow uniform, Russian or American, couldn't count on much of a welcome if he knocked on a Muscovite's door and asked for the phone number and business address.

Dean had presumed he'd have to call on the MOP computers to track down Viktor Gerasimov. But in an unexpected burst of good luck, the phone company had already done the dirty work: Gerasimov was already filed and available through information. Dean would begin his search for Gerasimov the next day.

Dean heated a frozen packet of Georgian shashlik for dinner and tuned in Vremya. He felt men became gourmet cooks in order to impress women with their spirit of equality, not because they genuinely enjoyed it. Luckily Vera despised home cooking, preferring the transient atmosphere of a restaurant or a railroad station snack bar.

To Dean's astonishment, Richard Gardner was on TV, his flesh tones a piercing crimson. Posed against the impressive background of the MOP homicide division's new computer graphics map of Moscow, he was delivering a press statement.

"Inspired detective work and plain old door-to-door footwork have resulted in my division identifying the Kosmos Hotel victim as one Andrei Pavlovich Bukharin, an employee of the Dawn of the First of May Scrap and Salvage Plant."

Gardner then responded to a volley of questions, answering each in a tone so obviously self-effacing it gave the impression that he alone had been responsible for this first breakthrough in the case. As Gardner basked in the glow of the television lights, smoothing the breast pocket handkerchief that, as always, was a match for his tie, he switched into fractured Russian. Dean switched off the set in disgust.

Disgust? That was jealousy. Dean angrily soaked up the mucus of sauce that clung to the shashlik with a shard of black bread, berating himself for the sudden envy he felt. He'd agreed to this assignment; he'd agreed to be the invisible backseat driver. Richard Gardner's shadow. What did he expect? That Gardner would announce his name on national television, that a major motion picture covering his crime-fighting exploits would be produced? What did he care about publicity or fleeting recognition? Those were emotions from the past, social-climbing emotions, corporate ladder emotions, ego. This was just another case.

Whom was he trying to impress?

There were five Viktor Gerasimovs on the list Dean obtained from information, and it wasn't until number three that Dean knew he'd found the former *tolkach*.

He was miffed at Gardner. His little press conference had blown Dean's cover. He could no longer pose as the tourist searching for his missing brother-in-law since everyone who'd watched the evening news now knew the brother-in-law was dead. His imagination was fuzzed from inventing fresh identities. He longed for the clarity of a rank and a badge, for the force of law. Tell me what I need to know, or go to jail for obstruction of justice.

By the time he reached Gerasimov's building, he still didn't know what his approach would be.

Gerasimov lived with his parents in one of those cities within a city that the Soviet government had termed microregions. Monotonous blocks of apartments were laid out along identical streets, each of which led to a central plaza like spokes on a wagon wheel. Each street had its own picked-over grocery store, its muddy patch of public park, and its streetlamps broken by rock-throwing teenagers. Each street was identical in its aura of fatigue and decay.

A man who Dean presumed was Gerasimov's father answered the door. A spindly, shuffling little man, he was a perfect complement to the sagging building in which he lived.

109

Dean figured the man and his home would become obsolete at the same time.

"Yes?" The voice was thin and brittle, like the walls.

"Mr. Gerasimov? My name is David Craig. From the Insurance Authority? My office phoned you?"

Mr. Gerasimov was approaching the age where forgetfulness looms like a fog. Maybe he had received a call from the Insurance Authority. Better to pretend he had than to let this stranger know his memory was going.

"Of course, Mr. Craig. What was this about again?"

"It's all rather unpleasant, I'm afraid."

"I'll get my wife."

Dean held back a chuckle. "Actually, it's your son, Viktor, I need to talk to. It's about the death of his friend and co-worker Andrei Bukharin."

The request seemed to fluster the old man. Surely he hadn't forgotten he had a son?

"Viktor? Viktor doesn't really see anyone."

"Oh? Is he ill?"

"No. That is—"

A stout woman in a smudged apron, one arm holding a broom, the other cradling a clutch of cleaning products, surfaced behind Mr. Gerasimov.

"Who is it, Aleksandr?" she asked, looking at Dean rather than her husband.

"It's a Mr. Craig. From the Insurance Authority. He wants to see Viktor."

"Did you tell him Viktor doesn't see anyone?" Again, without a glance at her husband.

Dean was forming a terrifying picture of Viktor Gerasimov: a frightening, overweight baby in his thirties who hadn't seen the sun in years, still wore diapers, slept in a crib, perhaps drank vodka from a formula bottle, and used a screwdriver as a pacifier.

"Am I speaking to Mrs. Gerasimova?" Dean asked.

"You are." She gradually nudged her husband out of the doorframe, planting herself like a gate guard. Perhaps she was afraid Dean would soil the apartment she was cleaning. "Our son is in the middle of a severe depression. We're screening his visitors at the moment."

"There might be some money in it for him."

"Money won't cure my son, Mr. Craig. Peace and quiet, home cooking, regular hours, a clean environment—that's what he needs."

"And I'm sure you do an admirable job of providing them. However, Viktor was named as beneficiary on Mr. Bukharin's policy—"

"I should be getting back to my work," said Aleksandr Gerasimov. "Would you excuse me, Mr. Craig?" Dean nodded, and Gerasimov drooped back into the apartment, leaving his wife to negotiate.

"His memoirs," she said. "My husband's been at them for three years. Just because he used to be a chauffeur to the *nachalstvo,* he feels he was part of history. Well, I encourage him, that's my job nowadays. Keep him away from the vodka, you understand? Now if you were a publisher, maybe from your Simon and Schuster—"

"Mother?" A male voice, a clear, penetrating baritone, called from somewhere in the flat. Not a baby's voice, certainly not an invalid's wheeze.

"Just a moment, please." Mrs. Gerasimova hurried away from the door in concern. Dean couldn't restrain his curiosity, and he edged across the threshold to where he had a clear view of the apartment.

Though daylight seeped through cracks in the walls, the Gerasimovs coped admirably with the shoddy construction. Their living room was warm and tasteful, comfortably cluttered with antiques, icons, and Bokhara rugs. Scores of wood-framed family photographs crowded the walls, turning them into a dizzying checkerboard. They made the apartment seemed cramped, but they covered the cold cement.

In one corner, beneath the living room's only window, oblivious of the wind whistling through cracked weather stripping, Aleksandr Gerasimov worked on his autobiography at a narrow secretarial desk, with barely enough surface for a sheet of paper and two elbows. Shelves, sagging beneath the weight of books and correspondence, climbed to the ceiling. Though his back was turned to Dean, Gerasimov could sense his presence.

"Come in, Mr. Craig. Don't stand in the drafty hallway. And close the door behind you, if you don't mind."

Dean reached into his overcoat pocket, thinking he would offer the old man a cigarette.

"Thanks just the same, Mr. Craig. I only smoke a pipe. And then only during the hockey matches, and then only if we're winning, and then only if it's the third period."

"How did you know I was going to offer you a smoke?"

"I spent twenty years as a chauffeur with my back to people. You develop a sixth sense about what's going on behind you. By all means, smoke yourself. And sit down."

Dean sat in a stuffed chair, facing Gerasimov's back, like a cooperative passenger.

"Quite an undertaking, your memoirs."

"Especially since I received no formal literary training. I've read the important autobiographies, of course; Khrushchev's, Stalin's, Brezhnev's—he was famous for producing an autobiography a year." He gestured toward the brimming bookshelves. "At last, I've made the leap into the intelligentsia—at seventy. I only hope I finish."

"Your son can't help you? It might be therapeutic."

"Oh, I wouldn't want to impose. After his loss I think the last thing he'd want to be involved in was a project which dredged up the past."

"His loss?"

"His family was killed in the war. He lost a wife and two daughters. Not a blow from which one ever completely recovers."

Dean suddenly felt numb. Wherever he turned in this case, he seemed to bump against tragedy.

"Listen, this is awfully insensitive of me intruding on your grief like this. Why don't I come back later? Better yet, maybe I can question Viktor about this Bukharin case over the phone sometime."

"Bukharin, Bukharin . . ." The old man reached for a box

marked "Viktor." "You see, Mr. Craig, my antidote to tragedy is activity. So please, don't feel you're intruding. The problem is, I can't recall any friends of Viktor's with that name. You say they worked together at the ministry?"

What ministry? Gerasimov had worked in a factory. Had he exaggerated his importance to his father? Or did Dean have the wrong Viktor Gerasimov?

"I may owe you another apology," Dean said. "The Viktor Gerasimov I'm looking for worked at the Dawn of the First of May Scrap and Salvage Plant—"

"That's our Viktor. He changed jobs a few months before the war. I got him a job as driver at the Ministry of Culture. It was the best I could do for him, you see. My influence didn't extend much beyond the garage. My only disappointment is that he remained a chauffeur. I'd always hoped one day he'd move to the back seat."

"If I may indulge in a piece of politics, it pays to remember that the man in the front seat has the controls."

Gerasimov smiled, enjoying the obvious flattery.

Aleksandr Gerasimov's eyes wandered over the tumult of his research. Then he turned to face Dean. "Of course, I'm still in the 1970's. I may come across this Bukharin as I work through the years. Perhaps you'd care to check back with me in a decade or so."

The old man was relaxing, delighted by the opportunity to reminisce aloud for a change. Just as he reached for the clear stem of a vodka bottle that peeked invitingly from behind a row of books, his wife entered from a dim hallway. He quickly snapped his hand back, as though it had been slapped.

"You'll have to be brief, as Viktor's show comes on in ten minutes," she said. "But he seems to think that a visitor might cheer him up. Please, I'll ask you again: Try not to upset him."

Dean got to his feet, shook hands with Aleksandr Gerasimov, and, almost guiltily, inched across the living-room floor.

"The door at the end of the hall," said Mrs. Gerasimova. "Knock first." Dean nodded and started down the corridor, toward the roar of a television.

Mrs. Gerasimova's shadow filled the hallway door behind Dean, virtually sealing him in darkness.

"If he needs anything, call me. If he falls asleep while you're talking, just slip out the door as quietly as you can." Dean nodded again. "And leave the TV on when you leave."

Dean raised his hand to knock at Viktor's door. The image of Viktor as a hideous baby was back, blood dripping from teething gums. It was a scene lifted from a Russian horror movie: the parents who kept the murderous, deformed child locked in his room, allowing him guests only at feeding time.

Dean's knuckles grazed the door. The baritone responded with "Come in, Mr. Craig."

Dean entered, half expecting to step into a puddle of drool and vomit.

Instead, Viktor appeared to be quite normal. Inquiring eyes were darkened behind tinted glasses. He looked Dean over with an open, winning face and a single gold tooth gleaming at the center of a perfect smile, unusual for a Russian. Wet-looking, straight hair was swept across his head at an oblique angle, dipping in an unruly wave just above his sideburns. He was comfortably folded into a chair beside a crisply made bed, one hand sipping a Budweiser, the other poised over a TV remote control.

Only his clothes were unusual, a mélange of styles and decades: tight faded blue jeans; Reeboks; a wide leather belt with a turquoise buckle; a T-shirt that read "Wasting away in Margaretaville"; a powder blue leisure suit coat with white stitching, a "Born in the USA" button pinned to the collar.

"Come in, come in." Gerasimov offered a firm handshake. "Would it be a major drag if we have the tube on while we talk? It's *USA Today*. I never miss it." Gerasimov's American accent and feel for slang were uncanny.

Dean closed the door, but his fingers lingered on the knob, not permitting it to latch.

"Leave it open if it'll relax you. Don't worry, man, we Russians do quite well in captivity. Look . . ." He waved his arms wildly, like a man stranded on a desert island trying to attract a search plane. "No straitjacket." He jumped to his feet and

114

closed his eyes, bringing the beer can directly toward his nose. "My equilibrium's perfect; I'm not on any medication. You're safe. How about a Bud?"

A beer had never sounded better, but Dean was determined to stay in character. "I'm afraid regulations forbid my drinking on the job."

"Regulations? I thought you Americans hated fucking regulations. He didn't need any regulations." Viktor pointed to a poster of Marlon Brando in his *Wild One* outfit. Like a teenage boy, Gerasimov had plastered his walls with portraits of larger-than-life American heroes. Sharing the room with men of action like Clint Eastwood and James Dean, were wizards of finance and industry: Lee Iacocca, Steve Wozniak, Ross Perot, and Paul Volcker.

"Well, Marlon Brando never had to put in eight hours a day at the Insurance Authority. Now, if I could just have a few minutes here . . ." Dean sat primly on the edge of the bed and opened his briefcase.

"Hold your horses." Gerasimov focused on the television, turning up the volume with one hand while reaching for a beer with the other.

The swell of a Russian male chorus blended into a rousing Sousa march, and Russia's most popular game show, *USA Today,* was on the air. Sponsored by the American daily paper, it was a poorly disguised attempt to whet the country's appetite for the paper's long-planned Russian edition. Every viewer was a potential subscriber. The occupation justified it as a way to introduce the average Russian to American culture, but that same average Russian appreciated it for the gaudy, hysterical quiz show it was.

Three Russian contestants—Americans could not participate—stood side by side at a red, white, and blue counter, facing the giant game board, which featured three outlined maps of the United States, one for each contestant. The game's object was to be the first to fill in the map with all fifty states. You did this by answering questions about America. For each correct response you were awarded a state, which swirled into view on a computer-generated tornado. But you still had to identify the state from its outline, before it was added to your map.

"Mr. Gerasimov?"

"Sssssh. Sssssssh. Here comes the first question."

Dean backed off. Perhaps this was how Gerasimov dealt with the loss of his family. Who was Dean to interrupt his video therapy?

The host, a former deputy press secretary from the Soviet delegation to the United Nations, bounded onto the stage. "In the 1977 American baseball championships, known as the World Series, this man hit four home runs, a series record that earned him the nickname Mr. October."

The contestants folded their lips in concentration.

"Reggie Jackson!" shouted Gerasimov. "Fuck, this show gets easier every day."

"You knew Andrei Bukharin, correct?"

"Yeah, yeah. At the scrap plant. Pathetic little guy, always sucking up to me. One of those people who walk around under a cloud. Sooner or later they get hit by lightning."

"Were you aware he listed you as a beneficiary in a policy he took out recently with us? We're not talking about a great deal of money here, but—"

Gerasimov motioned for silence. An unnamed state, one of those rectangular, anonymous midwestern states that Dean always found impossible to identify, whirlpooled onto the game board.

Gerasimov looked slyly at Dean. "You know it?" Dean shrugged his ignorance. "Nebraska," pronounced Gerasimov. He was right again.

"I don't get it. I hadn't seen Andrei Pavlovich since before the—I guess we're calling it a war these days. Why should he leave me anything?"

"That's what we're trying to find out. Were you aware of any enemies he had?"

"Mount McKinley and Death Valley!" Gerasimov answered. "The highest and lowest points in the United States."

"Look, before the war Bukharin was a nobody with a beer and vodka habit, a six-day-a-week job, and a mother who tucked him in at night. He never had two kopecks for a phone call. Why should he have enemies?"

"What about since the war?"

"Since the war he might have become the Godfather of Moscow with a million-ruble price on his head. I wouldn't know. The war is a line through people's lives."

"Boris Gelb. Anatoly Mintz. Nina Zinovieva. Did Bukharin ever mention those names?"

"Gelb, Gelb. Yeah, sure. Gelb worked on the line with Bukharin. Another loser. Nina Zinovieva: Bukharin and a woman? Forget it. Mintz? Sounds Jewish. Bukharin wouldn't know any Jews, wouldn't admit it if he did. Always going on about how he hated them."

"He was political?"

"He was careful. Now, let me ask you a question, Mr. Craig. You seem in the know. Who do the police think greased him?"

Dean nodded toward the television, where the craggy coastline of Chesapeake Bay danced into view.

"Maryland," Dean said.

"Virginia," corrected Gerasimov, right as usual.

"The police don't confide in me," Dean replied.

"I see. Could it be because you don't confide in them?"

"Our goals don't always coincide. Their interest in finding Bukharin's killer is purely statistical, another case for the computers. My interest is purely financial."

"Tell me. Who is Bukharin's prime beneficiary?"

"I'm afraid that's confidential." The first thing he taught his students back at the Farm: Keep your cover stories vague; details can turn on you. "Let's just say that person has been eliminated as a suspect to our satisfaction."

"And I haven't?"

"You've convinced me of your expertise in Americana; that's about all."

Gerasimov lowered the volume and leaned forward in his chair, dangling his arms on his knees. His sunglasses seemed to lighten.

"Look, Mr. Craig. Don't get the wrong idea about me. I'm not trying to make your job tougher. Obviously you can tell I

117

have a soft spot in my heart for Americans. It was a hobby of mine, learning about your country. I can name the Fortune five hundred companies in order every year since 1975. I can give you the leading NFL pass receivers for the last twenty years. I can tell a Plymouth Duster from a Scamp, a Chevy Biscayne from a Bel-Air. You give me any intersection, any two streets in a major American city, and I'll tell you where you are. Go ahead."

"Really, Mr. Gerasimov."

"Come on, make it a tough one."

"OK, OK. Beacon Street and Charles."

"Boston. I said make it a tough one."

"Sorry. Geography's never been my strong point. I'm curious, Mr. Gerasimov. This love for America. Did it just suddenly hit you, or was it a long, simmering process?"

"You know when it really hit me? My first day on the job as chauffeur. I saw first hand just how classless the classless society really is. Driving my boss to the Gastronome on Dzerzhinsky Street to pick up his caviar while the average Joe waited in line three weeks for a head of lettuce; dropping him off at private screenings of *The Godfather* and *Deep Throat,* little doses of cultural decadence they felt it was their duty to protect the average citizen from. Trumpeting down the main drags of Moscow in our own lane of traffic.

"You know what we used to do? The bosses'd be at some diplomatic reception getting blitzed on imported scotch, and we'd take out the limos. We'd pick up women, go drag racing. One night we played chicken on the Frunze Embankment; a friend of mine dumped an Academy of Sciences ZIL right in the Moskva."

"That must've earned him a trip to the Lubyanka," Dean said.

Gerasimov chortled. "Actually my friend cooked up some bullshit story about how a Politburo member had borrowed the limo to impress his French girl friend. His boss was so intimidated he let the whole thing drop." He crumpled his Budweiser can and sailed it into the wastebasket. "Bird sinks the hoop as the buzzer sounds, and we're into overtime."

Gerasimov opened another beer. "But I gotta say, since the armistice you Americans are really getting to me. You can't imagine the lineup of salesmen, con artists, and telephone solicitors that have been bugging us. Every hour of every day. And for a country that used to advertise itself as the most religious on earth, Sunday doesn't seem to mean shit when there's a buck to be made.

"So when another American knocks on my door and says there's money in it for me if only I answer his questions, I'm gonna be skeptical."

"You didn't need to invite me in. Your parents made it sound like you were unfit for human eyes."

Gerasimov raised the volume to mask their conversation. "Listen. Sometimes I may exaggerate a flu symptom, act a little withdrawn. Seem to require a little more attention. It's really for my mother's sake."

"So she'll feel needed? What a good son you are, permitting her to cook and clean herself into exhaustion for you every day."

"You know what a Russian mother wants more than anything? She wants someone to care for. Someone to dote on. Someone who's too sick, too depressed to look after himself. She wants to relieve someone's suffering."

Gerasimov pulled out a pack of Sputnik cigarettes and a nugget-size gold lighter. "Smoke?"

"Tell me," Dean asked, accepting one of Gerasimov's cigarettes. "Every Russian I've met lately seems to be carrying a chunk of gold around the size of his fist. I thought our black-market enforcement was pretty efficient. Where do they get it?"

"Speaking for myself, I've had years of experience obtaining the unobtainable. Just because something's illegal doesn't mean you can't shop for it as easily as coffee and cigs." Gerasimov returned his attention to the TV. "Have you ever noticed that Vermont is really only the mirror image of New Hampshire?"

"We were discussing Bukharin?" reminded Dean.

"OK, OK. We met in the Army. We were both from Mos

cow, so we ended up guarding the naval shipyards at Vladivostok. The Army did that to prevent regional loyalties from interfering with your duty to defend the motherland. Kazakhs went to Estonia; Lithuanians, to Turkmenia.

"It was a relationship that couldn't stand the strain of civilian life. In uniform he was my superior, able to hide his mistakes behind orders. In the real world he was hopeless. Plodding, jealous. The reality was, he couldn't give the orders anymore, and he had trouble dealing with that.

"I hadn't wasted a thought on him in years, until I heard on TV that he'd been knocked off. I mean, Andrei Pavlovich was the kind of guy who had to borrow a tie when he went to a snazzy restaurant. I can't picture him in the Kosmos Hotel."

"From what I've heard, you wouldn't want to picture it," Dean said. "It must have been a grisly scene. I'm glad I never went into police work. Give me forms in triplicate and a well-ventilated office, and I'm happy. Now, are you positive you're not overlooking anything noteworthy in Mr. Bukharin's past?"

"Look, I'll make a deal with you. I'll sift through my father's memoirs. Everyone who's walked in and out of our lives is there in his research. But in exchange, I'd like you to do me a little favor, Mr. Craig."

"I'll try."

"If you ever find out how Andrei Pavlovich ended up in that hotel suite, acting like he conquered the world, you let me know. Shit, if he can make it, I can make it."

A resounding knock on the bedroom door startled Dean.

"Are you all right in there, Viktor?"

"Mr. Craig was just leaving, Mother. I think I'll try to take a short nap after he goes."

Gerasimov smiled, indicating the interview was over. "Well, have a good one, Mr. Craig."

USA Today careened toward the final round. A fat man in a silk shirt so tight it formed his breasts into tiny turnovers that wobbled when he laughed had built up a commanding lead. The final mystery state of the night hurtled onto the screen.

"Ha, that's easy!" shouted Gerasimov. "Hawaii!"

"Guam," retorted Dean.

Gerasimov glared indignantly.

"Trick question. The fine print says, 'USA and possessions!'"

A Russian trivia expert hiding from the world. A missing dissident painter. A bitter factory worker who fashioned homemade knives out of scrapped missiles. A mother grieving for Russia. A pregnant woman seemingly determined to kill her own fetus. What did they have in common with an anti-Semitic loser who couldn't afford a phone call yet died in splendor?

Connections. He would have to make connections. He'd been saying that for days. Dean stood at a bus stop outside the Gerasimovs' building, watching the settling dusk. Dark, hunched figures, colorful shawls wrapped around their necks, hurried toward their apartment blocks, which loomed like movie sets in the dwindling light.

Connection 1: Viktor Gerasimov had once been a driver for the Ministry of Culture. The Ministry of Culture had presided over Soviet art, including painting. Anatoly Mintz was a painter. Connection 2: Andrei Bukharin was anti-Semitic. Anatoly Mintz was Jewish. Connection 3: Nina Zinovieva and Viktor Gerasimov both flagrantly displayed objects of black-market gold. Connection 4: Gelb, Bukharin, and Gerasimov all were employees at the same factory.

Connections, or coincidences? Why not go it a few steps farther? All were Soviet. All were human. All but one pissed standing up.

A bellowing rumble grew in volume, like the roll of kettledrums in a Tchaikovsky symphony. Dean joined the others at the bus stop in looking up at the clear black sky. Like a silver football, the Goodyear blimp appeared between two towering buildings across the plaza. Colored lights on the blimp's curved hull spelled out MAKE THIS A CHRISTMAS TO REMEMBER WITH THE AMERICAN EXPRESS CARD.

A bit premature, perhaps, since it was only late November. But Russians needed reminding. Christmas was a holiday they still weren't used to celebrating.

It reminded Dean how satisfying it would be to have the case solved by then—and how impossible.

CHAPTER TEN

The clear skies of the past week had been a warning. Order extra heating oil, fill the cracks in your weather stripping, tape your windows, reline your boots, because it's December now and this moderate weather is not going to last. Dean had ignored the warning and was now paying for his laziness. He drove with one hand, while the other, stiff and clumsy in a fur-lined glove, hooked out the window and swatted the falling snow off the windshield, doing the job of the wiper blade he'd neglected to repair

Richard Gardner, riding beside him, his face buried in a road map, was prepared for any contingency: fur hat; great-coat with fur collar; gloves with fur linings; supplemental galoshes; supplemental mittens; a survival kit that included a Russian dictionary, water purification tablets, flares, and bouillon cubes. He had quickly adapted to the Russian refusal to be intimidated by cold, taking a macho pride in his ability to endure the freezing wind, gloating with each degree below zero that the mercury dropped. To Dean the cold was to be avoided by huddling indoors with a good book, a boiling samovar, and a pint of bourbon, but to Gardner it was a test

Though they were barely two hundred miles southeast of Moscow, the drifting snow, wind, and desolate two-lane road promised Siberia around the next corner. Gardner had offered to arrange for a MOP Mercedes, but Dean had persuaded him to stick with his square, modest Zhiguli. The arrival of a massive foreign luxury car in a mud-soaked village in Mordovia would produce nothing but sealed lips and instant suspicion.

The car thumped across a set of train tracks, wiped clear of snow by the recent passage of a train.

"Could have been a gulag line," Dean said. "The camps had what amounted to their own private rail system. They might even have brought Mintz along this way from Moscow."

Gardner shuddered as he peered at the tracks, brown threads winding through a perfectly white landscape.

Dean hadn't wanted any company on this trip, but Gardner, filled with what old State Department hands disgustingly referred to as the "can-do spirit," had insisted on coming along. They might need to issue a subpoena; they might encounter official documents requiring his signature; they might need to make an arrest, in which case Gardner would have to take over. There was no duly authorized liaison in the area, whom Gardner could deputize in the name of the Military Occupation Police. "I intend to be a hands-on police officer," Gardner had said. "And that means I do my share of the dirty work."

Gardner had managed to identify the labor camp where Anatoly Mintz had been held following his conviction for "Anti-Soviet agitation." A computer search had turned up three of his fellow inmates, and Gardner had interviewed them himself. The first prisoner remembered Mintz as a loner, fond of rambling walks along the camp perimeter, a quiet inmate who did volunteer work in the *sklad* (camp storeroom), for which he was rewarded with pens and pencils he used to fill a sketchbook with vivid scenes of camp life. This prisoner had been impressed by Mintz's tenacity, devoting himself to drawings he knew would be confiscated by the guards before he was released. But they had not spoken more than ten words together, and this prisoner had no idea where Mintz could be found today The second prisoner Gardner had contacted had not known Mintz at all, but the third identified him from a photograph and gave Gardner the name of a guard with whom he believed Mintz had cultivated a friendship.

The small, inbred villages of the Mordovian autonomous republic, southeast of Moscow, were like company towns, sustained by the chain of gulags which stretched across the province. Men found work in the camps as guards; women, as cooks and doctors. The inmates were primarily political and artistic dissidents, held close to Moscow so their heresies could be monitored, so that they could not spread rebellion as they might have in the far-flung, isolated camps in Siberia. The inmates were not dangerous, the work was steady, and the opportunities to extract bribes from the prisoners were many. For these impoverished villages, neglected by the central government in Moscow, which concentrated its energies on urban planning, the gulags often meant the difference between extinction and survival.

A curtain of snow blurred the village of Nagorsk, hiding its secrets from strangers. Gardner and Dean looked at each other in silence as they slowed at the town limits, then peered at the white numb surroundings in trepidation. The sensation of leaving the smooth asphalt for the pitted, frozen dirt streets of the village was unnerving, like dropping off the edge of the world.

Sagging log houses faced the street, their tin roofs caked with dirty snow. The stark black-and-white of the village was relieved only by an occasional painted shutter or carved window frame. Black-wrapped peasants, curved in the wind like saplings, forced paths through the blizzard, some, incongruously, towing blocks of ice on sleds.

"Pipes must be frozen," Dean said. "River ice is the only way to get water."

Outhouse doors slammed in the wind. The streets were littered with objects blown loose from the yards: rakes; hoes; logs of firewood; a child's tricycle.

A coughing child knocked on the windshield, laughing as he held up a frozen cat, slapping its rock-hard tail against the glass. A satellite dish, undoubtedly owned by the village as a whole, had toppled over in the wind. A dog defecated in the snow, which filled the dish like soup in a bowl.

They were startled when a black, sizzling snake snapped into the windshield like a whip, then whopped against the roof as the car slid under it: a telephone cable, broken by the weight of the snow. The phones had been out for days; the village's only contact with the outside world was a ham radio at the local polyclinic.

"I'm not sure these people ever heard of the Second World War, let alone the last one," Gardner commented.

They stopped at the polyclinic, seemingly the village's only brick building. Dean got directions from the *feldsher,* the local health official, and they set off to find the house of Vitaly Zaitsev, the gulag guard said to have befriended Mintz.

Dean knew these villages had a timeless, muffled rhythm all their own. He was not surprised that the town bore so few traces of the occupation. The splintered church had reopened. A neat wood-frame building, the only two-story structure in sight, had once been the party headquarters. It was now abandoned, its windows and door stolen. A red flag was frozen in a permanent furl, icicles dangling from its frayed edges. But there were no signs of America. No angry protesters carrying YANKEE GO HOME signs, but no flower-bearing Russian girls to welcome the liberators either.

The village would survive. But life would not improve.

Zaitsev lived in a tidy, squat little house at the edge of the village. Dean wheeled into a clearing beside the outhouse and gratefully drew his arm into the car, attempting to shake warmth back into it. He debated leaving the motor running but decided against it. An empty car with the keys in it might provide too irresistible a temptation for some of the local teenagers, who had formed themselves into gangs every bit as brutal as those in the cities.

Gardner's hand disappeared into his overcoat, and Dean heard the snap of metal, a shoulder holster being opened.

"How often have you fired a gun in this kind of weather?" Dean asked.

"Never. But I consistently placed in the top ten in our Berlin shooting team. Don't worry about me."

Dean handed Gardner a pair of leather driving gloves. "Put these on. God help us if we get into trouble, and you're wearing those damn mittens. You'll never get them around a trigger, and if you use your bare finger, the frozen metal'll rip your skin right off."

Dean got out and knocked on Zaitsev's door as Gardner reequipped himself.

There was no answer. He knocked again, still without success. He looked through the glass, rimed with snow crystals. It was a one-room cottage, stuffed with homemade furniture, all facing a cast-iron wood-burning stove. Teacups, a bottle of brandy, and half a loaf of bread were scattered across an oil tablecloth. A hunting rifle and snowshoes dangled from a coatrack.

Gardner joined him at the door and knocked authoritatively. "Mr. Zaitsev? This is Detective Richard Gardner, from the Military Occupation Police. I'm here on official business regarding a homicide in Moscow." Gardner winked at Dean. "I know these small-town officials. They like to feel they're part of the action."

"Provided the small-town official's home."

Dean led Gardner to the back of the cottage. Fields of snow unfolded into the distance, where a black fringe of forest was shrouded in mist. Wood, a meticulous pile protected by a burlap tarp, was stacked up the wall. Barbed wire was coiled in the snow like a deadly ball of string, but there didn't seem to be anything worth fencing in.

"Looks like Zaitsev was planning on becoming a rancher," said Gardner.

"What was he gonna raise? Icicles?" said Dean, fiddling with the back door. Again there was no answer.

"I'll check with the neighbors," Gardner offered. As Dean continued his inspection of the shack, he watched in amusement as Gardner dealt with a suspicious woman who appeared at the cottage next door. He struggled through the interview, glancing down at his survival dictionary.

By the time Gardner returned, Dean had found what he was looking for. Two thin, parallel tracks led away from the cabin toward the forest. Only the overhanging eaves above the back door had prevented the tracks from filling with snow and becoming invisible. But no more than a foot away from the shelter of the eaves the tracks vanished in a sheet of white.

"Cross-country skis," said Dean.

"Maybe he's gone hunting."

"In this weather? You couldn't spot a bear if it was wearing a bull's-eye. Anyway, his rifle's in the shack." Dean checked his watch. It was 3:30. "Weather service is predicting twenty below tonight. I doubt if he's gone on a camping trip. He'll be back."

Bundled into every shred of clothing they had, they waited in the car, using the heater only sparingly to conserve gas. Gardner produced a Primus stove from the bottomless survival kit and heated them each a cup of chicken broth. Snow piled up on the hood; jazz crackled from tinny speakers, the faint voice of Radio Moscow.

No one was out now. A single car drove past, chains digging into the crunchy ice pack. Their breaths misted the glass; darkness crept in around them.

The silence made Gardner inquisitive. He wanted to know what had steered Dean toward a career in the Soviet Union. Was government service a family tradition? Was he motivated by a desire for détente, a commitment to defeat communism? Dean supposed the questions were to be expected from a student who runs into a teacher twenty years later and can finally talk to him on an equal basis.

"I guess it was my father's bomb shelter," answered Dean. The dim isolation of the car had brought it to mind.

He'd grown up in a sunny California suburb, American dream town, station wagon country, but, in its own way, as spiritless as the slabs of apartments that ringed Moscow. He'd grown up hungry for secrets in a world he was convinced had none.

There seemed to be no crime, no scandal. His parents

subscribed only to the local paper with its cheery, bland headlines. The world was brought to his family by *Huntley-Brinkley,* and that was only five nights a week. He'd grown up with the impression that politics and wars stopped all over the world on weekends, so everyone could get to the college football game of his choice.

Then he'd discovered the Russians.

One Saturday his father took him to the hardware store. Another routine home-improvement Saturday, he figured, buying paint and shingles and washers. Instead, they'd loaded up on cement and lumber and nails by the bucket. His mother had been sent to stock up on canned goods, dehydrated food, halazone tablets, flashlight batteries, and bottled water. They spent the next five weekends building a bomb shelter in their backyard, camouflaged beneath a patch of dichondra and a swing set.

It became his job to maintain the inventory, and he took to it with dedication and a secret hope that the bombers would soon come, to give shape to his daydreaming, to provide adventure. When his friends went camping or fishing, he hid out in the bomb shelter. He organized the neighborhood kids into resistance teams. They'd hole up in the shelter, where he rationed their food and executed traitors or hysterical cowards who just couldn't take the damp claustrophobia of the shelter. Ultimately, when his friends' parents found out just what kinds of games were going on down there—at the worst they'd expected clandestine smoking or furtive sessions with *Playboy*—he'd been forced to play all the parts by himself.

At school, when the children ducked under their desks during air-raid drills, he'd been the one who always volunteered to close the drapes to shield them from flying glass. Even the teacher had crouched symbolically at the head of the class. He drew out the procedure as long as possible, hoping to catch a glimpse of the bombers, red stars glistening on silver wings.

The Russians struck terror into the heart of the suburbs, and to Dean that meant they were worthy of fascination.

"By the time I grew up, I was better at languages than math anyway, so I wound up at Langley."

"You almost sound nostalgic for the days when the Russians scared the heck out of everyone."

Dean swirled the dregs of his bouillon. "Maybe I am."

They sat without talking for another ten minutes, Gardner fidgeting with the radio, attempting to tune in the week signal from Moscow. Dean was about to suggest they abandon the stakeout in favor of a warm café when he spotted a pale white glow in the tree line about a mile away. It was coming from the direction Zaitsev had gone. He pointed it out to Gardner, who surprised him yet again by producing a tiny pair of binoculars from his survival kit.

"Can't tell anything through these."

Dean pulled out the choke, and the engine wheezed to life. He backed gingerly out of the clearing, wheels spinning on the ice, and began to edge down the road that led out of the village.

"Keep it in sight," Dean ordered. "That's no campfire."

Gardner was grappling to read a local map under the overhead lamp. "What is it? A UFO? According to this map, there's nothing out there."

"I don't think you'll find it on any map." Dean drove with his knees, one hand serving as a windshield wiper, the other checking the clip on his automatic. The road was soon walled in by trees. The headlights were nearly useless to cut the swirling snow and descending darkness. But they were able to keep the flat white glare of the light in view.

The road curved to the left, and the light momentarily vanished. Dean braked to a stop and reversed; the light winked back into view. They squinted into the darkness and made out a thin groove of white, a side road which slashed through the woods.

Dean turned into it, creeping forward in first gear, keeping the light ahead of him. He felt as if they'd flown into a cloud in a small plane; all sense of direction had vanished, the horizon erased from the map. Only the light, now a frosty halo, let them know they were moving, as it bobbed behind the trees.

Suddenly a wall slammed out of the snowstorm, blocking the road. Dean fishtailed to a stop, spitting up a wake of dirty snow. They were confronted by a gigantic gate of solid iron, covered in rust and flaking green paint. A wooden fence topped with barbed wire extended from either side of the gate into the veiled forest. Headlights picked out a plaque covered with faded Cyrillic script: CHIEF ADMINISTRATION OF CORRECTIVE LABOR—CAMP NUMBER 7, SECTION 3. A tiny abandoned island in the gulag archipelago.

Both men shivered involuntarily. The light was coming from inside the camp.

Gardner's hand curled around his gun; Dean's did the same. He switched off the engine but left on the headlights. They could discern the fuzzed edges of buildings beyond the barbed wire. The light appeared to be coming from one of them.

"You think Zaitsev's here?" Gardner asked.

Something about the atmosphere of dread that gripped the place made Gardner whisper. Dean grabbed a flashlight and climbed out of the car. He kicked his way through the snow to the gate; he didn't even feel like whispering.

A twig was stuck through the lock, and Dean snapped it off. It took both men, shoulder to shoulder, to force the gate wide open enough for them to squeeze through.

They found themselves in a no-man's-land, a flat expanse of snow spiked with rolls of razor ribbon and cut by a wide culvert filled with ice and pine needles. Ten more steps brought them to a second gate and a second fence, both smaller. They forced open the second gate and pushed into the camp itself.

They walked uneasily beneath two boarded-up guard towers, black bunkers on stilts, that listed at precarious angles. The camp spread out in three directions. To the left were a kitchen and a brick hospital; beyond that was a football field, wind slicing through the shredded goal nets. To the right were what appeared to be administrative buildings. Facing them were three walls, all that was left of a communal shower. Water pipes sprouted from chipped tile walls; ice hung from their spouts like gargoyles.

Ahead was a broad footpath that led between rows of identical white barracks. Broken lights dangled from wires strung between the barracks, rocking crazily in the wind.

"There's a lot of ground to cover," said Gardner.

"You want to split up?"

"Do you?"

"No fucking way."

"Thank God."

They crept forward, the intensity of the wind seeming to increase with every step. The snow became wetter and heavier. Dean looked behind at their footprints, which filled with white powder within seconds. Ice slivers, driven by the rising wind, somehow scissored their way under his sleeves, freezing to his wrist. His gun had never felt so cold; even through his gloves, its steel handle sent a chill into his palm that rippled all the way to his ankles.

They clumped up a set of wooden stairs and peered into the first barracks. Dean played his flashlight beam through the rotting room. Metal bedframes were piled haphazardly in one corner, like a stack of old bones. Mattresses curled into twisted, mildewed shapes. No sign of life, no sign that anyone had been there for years.

They continued their rounds, investigating the barracks. Wind whined through splits in the wooden walls. With his imagination kicked into overdrive, Dean could hear prisoners scream in the agony of their wet packs, straitjackets of damp sheets that tightened around the body like a tourniquet, and the deafening hiss of air brakes as trains arrived with new inmates.

Dean signaled for a halt. He looked down the narrow corridor formed by two barracks, into the eddying snow. Had he seen a figure, a shadow, hunched over by wind, creeping along the fence?

If anything, a wolf, Dean told himself. He'd read how wolves'd made a comeback under the protection of the Soviet government. That's all it was, a wolf, distorted by darkness and snowfall into a human figure.

Then the light reappeared, and now it was clear and precise, a harsh fluorescent glare shining through a small window in the last barracks on the right. Definitely a lamp, perhaps a camper's butane lantern.

Motioning for Gardner to drop back to his left flank, Dean walked toward the barracks, index finger sliding back and forth across the trigger. Despite the chill, he loosened the top button on his shirt; the sweat of fear was beading along his collarbone.

He stopped at the barracks. A shade was drawn over the window.

He started gingerly up the steps, Gardner pressing too close behind him. His foot crashed through the top step, with a crunch of splintering wood.

He froze. The light did not go out. The noise had been disguised by the wind. He reached for the door, which seemed in good repair and was securely latched. To his surprise the wood was warm to the touch.

He inched open the door.

Wood collided with clattering metal.

Dean looked at his feet. The door had knocked over a pyramid of empty paint cans, which the wind whistled across the floor.

A small, crinkled man in baggy wool pants and a thick turtleneck sweater crouched against the far wall. He looked up in terror at Dean and Gardner as they stood in the threshold. He wore thick, wire-rimmed glasses, had wide, deep-set, shadowy eyes, a short, curly beard, and was totally bald. He was nearly hidden by piles of rags, gallon-size tins of turpentine and liquid soap. In his right hand, reddened and coarse, he clutched a lump of steel wool.

Behind him, stretching from corner to corner and from floor to ceiling, was a massive hand-painted mural. Though the lower half was buried beneath a coating of whitewash, Dean had no trouble recognizing it.

"Mr. Mintz?" Dean asked.

Before the painter could answer, a volley of gunfire spit out of the blizzard, burrowing into the rotting wood walls. A bullet struck Dean in the thigh, spinning him dizzily down the steps. He tumbled into the snow, gasping and bleeding, as footsteps ran toward him from out of the storm.

CHAPTER ELEVEN

His world seemed muffled. The ground throbbed with the heavy fall of bootheels. He clamped a hand over his wounded thigh; blood oozed, its sticky warmth trickling between his gloved fingers. He forced himself to his knees.

A figure was charging toward him. Dean was reminded of the desert, of a floating mirage that changes shape as you approach it. A mirage with a rifle.

He heard frenzied shouting, in Russian and English

"Dean, hit the deck!"

He twisted to look behind him. Gardner was at the barracks steps in a shooter's crouch, aiming at the rifleman. Dean saw a disaster about to ignite. Gardner would be no match for a professional sniper able to shoot to wound from a hundred yards in the middle of a blizzard.

"Put down the gun, Richard!" he screamed.

"What?"

"He's not trying to kill me. He's a prison camp guard. They're taught to aim for the legs."

Gardner vibrated with indecision: dying to pull the trigger,

133

terrified of the consequences. Anatoly Mintz hurried out of the barracks and called to the Russian rifleman. Dean heard the name Vitaly.

Vitaly Zaitsev emerged from the snow like an icebreaker. He was dressed in the tattered uniform of a gulag guard, one shoulder bent under the load of an ammunition case. His owlish eyes looked down at Dean contemptuously through misted glasses. He prodded Dean with the rifle barrel, as though he were a hunter checking if his prey were dead.

"You. What do you want here?"

Before Dean could answer, Gardner interjected: "Military Occupation Police. Surrender your weapon immediately." Gardner was still crouched, hands glued to his gun, face swollen with authority.

"Eb tvoi mat," Zaitsev snarled. "You're in my territory now. There'll be no arrest. You, get up."

Dean wobbled to his feet, hand pressed to his thigh. "Do you mind if we get inside before my blood freezes?" Dean grunted.

Zaitsev nodded yes. Gardner lowered his gun. Mintz disappeared into the barracks, and Zaitsev herded Dean and Gardner in after him.

Mintz stoked a wood-burning stove, conversing with Zaitsev in familiar whispers. Gardner and Dean sat on a sagging wood bench, scarred with knife-carved obscenities.

"The guy at the cemetery," Gardner said quietly.

"I know. There's something about the way a Russian tells you to fuck your mother; it's like a fingerprint."

Zaitsev, armored in his thick overcoat, every gesture a threat, was a long way from the intimidated poetry fan they'd surprised at the Vagankovsky Cemetery, yet it was definitely the same man.

Despite his looming presence, Zaitsev was clearly the servant and Mintz the master. The fire crackling to his satisfaction, Mintz turned to deal with his intruders. Zaitsev stood like an appendage to Mintz's left, the gun still zeroed in on Dean's chest.

"Listen, before he shoots me again, could you get me something for this?" Dean indicated his blood-spattered leg. "I like to bleed from one wound at a time."

"Of course. I'm sorry Vitaly attacked you. He's very protective of me, and really, he couldn't have known you were the police."

Mintz dropped a handful of rags in Dean's lap. He seemed anxious to keep as far away from the blood as possible. Gardner used a Swiss army knife to slice open Dean's pants leg. The slug had dug a black and red culvert across his thigh. Gardner watched with childish fascination as Dean cleaned and dressed the wound.

"You're trying to tell us you're not afraid of the police?" Gardner asked. "You're just hiding out here for old times' sake? A college reunion behind barbed wire?"

"A reunion you could call it, yes," Mintz answered. "Vitaly was the only guard who befriended me here. When I slept, ate, and pissed in this same room for four years."

"And it's just a coincidence that the day after a man is murdered at the Kosmos Hotel, a man you were seen arguing with, you drop from view. So frightened of returning to Moscow that you send Mr. Zaitsev into town to do your errands for you."

Mintz stroked his beard gently, forming his thoughts. "Am I under arrest?"

"That depends," Gardner answered. "We would like to ask you to accompany us to Moscow for questioning. We would hope you'd agree, sparing us the formality of an arrest." Gardner was a master of the conditional sentence.

Mintz looked at the bulk of Vitaly Zaitsev, then at Gardner, weakly trying to assert himself, and at Dean, grimacing with pain as he tried to shake away the numbing cold from his leg.

"But, sir, your partner is wounded and we have the rifle. Perhaps I should begin the questioning."

"I don't want this to degenerate into a show of force," Gardner said.

"An American occupier is telling me about force? An

135

American who imposes his democracy with troops and missiles."

"Now just a damn minute!" Gardner shouted. "Those missiles got you out of the gulag. Those missiles make it possible for you to paint whatever you want without being shipped off to Siberia every time you pick up a brush!"

"And for that I should be eternally grateful?"

Gardner allowed his temper to cool. When he spoke next, it was with deliberate precision. "I think you should tell us everything you know about the death of Andrei Pavlovich Bukharin, or you will be arrested."

Gardner looked at Dean, like a student seeking approval. Gardner had surprised him. Outgunned and frozen, he was still capable of righteous indignation.

"Look, Mr. Mintz," Dean said, "here's the point. We found you. That means someone else can, too. Whether it's the police, a homicidal art critic, whoever it is you're afraid of. You can't hold out here forever."

"Vitaly can hunt. He goes into the village for food. We have firewood. No one comes here now anyway."

"Fine. Say you last the winter. Spring comes. The snow melts. The mushrooms sprout. You've got picnickers and mushroom hunters swarming over this place. You going to shoot them one by one?"

"What is it you're terrified of?" Gardner asked.

Mintz chewed on a stray hair from his beard. His eyes were hidden behind twin images of the glowing fire, reflected in his scratched glasses.

"I'm prepared to offer you the safety of police custody. You have my word, no one can touch you," Gardner said.

"I don't trust them," Zaitsev spat out. "Stay here, finish the picture. I'll protect you like I always have."

Mintz looked tenderly at Zaitsev. George and Lennie, a Russian *Of Mice and Men.* Dean would have found it touching if he weren't looking down the barrel of a gun.

"You see, even if I were to accompany you, I can't leave Vitaly behind. I can't deprive him of the only role left to him in life."

"I'm sure he was equally concerned about you back when he was sitting warm and well fed up in his guard tower and you were freezing your balls off down here, surviving on black bread and kasha."

"I don't hold a man up to his past. One had to survive."

"You're awfully forgiving of a system that played havoc with your life," Gardner said.

"One fights, and one fights, and one grows tired. One accepts one's enemies. One eventually embraces them."

"There's a new system in place now, Mr. Mintz," Gardner said enthusiastically. "Why not give it a chance?"

Mintz shivered, then turned away. He and Zaitsev traded a few strained whispers, then wordlessly threw themselves into the task of making coffee, chipping away at the frozen beans with an ice pick.

"Can your system give me back what the old system stole?"

"What would that be?"

"My art."

Gardner and Dean had penetrated to the heart of Mintz's belief system. Politics, friendship, war, they all paled, washed out in the corona of the artist's ego. As the coffee bubbled and the wind snarled, Mintz began to talk.

"Do you know my work?" he asked, then answered his own question. "Of course, you've seen it in my workshop. Where you broke in. Where you undoubtedly confiscated my canvases with the same lack of respect police show artists everywhere in the world—"

Gardner was about to protest, but Dean stopped him.

"What did you think of it?"

"Impressive," Dean answered. "It gave me a couple of disturbing dreams, the intended effect, I guess."

Mintz nodded, accepting the compliment. "I call it 'Moscow Straitjacket.' A bit obvious in its symbolism perhaps, in its conviction that the real prisoners of Soviet society were outside the walls. Do you know how it was created?"

Mintz nodded toward the wall where he had been surprised at work. The same hollow-cheeked faces that filled the canvases in the workshop stared back at Dean with their

137

bludgeoned, stifled screams. Mintz was in the process of re-claiming it from the whitewash which had covered it.

"I spent two years on preliminary sketches, another year of work at night. Five minutes here, ten minutes there. At the end of the day, while others fell exhausted into their cots and boiled shoe polish for alcohol, I worked on that picture . . . from dinner to lights out."

Zaitsev served coffee, still gripping the rifle. Mintz sloshed some onto his sweater but ignored it. A man used to spilled paint, to living in work clothes.

"It was a work of memory, an attempt to duplicate the origi-nal canvas which was stolen from me at my arrest. I could see the colors of the original in the snow outside; the ground was like a canvas, swimming with shapes. At night I would rush to the wall before exhaustion dimmed my recall.

"I was nearly finished when I was released. Two months early. I would have had time to finish had my sentence not been shortened. It wasn't mercy; it was elaborately designed cruelty. I am certain I was the first gulag inmate who de-manded a longer sentence. I begged to be allowed to stay. I tried to be caught escaping. I fought with the guards, called Lenin a pederast, confessed to spying for Israel. I even offered to buy the wall with money I'd saved working in the store-room.

"They threw me out anyway. As I stood at the gate, holding a sack of possessions and a bundle of soiled paper work, they made sure I saw the Uzbek work crew hurrying toward my wall with buckets of white paint."

In the silence that followed, Mintz peered through the room's one window into the snowstorm, as though he dreaded the workers would return after all these years and cover again what he had so lovingly restored.

"When you were released, why didn't you go on to other paintings?" Gardner asked.

"Why does one become the victim of an obsession?"

Gardner shrugged. "Because it gets bigger than he is, I guess. He can't get away from it."

Dean, who knew a thing or two about obsession, had another theory. "Or he doesn't want to get away from it. He's afraid he can't succeed at anything else." Dean thought back to the Red Square sketch artist Valentin Orlov and his castigation of Mintz's paintings as "mediocre."

"You are quite right. 'Moscow Straitjacket' was the pinnacle of my career. Everything that followed was trash. A void. Dots and lines. Sadly it seemed I was doomed to one master piece."

"Where's the original?" Dean asked.

Mintz ignored the question. He poured them each another cup of coffee.

"Does your search for it have something to do with the murder at the Kosmos?"

"Indirectly, perhaps."

"Directly, definitely," Dean said. "You were seen fighting with Bukharin. Was he the one who stole your painting when you were arrested? If Van Gogh could slice his ear off for love, I can imagine you cutting a throat for art."

"I did not kill this man. I swear it."

"Don't swear it, prove it!"

"Dean, at this point I think we should make sure Mr. Mintz has a lawyer present before we put any more questions to him."

"Well, why don't I just run out into the blizzard and hire one!" Dean retorted.

Zaitsev smiled blandly as he sipped his coffee.

"You ever hear the word *blat*, Richard?" Dean asked. "It means 'pull.' It's the Soviet way of doing business that America, with all its idealism and efficiency, is trying to make obsolete. Let's say I'm a navigator with Aeroflot. I have access to plane tickets. You're a cardiologist at Moscow's best hospital; you're responsible for scheduling precious operating room time. I need open heart surgery; you need a vacation. If I go through channels, I may die. If you go through channels, you spend your vacation in front of the TV. So a deal is struck. Everyone's happy. We need a little *blat* right now!"

"If you're suggesting I offer this man immunity or a reduced sentence, you've seriously misjudged me. Not only is

139

it plainly corrupt, but it's beyond my jurisdiction, a decision for the military prosecutor to make. I won't exceed my authority."

"No, I suppose you won't. But I have no official authority, nothing on the record, so I have nothing to exceed, do I?" Dean turned to Mintz. "Mr. Mintz, I'm a series zero-zero-zero private investigator. Totally unaffiliated with the government. You hire me like you would a taxi. I'll find your painting for you—if you return to Moscow with us and help us solve this crime."

Gardner leaped to his feet. "Now just a damned minute here, Dean. I didn't authorize you to—"

"Of course you didn't. You didn't authorize me to do anything. You didn't hire me to do anything. I'm not even here, am I?"

Gardner retreated a step from his indignation.

"If we succeed in bringing Mintz in, I'm not going to take credit for it if that's what you're worried about. The public adulation, the news conferences—they're all yours."

"That was an unnecessarily cynical remark," Gardner said. "Publicity, positive publicity about the occupation police can only help our cause."

"Oh, sure. And the Russians believe every word of it."

"Opinion polls have led me to conclude that the Russians know we have their best interests at heart. They're starting to accept us."

"They accept whoever has the guns," Dean scoffed.

"Is it true? Can you find my painting?" asked Mintz, a momentarily forgotten participant in the conversation.

"If it's still in Moscow, and it's still in one piece, I've got a good shot," Dean answered.

"I'm certain it's in one piece. It's too valuable to destroy."

"You said it was confiscated. Maybe it was burned or something. On ideological grounds. Because it was too politically provocative."

"But that's precisely what made it so valuable. On the black market, of course. It was quite glamorous to own the work of a dissident. The more arrests a painter accumulated, the more expensive his work became."

The tone of Mintz's voice was warming, as he inched toward acceptance of Dean's offer. Gardner twitched with a growing fear that he was not going to figure in the deal.

"If I do allow this unorthodox bargain to be struck, you'd better come through with some damn good information, Mr. Mintz."

"I can promise you won't be disappointed."

"Just how can you promise that?"

"Because I saw the killer."

CHAPTER TWELVE

By dawn they were on the road back to Moscow. The storm had fallen apart; it hovered in pieces on the horizon, unable to re-form itself. The sky was a glaring blue; the sun, a white disk that turned the snow into a million needlepoints of light. It was a mini-Russian spring, testing the waters of winter. It motivated Mintz to tell the joke about the two worms in shit

"A mother worm and a baby worm live in a pile of shit. One day the baby emerges to find blue sky, green grass, puffy white clouds. The baby tells his mother about the marvelous world he's discovered outside the pile of shit. 'I know,' replies the mother worm. 'Then why don't we leave this pile of shit?' asks the baby. 'Are you crazy?' says the mother. 'This is our home.'"

"It's days like these the baby worm was talking about," Dean said.

"And days like these that give us the courage to continue living in shit," answered Mintz.

Mintz rode in the back seat, his right hand cuffed to the door handle With his left hand he doodled, endless variations on his familiar theme. Every few kilometers Gardner peered hopefully at the drawings, perhaps hoping for a sudden confession.

Once Mintz believed Dean could actually recover his masterpiece, a deal was made. Dean would find the painting, and Mintz would reveal what he'd seen at the Kosmos Hotel. Mintz had fled to the gulag because he was frightened. Of something . . . or of someone, he wouldn't say until his masterpiece was in his hands.

There had been a chill of sadness in the morning air as Dean and Gardner watched Mintz say good-bye to the guard Vitaly Zaitsev. They bear-hugged, cried a bit, drained a flask of brandy together. Then Zaitsev disappeared into his cabin.

"Zaitsev's a tough one to figure out," Gardner observed. "The way he could switch allegiances so quickly. One day he's taking orders from the camp commandant; the next, from the guy he used to guard."

"He's been taking orders for so long he's probably panicked by the thought of making a decision on his own. He'll probably hole up in his cabin until a new boss shows up with a new set of marching orders. Who knows? Maybe the Cultural Authority will turn the camp into a museum. He can get a job playing himself."

They reached Moscow around one and deposited Mintz in a MOP safe house, a dismal fourth-floor walk-up in the Chimki-Chovrino district, overlooking the main tracks of the Leningrad rail line. The view was of shunting freight cars and iron brown tracks, overlaid by the assault of clanging couplers, air brakes, and shouted obscenities. An American guard was posted outside the door. A Russian guard moved into the room with a rollaway bed, beer, and a sweater he was knitting himself. Mintz ironically noted that he could not commit suicide by jumping out the window; a safety net was bolted to the outside of the apartment house, an afterthought added by Soviet engineers to protect pedestrians from the bricks that occasionally tumbled loose from the shoddily constructed building.

Gardner bought Mintz a two-week supply of food, noting

the expense and retaining the receipt. Dean bought their prisoner paint, brushes, and canvas, in case his solitude proved inspirational.

"Find my painting, Mr. Joplin," Mintz said, "and you'll get more than information. I'll fill these canvases with sketches. Every suspicious face I saw at the hotel that night." He tapped his forehead. "They're all up here."

"Pssst. Iron Feliks's thumb? I'll sell it cheap. Comes with a certificate of authenticity." As Dean stepped off the number 24 tram, he was hounded by a teenage salesman in search of a sucker. Dean didn't buy, but he pressed a ruble into the boy's palm anyway. Gardner would have been proud; he was encouraging the spirit of entrepreneurship at the grass-roots level.

"Iron Feliks" was Feliks Dzerzhinsky, the Polish founder of Lenin's secret police, the Cheka. His iron statue had once stood arrogantly in front of KGB headquarters, presiding over the square that bore his name. During the tumultuous days before the armistice crowds had conducted vigils outside the Lubyanka, pleading for the release of their loved ones so that they could be reunited for the expected nuclear holocaust. Their agony was met by silence. Then, when the vigil continued, night and day, haunting chants focused on the stubborn edifice, water cannon were turned on the assembly. The demonstrators finally realized Moscow would see no storming of the Bastille, and they turned their hatred on the statue, splattering it with paint-filled balloons taken from the shattered display windows of Detsky Mir, the children's store across the square. Finally, Iron Feliks was pulled to the ground with tow truck winches.

Fragments of the dismembered statue showed up in antique stores now and then or in the hands of teenager hustlers who preyed on gullible tourists. During a two-week visit a tourist might get ten offers to buy "genuine thumbs," prompting a popular TV comedian to remark that if Iron Feliks really had as many fingers as were currently for sale in Moscow's streets, it was a wonder he ever lost his grip on power.

Dean walked across the renamed Detsky Square and into the graffiti-stained Lubyanka.

There had been talk of turning the place into a museum. But the KGB's work had been dim and shapeless, and no one really knew what would be displayed in such a museum. Some suggested razing the building and replacing it with a monument engraved with the names of the KGB's victims. But who were the victims? How could their suffering ever be categorized? That plan, too, was abandoned.

So the once-notorious building was now a mundane hive of researchers and computer experts from various occupation agencies, gamely trying to reconstruct what was left of the KGB files "for the sake of history."

In a dreary, cramped second-floor office, Dean encountered a smiling face.

"Dean!" shouted Sergei Borodin as he leaped up from his chair.

"Ssssh. Keep it down. I don't want anyone to know I'm here."

"Sorry. It's been awhile since I've had to keep a secret." Borodin chugged from behind his desk and forced Dean into a violent bear hug. "Jesus Christ and the Madonna, you look great!"

"And you look—"

"Tragic, I know." Dean sized up Borodin. He was still a fastidious dresser, in a tailored tan sports coat, maroon loafers with bow tie laces. But where there used to be muscle, there was now fat. His body sagged and bulged; his clothes fitted him like a sack of burlap wrapped around a pile of potatoes. The former judo aficionado now barely looked capable of supporting his own weight.

"You see," Borodin said, grabbing his overlap of fat like a butcher weighing a kilo of sausage, "you see what becomes of a man forced into early retirement."

Dean looked around the room, which was a dumping ground of dusty files and documents. "Come on, Sergei. This doesn't look like a rest home to me."

"You know what this is? It's bullshit. Baby food for the

mind!" Borodin kicked over a stack of papers, some embossed with a meaningless "Top Secret." "When the mind deteriorates, the body soon follows. Irina won't even touch me anymore. All those years in California, eyeing those tan, firm bodies, have spoiled her for the feel of solid, reliable Russian flesh."

Sergei was a former KGB field officer who had been assigned to the suburbs of California's Silicon Valley back in the 1970's. His cover as a Soviet "scientific attaché" allowed him to troll the high tech firms in San Jose, Cupertino, and Sunnyvale for traitors—young, burned-out geniuses who'd sell their companies' secrets for newer Porsches or second homes. They actually held auctions in Holiday Inns, jacking up the prices of hardware that Sergei dimly understood. The job made Sergei homesick, and melancholy, and he began to envy the boy millionaires, even as he grew to despise their morals. He started drinking heavily to conceal the embarrassment he felt at having to buy what his country couldn't develop itself. He'd eventually requested a transfer back to Moscow. Dean had met him during a deadly boring symposium on East-West technical exchange. Their California backgrounds, varied though they were, got them talking, and they became friendly enemies, relishing each other's uninhibited cynicism.

Now Sergei, gifted with near-photographic recall, labored in obscurity for the Americans. His assignment: to reconstruct from memory the biographies of the KGB officials with whom he had worked and the operations he'd guided.

"It can't be so bad, can it?" Dean asked. "It's sort of like writing your memoirs."

"Memoirs are for dying men. I'm fifty! At fifty Dostoyevsky was finishing *The Possessed. The Brothers Karamazov* was still nine years in the future." Borodin turned a dispirited gaze out the window toward the business end of the police garage, where mechanics were adding rainbow paint schemes to the KGB's dreaded black Volgas. Borodin, whose intelligent face spoke volumes, looked dead.

Suddenly he spun around. He ran to the door and locked it.

He turned off the intercom, then picked Dean up in his arms and began to sing. After a second Dean joined him. It was "Lara's Theme," but with words of their own design: "Somewhere, my love, somewhere in San Jose, there by the bay, that's where the Russians play."

They collapsed laughing on the couch. Files flew everywhere. Dean heard a crunch and pulled a shattered, glass-framed portrait of deposed KGB chief Vladimir Kryuchkov from under the cushion. Borodin flung the shards into the wastebasket.

"To the dustbin of history, where capitalism was supposed to end up," Borodin said.

"Listen, Sergei. I have a couple questions for you, and I'd like you to keep them confidential."

"Get me out of this bureaucratic asshole, and I'll carry your secrets to my grave."

"I can't hire you, Sergei. Much as I'd love to. I've got Natalie on half salary; I pay my informers with promises—"

Borodin winked. "You can pay me the other half of Natalie's salary."

"The other half goes to rent."

Borodin sighed. "Well, I tried. I'll be glad to help you any way I can, of course. It'll be refreshing to talk with flesh and blood instead of a computer."

"I'm interested in a dissident artist named Anatoly Mintz."

"Missing persons case?"

"Missing painting case."

Borodin's forehead creased in confusion. "Why come to me?"

"Mintz was arrested. At least twice that I know of. He did time in a labor camp. He would've been assigned a KGB monitor, probably someone attached to the Ministry of Culture. His paintings were confiscated after he was interrogated. Five years ago this month. In this building."

Dean handed Borodin a Polaroid of Mintz's "Moscow Straitjacket." "Recognize it?"

"No. And I wouldn't forget a drawing like this. Have you been to the Ministry of Culture?"

"You mean the Arts and Broadcasting Authority? Yeah, it was my first stop. The Russian employees say they were never infiltrated by the KGB. Why they insist on clinging to those old, transparent lies—"

"Perhaps they haven't been fed any fresh lies."

"Put the philosophy on hold and plug in that miracle memory of yours, OK. I need the name of Mintz's interrogator. The guy who followed him around Moscow in a leather coat. One name. I can take it from there."

"This painting. It's valuable?" Interest glinted in Borodin's eyes.

"That's what my client says."

"And that would be—"

"Confidential." Dean stood and shook Borodin's plump hand. He thanked him and headed for the door.

"Dean, I really need to get out of here, OK? If you get too busy, anything you can't handle. Even a lost dog. You'll let me know?"

Dean promised to do what he could. As he stepped into Detsky Square, a crowd was watching a crew of workmen unfurl a political banner across the facade of an office building: COMRADES, LET US WORK TO FULFILL THE MANDATE OF THE PEOPLE: STUDY DEMOCRACY. PREPARE FOR THE ELECTIONS. INFORMATION IS FREEDOM. The sign was painted in bold red letters, using phrases familiar to the Soviet man in the street to make the new messages more palatable.

As he turned to circumvent the crowd, he ran into a startled Emily Gardner. She had just come out of the Lubyanka herself.

They made an instinctive attempt to pretend they had not seen each other, averted their eyes as though they were searching for someone. Then their faces slowly met, and they traded frazzled smiles.

"Mr. Joplin," she said, her smooth-toned voice brittle with nervousness. "How nice to see you again."

"Good to see you, too. Though you're not the kind of woman I'd expect to see lurking around KGB headquarters."

"Oh? I don't seem like the lurking type?"

"Elegant women don't lurk. They pose coyly in doorways maybe."

She laughed, untied the belt of her raincoat, and opened it up in a gesture that reminded him of a striptease. She was wearing a baggy white cotton shirt with oversize pockets, a silver and turquoise belt, and faded jeans that delicately traced her long legs.

Dean noticed her furtively transfer a sheaf of papers to an inner pocket, but he said nothing.

"I'm not always dressed for dinner, you know. I do change my clothes occasionally."

"You changed your hair, too." The boyish curls were straighter, slanting across her forehead in a seductive black arc.

"Sweet of you to notice."

"I have a fantastic memory."

"For hair?"

"For women," he blurted. "And how are the kids?"

"Nice innocent transition, Mr. Joplin."

"Dean. And we can go back to flirting if you'd prefer."

"I don't think our conversation needs a road map. Why don't we just see where it ends up?"

They fell into silence. Dean kept expecting her to say, "Well, good seeing you. Got to run. Million things to do." Instead, she stood there wiping the new haircut out of her eyes, a beautiful, provocative invitation.

"What brings you down here?" he asked.

He saw indecision in her eyes. He read her next sentence as a lie. "Doing the sights. Just trying to see as much of Moscow as I can."

"Sounds awfully educational."

"I try to make it entertaining. I like discovering little tidbits the guidebooks overlook."

"I know a great bar that's definitely not on the tourist path. I'm on my way there now if you want to join me."

She looked around the square as if she were waiting for the crowd's permission.

"Well . . ." she said, drawing the word out into three syllables.

"Call Richard. Have him meet us. If that's what you're afraid of."

Dean imagined he could see her spine stiffening beneath her raincoat. "I'm not on a leash, Mr. Joplin. However, considering my husband's position, I don't know if it's appropriate for us to be seen in the middle of the afternoon, slinking into bars like lovers."

"That's your imagination at work, not mine. Listen, why don't we go into Detsky Mir? Christmas is coming. Your husband's former teacher is taking you toy shopping. How more aboveboard can you get?"

She smiled. "Lead on."

They were threading through the crowd toward Detsky Mir when Emily stopped abruptly. "You taught Richard how to avoid surveillance, right? How do I know this isn't just one of your techniques?"

"You don't."

Detsky Mir, the country's largest toy store, was in the middle of an identity crisis: Management couldn't decide whether to emphasize the traditional Soviet New Year's buying season or the newly legalized Christmas spirit.

An Americanized Santa Claus had set up shop in one corner, and a throng of curious Russian kids studied a list of instructions posted on his workshop door before hopping tentatively onto his lap. His Russian equivalent, Grandfather Frost, strolled the aisles, advising parents on this year's smart purchases. Trees were everywhere, but in one part of the store they were called New Year's trees, in another part, Christmas trees.

Thanks to the revival of the Russian Orthodox Church, manger scenes sold out faster than they could be manufactured. But sociologists liked to point out that despite the armistice and the return of religion to the Christmas season, the country's most popular toy continued to be the machine gun.

"I guess you haven't gotten around to war toys yet," Emily said.

"What?" Dean had missed the question, taking the opportunity to watch Emily in the store's mirrors.

"The Disarmament Authority? Your job, remember?"

Dean realized she'd caught him staring. "I'm sorry. I don't want you to think that all retired spies turn into voyeurs."

"You're quite taken with me, aren't you? Don't apologize. I think I like it. Now, shall we continue with our cover story?"

As they eddied through the packed store, they exchanged get-acquainted talk, often forced to shout above the squawks of the intercom and the squeals of excited children. Dean learned that Emily's maiden name was Amelia Benes, that her mother had been a secretary in the American Embassy in pre-revolutionary Havana, her father a Cuban employee in its political section. As Castro marched out of the Sierra Madre, Señor Benes marched his family to Miami and later to Washington, D.C. His impeccable anti-Castro references landed him a position with the State Department's Bureau of Consular Affairs, where he helped write and rewrite the Byzantine laws governing American travel to Cuba.

"But your accent's pure Midwest," Dean observed as he loaded a New York police car into his shopping basket.

"My father went on a crusade to erase his Latin roots. He drilled us in exercises to lose our accents. Convinced me to Americanize my name. Since *The Wizard of Oz* was my favorite movie, I'd always wanted a Kansas accent. So my father hired a tutor from Wichita to give me one."

"Did he go back to Cuba after the war?"

"He resisted. Said he'd become so Americanized he couldn't tell a plantain from a peanut butter sandwich. But it lasted only about a week. The Cuban inside him had never really died; it was just taking an extended siesta, as he called it. He and my mother both moved back. As far as I can tell, he's in heaven. He got a job at the new American Embassy; he even found his old desk in some basement. He prowls the streets of Havana in a brand-new guayabera, spends the evenings sipping café cubanos and catching up on thirty years of gossip."

"Sounds like you miss him."

"Of course, I miss him. But I think I envy him more. His fight is over."

It was a telling remark. Dean wanted to press for more, but Emily made for the escalator, signaling a change of subject.

"When did Richard come into the picture?"

"My father convinced me that my future lay with the government that had taken him in as a refugee. 'With your mother's brains and your father's charm, you'll make a great first lady.' Translation: If I hung around the corridors of power long enough, I'd attach myself to a future President.

"One night we were at a party at the Czechoslovakian Embassy—it used to handle Cuba's affairs back then—and my father heard what sounded like John F. Kennedy giving a speech. JFK's a combination of Jesus Christ and Joe DiMaggio to my father, so he had to know what's going on: Kennedy'd been dead for seven years after all. It turned out to be Richard, semitanked, doing a letter-perfect JFK impression. But it was respectful, not bitter. It turned out Kennedy was Richard's idol, too.

"Well, it was one of those nights when everything seems plotted by a romance novelist: Richard was handsome. His uniform was the whitest single article of clothing I'd ever seen on any man. His gold epaulets gleamed in the chandeliers . . . and he worshiped John Fitzgerald Kennedy. My father and I both fell in love."

Her reverie was broken by a squad of boys charging past on their way to a fresh shipment of Erector sets that had just been set on the counter.

"We'd better get Bryn one of those, too. Don't want her to call me sexist."

Dean tangled with the boys and their fathers, in the jostling, shouldering Moscow shopping style that no one considers rude, and managed to snag the last Erector set.

Then he realized Emily had disappeared. He scanned the store, assuming she'd continued with her shopping, but he didn't see her. He walked through the girls' section, but she wasn't there either.

He rode upstairs to the children's clothing department. No

sign of her. Perhaps she'd run into her husband. Or some other acquaintance she felt she could not introduce to him.

He was about to leave when he noticed a commotion across the store. Kids clustered around the doors to the changing rooms. A blond girl with a strand of bubble gum clinging to her cheek, pounded on the door with an ice skate, gouging a streak in the paint. Apparently some stubborn kid had locked himself in the changing room and refused to come out. A harassed salesgirl arrived and began berating the girl for scratching the door. Another boy dropped to his knees and attempted to probe under the door with a hockey stick.

He jumped back, jolted by a clatter of falling objects from inside the changing room. The police car Dean had bought exploded from under the door and whined across the store, pursued by a dozen boys.

Dean hurried to the changing room and knocked.

"Emily? You OK?"

After a deadly pause she answered with a tremulous voice, "I'm fine. I just had to get away from that fucking noise."

"You need any help?"

"No."

"You sure? You want me to call Richard?"

"No!"

Dean looked into the strained face of the salesgirl, who motioned to the line of kids and parents waiting to try on winter clothes. "Sir, if you can't get your child out of there, I'll have to call the manager."

"Emily. Unlock the door. I'm about to be crucified out here."

He heard the latch slide open. Dean squeezed through the door and locked it. Emily, her eyes red, her hair limp, her cheeks dewy with sweat, was coiled on a bench, her head lolling against a mirror she seemed to have cracked. The toys she'd bought were strewn on the floor.

"What is it? Are you sure you're all right?"

"I'll be fine. I think I'm slowly returning to normal."

"I guess this is what a nervous breakdown looks like," Dean said.

"I wouldn't know. When Richard had his, I was too busy to have mine."

"When was that?" Dean asked, taking a seat beside her.

"When we first moved to Moscow. It got a little nightmarish. He spent some time in a hospital. When things finally threatened to get out of hand, we agreed I should take the kids on vacation. We went to visit my parents in Havana. When we returned a couple months later, he seemed OK. But different somehow. Like parts of him had been replaced. He never talked about it, and I didn't ask. A spy's wife, you know?"

Dean curled an arm around her. Her body felt strong and warm, despite the occasional shudder.

"You don't need to prop me up, Dean. I'm embarrassed enough to do it myself." She stiffened and straightened her clothes. She bent over to gather the toys.

"There's nothing to be embarrassed about. Sometimes things get to be too much, that's all. Especially in a crowded Moscow toy store around Christmas."

"I've no right to unload my problems on you."

"It's OK. I'm a good listener. Eavesdropper, to be more accurate. Do you want to tell me what caused you to run in here? Or do you just want to forget the whole episode?"

The salesgirl began pounding on the door again.

"Forget the whole thing?"

"You got it."

When they emerged, they faced a gauntlet of smoldering kids and parents, who raised their eyebrows in disapproval of the erotic encounters they imagined had taken place behind the changing-room doors.

Outside the store Dean reluctantly let his arm fall away from Emily.

"You won't tell Rich about this, will you?" she asked.

"Not if you don't want me to."

"I didn't plan it this way, our keeping secrets from my husband."

"I don't mind. Discretion's what the government used to pay me for. It's a tough habit to break."

154

She brushed his mouth with her lips. "Thanks for riding to the rescue, Dean. Next time you see me, I promise I'll be good as new."

"Don't be too good," Dean retorted, but she was already gone.

Dean stared into his glass of green tea, as opaque as his encounter with Emily had been. Though he was planted on a cold barstool in the White Palm, his thigh still burned from where their legs had touched in the changing room. He turned the beautiful but opaque figure of Emily over in his mind, searching for the crack that would let him look beneath her surface. All he saw was his own reflection. A good Samaritan, anxious to soothe her pain. Cross that out. A horny good Samaritan, with Gardner peering sternly over his shoulder like goddamn JFK. "Ask not what my wife can do for you, but what you can do to my wife."

"What's that?" asked Gennady Yurchenko, the bartender.

Dean shook his head, and Gennady went back to fuming at the television. American and Russian dignitaries were toasting each other, prior to ground-breaking ceremonies on the Leningrad Stock Exchange.

"Look at their form, their style. It's pathetic! If that's the best you Americans have to offer—"

Dean finally became aware of Gennady's tirade.

"Gennady, what the hell are you raving about?"

"I'm talking about toasting, fuck your mother! You want to see how it's done? Watch this. You start small. None of this 'Let's drink to the peace of all peoples.' You build, you enlarge, but you must begin on a personal note. For example, 'To Dean Joplin, my friend and confidant, who looks like he's having woman troubles . . . may they soon vanish like a pack of wolves fleeing a shotgun.'"

Gennady lifted the glass to his lips in a graceful arc, exhaled a bullet of air, threw his head back, and emptied the glass. Dean could follow the vodka's trickling progress by the bulges that moved down his throat.

Gennady Yurchenko was a unique species of Soviet man,

the only bartender ever removed from high office for violation of Article 70—"anti-Soviet propaganda." An essentially apolitical man, he had been the operator of a wine cart in the Kremlin's Palace of Congresses. He dispensed liquor during intermissions of the Bolshoi or between speeches whenever the Supreme Soviet met and the fifteen hundred delegates, many of them Moscow-awed provincials enjoying what was basically a paid vacation, slipped into the lobby to recharge themselves. Nothing reactionary per se in that, but it was the customized cocktails he mixed for the party bosses that proved his downfall.

Following Gorbachev's crackdown on drinking, hard liquor had been banned from the Palace of Congresses, and the country's dedicated deputies were expected to slake their thirsts on wine and fruit juice. But for the right man and the right price, Gennady could spice up a "woman's drink" with something stronger from a specially tailored pocket his wife, Natalie, had sewn into his smock.

Still, it was not his violation of the vodka ban which precipitated his fall from grace, since even senior officers of the KGB took advantage of his clandestine services and would not have dreamed of disrupting the vodka's flow by arresting its source.

It was the names Gennady gave to his concoctions.

"Lenin's Asshole": part lime juice, part Armenian brandy. "Andropov's Limp Prick": 110 proof Krepkaya vodka adulterated with orange juice. "Porizhkov's White Palm," a milky mixture of cherry vodka and cream, which everyone knew referred to Brezhnev-era hack Sergei Porizhkov, a wonderfully bribable functionary whose widely publicized but hollow attacks on corruption were better known as "Porizhkov jerking off."

A pity, then, that Mrs. Porizhkova, during a matinee performance of Vinonen's *Flames of Paris,* overheard Gennady offer her husband's namesake to a thirsty old veteran of the Great Patriotic War.

For his alcoholic homage Gennady was rewarded with a year in a regional jail and six months "on potatoes," a conscript in a brigade of prisoners bussed to collective farms around Moscow to help with the potato harvest.

Gennady's baroque past made the White Palm a success. Tending bar in the blue velour jumpsuit he wore around the clock, he was still one of Moscow's most entertaining personalities. "Too many melancholy Russians" was his motto.

"Natalie has mail for you, Dean," Gennady said. "Christmas cards *and* presents. From your family."

"Christmas. Already?"

"The ruble will be convertible for two weeks this Christmas. They expect the postal system to be overloaded, so they want people to mail early. It was in the papers. Don't you read *Pravda* anymore?"

"Not since it started telling the truth."

"Don't you want to answer the cards yourself this Christmas?"

"Natalie does a better job than I ever could."

"She's laid off, remember?"

"For that, she's laid back on. I'll bring by a check tomorrow. She can shop for Molly and Patrick this weekend."

"Dean, just once, why don't you write them yourself?"

"Why don't you bring me a beer and a phone? The sooner I get back on this case, the sooner I get paid, and the sooner Natalie goes back to work full-time."

Vera was back in Moscow. Dean picked her up at the Rossiya Hotel, a Pentagon-size monstrosity opposite Red Square. The Rossiya had claimed to be the world's largest hotel until it was toppled from first place by a hotel constructed for the 1980 Moscow Olympics. Vera lived there for its anonymity. It was not a homey bed and breakfast, where the personnel addressed you on a first-name basis, had the paper waiting for you at your favorite table in the morning, your usual drink poured at the bar after work. Your identity was a number between 1 and 3,150. You were handled on a transient basis, with efficiency but not friendship. You were expected to be on your way soon, to another hotel, another city. Which was how Vera preferred it. Which was how Vera loved it. The restaurants, the bars, the room service, the coming and going of tourists and businessmen all combined to re-create the effect of the road. She continued to travel, even while standing still.

Dean was surprised that she wanted to move, but the situation became clearer when he learned where she was headed.

"Sheremetyevo Sheraton, please," she said, giving him a tired kiss, tossing her two battered suitcases into the back seat. An airport hotel, the ultimate transient stopover.

"Come on, Vera . . . I can't even pronounce that. And now you want to move there?"

"You don't approve? Did you have something else in mind for me?"

"Look, when you called, you said you were ready for a change. I assumed that after all this suitcase living, you'd want to hang your dress in a closet for a change."

"Anyone's closet in particular?"

"Mine is two thirds empty, for example."

"There are closets at the Sheraton," she huffed, folding her arms.

"Pardon me," Dean said. He slalomed through the taxi ranks and turned onto the Moskvoreckaya Quay, intending to follow the river to the Sadovoya. He focused on the road while they sat in icy silence. Finally, Vera smiled, slid warmly across the seat, and curled into his arms like a teenage girl at a drive-in.

"I'm sorry, Dean. This tour was awful. All Americans, all psychiatrists from Los Angeles. Their demands didn't stop until two in the morning and started up again at six. They're such infants. How can they help all those crazy people in Los Angeles if they can't find their way to the toilet down the hall?"

"You'd be surprised what you can find for a hundred bucks an hour."

"Seriously? Maybe I should consider that as my new career."

"What new career?"

"Didn't I tell you? I quit Mostours. In Yakutsk."

"Yakutsk? That was three weeks ago."

A malicious smile crept across her face. "Now they know what it was like to be banished to Siberia. A real Russian tour. I should have charged them double."

"You just left them there?"

"In the museum of the Frost Research Institute. If I had to translate one more menu or show one more American bitch how to plug in her hair dryer—"

"So what now?"

"Ne znayu." She shrugged. "I'm moving to the center of the country. Where all the important people arrive and depart. Maybe I'll meet a diplomat or an airline pilot. Maybe I'll become a stewardess"—she looked slyly at Dean—"or a spy."

"Who the hell would you spy on?"

Vera considered for a moment. "The Chinese? We still don't really trust them."

"Vera, come on. You've been wandering around for three years. Why don't you simply stop for a while? See what it feels like."

Dean turned north onto the Mira Prospekt.

Vera cocked her fist into the shape of a microphone. "Up ahead, the Exhibition of Economic Achievements, a sterling reminder of the great technical strides made by the Soviet people and a forecast of the progress still to come under the occupation."

Whenever Vera wished to avoid an issue, she launched into one of her tour guide lectures.

"Vera, goddamn it. I'd like to settle this."

She reached across his thigh and plucked the keys from the ignition, burying them in her purse. The car slowed, igniting a blare of horns behind them. Dean maneuvered to the curb, the tires screeching against the cement.

"You get the keys back when you agree to stop pressuring me. What happened to you while I was gone? I don't recognize you anymore."

The car dragged to a stop. Dean forced his arms out straight, like a racing driver tensing for the starting flag. Drivers threw him nasty looks as they hurtled past.

Dean knew what had happened: Emily Gardner was cutting away at the leisurely, complacent pattern of his life. Gouging him, luring him, tripping him up. She inhabited his dreams now, too. Maybe he just wanted a little protection from her. If

159

Vera moved in with him, it'd be business as usual; she could tempt him away from temptation.

"You know, Dean, you really are a typical American. Our treaty's barely a year old, and already you want to break it."

When they first met, they'd hammered out an agreement governing their relationship, SALT 1, their Strategic Alliance for a Limited Term. It was their personal equivalent of the grandiose reforms that follow revolutions.

The treaty precluded marriage, community property, children, or dominance in the relationship. It specified total freedom and aimlessness. It sounded like a load of sixties mush, but it had made sense until now.

"I know what this is all about," Vera said. "You're bored. Lonely. You feel useless. You want to reconstruct your family."

"Bullshit."

"No, no, no. I'm on to something. I spent six weeks with those psychiatrists, remember. You want that picture on the TV."

Dean was lost. "What picture?"

"You know. All Americans have one. The family portrait on the television. It sits on the lace doily the wife inherited from her mother. In the picture the husband has his arm around the woman, protecting her, and another hand on the shoulder of his fat little boy, who's wearing a baseball uniform. The wife has her hand on the little girl's shoulder. They're all giving the camera that same stupid, squinting smile. Admit it. You want to start a new picture with me."

"And then put us up on the TV?"

"Right."

"Not on the radiator, not on the water heater?"

"I'm trying to be serious."

"OK, let's suppose your amateur hour analysis is true. Russians love families. What the hell is so damn frightening about starting a new one with me?"

"Don't you see what a disaster that would be? You want to start a second family when you couldn't even hang on to your first one!"

Vera tossed him the car keys. She plucked her bags from the back seat and shot out of the car. Studiously avoiding a backward glance, she merged with a flock of pedestrians crossing at a light. Dean watched her start down the Mira Prospekt, perhaps heading back to the Sadovoya and a bus to the airport.

He could have caught her. Traffic was stopped by lights in both directions. It would have been an easy U-turn.

Instead, he shoved the Zhiguli into gear and headed west, following the thin, fading light.

Sergei Borodin had come through with an address, not a name, an address he'd found on yellowed bills of lading which recorded the confiscation of slanderous works of art and noted their destinations. On the phone he told Dean that an oil painting titled "Moscow Straightjacket" had been delivered to a dacha in Zhukovka, a small village about twenty miles west of Moscow. He didn't know who owned the dacha, since property records had been transferred to the local MOP headquarters.

Dean thanked Borodin and jotted down the address.

"Anytime. And keep thinking of a way to get me out of here."

That same afternoon Dean drove through the quiet pine groves that sequestered the village of Zhukovka. He passed the Russian version of a revival meeting. But this was a revival of the Russian past, led by Aleksandr Solzhenitsyn, returned from his Vermont exile to guide his Rodina party to victory over the "godless capitalism" that had replaced "godless communism."

Men in soiled peasant clothing and dark, roiling beards forced Dean's car to slow as he passed the meeting, which was being conducted in a soccer field. People were arriving on horseback. Like the Amish, the Rodina party turned away from the internal-combustion engine. Solzhenitsyn called for a return to traditional Russian values, for a dictatorship of church and village, and he traversed the country, trying to mobilize the people for the upcoming elections. Dean scanned the lectern for a glimpse of the oaky, commanding presence of Solzhenitsyn himself but saw only his acolytes struggling with a stubborn microphone. Desperate to be authentic peasants, they competed to have the dirtiest, most unruly beards, the roughest, most uncomfortable clothes, and the most tragic faces.

There was something Hollywood about the Rodina movement, Dean thought, as he passed a horse and buggy with a burst of gas and was rewarded with a hail of gravel hurled at his rear windshield.

The unpreposessing village of Zhukovka, on the surface all log cabins and tidy vegetable gardens, concealed money, bodyguards, and limousines. We are the victors, and here are the spoils, Dean thought. Rambling wooden cottages and four-story marble-floored hunting lodges stuffed with black-market treasures peeked out behind electrified fences at a curve of the Moskva River. Brezhnev had once had a home here. Kosygin. Khrushchev. Gromyko. Solzhenitsyn and Sakharov, before their falls from grace. Shostakovich and Rostropovich made beautiful music on beautiful, state-owned instruments here. Zhukovka had been Moscow's Malibu. Now the country homes that had belonged to the Soviet elite were weekend retreats for American bureaucrats, who were clearing the forests for golf courses.

Dean turned onto a side road, beside a brand-new 7-Eleven store. RUSSIA LOVES THE CONVENIENCE, trumpeted the sign. The sour looks on the faces of the Russians in line said otherwise.

He parked in the lot and walked down the lane, just another afternoon stroller.

The dacha was small, seafoam green clapboard, its shutters decorated with hand-painted doves. It was a peaceful setting. Smoke from nearby chimneys hung in the air. Hunting dogs barked in the distance.

He knocked on the front door. There was no answer, no noise from inside, no name on the brass nameplate. He circled the cottage. Peered in a garden shed. A model railroad gathered dust and cobwebs. Märklin, Dean noted. Foreign. Expensive. The rarefied hobby of a spoiled kid . . . or a privileged adult who enjoyed children's toys.

Dean thought about questioning the neighbors but decided that would produce more suspicion than answers. He tried the back door. Locked, of course. He squinted through hazy windows, but the angle of the sun turned the interior to gloom.

Then he had a flush of inspiration, one of those puzzle-piece coincidences his subconscious grudgingly rewarded him with now and then.

He rushed to the car and sifted through the box of Andrei Bukharin's possessions. He dug the key ring from under a stack of ration cards.

The third key he tried fitted the dacha's front door.

CHAPTER THIRTEEN

He always entered a stranger's house with a mix of fear and fascination: fear because he could always bump into a shotgun or a fist; fascination because he was an inherent voyeur, who loved sifting through people's lives.

On the Soviet scale of privilege, the dacha suited a mid-level KGB officer, one responsible for cracking the whip on dissident artists. The owner had gone out of his way to advertise his access to imported goods. The furniture was Scandinavian, positioned so the designer labels were clearly visible. The liquor cabinet was wall-to-wall prestige: Kentucky bourbon, French cognac, even Finnish vodka, in the land of Stolichnaya. The bookshelf drooped under the weight of gleaming American and French dust jackets. Solzhenitsyn, Nabokov, Pasternak, and other homegrown, but banned, authors were stacked on a coffee table like an opulent display of jewelry.

Soviet nouveau riche and the accumulation of booty from the West.

Dean scoffed at the irony. With most of the articles in the dacha now freely available, their status was gone.

But who was the owner? Bukharin? The more Dean learned about him, the more plausible it seemed.

He continued his inspection. A photograph glued to a mirror showed an unidentified, sun-burnished young man with a beaklike nose, a confident grin, and slicked-back hair, wearing the uniform of a private in the Red Army. He had his arms slung around his parents. A bus was loading soldiers in the background. It was draft day, the first day of Russian manhood. Dean pocketed the photo and moved on.

He heard a precise male voice speaking Spanish in the next room.

"Me gustaría hacer un viaje por avión." Dean drew his gun and tried to summon his high school Spanish. *"Por avión."* Something about an airplane? He approached the doorway, his boots cracking the brittle floorboards like dried bones.

"Me gustaría hacer un viaje por avión."

He swung clumsily into the room.

It was empty. But above the bed a painted-over window was raised just enough to permit an escape. He rushed to the window and darted a glance outside. No one.

He squeezed through the opening anyway and plopped onto the snow like a sack of mail thrown off a train. The ground was hard, no footprints. He flipped a mental coin and veered to his right, edging through a stand of pine trees until he came to the white sheet of the Moskva River, mirroring the anemic afternoon sun.

It was a scene to make a Russian cry. Sky, water, forest. Smoke curled from dachas across the river; wide plains swept invitingly toward Moscow. A trio of sailboats coursed upstream, searching for wind, enjoying a final cruise before the river froze.

He looked up and down the bank. Deserted, no trace of the fugitive. A few docks poked into the river; neat, brightly painted speedboats bobbed gently against their moorings. He felt becalmed by the setting. The tension drained out of his stomach. He gulped in the crisp air and squatted at the river's edge, swirling the icy water with his hand.

A motorboat choked in protest, and the smell of diesel fuel cut through the pines. At the edge of his vision Dean caught a fast-moving burst of orange—a speedboat hurtling along an inlet behind the dacha. Dean crashed through the trees, trampling the remains of a summer vegetable garden, and reached the inlet. The boat's driver was impossible to distinguish as it blurred into the distance. Dean watched helplessly as the boat disappeared, kicking up a brown, twisting wake.

He slapped his thigh in frustration and made a brief inspection of the homemade dock. Rags, empty fuel cans, a pile of tools. A shredded life preserver stenciled with the name of the boat: *Aleksandr Nevsky.*

He returned to the dacha, fitting himself through the open window.

"Donde está la estación del ferrocarril?" Dean spotted a language cassette spinning behind the smoked glass of a state-of-the-art Japanese recorder. Dean popped out the cassette, *Spanish in 20 Lessons.* The unidentified pupil had been in the middle of lesson 6. Blank cassettes were stacked on top of the recorder. Next to the tapes were a Hallwag map of Russia and a Young Pioneer compass. Odd tools for a language student, Dean mused.

The rest of the room had been looted. Floor-to-ceiling shelves were barren; a chest of empty drawers stood against the wall like a pilfered cash register. Paintings were missing from the walls; the sheets and pillowcases from the double bed were gone. A floorboard had been pried up; whatever treasure it once concealed had been liberated.

He went out to the garden shed and opened its rusting padlock with another of Bukharin's keys. It was like stepping into a young boy's vision of heaven. The villages and steppes of Russia spread out before him, traversed by the sleek red trains of the Baikal—Amur Mainline, all in HO scale. The model railroad, coated with dust and disuse, still glittered with the money that had been lavished on it, perhaps spent by an adult compensating for a childhood deprivation.

Dean strolled around the layout. He couldn't resist the urge to push the locomotive through a tunnel.

He bent under the railroad to examine the wiring and discovered a wide shelf, stacked with plastic-wrapped paintings. Dean ripped off the rope binding and slid out the pile of canvases.

Abstracts. Nudes. Landscapes. All by different artists, none particularly haunting or beautiful; few were even competent.

Halfway through the stack, he found Anatoly Mintz's "Moscow Straitjacket," shrouded in its own protective cloth. As he ferevishly unwrapped it, he realized how large it was, nearly equal to the dimensions of the room itself. He tore the last fragment of cloth away and held it up to the low afternoon sunlight.

The dim, shabby surroundings did not diminish the intensity of the work. Mintz's brushstrokes, slashing, adventurous, like a figurative Franz Kline, led the eye to the center of the painting and its tortured inhabitants, then out to the canvas's borders and beyond, as though Mintz were forcing the viewer to confront the world outside the painting.

It was too big to be moved as was. Dean unstapled it from the stretcher bars and rolled it up, careful to keep the cold paint from flaking.

Mintz's masterpiece secure in his trunk, Dean drove to the local MOP precinct. He presented himself as a senior VP with Merrill Lynch Realty, anxious to purchase vacation homes for American business executives stationed in Moscow. Could he inquire as to the owner of the charming little fixer-upper at 14 Krasnoarmeiskaya Street?

The officer of the day, a young Texan who seemed genuinely perplexed to find himself planted in the middle of Russia, performed a fast finger tapping at his computer keyboard and frowned.

"Awful sorry, sir. Looks like you're out of luck. Number fourteen Krasno—Krasnowhatever is under protectorate. Ain't gonna be nobody's dream house, looks like."

"Protectorate?"

"I guess you're new to the Russian real estate game, sir. The occupation took over certain assets they think ought to go back to the people. Country homes, estates, boats, planes. You know, ill-gotten gain, the kind of thing your Texas oilman brags about but your good Russian Communist ain't supposed to have. We put 'em under protectorate until we can figure out what to do with 'em. Meantime, they ain't for sale."

The Texan's fingers hopped over the keyboard. His frown deepened. "Let's see. Looks like the owner's deceased. Identity unavailable. Uh-oh, your little fixer-upper's a Code A. Means it used to belong to a KGB bigwig." He threw Dean a home-on-the-range grin. "Means it definitely ain't for sale."

"There was a boat. The *Aleksandr Nevsky.* Maybe you've seen it around?"

"Same story with the boat. Goes with the house. They all got 'em around here. You ever water-ski the Moscow River? Not half bad. Ain't South Padre, but it's wet."

Dean shook his head in resignation. "Another day, another deal down the drain. Thanks for your help anyway, soldier."

"That's what we're here for, sir. You ever get out to Dallas, my cousin's got a condo he'll sell you. Used to belong to Roger Staubach."

Dean parked outside the dacha at Krasnowhatever for an hour, smoking and watching the dock, hoping the *Aleksandr Nevsky* would return. But its owner seemed scared off for the ght, so Dean reluctantly pointed the Zhiguli back toward Moscow.

An infinite black sky was crowded with stars by the time Dean reached his apartment building. The stars didn't twinkle or inspire awe like cliché stars. They were vicious little dots of light. Getting weaker, moving farther away, making him feel left out. The window of his apartment was a dark, brooding square. The light he usually left on must have burned out. He couldn't imagine a more hostile environment at that moment than his own living room.

The lobby light was off, too. Both lights burned out? What were the chances of that? As he cautiously pushed open the lobby door, he heard something drop to the ground.

He slapped at the wall switch, and the light flared on. The lobby was empty. He checked the basement door; it was secure. His suspicious glance flew to his mailbox; it, too, was locked.

He bent down to pick up the object that had fallen. It was a beer coaster, and it had been wedged in the door to keep it from locking automatically. A tenant who'd forgotten his key? Or a burglar's escape hatch?

Should he call the police? If they surprised Dean and got there in time, there'd be too many questions. If the burglars were connected to the Bukharin case, his cover would be blown.

He had to draw the burglars out somehow.

He slipped back outside. Looked up at his window. It seemed to glow, then darken, like the evaporating glimmer of a flashbulb. Had someone just turned off a light?

He pressed the button next to his name on the outside intercom and growled into the speaker: "Hey, Dean. It's me, Tony. I got a buncha the guys down here and a fifth with your name on it." Then, in Russian: "Break out the ice, comrade, we're coming up."

Dean returned to the lobby. Turned the light back out. He waited until his eyes adjusted, then took cover behind a stack of pipe. The building had no back doors. Whoever was up there would have to leave by the stairs or the elevator.

Two minutes passed. They're awfully unperturbed, Dean thought. Then the elevator clunked into gear and began its descent. Dean drew his gun, felt his stomach constrict. His breath rose in thin, anxious clouds.

The elevator reached the lobby with an echoing thud. A woman's voice swore. Then the grate flew open.

Natalie. She screamed as Dean's shadow floated toward her out of the darkness.

"Natalie, it's OK. It's me."

He rushed to turn on the light. Her face was chalky with shock; her arms were burdened with Christmas presents, which glittered like giant ice cubes.

"God, you frightened me. I thought it was a New York mugging for sure . . . the lights shot out in the lobby, the old lady alone with her Christmas presents—"

Dean couldn't disguise his smile. "I'm sorry. I had no idea you'd be here. I can't believe you're done shopping already."

"Unemployment seems to have given me extra energy. I decided to get it over with in one afternoon. You're going

Russian this year: fur hat and gloves for Patrick, amber necklace for Molly."

"You put that beer coaster in the door?"

She nodded. "I had to make two trips. I didn't want to be locked out. Lot of good it did me. I forgot the key to your apartment, so—"

"Wait a minute. You haven't been inside?"

"I just told you—"

A giant shadow seemed to launch itself at them from the stairs. Then the shadow split in half. Two gray-coated men in fur hats butted Dean against the door, spilling him onto the street. Natalie shouted and battered the Christmas packages against Dean's attackers, shredding the ribbons. The taller of the two, blond with creased skin and ice-blistered lips, swore in Russian and swatted her indignantly.

Dean coiled his fist and pivoted it into the shorter attacker's stomach. Warm, garlicky breath spouted from his surprised lips. Dean saw Natalie sprawled on the sidewalk, her packages trashed around her.

He had to tangle with both the muggers now. As he was hurled against the cement wall, he dropped the painting. A jagged cornice tore into his back. Fists crash-landed on his jaw; knees pumped into his groin. He shouted weakly at a passing taxi, but he could easily imagine what the driver saw: a typical Moscow late-night street scene, three drunks squabbling over a bottle, a fourth collapsed in an alcoholic stupor.

Dean kicked, groping hazily for a shin or a kneecap. Then he spotted the black curve of a gun handle protruding from Garlic Breath's belt. Suddenly, charitably, he was reaching for his wallet.

"Look, I've got a few rubles, a MasterCard, a Moscow residency permit. You can make a fortune forging it. Just let up, OK? And keep that cannon holstered." Dean waved his wallet like a white flag.

Garlic Breath slapped it away. His fingers knotted around his gun handle, while his accomplice picked up Mintz's picture. He examined it with probing eyes, held it up to the pale streetlight. He squinted at the unpainted back, as though hunting for invisible ink.

"Go ahead, take it. My uncle's an amateur painter, it's just a piece of crap anyway."

Dean's reverse psychology backfired. "We'll take the *kartina* and your wallet," said Garlic Breath, his voice a rasping, asthmatic wheeze.

The two whispered in Russian; Dean picked out the word "witness." Garlic Breath pulled out his gun. The barrel looked as if it would never end.

Oh, fuck, this is it, Dean thought. This isn't a break-in; this isn't a mugging. They want the painting; they know what it means. They understand the crux of the case, while I flounder in darkness. They know what I should know.

His mind stalled, fogged over, blackened. His knees weren't weak; they weren't there at all. His throat pinched until he felt as if he were going to choke.

They dragged Natalie to her feet. They weren't going to kill her, too? She howled at them in Russian, obscenities so elaborate they made the two killers blush. They balled up a handkerchief and stuffed it into her mouth.

Dean and Natalie were forced toward an illegally parked gray Volga sedan. Dean peered up the empty sidewalk. Was it too much to hope for an overzealous traffic policeman? An autobus clattered by, its passengers happily ignorant behind steamed glass.

Then Natalie began to cough. She hunched over, spitting in agony. The two men rushed to support her. She wilted in their arms, a package of dead weight.

But her eyes caught Dean's for a trace of a second. They widened meaningfully, focusing their intensity on Patrick's Christmas present, on the brown shoelaces coiled in the wrapping paper.

Natalie knew her message had been received. She swooned in the street, pulling the blond with her. Garlic Breath's attention divided momentarily, long enough for Dean to snap his hand into the gift box. His fingers hunted for what seemed like hours, until they fastened on a heel of shoe leather.

He dug the ice skate out in a snapping arc, and like a pitcher unleashing a curve ball, he cracked his wrist as he swung.

The ice skate's blade, sharpened like a razor just hours ago by the Detsky Mir sporting goods staff, slashed into the back of Garlic Breath's neck with a sound like ripping cloth. He whipped toward Dean instantly; as he did, the blade continued its path toward his Adam's apple, unleashing a geyser of warm blood.

Dean's vision went black. He wiped the blood from his eyes, and felt it chill as it splattered onto his cold skin.

Hands clamped to his neck, Garlic Breath spun into the middle of the street, dropping his gun. The blond came up with it first, but the sight of his friend pirouetting uncontrollably down the center divider, blood spraying into the night, paralyzed his trigger finger. Somehow he gathered the presence of mind to grab Mintz's painting. He balled it up as if it were a pile of old newspaper and stuffed it into his jacket.

As Dean helped Natalie to her feet, the attackers retreated toward the Volga. Garlic Breath staggered. He grasped the radio antenna for support. He collapsed in the front seat, still jerking as if he'd been electrocuted. As the car squealed off, blood jetted onto the rear window, painting the glass a dirty red.

"Goddamn it, we were ten breaths away from a firing squad. They were going to execute us, there's no other word for it."

Words exploded from Dean's mouth, blocking Gardner from so much as a grunt in reply.

"They were ready to kill for a painting. Why would they kill us for a fucking painting?"

Dean stood at the window, receiver in one hand, glass of brandy in the other. He was unable to take his eyes off the street, watching as the tires of passing cars ground the bloodstains into the pavement.

After the attack Dean and Natalie had been stunned into activity. They'd gathered the Christmas packages, hurried into his apartment, boiled water for tea, locked doors, called Gennady, who was on his way, and even scrubbed the blood off Patrick's skate. Then they'd sat on the couch, holding each other, shivering as they listened to the building shut down for

172

the night, the gradual dimming of televisions and radios, the kettledrumming of bad plumbing, the murmur of exhausted voices.

"My secretary was nearly killed. I slashed a man's throat with a goddamn ice skate. Richard, is any of this sinking in at all?"

There was nothing but a pained hollowness on the other end of the phone.

"Richard!"

"Mintz has just been murdered."

When Gardner met Dean outside the safe house, he slapped firm hands on his shoulders and looked him over like a football coach relieved his star quarterback has survived a vicious sacking. He levered Dean's hand and spouted apologies, desperate concern, offered the services of his private physician . . . and more money.

Gardner ordered a city-wide search for the bloodstained Volga and sent detectives to Moscow emergency rooms in case Dean's attacker staggered in for treatment.

He led Dean through the straggling curiosity seekers and up four flights of stone stairs, smudged with mud and ice by police boots.

Another empty room after the body, the murderer, and the police had gone. This time a metal and Formica elevator car, frozen at the fourth floor.

"I can see the headline now: SHOT TRYING TO ESCAPE," Dean said as he squatted in the corner, examining bullet damage to the floor.

"Don't even joke about that," Gardner said. "You have no idea how heavy this is going to hit down at HQ." He looked pale and shrunken by tension. Great weight-loss program, Dean mused, investigating a fresh murder every two weeks.

"What the hell was he doing in the elevator?" Dean asked.

"You weren't far off with your first impression. I figure he was trying to escape the gunman."

"Anyone hear the shots?"

"Everyone heard the shots. No one saw a thing. We've questioned everyone in the building."

The elevator was pocked with bullet holes. At least two shots must have gone astray, ricocheting through the confined space like electrons.

"But where the hell were the guards we posted?"

Gardner's face slackened. He removed a pipe from his pocket and began to stuff it with tobacco, his hands flittering, brown leaves wafting to the floor.

"You ought to take up cigarettes, Richard. You don't have the nerves for a pipe."

"The guards were missing. I can only assume one of them killed Mintz."

"Or they were bribed by the killer to look the other way. But why go for Mintz tonight? We've been holding him for three days."

"Mintz didn't finish his sketches until tonight."

"They're gone, too, I suppose."

Gardner cleared his throat, as if he were preparing to give a speech. "Every now and then my foresight manages to beat out my hindsight. I took them home with me."

Abruptly Dean's thoughts veered to Emily and the Gardner children.

"Get a guard on Emily. Someone you've double- and triple-checked. Better yet, send her on vacation."

"Taken care of. I've posted a twenty-four-hour uniformed guard at our front and back doors. As for your second suggestion, I appreciate the concern, but how would it look for the wife of a homicide detective to head for the airport with her tail between her legs just when things heat up? What kind of message would that send to the Russians?"

Dean rode with Gardner to his apartment and waited in the car while he retrieved Mintz's sketches. He traded suspicious stares with the militiaman posted at the door, a young brute with a weight lifter's body, who rhythmically cracked his white baton into his palm—a signpost of intimidation or a ploy to keep warm?

They drove to Gardner's office in the former Ministry of

Internal Affairs building and provisioned themselves with food, drink, and cigarettes.

Dean did sit-ups and push-ups, trying to keep his mind alive as the dead hours of morning pressed down on him. Gardner sat at his desk, sifting through the evidence, headphones playing the collected speeches of John F. Kennedy. "Listening to JFK triggers ideas, gets the mental juices flowing," he explained.

The day before the murder Gardner had lured Mintz into conversation. But it turned out to be a rambling background monologue, rather than a confession.

"The way Mintz told it he'd been wandering the streets of Moscow since the war, scaring up odd jobs. He haunted antique shops, art galleries, on the off chance his masterpiece would turn up. He'd given up hope long ago, but he didn't really have anything else to fill his days, so he kept looking. The afternoon of the murder he's prowling through an antique shop on Arbat Street, when a man comes in and sells a sketch—one of his sketches. The man refuses to identify himself. There's a squabble. Mintz takes a swing at the fellow and pushes his fist right through the antique store's window. The owner calls the MOPs, the man disappears, but Mintz follows him—"

"To the Kosmos Hotel," Dean interjected.

Gardner nodded. "It's our man Bukharin. Well, Mintz makes quite a pest of himself. He harasses Bukharin in the lobby and gets tossed out by the desk clerk. He comes back when there's a new man on duty and finagles Bukharin's room number. At this point, I thought, Good grief, he's going to confess right here. But Mintz claimed he was only going to talk to Bukharin, to make a deal to get his painting back.

"He's told to wait in Bukharin's sitting room. Bukharin has a stream of visitors, and being the curious type, Mintz can't resist a peek or two. A couple hours later Bukharin's business seems to be concluded, and he's in a generous mood all of a sudden: He promises to hand over 'Moscow Straitjacket' the next day."

For the hundredth time Dean looked up at the four charcoal

sketches tacked to Gardner's tidy bulletin board. Two were of room service waiters Gardner had already interviewed; the other two were of Viktor Gerasimov and Nina Zinovieva!

None of them seemed capable of sawing a man's throat open. "You make any progress with those numbers?" Dean asked.

"When the computers aren't down, they suggest that the numbers might refer to the prize money at last year's Kiev open tennis tournament."

"I can see we're not going to get much help from IBM. It's fucking inconvenient that the two who attacked me didn't show up on Mintz's sketchpad. Why the hell did they want that painting?"

"If it's as valuable as Mintz claimed—"

"They wouldn't know a masterpiece from a master cylinder," Dean answered. "They handled that painting like an old sweater. It's got to have some other value that we're just not seeing."

His eyes wandered to the charcoal faces of the suspects.

"Maybe one of them knows."

During the next three days Dean responded to the violent developments in the Bukharin case by making a few changes in his routine. He installed new locks on his front door. The gun he casually carried in his glove compartment under a pile of Moscow street maps found a new home in his shoulder holster. Unable to keep the case secret from Natalie, he used Richard's raise to restore her salary. Feeling guilty for the danger he'd exposed her to, he offered her a month's vacation. She turned it down, preferring danger to boredom.

The next week passed in bits and pieces. The case led in so many fraying directions that a focused day's work was impossible. He and Natalie spent thirteen hours in dank basement archives, failing to determine who owned the *Aleksandr Nevsky,* the launch Dean had seen speeding away from the dacha in Zhukovka.

He bought twenty-five pounds of horsemeat and sliced into it with saws, knives, razors, and broken bottles, attempting to duplicate Bukharin's throat wounds. At the end of the week his office bristled with useless, exotic tools, he'd run out of recipes for horsemeat, and the murder weapon was still unidentified.

One afternoon he rushed to the parking lot of the Kiev railroad station, where a blood-spattered gray Volga had been reported abandoned. The blood turned out to be from a chicken, stolen by a vagrant from a freight train and sloppily slaughtered in the back seat of the car, where he made his home.

Lab reports arrived from Gardner. A thorough fingerprint dusting of Mintz's graveyard workshop uncovered no prints other than his own and Zaitsev's. The paintings had been done within the last few months, shooting down Dean's theory that they had just been window dressing for some illegal activity.

The clues massed in front of Dean like soldiers assembled on a parade ground to receive their orders. But Dean found it impossible to get them marching; he couldn't even decide whether to lead with the left foot or the right.

CHAPTER FOURTEEN

Elections mean hoopla in the States, so the Election Authority decided that the first Soviet dance steps in democracy should be loud and *Music Man* brassy. Election day should be a garish, seductive package that the population couldn't wait to tear open. The yes or no candidate approval system which constituted Soviet voting before the occupation had never been big box office. Voting had been a drudge, a household chore like scouring the toilet. You did it to get ahead because the party authorities counted on a 100 percent turnout. Vera had told Dean how the tenants of an apartment building would chip in for a bottle of vodka and hand over their voting cards to a single designee who'd vote for everybody.

This was the attitude the Americans wished to erase. The first elections were going to be held on the republic level, appealing to the exploding nationalism of the non-Russians. The hated ethnic Russians had retreated from the Baltic republics, from Kirghizia and Turkmenia and Kazakhstan, leaving a power vacuum it was hoped the locals would fill. The republics would elect their own leaders and representatives to a new national congress, which would hammer out a democratic constitution. (They didn't know that the constitution had already been rough-drafted by a handful of prestigious Washington and Los Angeles law firms, which had collected astronomical fees for their work.)

But politics alone could not ensure a healthy voter turnout. To sugar the medicine of democracy, the Election Authority had scheduled parades, block parties, sporting events, and cultural exchanges, from stand-up comedians to virtuoso violinists. "Elections Are Fun!" Soviet citizens, conditioned to following dictates from the top, grimly set out to enjoy themselves.

One of the ways a select group of Russians enjoy themselves is by dipping their bodies into the Moskva River when the temperature hovers around fifteen degrees Fahrenheit and a swimming hole must be bored through the ice. This year the gathering of the Moscow Walrus Club was to be multinational, a chance for officials in the occupation and their Russian counterparts to outtough one another. There would be speeches by Russian candidates and politically themed entertainment. The entire event would be sponsored by McDonald's. Dean was not surprised that Richard Gardner, as a representative of the MOPs, was going to participate in the swim.

It was one of those knife-edged winter days when the sunlight feels colder than the shade. Moscow had seen its third snowfall, the unofficial signal that winter had set up shop for good. Viewing stands had been erected along the Frunze Embankment; across the river a standing-room-only crowd knotted in the frosty grass of Gorky Park. The Walrus swim, which had once been informal, was now corporate and organized. The swimmers wore numbered trunks stenciled with the McDonald's logo. A golden arch spanned the Moskva River, guiding the eye to a stage where Russian rock bands Zvuki Mu and Brigade C would play after the swim, to warm up the audience for the speeches.

Dean watched the Russian swimmers perform calisthenics on the dock which jutted into the ice-flecked water. Flabby

179

and middle-aged, white, spotted skin drooping over tight tennis shoes, they were briskly enthusiastic and seemed impervious to cold.

The handful of Americans trotted toward the dock in sweatsuits. They were trim and steely and appeared outrageously fit. They also looked as if they were freezing to death.

Dean stood at the river's edge, sipping tea from a glass. He returned the empty glass to the vendor, who refilled it for his next customer. An American health inspector would have gone berserk.

Dean wasn't sure why he was there. He needed a day away from the case, and the Walrus swim was always amusing. But he suspected deeper motives in himself. A desire to glimpse Richard Gardner in his native habitat? A voyeuristic glimpse of Emily? Maybe he could uncover a concealed rift in the Gardner marriage. Maybe he could see disenchantment or boredom or resentment on their faces, a situation he could exploit by chivalrously rescuing Emily from a dead relationship.

He spotted Emily and the children traipsing along the embankment, shivering as they passed through the shadow of the Church of St. Nicholas in Khamovniki. Surprisingly Emily wore a fox fur coat; it didn't suit her personality or her income. Dean felt a tingling in his thighs as he watched her climb the grandstand to her seat. The fur coat didn't disguise her figure or make it seem bulky; it rippled and breathed with her coiling body movements. The way Emily wore the coat made Dean feel the fox was still alive, still sleek, still a hunter.

He didn't see Gardner in the crowd. Feedback and wind whistled through a microphone, as a McDonald's representative said a few fatuous remarks about democracy and the American hamburger. Would the swim go off without Gardner's seizing the chance to prove his Russian machismo?

Then Dean spotted him, hurrying away from a taxi parked in front of the Frunze Quay housing project. Dean ducked into the crowd, and Gardner bustled past, his number trailing from his fist like a kite tail.

Dean was more interested in the second man who climbed

out of the taxi, yawning contentedly, as though he'd just awakened from a nap; it was the same man he'd seen Gardner arguing with outside his building.

In crisp sunlight Dean examined the man he'd seen only in shadow. He wore a brown suede jacket, unbuttoned to display a silk western shirt bisected by a turquoise and silver string tie. His pants were tailored wool, ending in a pair of ostrichskin cowboy boots. His face was square and alert, burnished by a desert suntan. The man's hair was the color of polished aluminum, and it looked sculptured by highly paid hands. He held a hand to his forehead and used it as a visor to peer at the icy glare of the Moskva.

Here is a man who sees the world through guarded eyes, Dean thought.

He approached him as though they were old friends, his hand extended with a salesman's enthusiasm. "Sorry, but I don't remember your name. I'm Dean Joplin. I think we met at Richard Gardner's."

"My memory for faces is impeccable. I'm afraid I don't recall yours." There was a trace of the Bronx in the man's accent, not the western drawl he'd expected.

"Maybe we met at MOP headquarters."

"It's possible. I'm Taylor Willis, Mr. Gardner's attorney."

"Well, that explains the photographic memory. All those years studying the fine print."

Willis smiled indulgently, like an adult forgiving a misbehaving child.

"Lawyers make a decent living in Moscow?"

"As you may know, the law's in a state of flux here. You have Soviet law, military law, and American law, all butting heads. Wherever there's confusion, we lawyers thrive."

"Well, your suntan certainly seems to be thriving."

"I try to get back home to Arizona every few months. Frankly I'll be glad when I've gotten our firm's Moscow office on a sound footing. I miss those wide-open spaces, not to mention the fact that I've yet to find a competitive golfer in all of Russia."

"Just what is it you do for Richard?" Dean asked.

181

"Protect his privacy, for one thing."

Dean laughed. "OK, guilty as charged. I thought lawyers liked questions."

"Only when we're asking them, Mr. Joplin." He gave Dean the indulgent smile again. "And what's your connection to our would-be Walrus?"

"We met in the CIA. I taught him everything he knows about bugging, debugging, shadowing, and shaking a tail."

"Then I know whom to call if he runs out on his bill. I see the festivities are about to begin. Shall we?"

The American Walruses had stripped off their sweatsuits and were slapping their arms against their chests for warmth, surveying the river with all the enthusiasm of a cat confronting a bath. Gardner waved to his family and pumped his meek body into a V.

Willis forced open his eyes and dosed them with a few drops of Murine. "Smog doesn't get to me, but this clear winter air does. I just wasn't built for the cold." He marched toward the bleachers with the innate confidence of a man who knows no one would dare stab him in the back.

He took a seat next to Emily and attempted to engage her in conversation. She rebuffed him with a frosty smile and shifted her body so that Bryn and Jack were shielded from any contact with Willis. Dean chuckled in approval. No sense in exposing children to the legal profession any younger than necessary.

A drumroll thundered across the river and was absorbed into the thick clothes of the audience. Several candidates for the Russian state assembly were announced, and they skirmished to have their pictures taken with the hardy Walruses. Dean noticed the candidates were comfortably bundled and did not even bother to remove their gloves for the ceremonial handshakes.

One by one the Russian Walruses plopped feetfirst into the water. They panted and hooted like coyotes, as they backstroked away from the dock. They swam toward the center of the river, their pumping elbows poking against floating ice shards. Some smiled dutifully, the pain and cold obvious in their eyes; others truly seemed to relish the experience. After no more than thirty seconds they clambered back onto the dock, where they were met with blankets and scalding cups of tea.

The crowd cheered as their heroes waved flabby arms in victory.

Egged on by the smug grins of the Russians, the Americans dangled toes in the water, postponing the torture. Finally someone shoved dramatically toward the head of the line and posed at the edge of the dock like an Olympic diver. Gardner!

He pushed off, arced smoothly through the air, and cut into the water without a splash. The audience crowed in delight. Dean saw Emily and the kids lean forward anxiously.

Gardner's head bobbed to the surface, and he waved, forming his fingers into a V. The Americans applauded, hugging each other like a victorious football team.

But something was wrong. Gardner's arm suddenly collapsed into the water, and his head lolled back. A chip of ice floated into his mouth, and he made no effort to spit it out. The wake from a passing speedboat pushed an ice mass between him and the dock, cutting him off.

Gardner started to panic. He windmilled his arms, choking on ice water. Dean knew what would happen if they didn't get him out immediately. He'd grow numb and drowsy, would lose control of his muscles. As his body temperature lowered, his heart would slow. Eventually it would stop.

Dean shouldered through the shouting crowd. Two Walruses ran to the embankment and splashed into the water, fighting their way through the ice toward Gardner. Lifelines snaked through the air; a rescue boat picked a tedious course through the ice.

One of the candidates grabbed the microphone and attempted to restore order. "Everyone, stay back, please. Let the rescuers do their job."

Television crews burrowed through the spectators, trying for a shot of the tragedy. One cameraman, his point of view blocked, turned his lens on the podium, and a candidate straightened his tie and dashed a comb through his hair.

Bodies bumped against Dean. One of them was Emily. They traded dark, charged looks. Dean instinctively drew her to him, holding her gloved hand so tightly he could feel her tingling skin beneath the leather. A second later she was gone, pressing through the crowd.

There were four Russian Walruses in the water now, and somehow, they had managed to carve a path through the ice. Keeping Gardner's head above water, they towed him to shore, two on each side like pallbearers.

Two stocky women took charge. Doctors, Dean presumed, since most Russian doctors were women. Shouts of advice in Russian and English crackled like static.

"Rub his fingers and toes or he'll get frostbite."

"No, don't rub. Firm pressure, just firm pressure."

"Get him some brandy. Some vodka!"

"No alcohol. Tea. And a thermometer!"

One of the Russian doctors slammed a thermometer into Gardner's mouth. Dean saw his chest rise. At least he was alive, though he hadn't regained consciousness.

"Eighty-three degrees. What's that in Celsius?"

Dean remembered reading that if the human body dropped to seventy-seven, you were dead.

The doctors tore off Gardner's sopping swimsuit. Emily watched as her husband's blanched, naked flesh was exposed to the gaping television cameras. A little boy pointed a laughing finger at Gardner's penis, which the cold water had shriveled into a pink bullet.

The doctors mummified Gardner in layers of heavy wool blankets. Emily knelt by her husband's side, as Jack and Bryn worked toward them.

"What is it?" Jack asked. "Is Dad OK?"

"He looks like a fish," Bryn observed.

"He'll be fine." Dean consoled them. "He just got knocked out."

"Hey, Mom, it's the guy who's the bad liar."

"I'm not lying this time, Jack. Your dad'll be fine. Look."

Gardner's eyelids fluttered, and the doctors immediately began to pour tea over his white, blistered lips.

184

"We should get him into a bathtub and start warming him up," Dean said. "I live near here, we can take him to my place."

Dean helped ferry Gardner to his car, while the crowd bunched around like autograph hounds. Still embalmed in blankets, he was propped up in the back seat, between Emily and the kids. Dean drove as Emily force-fed him hot tea from a thermos.

Gardner began to sputter apologetically. "I'm sorry to put you all through this—"

"Ssssh. Honey. Don't talk. Just drink your tea."

"I just wanted to be like them. To prove we could assimilate. That Americans are team players, not dictators. I'm afraid I made us look awfully foolish."

"Or awfully tough," Dean said. "Peter the Great was killed diving into ice water in the Gulf of Finland; you lived to tell the tale."

"I'm just trying to build bridges to the Russians. That's important, don't you think? Building bridges?"

At Dean's apartment they helped Gardner into a tub of water, using a thermometer to maintain the temperature between seventy-eight and eighty-two. Emily stayed with her husband in the bathroom, while Dean tried to entertain the kids. They were soon embroiled in an argument about their father's exploit.

"It's embarrassing. It's gonna be headlines. The kids at school are gonna be all over me," Jack declared.

"It was neat," Bryn said.

"Why do you think it was neat?" Dean asked.

"Because Dad wants to be a Russian."

"Oh, perfect. Dad wants to be a Russian 'cause we're in Russia. In Germany he wanted to be a German. He wanted to be a war hero when Grandpa was still alive. I just wish he'd make up his mind," Jack said.

"You guys loved your grandfather, huh?"

"We never met him. He died," Bryn answered.

Jack's face glowed at the mention of his grandfather. He dragged Dean to the couch and rooted through his pockets.

185

He produced a wrinkled snapshot, smudged with youthful thumbprints. "Here he is," Jack said. The photo depicted a craggy, determined face that could have adorned a Navy recruitment poster. Lieutenant Commander Harrison Gardner fixed a blue-eyed stare at Dean from a full-sail untainted past. He was as trim and crisp as his dress whites, as spit-shined and bristling with arrogance as the ships he commanded.

"He got killed in Vietnam, in 1971," Jack said. "They made him a hero. Nixon even phoned my mom. We have tapes he sent Mom and Dad from the war. Sometimes we all listen to them."

"You should come over sometime," Bryn offered. "It's funny when Dad cries."

"It's hilarious," Jack muttered.

Emily appeared at the doorway to his bedroom, backlit by frosty sunlight. "Ninety-eight-point-six."

"Great," Dean said, getting to his feet. "Anything more I can do?"

"You can lend Richard your bed for a couple of hours. He's pretty well exhausted."

"No problem. Hang the clothes over the radiator. They'll be dry by the time he gets up."

"Bryn. You want to take a nap with your dad?"

Bryn bounced to her feet and sped toward the bedroom. She braked at the threshold, performed a wide, theatrical yawn, then hurtled to join her father.

"I'll be out of your hair by sunset, Dean," Gardner's thin voice called. "In case you have a date this evening. Wouldn't want to scare her off."

"Don't worry about it. I scare them off myself sometimes."

Emily vanished into the bedroom, and Dean imagined her brushing her lips against Gardner's in a nurselike kiss, tucking Bryn in next to him and drawing the shades. She reappeared and shut the door behind her. Dean caught a flame in her eye as she gave Jack permission to play in the park across the street.

Soon they were alone, except for the deep, exhausted breathing from the bedroom. Even the traffic on the ring road was discreet, unusually sparse.

"Events conspire sometimes, don't they?" Emily asked.

"If you let them."

"Will we let them?"

"If we do, we should whisper. The walls are paper-thin—shoddy Soviet construction, you know."

"More secrecy. The story of my life." Emily avoided Dean's frank stare and paraded around the living room, appraising the surroundings with the calculating eye of a realtor.

"You live very starkly, Dean."

"My ex-wife and son were supposed to join me. They would have made it less stark."

"Even so. No pictures, no mementos, no souvenirs. One might think you'd spent your whole life in this apartment without ever venturing into the outside world."

"It's a holdover from my days with the Company. I spent years learning to be anonymous. That meant no incriminating family photos, no hobbies, no personal baggage. My clothes had no store labels; my desk was a vacant lot—no receipts, no credit card bills, no traveler's check records. No paper trail."

"No junk?"

"No junk. I was the only person on my block who actually had room in the garage for his car."

"No scars?"

"None visible."

"No distinguishing features . . . the perfect spy."

"Not perfect. That would have called attention to me. I was average."

Emily leaned against the flat whitewash of Dean's wall, palms pressed against the plaster, one foot hooked around the back of her calf. Despite the bleached winter light, her tan skin held its color, her obsidian hair sparkled.

"You look outrageously exotic standing here in my drab apartment."

"That's me. The Latin spitfire on a mission to stir up the humdrum lives of WASPs everywhere."

"That why you flirt with me? 'Cause you think my life needs stirring up?"

"You don't like it?"

"I'm enjoying it tremendously."

There was a heavy pause as Emily drew her nail across the wall. "Me, too. I feel . . . comfortable."

"Comfortable! An old sweater's comfortable. Grandmother's samovar's comfortable. Not someone whom you're attempting to picture in bed."

"I'm imagining you in bed?"

"I hope so. I'm imagining you."

"What's it like?"

"Well, it sure as hell isn't comfortable. Not until afterward, anyway."

"May I have a drink, Dean?"

"Alcohol-free beer?"

"Cognac, if you have it."

Emily moved to the couch. Dean watched her legs cross, her hands push away the delicate spray of bangs that immediately fell back across her forehead. As he poured the drinks, his eyes caught the gray fox coat, and he imagined making love to her on it.

"What I mean is, I don't feel tension around you. I don't feel you have this nagging need to be somewhere else. When I first saw you, what was so remarkable about your face was the lack of strain in it. It was placid, confident."

"What you mean is I'm sedentary. Devoid of ambition. An old hunting dog retired to a rug in front of the fire."

Emily laughed. "It's not an insult. You're a man who's not fighting for things beyond his reach, things he knows he can't have. Life's not a war for you."

"I'm just a postwar kind of guy, I guess." He joined Emily on the couch with the drinks. "Is that what life with Richard is like? A war?"

She sipped carefully, considering her answer.

"Not between us, really. Between him and the world. Between him and the waterlogged ghost of his goddamned father."

"The war hero."

"Right. One of those larger-than-life men. Held the rushing record for the Navy football team, the second-highest grades in his graduating class, one of the youngest lieutenants to

188

command a destroyer in the Second World War, the oldest officer to command a ship in the Vietnam War."

"Cradle-to-grave perfection," Dean said.

"Not quite." Emily smiled, guiltily. "He died in bed. In his bunk on the destroyer. He'd been on the bridge for three straight days without sleep. Apparently he went down to grab a nap, and they came under fire. He'd forgotten to arm some radar system, forgotten to delegate authority. Everyone sleeping in the crew's quarters was killed. He might have been court-martialed if he'd survived. But Harrison had cultivated a number of important friends in the government over the years, and he'd been decorated so many times that they overlooked his falling asleep on the job. He got his burial at Arlington, and Richard's mother got his medals."

"Didn't that destroy the myth for Richard?"

"No, I think it humanized his father for him. It gave him an opening to exploit. There's a hole in his father's legend, and Richard thinks maybe he can slip through that hole and become his father's equal."

Emily finished her cognac and leaned back in the couch, her eyes scanning the ceiling as though it were a telescope pointed toward clues in her past. "What Richard doesn't see is that his father got fed up with being a hero. You can sense it from the tapes. If you listen to them in sequence, you can hear his voice change. It gets weaker, kind of hoarse. His sentences trail off . . . until it's no longer a voice you can imagine giving orders. I think Harrison Gardner got tired of being perfect. The night his ship was attacked, he just said, 'Fuck it, I'm getting some sleep.'"

Dean refilled their glasses. The dwindling afternoon sun sucked light out of the room and replaced it with silence.

"How does Taylor Willis fit into Richard's life?" Dean asked.

"What an odd question."

"Not really. I met him at the festivities today. I am just curious."

"From time to time people whose functions are a mystery to me appear in Richard's life. He met Taylor about a year ago, brought him home to dinner, introduced him as our lawyer. I hadn't been aware we needed a lawyer. He basically offered him carte blanche to our lives."

"What do you mean by that?"

"He calls at strange hours. Drops by unannounced, and they slink off into the den for long conversations. Richard locks the door behind them. I have never, never been locked out of a room in our house before. Willis presumes on my hospitality. Then, when he senses I'm becoming resentful, he retaliates by showering me and the kids with gifts . . . that fur coat, for example. I don't like people who manipulate my emotions so overtly."

"He is a lawyer after all."

"Well, I wish he'd confine his antics to the courtroom."

"You know, I'm one of those people," Dean said.

Emily tilted her head quizzically. The somber light that had clouded her eyes during her discussion of Harrison Gardner lifted.

"I show up in Richard's life from out of the past like a long-lost relative. I come to dinner, I take you shopping—"

"Watch me have a fit at a toy store."

"I told you not to be embarrassed by that. Sometimes the engine just quits, that's all."

"Shall I tell you something that's haunted me ever since that day?"

"Will I need another drink?"

"It depends on how much flattery you can stand."

"I can stand a fair amount," Dean replied.

"OK, here goes. Even while I was sitting in that dressing room, throwing Jack's toys at the mirror, even while I was shivering with embarrassment, I felt relieved. I could never have allowed myself to short-circuit like that with Richard, but around you I somehow felt I had permission. I was with a man who'd let me have a nervous breakdown. It felt absolutely amazing. I was very grateful to you . . . and very attracted."

Emily finished her cognac and held a hand against her forehead. "It's hot in here, isn't it?"

"I turned everything on full blast. To thaw out our frozen fish in the next room."

"We should leave it on. Do you have anything cool?"

"Every Russian host keeps a chilled supply of vodka on hand."

"I don't think I need any more alcohol. I feel my addictive side emerging."

"I'll come up with something." Dean backed into the kitchen, watching Emily loosen her blouse.

He threw open the refrigerator door. Cheese, salami, yogurt. Nothing to drink. He felt like a college student who has lured a girl to his room with the promise of exotic cocktails and is reduced to serving her flat Diet Pepsi.

Then an idea struck him. He opened the freezer and scraped away a blanket of ice from four chilled pewter vodka tumblers. He returned to the couch, hands tucked behind his back.

"Close your eyes, and prepare for a little bit of o' Siberia."

Emily clamped her eyes shut and threw back her head. Dean lightly touched one of the tumblers to the silk of her neck. She flinched but kept her eyes shut. She sighed softly as he sledded the chilled metal up her throat, across her lips, beaded with cognac, and over her cheeks. The cool sensation translated to heat in his mind, and he felt jolted, as if they had just shared a hungry kiss. The haze of cold evaporated from the tumbler as he held it to her forehead.

"Shall I do the other side?"

She nodded. She held her hand over his as he trailed the second vodka cup across the slope of her cheekbones, brushed it against her eyelid, then pressed it against her forehead.

"It's already warm," she said, opening her eyes. "But it was good while it lasted."

She tightened her grip on his hand and kissed him.

Sharply. Not a soft, yielding kiss, it was more like an attack. He surrendered, dropping the cups to the floor.

"This isn't doing much to cool us off," Dean whispered.

Emily answered with an angrier kiss and pulled his shirttail out, snaking her hand up and down his back.

"I want to feel your skin. Some part of you that's usually

buried under clothes. Something to satisfy my sense of touch, something to make the guilt worthwhile."

The word "guilt" detonated in the close, hot room.

As Dean recoiled from Emily, her nail knifed electrically across his back. His hearing suddenly seemed more acute. He could hear Richard Gardner in the next room. Breathing. Coughing. Listening?

"Are we really ready for this?" Dean asked.

"You mean, from the neck up?"

Her joke came as a relief, tempering the desperation of her kisses, freezing his own urge to act out his fur coat fantasy.

"There's a lot I don't know about you," Dean said. "I mean, this is more than just two groping people who are attracted to each other. More than just a bored housewife coming on to her confidant."

Dean edged away from Emily and tucked in his shirt. She halfheartedly buttoned her blouse, still in a languid pose, a challenge to any man's willpower.

"I guess we're both hunting for something," Emily said.

"Well, I can get laid on Gorky Street. Guilt free and quite cheaply. So it's not sex—not that I wouldn't make a glutton of myself under different circumstances."

Emily stood, again telegraphing the image of a swimmer emerging from the waves. That ability to appear naked even under the heaviest of clothes was her most erotic feature.

"I should wake my husband and collect my kids."

"You haven't told me what we're after."

She grabbed him around the thighs and gave him another razoring kiss. "You have fantastic skin!"

"Emily."

"I explained to you that secrecy is the story of my life. I've even developed the ability to keep some things secret from myself."

They revived Gardner, who accepted a mug of hot tea with lemon, while continuing to issue apologies.

"You're exhausted, Richard," Dean consoled. "Overworked. A body under that kind of stress can't cope with shock. Take some time off."

"Next lifetime. Half the U.S. Congress'll be in town for election day, and they want to see crime-free streets."

"They don't expect you to accomplish what Stalin couldn't."

Dean escorted the Gardners to the elevator, Bryn anxiously tugging at his pants, asking if she could come back sometime for another nap.

He accepted the Gardner secrets as the door clanged shut. From Emily a furtive hand squeeze that became a lacerating caress. From Richard, a whispered question: "You didn't tell her anything, did you? After today I couldn't bear her knowing I'm not doing my own police work."

Dean gestured that their arrangement was still confidential. He watched the elevator car descend into the dying light, trying to read the signals from two pairs of Gardner eyes.

CHAPTER FIFTEEN

M oscow after hours: no competition for New York, Berlin, or Amsterdam. By midnight the curtain had fallen on the ballets, concerts, and poetry readings, and bartenders had hustled their last customers out the door. Moscow had always been a straitlaced city, and under the occupation it was little different. The explosion of sex clubs, red-light districts, and all-night parties that often followed a dictator's dismissal (Franco's Spain, for example) had never happened in Moscow. Night life was earnest—and safe. Serious American jazz, enjoyed by serious, painstakingly informed Russian jazz fans. Serious Russian rock groups, performed for serious teenagers. It was as though the city wanted to be unfettered and outrageous but simply didn't know how.

Dean walked to the river's edge, through the tatters of the Walrus Day celebration, and listened to the Moscow night.

He heard the rumble of buses as they streamed in from the airport, each stuffed with Russia-mad Westerners. Moskvich and Zhiguli horns dueled in a traffic jam outside the Gorky Park McDonald's. A dirty armored car rolled eastward across the Krimsky Bridge, perhaps heading for the Moscow Bank for

194

Foreign Trade to deposit the day's tourist income. A prostitute limped past Dean, one heel on her winter boots broken, the teeth missing from the ratty sable stole that coiled around her neck. Icy breath shot from her lips as she whistled up a passing pedestrian.

Everywhere Dean turned, he heard the sound of money.

He walked north along the embankment, trying to remember where he'd seen it. Wind gusted off the ice floes, slapping against an election banner. The chill sent a pair of lovers scurrying for their car, leaving Dean alone.

A rusty hinge creaked to his left.

There it was. Five paces brought him to the square metal box, which resembled an old washing machine. Stenciled across it were the words "Moscow Swimming Club." The doors hung partly open. Dean pointed a penlight through the crack. Life preserver, rope, blankets, towels, lane dividers.

His light caught a line of jagged steel teeth. He closed his glove around the teeth and withdrew a metal saw, about the length and width of a yardstick.

It resembled an old-fashioned logger's saw, its teeth sharply angled and widely spaced. A cracked wooden handle was riveted to the blade at one end, the other narrowed to a point.

He'd glimpsed the saw in the hands of a Russian Walrus, who'd used it to slice away the ice during the attempt to rescue Gardner. Dean forced a section of the saw into a block of paraffin, capturing the pattern of its teeth in wax; he did a couple of rough sketches and noted the manufacturer's name. He replaced the saw and walked briskly home to test his theory.

The apartment still resonated with Emily Gardner. The impression of her thighs still indented the couch. A scarf dangled from the coat rack, like a seductive hand urging him to come closer. He shook his head, impatient with himself. "Never get involved with a client" was one of the earliest resolutions he'd made when he opened the agency. So far it was a vow he'd kept. Never get involved with a client's wife—that was such an improbable situation, he'd never felt the need to guard against it.

He distracted himself with pictures of blood. The files on Andrei Bukharin contained photographs of his slashed throat, abrasively lit close-ups from a needless variety of angles. At first glance it seemed possible that the wounds could have been inflicted with the Walrus saw, provided angle and momentum were just so. He worked for a few minutes with a ruler, comparing the size of the teeth in the wax impression with the wound measurements detailed in the autopsy report. Maybe, maybe not.

Dean smiled at the irony. Gardner's stumbling attempts to match the Russians' icy machismo might have led him to the murder weapon.

Dean sat at his desk, glumly considering Nina Zinovieva and Viktor Gerasimov. If Mintz's sketches were to be believed, what were they doing in Andrei Bukharin's hotel room? It seemed they both had something to hide—if not murder, then some personal indiscretion—which would make it doubly difficult to take a second crack at them.

Natalie crashed his thoughts, charging into his office, a stack of magazines cradled in her arms.

"Do you always run everywhere, Natalie?"

"I'm like a battery. I've stored up energy during my time off."

"You bringing me good news?"

"Your saw is made in Yakutsk," she answered. "The local people there use it to cut fishing holes in the ice."

"Can you buy this thing in Moscow?"

"Sorry. This particular model is only available through the mail. However . . ."

She dropped the magazines on his desk. They were brochures from Moscow sporting goods stores that specialized in ice augers and winter fishing equipment. "Others like it *can* be found in Moscow."

Dean read through the brochures, eliminating them one by one. Nothing matched the specifications of Bukharin's wounds. Only the Walrus saw was a likely murder weapon. Did this mean he'd have to interrogate every winter swimmer

196

in Moscow? Or had the killer brought his own saw from Yakutsk? Maybe he was a local resident who'd purchased it by mail.

Dean ground down his pencil lead in discouragement. He squared off the brochures on his desk and sharpened the rest of his pencils. He buffed the dust off his glass paperweight, which contained a miniature Kremlin. Unlike Western snow domes, when you held it upside down, it rained sunshine. Wishful thinking, Soviet style.

Natalie puffed herself up, trying to appear optimistic. "I think we may have a new job," she said. "The Omnicom group sent us an inquiry in this morning's mail."

"Well, what is it this time?"

"They believe someone is selling the drawings of a new campaign to a rival firm. They would like you to go under-cover to find the suspect."

Omnicom was an international advertising agency whose tentacles now reached Moscow. Its lobbying muscle had helped push the occupation Arts and Broadcasting Authority into permitting total advertising freedom on TV and radio. An-ticipating (mistakenly, Dean felt) Russia's pent-up thirst for advertising, Omnicom had been grinding out copy and com-mercials for over a year, and Dean had occasionally done se-curity work for them.

"OK, let's see what they want me to risk life and limb for now." Dean skimmed the letter from Omnicom's chief of mar-keting, then glanced at the artwork. A blond, Slavic gigolo poured a glass of champagne for a pink-cheeked beauty, while a birch fire crackled in the fireplace. Their eyes seemed slightly crossed; maybe they were on their second bottle. The slug line read: "Shield, safe as a state secret."

Shield appeared to be a deodorant.

Dean exhaled wearily. It was the type of assignment that he'd always considered lucrative, if insignificant. Now it just seemed insignificant.

"I say we pass on this one, Natalie."

"Pass? But why?"

"Who fucking cares if their deodorant gets stolen?"

Natalie smiled mischievously. "Don't tell me. The need for significance has entered the life of Dean Joplin."

"Maybe I don't need significance. But it wouldn't hurt to believe in my clients now and then, would it?"

Natalie frowned. "Take the job, don't take the job, but don't attach so much importance to your decision." Her scolding manner softened. "Don't become another melancholy Russian, Dean."

He nodded, and picked up his overcoat. He began to sing "O Chochornya" in a low, rolling bass. Natalie laughed and threw her scarf at his back.

Like a student cramming for an exam, Dean sat in his car, listening to a tape of Gardner's second interview with Viktor Gerasimov. Gardner had tracked the former *tolkach* to the Rogoshski Cemetery, where he'd been visiting the graves of his wife and daughters.

Trains clattered in the background; nearby a priest mur mured his way through a funeral.

"I don't understand, Mr. Gerasimov. You didn't know Andrei Bukharin was staying at the Kosmos Hotel, yet you were seen in his room."

"What? Who handed you that crock of shit?"

"We have it from a reliable source."

"The infamous 'reliable' source First, you have the audacity to question me here; second, you don't permit me to confront or even know my accuser This is the kind of trial Stalin would understand."

"This isn't a trial, Mr. Gerasimov."

"Not yet."

"Look, please don't turn this into a political debate. I'm just trying to do my job, trying to come up with some answers—"

"I know the police. When they can't find the answers, they begin to make them up."

"Soviet police, maybe."

"All police."

Gardner sighed, creating a crackle of static. "I'm prepared to make your worst fears come true, Mr. Gerasimov I have

enough evidence to bring you in for a more rigorous ques
tioning."

"Democracy in action."

"It's not a democracy quite yet. You have an election on
January twentieth. You can elect men who'll empty the jails
and abolish the police force for all I care. But until then I have
the legal right to detain you for thirty days if you don't coop'
erate."

"I'm my parents' sole source of support. My father's pension
is lost somewhere in your goddamn bureaucracy. A thirty-day
absence would be impossible."

There was a gap of silence. Then Gerasimov spoke again.
"Look, there are certain aspects of my life that I don't want
the cops to find out about, you follow?"

"Whatever's not pertinent to my investigation I'm prepared
to ignore. Now, shall we get to the point?"

There was another pause, then the scrape of feet as the two
men began walking.

"Your connection to Bukharin?" Gardner prompted. A swag-
ger had entered his voice, as though he were proud of the
way he'd exercised his authority.

"I have a reputation as a guy who's good at getting his
hands on things."

"You were the *tolkach* at the Dawn of the First of May
Scrap and Salvage Plant; it's in my report."

"It was no picnic dealing with scarcity. But it could be a
kick as well. We'd have contests, what you'd call scavenger
hunts. All the *tolkachi* in the region would compete to find a
defitsitnyi item, and each factory would bet on its own
tolkach. Whoever found the item first was declared the winner. I'll say this: I never lost a kopeck of my co-workers'
money."

"And that's how you make your living today?"

"Right. I look for things."

"Some of which may simply be scarce, others illegal,"
Gardner said. "What did Andrei Bukharin want you to look
for?"

"Aviation fuel. One hundred low-lead'"

199

Private ownership of airplanes and the fuel to fly them was forbidden under the occupation. The country's forty thousand miles of borders were still technically sealed, to prevent political criminals and others the occupation wished to prosecute from fleeing the country. War and sabotage had torn great gaps in the radar curtain that had once protected Russia, and a quick hop over the border in a rented Yakovlev trainer might never be noticed.

"You find it?"

"Is Lenin a mummy?"

"Where?"

"Tushino Airfield. Sealed in the warehouse of a disbanded flying club."

"I'll check to see if you're telling the truth."

"Go ahead. Check with the warehouse manager. Maybe you can drive a harder bargain than I did."

"And that's why you visited Bukharin's hotel room? To tell him you'd located the stuff?"

"To get his approval for the deal I'd negotiated."

"Did he say why he needed the aviation fuel?"

"No. And I didn't ask. Curiosity is not an asset in my business."

"How long were you in his hotel room?"

"Ten minutes. Maybe a quarter of an hour."

"Did he get any calls while you were there? Any other visitors?"

"No."

"What time would you say you left him? Approximately."

"Around ten."

The coroner had fixed the time of death between eleven and midnight. The MOPs had kept this a secret in order to verify alibis. Gerasimov hadn't cleared himself as far as Dean was concerned; the killer would know the time of death more accurately than anyone.

"Then you went straight home, where you spent the rest of the evening, as, of course, your parents can verify."

"No. I'm sorry."

"Do you have anyone who can confirm your whereabouts for the next two hours?"

"Not unless gravestones can talk."

The rest of the interview was uninteresting, devoted to the facts and figures of Gerasimov's biography.

"He despises the police," Gardner had told Dean. "I think you'll have more luck with him than I did."

"I think my luck will depend on a nice round figure. How high can I go?"

"Keep it under twenty-five hundred occupation. We can go higher if it looks like it'll buy us something worthwhile."

As he had on Dean's last visit, Aleksandr Gerasimov answered the door. He seemed more frail than before, stooped over as though he were afraid the ceiling were pressing down on him.

"Ah, Mr. Craig, from the Insurance Authority."

"Good afternoon, Mr. Gerasimov. I'm surprised you remember me."

"Everyone I meet is a potential character in the story of my life."

"Well, I hope I'll be nothing more than a footnote."

"Don't be too sure. I've been investigating a distant cousin of mine, a party official purged by Stalin. All mention of him was expunged from party records, his name disgraced. Then, while doing some research at the old Central Committee Library, I found my cousin was named a Hero of Socialist Labor. Twice. I began a full-scale investigation, and now one of my prime missions is the restoration of this man's reputation. You see how history operates in Russia: To one generation you are a hero; to the next, a name people are afraid to mention in public."

"I wonder how history will judge the Americans."

"I would say it depends on who writes the books."

Gerasimov directed Dean to the basement, where he found Viktor at work in the piercing glare of a bare light bulb. The room was a mixture of pawnshop and garage sale, and Viktor, dressed in creased white slacks and Hawaiian shirt, appeared to be noting its contents in a notebook.

"Barracks and Decatur," Dean said.

"New Orleans," Viktor snapped, without looking up.

"It was a bit obvious, I guess. How have you been, Mr. Gerasimov?"

Dean extended his hand, which Viktor shook limply. "Busy, as you can see."

"Then I'm doubly grateful for your time."

"How about showing your gratitude with that insurance check, Mr. Craig."

"I might be able to do just that—if you can clear up a few more details for me."

"Is there a problem?"

"Frankly, yes. We still can't understand why Andrei Pavlovich would name you as a beneficiary in his policy if you hadn't seen him for years."

"Russian friendships endure time and separation."

"Even one-sided ones?"

"What are you driving at, Mr. Craig?"

"Just this. My superiors would feel a lot more comfortable if they could see some evidence pointing toward a closer relationship between you and the deceased. A renewal of your friendship since the war. Personal contact of some kind. Otherwise, they may begin to suspect that the insurance policy was tampered with somehow."

"I'm not a lawyer. How could I get hold of Andrei Pavlovich's policy?"

Dean gestured around the cluttered basement. "There doesn't seem to be much in Moscow you can't get hold of."

Viktor turned an appraising eye on Dean. Suddenly the hair that lay slack jumped like a sail, as a blast of hot air burst through a dingy wall vent. The palm trees on Viktor's Hawaiian shirt rippled, as though stirred by the trade winds.

"Sorry about the heat down here. I keep the boiler cranked up when I'm working. It's one of the few chances I have to wear my Hawaiian shirts. Maybe you were admiring this one: vintage silk, from the forties. Part of a collection I nailed down in trade   . How much did you say Andrei Pavlovich left me?"

"I didn't."

"It must be substantial, or it wouldn't be worthwhile for the Insurance Authority to send you out here twice "

"Maybe I just work cheap," Dean said.

Viktor began to sort through a pile of women's dresses. He jotted a note on his clipboard, then nodded as though he'd just settled some mental debate. He pointed toward the basement window, which provided a street-level view of passing shoes and pants cuffs. A woman's shapely ankle pranced past, parrot green high heels dancing through the slush.

"American ankles," Viktor said. "I have female customers who'd kill for a pair of heels like that."

"Viktor, do yourself a favor. Answer the questions."

"OK, OK. I did see Andrei Pavlovich a few times since the occupation began. Just not in a capacity I like to brag about, that's all. So I'd appreciate it if you'd keep this under your Stetson."

"I'm not here to moralize. We just need to see a logical reason for Bukharin to have left you the money."

"I used to find women for him."

Dean fussily straightened his tie. He gulped in quiet embarrassment, keeping in bureaucratic character.

"How did that . . . arrangement come about?"

"The rewards of life always seemed out of reach to Bukharin. He'd spent his whole life working in a scrapyard, tearing old, useless things apart. He dreamed of remodeling himself. He wanted to be sleek, attractive, new. But he wanted it too desperately. Frustration dripped off him like water off a dog. Women gave him a wide berth."

"So he came to you?"

"About six months ago. He wanted to renew our friendship. The brotherhood of the military, buy your old sergeant a drink, that kind of bullshit. He was having a hard time meeting women and wondered if I could help. To him, women were just another *defitsitnyi* commodity that you could scare up for the right price. I knew a few women like that from my days as a *tolkach*. Some of them had aged gracefully; most of them were broke."

"Where did he get the money to pay these women?"

"The same place he got the bread to stay at a place like the Kosmos—thin air "

"Interesting that he left you the money, not the women."

"Maybe I did my job better than they did theirs."

Viktor continued his inventory. Beyond the women's dresses were a box labeled "Children's winter clothes," a tower of snowshoes, pyramids of canned goods, and a shelf brimming with miscellany, including several hand-size devices which resembled voltage meters.

"You get many requests for Geiger counters?" Dean asked.

"Occasionally. People traveling to the NUCDET sites to visit relatives. They don't really trust the government screening procedures, so they want a little portable reassurance. I can just picture them sitting down to dinner, pulling out the counter to check their chicken Kiev."

Dean continued to probe Viktor for details of his meetings with Andrei Bukharin but learned nothing new. Viktor's description of his visit to the Kosmos was identical with the version he'd told Gardner, almost as though he'd expected his two interrogators to compare stories.

"Now that you've put me through the third degree, do I get my money?"

"I should go over this with my superiors."

"What happened to American initiative?"

"Good question. I've never run into it in my office. I'm wired to my boss like a light to a switch. I suppose I could just say you had an ongoing and lucrative business relationship with Mr. Bukharin, and he showed his appreciation by naming you as a beneficiary. I don't need to go into the details."

"Now you're talking."

Viktor had returned to his clipboard when the boiler shut down with a clunk. The streamers on the heating vent went limp, and a sudden chill seeped in through the porous cinderblock walls.

"Automatic shutoff," Viktor said. "Landlord doesn't let me run the heat on high for too long." He hugged his bare arms to his chest and shivered. "Guess my vacation in Waikiki is over for the afternoon," he said, leading Dean to the basement door. "You know, there is this one woman he used to see."

"I thought you said—"

"I know, I know. He couldn't get to first base with a girl. But this girl . . . blond, tough-looking, unhappy. I think she was a ghost from his past. And believe me, he'd gotten farther than first base with her."

"Meaning?"

"She was pregnant. He'd used Soviet condoms, so he really only had himself to blame—especially since I could've gotten him a good price on a European brand."

Dean followed Viktor up to the lobby, where the last traces of sunlight bunched against the front door. A rat crouched in the bright spot, trying to soak up the fading warmth. Dean absently returned Viktor's handshake and heard himself promise to send the insurance check.

He was certain Viktor had just described Nina Zinovieva.

CHAPTER SIXTEEN

There was a waiting list for funerals in Moscow.

One of the first official acts of the occupation had been to free the Russian Orthodox Church from government control. The country's seventy-five hundred churches doubled, then tripled in worshipers in a few short months as the religious resurgence, already going strong before the war, accelerated. Attendance at religious ceremonies, while not officially proscribed, had always been a black mark on a worker's résumé, so only independent thinkers had chosen church weddings, baptisms, and burials. Now, with no one looking over their shoulders, with the KGB-inspired gangs of thugs cleared from cathedral doors, Russians crowded the churches to admire the gilt, inhale the incense, and transport themselves back to an ornate, mystically codified Russian past.

But until new churches could be constructed, or the old ones which the state had turned into museums or warehouses, renovated, the Moscow patriarchate could not keep up with the masses of citizens who wanted to baptize, marry, or die in Orthodoxy. If you wanted a church service, you had to take a number.

On December 10, more than a month after he was murdered, Andrei Pavlovich Bukharin finally got his funeral.

Dean had stopped by the communal apartment Nina Zinovieva shared with Mrs. Bukharina and been directed by one of the other tenants to a small chapel in the Fili-Mazilovo district, a suburb of eastern Moscow.

The chapel was squeezed into a narrow lot between two concrete apartment blocks. Fumes from cars and buses blackened the whitewashed walls and settled on a trampled patch of snow, which set off the church from the sidewalk.

Despite the years of neglect, the church still retained a veneer of dignity, its purpose never in doubt. Squatting in the night, its single stained glass window burnished with light, it reminded Dean of a tired candle that had dripped down to a stub, but refused to be blown out.

Dean walked to the front doors, passing two old ladies and a leather-clad teenager planting birch saplings in the frozen soil, melting the ground first with water boiled in an electric samovar.

Dean inched through the door and was met by a coiling cloud of censer smoke and the drone of a priest chanting a eulogy.

To his surprise, it was standing room only. Three rows of winter-coated parishioners faced the altar, several holding candles. A priest in a blue, silver-trimmed cassock was flanked by two acolytes as he read prayers over a closed coffin. Bukharin had been buried immediately after the autopsy, so Dean surmised the coffin was empty, a reusable demo.

Dean struggled to understand the Russian until he realized the priest was speaking in Old Church Slavonic, a dead language the clergy was reviving. As the priest led the congregation in a hymn, Dean whispered to the woman next to him. "Is this the Bukharin funeral?"

"I'm not sure," she replied. "It's either this or the next one." After a moment she added: "Or the last one."

"Then you didn't know Andrei Pavlovich?"

"Oh, no. I don't know anyone here." She watched raptly as the priest plucked a piece of paper off the coffin lid and scrolled it up ceremoniously, prayers for the dead. "I'm just a spectator. I like church ceremonies. I saw a baptism here this morning." She lowered her voice. "Beautiful parents, ugly baby. I've heard there's a wedding tomorrow. A couple from Zagorsk who can't get a reservation in the cathedral there. I hope I can get off work in time."

He saw Nina Zinovieva and Mrs. Bukharina separate from the crowd and kneel in front of the priest, who performed an elaborate blessing and addressed them in a subdued voice. The two women stood, exchanged fussy kisses with the priest. They seemed to argue briefly. Then he handed them the scrolled prayer sheet—the only tangible souvenir of the ceremony—and it was over.

Convulsed with tears, Mrs. Bukharina knelt at the coffin, gliding her hand along the lid as though she were trying to resurrect the emptiness inside.

The spectators mumbled among themselves as they filed to the door, comparing notes on the funeral like a first-night theater audience.

"I felt it lacked sincerity"; "The Ogarkov affair was much more dramatic"; "The priest seemed bored tonight"; "The old lady, Mrs. Whats her name . . . did you see the way she was dressed? You think she could do better for her own son's funeral."

Dean blended into the dispersing crowd as they pushed out the door and scrunched through the snow to the street. They all were spectators; only Nina and his mother had come to mourn Andrei Bukharin.

The two women came out of the church arm in arm, and after a few further words of condolence the priest closed the door behind them. Almost immediately the light in the chapel blinked out and the warm blue glow of a television appeared in the priest's living quarters.

Not wanting to intrude on Mrs. Bukharina's grief, Dean decided to question Nina Zinovieva alone. He figured she would escort Mrs. Bukharina home, and he would wait a respectful interval for the old lady to go to bed before knocking on their door.

Instead, Nina flagged a taxi for Mrs. Bukharina. They hugged distantly, before the old woman folded herself into the back seat and, without a look back, ordered the taxi to drive off.

Dean decided to approach Nina right there. But then she reached into her pocket, extracted a Sony Walkman, and fiddled with the volume. He heard a spray of static, then a deliberate male voice speaking Spanish. The sentence was sliced off as Nina fitted the headset around her ears and clamped on an earmuff. Equipped for her Spanish lesson, she set off briskly toward the Pionerskaya metro station.

Keeping a safe distance, Dean followed her into the station, joining the handful of passengers hurrying beneath the giant red *M*. Caught at the turnstile without a five-kopeck piece, Dean lost sight of Nina as she plunged down the express escalator while he hunted for a change machine.

He rode down the wooden escalator on his toes, straining for a glimpse of Nina. It seemed to descend forever. The metro was deeper than the London underground, deeper than the New York subway, its exact depth once a military secret. The passengers were strangely mournful, like coal miners returning to work after a cave-in.

He pushed politely through a wall of winter coats in time to see Nina's blue earmuffs disappear into the last car of an Arbatskaya train. She found a seat at the head of the car. Certain she hadn't spotted him, Dean fitted himself into a group of men standing near the entrance holding cross-country skis.

The train pulled out smoothly, and Dean watched the yellow walls of the station whip past, the vaunted marble columns and filigreed ceilings now placarded with ads for Hilton Hotels, instant coffee, and a new line of frozen Russian diet dinners named Slenderella.

"Look at this. Leon Trotsky. Have you ever seen a better likeness? They even got the glasses right."

A man with a jutting jaw and a huge forehead that sloped like a steep cliff up to a wayward patch of hair, burdened with shopping bags, wove toward Dean. From his breath Dean decided he'd done more drinking than shopping. He waved a small plaster bust of Leon Trotsky.

"Very nice," Dean said.

"Got Khrushchev in here, too. Lavrenty Beria, fuck your mother."

The man produced a cheaply framed portrait of Beria, Stalin's officially disgraced secret police chief. "There's a warehouse outside the city . . . do you know it?" the man whispered. When Dean said he didn't, he was treated to a travelog. "It's filled with busts and paintings, officially commissioned works that could never be displayed because all the men had been purged."

The man drew out an assembly line of socialist realism sculpture and handed the busts to Dean one by one. "Here's Nikolai Bukharin, Lenin's right hand, Georgi Malenkov Vyacheslav Molotov . . . I can let them go for twenty-five: my cost, plus ten percent."

"No, thank you."

"Do me a favor. New Year's coming. Just take one."

"Please, I'm not interested." Dean had his eyes on Nina Zinovieva, who stared out the window at the blurring stations.

"Come on. Here's Aleksandr Kerensky, our only president. I'm sure you're interested in him; he moved to California after the revolution." The salesman was growing abrasive. He pushed his bulk into Dean's line of sight and forced the Kerensky statuette into his hand. Dean recoiled, and the plaster bust dropped to the floor and shattered.

The salesman growled a torrent of insults. Nina, cocooned in her language tapes, didn't hear a word, but the commotion drew her gaze straight at Dean.

He dropped to a crouch, shielded by knees and winter boots.

"Well. Now that you've broken it, you'll have to pay for it."

Dean gathered the shards together, pretending to reassemble it. The train slowed. Through the forest of legs Dean saw Nina stand and join the rush for the door. The intercom coughed, and the driver announced their arrival at the Kievskaya station. Three metro lines converged here. If Dean lost her now, he'd never pick up her trail again.

Dean got to his feet, cradling the remains of Aleksandr Kerensky. The faces of the cross-country skiers were severe, as though they were prepared to come to the salesman's defense against the boorish American.

"Look, I don't have much change."

"I take American Express, comrade."

The salesman cracked a gloating smile, which infected the skiers with laughter.

The metro whistled to a smooth stop, and the doors parted. Dean dropped a fistful of coins in the salesman's hands.

"Look, just let me by. This is my stop."

The salesman contemptuously let the coins drizzle to the floor. A couple of kids battled for the money. Nina Zinovieva was already out the door and heading for the escalator.

The salesman stood his ground, determined to create an international standoff. The skiers, muttering among themselves, formed a barricade between Dean and the door.

"Look, mister," the salesman snarled, "you may have won the war, but it doesn't mean you can come over here and pick our pockets, too. Now twenty-five rubles is a fair price."

"But I don't have—oh, shit!"

The doors closed after the last of the exiting passengers. The intercom called, "Next stop, Smolenskaya," signaling the train was about to depart.

Dean tore a hundred-ruble note from his wallet and forced it into the salesman's breast pocket. He grabbed the entire shopping bag and surged to the door, the fallen Soviet heroes rattling at his side.

Dean scuttled through the terminal after Nina and followed her into another train, heading for the Mira Prospekt. The car was nearly empty. Burying his face in his shopping bag, he took a seat in the corner.

At the Mira Prospekt Nina changed to the yellow line, heading north toward Medvedkovo. She got off at the Exhibition of Economic Achievements, known to Russians by its initials, VDNKh. Dean tailed her up to the street and into the eye-stinging cold.

Dean watched her from behind a *Pravda* display case, as she perched on a bench and rubbed her hand over her swollen stomach. Several passersby expressed concern or delight over her pregnancy, but she waved them off. He followed her gaze up the Mira Prospekt. She was staring at the Kosmos Hotel! It was a tower of glass and light, its two-hundred-dollar rooms an unaffordable temptation to the cold pedestrians who hurried past its lobby. Was Nina dreaming about luxury or contemplating a return to the scene of the crime?

Dean debated calling Gardner. Nina settled the question by getting up and heading west along Ostankinskaya Street. Dean kept up with her, wrapping his face in a shawl in case she looked back. She walked more quickly now, her toes kicking away dead leaves and slush.

Up ahead the Ostankino television tower was shrouded in mist. The cloud cover can't be that low, Dean thought.

Then he realized that it wasn't a cloud cover; it was smoke from the cooking fires in the Dzerzhinsky Park squatters' camp. Dean thought of the well-tended diners in the Seventh Heaven restaurant at the top of the television tower, unbuckling their belts after an imported meal, coaxing the last drop of French champagne out of the bottle as they looked down on the tangled, smoky misery of the camp. They were probably grateful that the restaurant revolved; at least part of the time they had a consoling postcard view of Moscow's nightlights.

Nina headed up an alley to the camp's southern perimeter. Dean set down the shopping bag, which he suddenly realized he was still carrying, and blended with a knot of people lining up to enter the camp.

Chain-link fence, topped with barbed wire, stretched between cement uprights on either side of a pedestrian gate. MOPs and Russian militiamen frisked visitors under the glare of halogen security lamps, inspected IDs with flickering penlights. There was light everywhere but in the guards' bleak faces. Many of the visitors carried bundles of clothing and coolers stuffed with meat and produce, which they were bringing to friends and relatives in the camps. Occasionally the guards helped themselves to a delicacy as a reward for expediting the paper work.

212

Nina was evidently a frequent visitor. The guards waved her through without a glance at her pass. With Dean they were more precise, demanding his Moscow residency permit, his driver's license, cracking a few stale jokes about his detective's license, as they ran his name through a computer.

"Sign here, Dick Tracy," said a young American MOP, handing Dean a logbook for his signature. "Enjoy your stay in the South Bronx East. You run into trouble, look for the MOP jeeps with the cherry tops. They'll help you out if they're sober."

Dean joined a line at an airport metal detector, which listed crazily in the mud. People walked through it at an angle, their bodies tilted as though reflected in a fun house mirror.

The camp sprawled before him. Once a gentle green oasis dotted with museums and boating lakes, centered on a one-thousand-acre botanical garden, it was now a despairing tent city, colored brown and black. Somewhere Dean had read that it had recently surpassed the Gaza Strip as the most densely populated area in the world.

It reminded him of a nineteenth-century painting of a military camp the night before a battle. Tents, sagging with snow, formed rows of canvas tenements, fronting mud streets. In front of the tents, families cooked dinner, the lucky ones over small government-issue stoves. The rest set garbage fires, which burned energetically but spread a sour stench that coated the food, the nostrils, the air.

A gang of teenagers fought with rocks and knives. They crashed into Dean as they charged down the streets in hysterical laughter.

Dean hurried after Nina, who knew her way through the labyrinth. Immediately spotting Dean for an outsider, a teenage boy tried to sell him a map of the camp: "Please, sir, it's accurate down to the last tent pole. I've lived here for two years. It'd make a great souvenir. I drew it with my own blood."

Dean snaked away from the kid and followed Nina down a broader avenue. The tents here were stores and businesses. Signs in Russian advertised "groceries," "fuel," "boots," even "legal assistance." A spry old man specialized in picture postcards of prerevolutionary Moscow. A curious greeting was stenciled to the side of the old man's tent: "This tent a gift from the Yellow Springs, Ohio, Boy Scouts, Troop 17." In smudged felt pen, Scouts had signed the olive canvas, the scoutmaster had added the only Russian words he knew: *Na zdorovie* (Cheers).

Suddenly a strange silence descended on the street, and people darted into tents. The silence was momentary, shattered by shouting, the sound of running boots, and a heavy mechanical growl.

Dean peered into the grimy distance. The endless canopy of tents began to glow with a radiant white light, as though it were targeted by a moonbeam. But the moonbeam moved, and the metallic chatter grew deafening.

It was a searchlight from a MOP helicopter, pinpointing some fugitive from the air. Dean backed into the shadows as headlights swished onto the street, followed by the grinding gears of a MOP jeep.

The jeep stopped, its silver-helmeted occupants and their AK-47's backlit by the searchlight. Another jeep appeared at the other end of the street, high beams burning. It, too, slushed to a halt. The street was closed off. Pedestrians, including Nina, were forced to wait out the police action.

The chopper hovered closer, an unearthly sight as it dipped in and out of the smoke that stratified above the camp. The cockpit lights burnished the two pilots in a hellish orange glow.

Black, infrared goggles protruded from their foreheads like insect eyes. Dean realized they were forcing the fugitive through the warren of tents to the main street, where they could box him in between the jeeps.

There was a commotion across the street. Tents wobbled, and a group of people tumbled out of a narrow alley and split off in different directions.

The fugitive was right behind these innocent pedestrians caught in the chase. He exploded onto the main street in a whirl of panic. In the angular web of the searchlights, his face was white and shadowless. He was in his early twenties, with bony features and eyes round in catlike confusion. He wore scraps of discarded wardrobes: pinstriped banker's slacks, a New York Yankees sweatshirt, and a gray overcoat festooned with Orders of Lenin.

He yo-yoed up and down the street; the jeeps crept toward him; the MOPs unhinged the safeties on their Kalashnikovs.

He tried to fight his way into the dubious protection of the tents but was battered off by frying pans and sticks of firewood. He skittered in the mud, looking for an escape route, screaming in Russian for help. The helicopter descended like a deadly chandelier, rotors whipping up a tornado.

Dean felt an impulse to rush to the young man's rescue, but the odds were too overwhelming. Dean salved his conscience. If the MOPs were so desperate to capture him, he must have committed a dozen murders.

The chopper set down in the middle of the street. Mud was sucked into the airstream and sprayed onto the tents. Dean cringed as muck mixed with sewage splattered his shirt.

The MOPs vaulted from their jeeps and marched toward the fugitive. He was covered in grime now, nearly exhausted, yet he kept up his dance, searching for escape. The helicopter pilots followed him with their searchlight, and for the first time Dean saw the faces of the spectators. They were stoic, nearly uninterested. No one shouted hatred at the MOPs; no one pelted them with rocks or pleaded for the young man's freedom. To the camp residents it was a television show, and not a very compelling one.

The young man picked up garbage and flung it at the soldiers. The helicopter door swung open, and an imposing dark-suited figure in a heavy overcoat emerged. Dean recognized him as a *dolgozhiteli,* a long lifer from one of the Caucasian republics, where men lived well past a hundred, thanks to a hard life, a healthy diet, and natural springwater. He had a taut, tanned face that was old but not wrinkled, a commanding white mustache, and black, incisive eyes. His shoulders were upright, not sloping, like those of many old men. He carried an inconspicuous handgun, and a silver ceremonial sword dangled from his belt.

215

If he was supposed to take command of the situation, he failed. As he reached for a bullhorn, the fugitive's nerve ends burned up.

He rushed the nearest soldier, overwhelming him with surprise. The young man grabbed the AK-47 and pointed the barrel at his stomach. He clamped his hand on the soldier's, forcing him onto the trigger.

The machine gun erupted. As a stream of bullets tore into him, the young man shuddered, like a flame lashed in a windstorm. For a deafening second, killer and victim were linked by the gun. It shook them both, as it spit out rounds, grinding away on instinct, the weapon controlling the soldier.

Then the young man fell away from the gun and dropped into the mud. For a few moments a pall of shock gripped the scene. It was broken by a group of children, who charged out of the camp's dark corners, unintimidated by the soldiers. They rooted through the mud, fighting for souvenirs—the bullets that had torn through the fugitive's body.

The long lifer strode to the body, slicing through the bunched soldiers. He presented them with an ID, then knelt over the corpse. He used a black handkerchief to mop mud off the dead man's face. The long lifer's mustache twitched. His face set into a scowl.

"This is the wrong man," he announced. "The dental work is wrong, and the eye color does not match the description."

The commander of the soldiers protested feebly. Arguing broke out among the MOPs as they passed the blame. One jammed a gloved hand into the dead man's bleeding mouth to inspect the teeth himself. The long lifer, uninterested in excuses, walked back to the chopper. The pilots were sharing a thermos of coffee, infrared scopes pushed back in their hair like sunglasses.

Through the Plexiglas Dean saw the pilots shrug, as the long lifer climbed aboard to explain the mistake. They offered him a cup of coffee, which he declined. Unhealthy, Dean mused. Probably waiting to get home to his raw vegetables and kefir. The helicopter lifted off unceremoniously, its searchlight striking the corpse for a second, before the pilot switched it off.

216

The helicopter banked into the smoke, its whopping blades continuing to stir the air long after the red and green navigation lights had disappeared.

Dean asked the nearest soldier for an explanation. He received a stony look in reply.

"The long lifer, the Georgian. Who was he?"

"Hey, man, I'm from Milwaukee. What do I know?"

"What do you mean? He orchestrated the whole chase. He flew off in a MOP helicopter."

"I'm paid to carry a gun, not ask questions," the soldier snapped. He hurried back to the safety of his group. They stood guard around the body, like football players in a huddle, until an ambulance careened onto the scene. Were they merely protecting the corpse from looters, or were they trying to cover up the evidence of their tragic miscalculation?

As the ambulance pulled away, squatters filtered out of their tents and returned to their cooking fires.

No one could or would answer Dean's questions. The circumstances behind the botched arrest remained obscure; the identity of the sword-wielding Georgian, unknown.

Dean saw Nina waiting in the crowd for the MOPs to lift their roadblock. They checked a few identity papers with lazy arrogance, then fishtailed away.

Nina took off at a brisk clip, her knee boots an advantage over Dean's low shoes. A few minutes of fast walking brought them to the edge of a small lake.

In the social structure of the squatters' camp, the tent pitched along the lakeshore belonged to the aristocracy. The mud alleys were wider; the tents and shanties, more spacious. The black waters of the lake, stretching toward a pine and spruce forest which had been thinned for firewood, gave a welcome feeling of openness; it was the one spot in the camp where one could escape the relentless overcrowding.

Nina entered a large shack, whose back wall was constructed from the hull of one of the tourist sailboats which had once plied the lake. Through a crack in the hull Dean could glimpse the shack's interior. A fire blazed in a wood-burning stove. In the sallow haze of a kerosene lamp Nina carried mugs of coffee, one of which she handed to someone below Dean's field of vision.

He crept along the rear of the shanty. A smudged car window had been jerry-built into the shack. It still bore an *Ingosstrakh* insurance sticker, meaning it had once belonged to a foreign tourist. Maybe with a little imagination, the people in the shack could look out the car window and see Sweden or France.

He risked a glance through the window and saw a makeshift bathroom. Its centerpiece was a tub, unconnected to any plumbing. Several Rubin televisions, useless without electricity, had their picture tubes smashed in and did duty as storage space. One was brimming with medicine bottles; another, with foreign perfumes.

He heard distorted rock music. He was attracting the suspicions of a group of teenagers, gathered around a mountain of burning tires, which served as a communal heater for those so poor they had to sleep outside.

Dean decided a bluff would at least buy him a few minutes with Nina and the stranger. He went to the front door, which was from a BMW, and knocked brazenly.

Nina opened it. She seemed to be trying to recall his face.

"Miss Zinovieva? Do you remember me? I worked with Andrei Bukharin?"

Her face was blank; her voice, flat. "Come in, please."

Dean bent his head and entered. The door shut behind him with solid German authority.

"I know this may seem totally insane, my coming here like this . . . you don't remember me, do you?"

"I remember you."

Toneless. Chilled. But not one note of surprise. Dean's skin began to tingle. Something's out of whack here, he thought.

He inched into the shack, ice cold despite the fire. Against the back wall, a cot was set into the curve of the sailboat. A tall, coughing man was buried under layers of blankets, his face in shadow. Dean made out a mustache and the red dot of a smoldering cigar.

The smell of sewage, strong outside, was overpowering in

the shack. It came in waves, only occasionally tempered by the aroma of fresh coffee.

"Bring him over here, Nina," ordered the man.

Dean hesitated.

"Go ahead. Vladimir's the one you really came to see," Nina said.

Dean walked across a thatch of timbers that bridged the muddy floor. Vladimir propped his head up against a car seat cushion. In the hissing kerosene light they inspected each other. He was large-framed, but his tattered silk Yves Saint Laurent pajamas hung loosely on a body that had lost both weight and muscle. His face had once been handsome and defined, but now his skin drooped and puckered like a dried apricot. His teeth were stained—not with tobacco but with dried blood. His eyes were clouded and dim, like two dying flashlights. Most frightening of all, when he ran a skeletal hand through his musty hair, tufts of it pulled out and floated through the shack like dandelions.

"I'm a child's nightmare, am I not?" asked Vladimir. He fixed Dean with an acrid stare. "You, I'm gratified to see, are a true cliché. Maybe you like our Russian food a little too well, but otherwise you seem fit, able to handle yourself. Just as I always imagined an American private detective would look."

CHAPTER SEVENTEEN

"You're shocked that I know? I'm pleased. Perhaps I haven't lost my ability to surprise. Maybe I'll surprise everybody and live another year."

"Vladimir, come on. Don't start this morbid chatter again," said Nina.

"Go fuck yourself—if everybody on the outside isn't already doing it for you."

Nina ignored the taunt and leaned against the far wall, waiting.

"And by the way, coffee isn't good for expectant mothers," Vladimir added.

Nina patted her stomach. "I'm sure little Joaquin won't mind."

"Joaquin? He's a boy? That's the first I've heard of it."

"I renamed him. After Joaquin Rodrigo. The music we were listening to when he was conceived."

"I don't recall any music. I think I was too preoccupied with calculating how much a fuck with you was going to cost me."

The insults didn't even reach Nina, who seemed to have

heard them all before. They just hovered in the air, with the flies that swirled above Vladimir's cot. They were a couple that couldn't seem to decide between bitterness and affection, so they lived with a mix of both.

Vladimir thumped an unopened bottle of Chivas Regal against the wall.

"Pavel, get the hell in here!"

A scrawny, depleted teenager slouched into the room, a ghetto blaster perched on his shoulder. Dean recognized him as one of the gang who had crashed into him near the camp entrance.

"Let's have that wallet."

Vladimir attempted to snap his fingers, the gesture of a man accustomed to servants tuned to his whims—but his hand was weak, his joints unresponsive.

"Another part of the machine has become obsolete," he said. Pavel handed him Dean's wallet and disappeared, trailing a wake of distorted music.

"What kind of game is this?" Dean said.

"I noticed you following me, so I told Pavel to pick your pocket. We have expert thieves in the camps," Nina explained.

"Driver's license, gun license, Moscow residency permit, private investigator's license," Vladimir recited, leafing through Dean's wallet. "You're licensed for practically everything, Mr. Joplin. Too much freedom for one man."

"Freedom equals anarchy? A true Soviet," Dean said.

"A jealous Soviet, maybe. I'm a prisoner in my own country while you roam luxuriously through Moscow driving big cars and firing off guns."

"A 1975 Zhiguli and a used thirty-eight. Talk about luxury."

Vladimir's features began to sort themselves into a familiar picture. Dean knew he had seen the face somewhere before.

"Why were you following Nina, Mr. Joplin?"

"I wouldn't be a very private investigator if I told you."

"Are you working for the police? Is Nina suspected of some sort of crime?"

"Private detectives and the police don't always get along, Vladimir."

"In my experience, everyone gets along with the police in Moscow. And call me Mr. Raikin. You're in my house, so grant me a little formality."

"What are you doing, Vladimir?" Nina exploded. "Let's just ram a gun down his throat until he tells us what he knows."

"Nina, please. Who is the experienced interrogator here?"

She shifted her shoulders in disgust and stalked to the stove. She ripped up a section of floorboard and used it to stoke the fires. On a shelf above the stove, mixed in with jars of flour and sugar, Dean saw a row of perfume bottles: Chanel No. 5, Opium, Obsession. A curious oasis of indulgence in the wasted decay of the shack.

Then Dean knew where he'd seen Vladimir before.

"You see, Mr. Joplin, we're reduced to burning our own house to keep warm. An apt metaphor for the Soviet Union, wouldn't you agree?"

"Throw a little Chanel on the fire. That oughta burn," Dean said.

"You spotted our little collection. Luxury goods we manage to trade for now and then. They're almost like currency when you barter them for food."

"When you combine it with the treasure trove in your dacha, there's no reason you should go hungry."

Vladimir smiled indulgently, through blood-flecked teeth. "Of course, my country home. You know, Nina, I've been thinking it's about time we took off for a little vacation. Throw a few things in a suitcase, hop in the car, and tell the camp guards to feed the cats."

"Irony doesn't suit you, Vladimir. I saw your picture in the dacha: twenty years younger, twenty years healthier. A young man saying good-bye to his proud parents as he marched off to serve the motherland."

Nina stiffened but kept her back turned to Dean. Raikin's face weakened momentarily, but he recovered, calmly relighting his cigar.

"So. I've seen your cards, and you've seen mine. I prefer it

222

this way actually. We can talk frankly now, without a lot of bullshit. No irony, I promise."

"How's this for frank? Your girl friend here—I'll call her Miss Zinovieva to keep you happy—was spotted leaving a man's hotel room the night he was murdered. The police have her at the top of a very short list of suspects."

"Then why haven't they arrested her?"

"The military courts still haven't decided what constitutes sufficient evidence to issue an arrest warrant. The MOPs don't want to pull someone in if they're just going to have to let her go on a technicality."

"The police in the camps aren't subject to the same laws," Vladimir pointed out.

"You're right. They don't seem subject to any laws that I can see. Maybe I should call them."

Raikin propped himself up on spiny elbows.

"Or . . . you could tell me what you know about Andrei Bukharin," Dean added.

Vladimir fitted another pillow beneath his head. "I'm afraid I don't know the name."

"Of course not. Neither does Nina. That's why she's been living with his mother. When she's not staying at your dacha, practicing her Spanish." Dean saw this last bit of information surprised both Nina and Raikin. "Don't keep testing me, Vladimir. I know enough about both of you to know when you're feeding me shit."

Raikin sighed. As he exhaled, a knot seemed to tighten around his midriff, corkscrewing his body in pain. Blood squirted out of his mouth and trickled onto his pajamas, staining Yves Saint Laurent's stately monogram. Nina dragged a bundle of newspapers from under the cot. She crumpled the front page of a month-old *Evening Moscow* into a ball and fed it to Raikin. In a minute he pulled it out of his mouth, sopping red. It took three more pages before the bleeding had stopped sufficiently for Raikin to speak.

"You'll have to forgive me, Mr. Joplin. My body is beginning to leak. There doesn't seem to be a single fluid that I'm capable of controlling."

"What is it?"

"A couple of camp doctors have told me it's cancer. But who knows? They'd say anything for a bottle of my whiskey."

"For a case they'd tell him he was cured," Nina said.

"So you can see, I live in a bartering society. What do you have to trade for my information?"

"Maybe I could arrange a *propiska*, a Moscow residency permit. A temporary one so we could get you out of here to a specialist."

Raikin waved the offer aside with a blasé shrug. But Nina seemed interested.

"Could you really manage that?" she asked.

"Nina, he's bluffing—"

"Then let's test him. What have you got to lose?"

"Maybe he's not after you. Maybe he came for me. Think of that for a moment. Maybe the whole Bukharin investigation is just another cover story. An excuse to get me into some occupation hospital with bars on the windows and American prosecutors feeding me truth serum."

Nina impulsively snatched Dean's hand. She led him through a Soviet flag curtain into the bathroom.

"Nina," Raikin called. She didn't answer.

"Can you really get him out of the camps? Into a cancer clinic?"

"Look, I can't promise anything. You know how the occupation works. But I have a few connections. I can persuade, I can lobby—"

"How soon?"

"That would depend on the quality of the information he gives me."

Nina perched on the edge of the bathtub, which Dean saw was filled with loose cigarettes. She plunged a hand into the lake of cigarettes, which rose to her elbow, and pulled out a Marlboro.

"He won't say a word. He's too ashamed of his weakness; he won't acknowledge his disease. He won't bargain with you for his life."

"He was a KGB officer, wasn't he?" Nina hedged. "I've been

to the dacha, Nina. I saw you take off in the speedboat. It's not something you can hide anymore."

She parted the curtain and looked in on Vladimir, who was bent over in a coughing attack.

"He worked for the Committee for thirteen years, and now he's terrified of reprisals. He has a recurring nightmare: He's lying on a cutting board in a butcher shop. Dissidents, hooligans, parasites—all those ridiculous names for people he arrested—they're all putting on aprons and sharpening knives. Here in the camps no one knows his real name or anything about his past."

"So he sends you to the dacha. You've been selling off his luxury goods bit by bit and bringing him the proceeds."

She nodded.

"OK, we'll come back to that. How did you meet?"

"After the armistice I tried to work my way toward Moscow."

"By work, you mean—"

"Sure, OK, I was a whore. The situation in the countryside was catastrophic. Millions of people were trying to get to Moscow, and I didn't have any money or gasoline to pay my way. We knew NATO would seal off the city once they stopped squabbling at the Geneva Conference. The collective farms emptied; divisions of soldiers took to the road in stolen trucks and tanks. We drove day and night. Through blizzards. A man I'd fucked the night before froze to death on top of me by the next morning.

"We'd been traveling for a month when Vladimir wandered into our camp one night. He didn't say where he was from, wouldn't talk. For three days he didn't say a word. He rode with us in an armored personnel carrier, paying his way by cooking.

"When he finally opened up, I realized he was from Moscow. I knew he'd been well off, a party *nachalstvo,* a major in the KGB. I was thrilled. I fell in love with his status and the grandiose life I imagined he'd led in Moscow. I spent my whole life on a kolkhoz so small we had no TV, no cinema, no library. For me, the war was a chance to get to Moscow, and here was Vladimir, my own personal Muscovite.

"He had money, too. Rubles, francs, dollars, pounds. Sewn into his clothes, glued into the soles of his shoes. I'd never seen foreign money before. At night, when the others were asleep, I would make Vladimir show off the banknotes in the glow of the headlights.

"Vladimir never intended to return to Moscow, where he had so many enemies. We planned to head north, to cross the border into Finland. But the occupation forces systematically rounded up war refugees and funneled us into the camp here. Now we wait, while they try to decide what to do with us. Moscow can't absorb us; the countryside can't provide us with a decent living. You Americans don't want two million new immigrants. Sometimes I think the only solution is to start another war and throw all of us into the Army."

"But you got out."

Nina stubbed out her cigarette in the mud. She reached into one of the shattered television sets for a bottle of Chanel. She daintily sprayed a wisp behind her ears and on her neck, then replaced the bottle with reverential tenderness.

"Yes, I got out. And now I finally have my Moscow life of luxury, as you can see."

"How did you manage it?"

"I've told you how I make my living."

"Who did you sleep with? The camp commander?"

"I got married. There's a law, part of the family reunification act. If you marry a Moscow resident, you automatically become one yourself."

"What's your husband's name?"

"My late husband."

There was a long pause.

"Andrei Pavlovich Bukharin," Dean said.

Nina plucked another cigarette from the bathtub. "Andrei Pavlovich was Vladimir's cousin. A black sheep, as you would say in America. The one straggler in a family of accomplished people—"

"Nina?" Raikin called, his voice brittle and fading. "Bring the

226

damn prisoner back in here. I'm not through questioning him."

Nina smiled, as though Raikin were just a child begging for an extra dessert.

"But Andrei was not totally worthless; he had that residency permit. It was a real arranged marriage, like those in Azerbaijan or Turkmenia."

"Love never entered the picture, I presume."

"I despised Andrei Pavlovich; he tolerated me. It looks like I had a reason to kill him, doesn't it? I'll confess to the murder if you'll arrange to get Vladimir to a hospital tonight."

Dean ignored the offer. "Did it seem like he was afraid of anybody? Any old enemies out to settle prewar scores?"

She gave a blank shake of the head.

"Anatoly Mintz. Viktor Gerasimov. Boris Gelb. Did he ever mention those names to you?"

Another no. But this time it was accompanied by a minute glow in the eyes that was gone the moment Nina blinked.

"That leaves you, the desperate woman who marries to escape the camps, then, once she's fulfilled her lifelong dream of Moscow residency, kills her drudge of a husband. But that sounds much too programmed to be human behavior. That leaves Vladimir—"

"Do not try to connect him with this crime. He's suffering enough as it is."

"Just how long has he been sick? Has he ever managed to sneak out of the camp?"

"No more questions now." She stalked toward the curtain.

"Why was your husband staying at the Kosmos?"

"No more! You give me your phone number. I'll call twice a day, morning and evening, until you have a hospital bed and a transit pass arranged for Vladimir. Then maybe we'll talk again."

"I could have you arrested. I think you've told me enough to justify a warrant."

"And then?"

"The police would require you to talk."

"How? What could they threaten me with? Is there some

new form of pain they can inflict that I haven't already endured?"

Back in the "living room," Vladimir Raikin was fading into delirium. Whatever drugs had powered him had lost their force. He waved a hand at an imaginary prisoner.

"You Zionist shit, renegade, turncoat, speculator, Hitlerite. We have a special place for you in our society!"

Even under the hex of cancer, the life literally draining out of him, Raikin could not accept his stripped position. His state-sponsored powers to degrade and vilify were gone.

He was a torturer only in his dreams.

CHAPTER EIGHTEEN

It was taking days for Gardner to arrange a residency permit for Raikin. Nina Zinovieva phoned every morning and evening, but Dean could only give her typically Soviet answers: There was a work slowdown at the office which printed the permits; there were no openings in Moscow's cancer wards.

Christmas came in a sodden week of damp snow and lowering skies. Dean celebrated Christmas Eve with Natalie and Gennady, continuing the gift-giving compromise they'd worked out a year ago: He got his present on Christmas; they received theirs on New Year's Day. This year they'd bought each other the same thing: gift certificates redeemable for eighteen holes of golf at the Moscow Country Club, due to open in May.

Dean hated the artificial void created by holidays. He found it impossible to relax in his apartment, impossible to dismiss the case from his mind. On Christmas morning he swung by Nina Zinovieva's apartment building to check on the security arrangements Gardner had made. A surveillance team was in place, ready to follow her if she made a sudden move. One guard smoked a *papirosi* as he studied the *Pravda* headlines;

another listed drunkenly in a doorway, prop vodka bottles strewn at his feet.

Dean had an urge to introduce himself to these men. To describe his progress in the case, to exchange tradecraft anecdotes, to share hunches and war stories.

But the shadow cop knew his place. Dean slowed the car but didn't stop. He drove to his empty office to wait out the holiday.

The next morning Gardner phoned to say the residency papers would be delayed another week.

"Goddamn it, Richard, we have to get Raikin out now!" Dean shouted. "He's the key to the whole case!" Dean could almost hear Gardner grappling with his instincts on the phone line. His New England military upbringing had instilled in him a fear of authority and an unholy respect for channels, but there was a spring of rebellion in him that was tightening, a growing conviction that toeing the line was unmanly. "Don't be an asshole, Richard. You want a promotion, then show some initiative for a change!" A needling from the former teacher seemed to work. Gardner promised they'd go after Raikin the next morning, with or without the proper papers.

In the meantime, Dean recruited Sergei Borodin, who was so excited about being sent into action again that he brought along his wife and mother for a celebration dinner at the Gorky Park McDonald's.

They waited patiently at the drive-through window, Dean and Borodin in the front seat of his cramped Zaphorozhets, wife, Tanya, and mother, Aleksandra, in the back. They ordered Big Macs, fries, and a half liter of vodka. They ate in the car, a social grace that had become the rage of Moscow. Between toasts Dean told Borodin he wanted a complete background check done on KGB agent Vladimir Raikin, as much information as he could assemble from memory and the tattered KGB data banks.

By sundown and their second liter of vodka Dean realized that the theory of fast food was going to be a cultural impossibility in Russia. Russians loved to linger over their meals. The dinner table was the family social center, the focus of cramped communal living, the only place where they could express uninhibited opinions. Russian meals traditionally stretched on for hours, and the Golden Arches couldn't change that. It was going to be tough to reach "40 billion served" in Moscow.

At eight the next morning Gardner picked up Dean in a cornflower blue Volvo.

"Emily's car," he explained. "The MOP motor pool's a joke. Frozen batteries, frozen radiators. No one knows what they're doing."

The scent of Emily gripped the air. Her perfume? He didn't think she wore any. Her skin? Her clothes? Her hair? Whatever it was, it filled Dean's blood with a pungent longing. Her stockings taunted him from the floor. The earrings she'd worn at his apartment glinted seductively on the front seat, then slipped behind the cushion as Gardner shifted his position.

Dean's desire for her began to suffocate him, and he rolled down the window. Think of murder, he told himself. Think of the Raikin case. Think of blood, and knives. It didn't help. In his mind Emily was woven into thoughts of homicide. Flashes of crime led to flashes of sex.

"What's the matter?" Gardner asked. "You feeling nauseated?"

"Lack of sleep, I guess. You look pretty ragged yourself."

Gardner's tie was sloppily knotted, his hair a maze, his eyes a web of squint lines. For a man so outwardly fastidious, they seemed signs of an internal breakdown.

"I'm fine."

"You and Emily OK?"

He shot Dean a sour look. "Why wouldn't we be?"

"You're under a lot of pressure. You know how it is."

"Did she tell you we weren't getting along? That day I conked out at your apartment?"

"Of course not, we just made small talk."

They rode in frosty silence for a minute.

"Emily's become rather secretive, that's all."

"You don't need to go into this."

"No, no, I don't mind. Perhaps talking a bit about it will

231

enlighten me." Dean had to hand it to Gardner. Despite his obvious pain, he still slipped words like "enlighten" into a conversation.

"She disappears after dinner. Just leaves the house without a word of explanation. Sometimes for hours. And this collection mania of hers is getting out of hand; it's automobile hood ornaments now. She buys them right off people's cars, for crying out loud.

"She can't sleep. It used to be one of life's inescapable pleasures for her. She'd even rate nights of sleep on a scale from one to ten. And when she can't sleep, I can't sleep."

"As a reformed insomniac I can assure you, it's only temporary."

"It's not just insomnia. I'll catch her going through my papers, crying over old scrapbooks. She makes long-distance calls in the middle of the night, then intercepts the phone bill before I see it. You can imagine how confused the kids are by all this. She'll virtually ignore them for a few days; then she'll assault them with attention. They'll go to museums and plays. She'll take them to snazzy restaurants they can't possibly appreciate. 'I just want to expose them to the rest of the world,' she says. Now what's that supposed to mean?"

"Classic symptoms of family fatigue," Dean said. He sensed Gardner wasn't after serious solutions. A blithe expression of sympathy would do. "I prescribe a vacation."

"That's impossible at the moment."

"Things will only get worse."

"I did not make things bad!" he declared. "But I'm the only one who can make them better. I'm the compass needle for this family, Dean—and I set the course!"

Gardner sledgehammered the gas pedal, and the car blazed through a red light. Blood surged to the surface of his knuckles. Gardner the hero, the breadwinner, the man determined to do it all. Dean recognized this family, and the boxing up of its secrets, the tightening of its obsessions, the longing for escape.

At the squatters' camp entrance, Gardner identified himself and explained their mission. The guards protested. Argued

232

among themselves. Phoned superiors. Finally they agreed to let Gardner "extract a camp resident without accompanying Transit Forms 1765 A and B," provided he accept sole responsibility for this bureaucratic deviation.

Dean led Gardner through the camp and could see the shock and abhorrence on his face. The camp was less frightening and gothic in daylight, but more desperate, as sunlight accented poverty the darkness hid.

Gardner didn't have the calluses to march coldly through the streets. By the time they reached the lakefront, he'd doled out handfuls of change to beggars and bought a basketful of useless sundries, including a gold pen its seller claimed Gorbachev had used to sign the first INF Treaty in Washington.

Distracted by his purchases, Gardner collided with Dean, who stood in the street, frigid with amazement.

Vladimir Raikin's shack was a smoldering ruin.

"Is this it?"

"This was it."

Black, smoking timbers jumbled in the mud were all that remained of the shanty; the bathtub, the car doors, the stove had been carted away by looters.

Dean picked his way through the debris, little more than a dying campfire. "This was the bathroom; this was the stove." Dean knelt and ran his fingers through the mud. "I interviewed Raikin on this exact goddamned spot!"

As Gardner scanned the shantytown, something caught Dean's eye, and he picked it up: a vial of pills, melted by the heat into a twisted stub.

"Maybe you got disoriented. Everything kind of runs together out here."

"No, this was it. I'm certain. Someone knew we were coming and torched it." His gaze fell on the homeless teenagers who clotted together at the nearby pile of smoking tires.

"Hey, listen," he shouted. "Am I crazy, or was there a shack here a week ago?" They gave him dead, uncaring looks. "It was made out of a sailboat, remember?"

Dean and Gardner approached the gang like hunters surrounding a wounded tiger.

"We're not gonna hurt you; we're not after anything. We just want to ask a couple questions."

The kids, skeletal and bent, wore cast-off Red Army uniforms, their feet slipping in boots several sizes too large. They backed away as Gardner approached.

"You help us out and I'll give you"—Gardner scavenged through his purchases for bait—"a gold pen. What about it? Razor blades? Shoelaces, postcards?"

They turned their sullen backs and trudged away. A teenage girl remained. She had a feline beauty that war and deprivation had smudged but not erased. Her hair hung in matted ringlets around a soft face. She had sly, smoky eyes and an acrobatic tongue that danced over blistered lips in a gesture she hoped was sensual.

"What about you?" Dean asked. "Just a couple questions? Name your price."

She hesitated. Then she spoke in a brutal Ukrainian slang that Dean had to translate for Gardner.

"Well," he said, "that's a new one."

"Come on, what is it? What does she want?"

"She wants to kiss you."

Gardner coughed. "Oh, for heaven's sake." He shifted his shoulders in embarrassment and looked into the teenager's ravenous eyes. Her delicate fingers suddenly curled, as though she'd sprouted claws.

"It's for the good of the cause," Dean prompted.

Gardner gave in and presented a chaste cheek to the girl. She sputtered in Ukrainian again.

"On the mouth, Richard. And she wants you to use your tongue."

"Honestly."

Before Gardner could retreat, the girl pounced. She curled around him, her tongue invading his startled lips. In a rough parody of a ballet move, she arched onto one toe and laced her other leg around Gardner's thigh, tightening it in a rasp of stocking.

Dean loved Gardner's reaction: his exploding eyes, then the gasp of astonishment as the girl plunged her hand down his pants. She let out a predatory growl and licked her way across Gardner's face, like a cat scouring an empty bowl of milk.

Finally Dean pried the girl away. Gardner reeled and swiped a hand across his face. The girl collapsed onto a mound of garbage. As she panted breathlessly, she pushed a cigarette butt into her mouth and chewed on it.

She said something to Dean, and he translated. "She says you taste like coffee."

Gardner took a moment to gather his thoughts. "Tell her she tasted like cream."

The girl smiled, acknowledging the compliment. Dean pulled up a tractor tire and sat next to her. "What's your name?"

"Barbara." To Dean's questioning look, she added, "We've all changed our names. She nodded to her friends, who watched from a distance. "I love the sound: Ba . . . ba . . . ra. . . ."

"OK, Barbara. Did you see who burned down the shack?"
She nodded.

"When?"

"Two nights ago."

"Who did it."

She frowned.

"You won't get in trouble by telling."

"Neighbors."

"People from the camp burned it down?" asked Gardner incredulously. "Why?"

"Maybe they were afraid they would die, too."

"Are you telling us Mr. Raikin is dead?" Gardner asked.

Barbara looked perplexed.

"The man who lived in the shack."

"An ambulance came for him in the night. Then the police came in radiation suits and measured the shack with some sort of instruments."

Dean drew a picture in the mud of a square box, with a handle and a clock face.

"Did their instruments look like this?"

Barbara's eyes glinted, and she nodded.

"War survey meters," Dean said to Gardner. "They measure ambient radiation. They're heavy-duty; some of them go up to five hundred rems an hour."

"She's telling us Raikin died of radiation sickness. You met him, Dean. Does that seem plausible?"

"It all fits. The hair loss, the cancer, the cataracts. And I found this buried in the mud." Dean showed Gardner the vial of pills, its scorched label barely legible. "He had a regular pharmacy, hundreds of bottles of the stuff."

"Potassium iodide?"

"A thyroid blocker. It interferes with the absorption of radioiodine by the thyroid gland. Iodine one-three-one, for example. It's a radioactive isotope that can enter the body through contaminated food or water. There's no evidence that I know of to show that potassium iodide does any good after exposure, but try convincing someone who's dying of that. I figure the neighbors learned what killed him and panicked."

"But radiation sickness isn't contagious," Gardner said.

"Not at this stage. Not without fallout present."

"So the neighbors either acted out of defiance of scientific fact—"

"Which is highly likely, considering scientific fact brought them World War Three."

"Or Raikin had something in his possession that was truly radioactive. Plutonium, for example. Maybe he stole it from a weapons plant or a nuclear reactor."

"But he's been in the camp for two years. Where the hell would he get it?"

"He might have had it with him all the time. Nina told you he appeared out of nowhere. His activities during the war were a total blank. He was a high-ranking KGB agent. He might have had access to military secrets, even radioactive materials."

"And he just sat on it for two years, maybe selling a little bit here and there—to who I can't imagine—until it gradually killed him? I don't believe it. Raikin was desperate that he'd lost control over his life, over other people. He was not the kind of man who'd knowingly be the cause of his own death."

"Then you fill in the blanks for me. You tell me how he managed to die of radiation sickness. Then you tell me what all this has to do with the two unsolved murders I've got on the books!"

Dean had no answers. He was as empty and as thwarted as Gardner. He returned his attention to Barbara.

"Thank you, Barbara. You've given us a lot of help. Come on, Richard, give her another kiss, and let's go."

Gardner managed to stifle his impatience. He leaned warily toward Barbara, expecting another attack. Instead, she gave him a slow, tender kiss. Gardner responded and brought a palm to the back of her pale neck. He broke the kiss and clumsily handed her a wad of occupation rubles.

"Use this to buy some warm clothes, OK? It's a long ways till summer."

Gardner backed away from her, hands tucked in his pockets like a shy teenager. As he and Dean moved off, her friends joined her, peppering her with questions. She continued to watch Gardnner, her eyes still ravenous. Then her mouth curved into a smile.

It took several hours of bureaucratic tinkering before they learned the circumstances of Vladimir Raikin's death.

A neighbor had found him one morning, facedown on the floor, blood from an internal wound pooling next to him, a pot of coffee boiling over on the stove. A camp coroner's wagon had transported the body to the temporary morgue in the Museum of Serf Art on the southern flank of Dzerzhinsky Park.

Initially no autopsy had been planned. After a brief waiting period in which relatives could claim the body, provided they could pay for burial, the corpse was to be cremated. But a sharp-eyed paramedic had found a discarded radiation dosimeter in the garbage outside the shack. An autopsy was hastily arranged. The official cause of death was listed as "chronic granulocytic leukemia." The body also displayed significant tumors of the thyroid and salivary glands. A suspicious coroner had taken a bone marrow sample and found traces of the radioactive isotope strontium 90.

In the final unhinged spasms of the war, the Soviet Union had absorbed several nuclear missile strikes against missile silos and oil refineries in Siberia. The government had been familiar with the effects of ionizing radiation since the Chernobyl disaster. It knew how to determine the effect of wind on fallout patterns, how to measure blast shelter protection factors, how to compute radiation absorption rates; many Russians knew the mathematics of radiation-induced genetic mutations, the percentage of the population that could expect to succumb to cancer twenty, thirty, even fifty years after the missiles had fallen. To that end, to prevent mutations from entering the general populace, the NUCDET zones were sealed off. Russians had always lived with draconian governmental decrees; it was better to err on the side of safety. The Russians transferred their paranoia of Western contamination to a determined effort to quarantine the future.

News of the autopsy findings spread through the camp. A mob formed. Ignoring the MOPs' claims that the area was perfectly safe, it set the torch to Raikin's shack.

For the second time in two weeks Nina Zinovieva attended a funeral. She and Dean stood on a hill outside Moscow, their faces bitten by wind, which gathered speed as it rushed up the slope. They were the only witnesses to Vladimir Raikin's final interment. Nina watched through binoculars for a moment, then passed them to Dean. He saw barbed wire, glittering in sunlight. Behind it, blurred figures moved among small trucks and earth-moving equipment. Rusted drums of toxic chemicals pyramided to the skies, their cheerful paint schemes belying their noxious contents. His remains refused by every cemetery in Moscow, Vladimir Raikin was being sealed in frozen ground amid the toxic exhaust of Moscow's chemical plants.

He'd asked Nina if she wanted a priest.

"Vladimir spent his whole life trying to bully the church into submission. I don't think he'd appreciate having a priest hovering over his body, whining forgiveness, and searching for his imaginary virtues."

"You could have made this easier on yourself," Dean said. She looked at him questioningly.

"Dead men make the best suspects. You could have put the blame on him. Claimed he'd sneaked out of the camp and murdered Bukharin. Maybe he was jealous; maybe he simply envied Bukharin's health; maybe the cancer caused his mind to snap."

"You don't accuse someone you love. I know, I know, you must be wondering how I could love a man who had no good side to him."

"The priest would have told you there's a little good in everyone."

"That's shit, and you know it. I loved Vladimir because he made me promises." She wrapped a muffler around her face until all Dean could see were her eyes, tearing in the wind. "He said when he got out of the camp, he'd take me to Spain. To Madrid. He'd been assigned to the embassy there years ago."

"You think a man with no good side intended to keep his promise?"

"It doesn't really matter, does it? Even if it was just another fucking lie, at least he took the time to make it a good one."

The distance made it impossible to determine the exact moment Vladimir Raikin was buried. With nothing to watch or wait for, Nina walked back to the car.

A MOP car was perched at the edge of a salted two-lane road. Richard Gardner stood next to it, feeding dead grass to a goat, which poked its hungry head through a wooden fence. Nina stoically held out her hands as Gardner clamped the handcuffs on her.

On the way back to the city Gardner was the first to break the silence. "We're going to indict her. I spoke to the district judge. He thinks we have enough to develop a case."

Dean was startled. "Come on, it's paper-thin, Richard."

"Now wait a minute. Just think it through, Dean. First of all, Mrs. Bukharina can't account for Nina's whereabouts that

239

night. Neither can anyone else. The hotel personnel knew her as Bukharin's wife, meaning she could have come and gone unimpeded. And we have Mintz's sketch, which puts her in the room."

"That's it?"

"We have a motive: She wished to extricate herself from a marriage of convenience. She's admitted she despised Bukharin."

"If I didn't know I was dealing with Mr. Democracy, I'd suspect a frame-up. This whole case is awfully brittle, even for the military occupation courts."

"Think what you like," Gardner snapped. "But that's the game plan."

"What about the attack on me and Natalie? The stolen painting, the Mintz murder? How the hell are you planning on attaching Nina to that?"

"Maybe I can't. The prosecutor has advised us to build our case one step at a time."

"That's insane" was all Dean could think of in reply.

Where did Gardner's newfound smugness come from? Dean appraised him: his set jaw, straight-ahead eyes, gloved hands gripping the steering wheel at ten o'clock and two o'clock, the same secure, regulation grip he held on life. Dean checked the speedometer: They were always within half a kilometer of the speed limit. He appeared to be the same steady-as-she-goes Richard Gardner, but his obsession with prosecuting Nina was uncharacteristically reckless.

"You ought to give yourself a pat on the back, Dean, instead of throwing your pessimism all over the case. It was your persistence and legwork that led me to Nina."

"Despite what you're undoubtedly going to tell the media."

"That's uncalled for. It's a public job, and the public likes to see their institutions perform effectively. If we don't brag about it, they have no way of knowing. Besides, you knew your role was to be uncredited. Don't go trying to change the rules now."

"I don't care about the goddamn rules. And it's not my role

I'm concerned about. It's yours. I wonder how you're going to play it when Nina is acquitted because the cops didn't take the time to prepare an effective case."

He glanced back at Nina, enclosed in her Spanish-language earphones, unaware of the hangman's noose Gardner was knotting in his mind for her.

CHAPTER NINETEEN

I t was three forty-five in the morning, December 28. When the phone rang, Dean snatched it up after the first ring, half expecting a belated long-distance Christmas wish from his ex-family.

"Hello?"

"Dean Joplin?"

"Yeah, who's this?"

"There was another sketch," said a husky American male voice.

"Wait a minute. What was that?" Dean sat up and groped on the nightstand for his cassette recorder. He flipped it on and held it next to the phone. "I'm sorry, you got me out of a dead sleep. What did you say about a fifth sketch?"

Dead batteries. Again, he found himself longing for the high tech equipment Congress had almost forced on the CIA back in the agency's salad days. One push of a button, and he could have a squad of computers tracing this call.

"I was one of Anatoly Mintz's guards at the safe house. He did another drawing, but it was destroyed."

Dean grabbed a pencil and paper.

"Who is this?"

"My career is ruined. It would serve no purpose to give you my name. I just thought someone should know, that's all."

"Hang on. Let me meet you somewhere. Total anonymity, I promise."

"I'm not in Moscow. I may not even be in Russia."

"OK, OK . . . Don't worry about it. I don't need your name. Just tell me one thing: Did you recognize the sketch?"

There was a long pause. A sigh, a cough.

"Yes."

"Who was it?"

No answer.

"OK, let me try this: Do you know who destroyed the sketch? Do you know why?"

The line went dead.

Dean held the receiver in his hand, unwilling to hang up.

Was this a bluff? A joke?

Some joke, at four in the morning.

Gardner had told him the guards were missing. Had one been seized by guilt for his role in the Mintz murder? But why call Dean, not Gardner?

Unless Gardner was involved.

The silence unnerved Dean. He looked around the bedroom. In the darkness every stick of furniture seemed to have acquired a grotesque shadow.

The window rattled. The snowfall which had begun just before midnight had intensified into a bitter flurry.

He was startled by a deafening series of clicks in the receiver, followed by a buzz of static. Dean recognized the signs. This wasn't just cheap Russian wiring.

He parted the curtains. Somewhere out there, between the slabbed high rises, in the middle of the dwindling lights of Moscow, someone was listening.

A car was parked across the street. So what? A neighbor's late-night guest. It had been there all night, hadn't it? But every other car on the block wore a thick mantle of snow; this sedan's roof was clean.

Dean hung up. He unscrewed the receiver and shook it like

a clogged salt shaker. It looked clean. He followed the phone cord to the wall, where it connected to a boxy 1950's vintage outlet. He ripped it apart. Nothing suspicious. The line led up the wall, a bulky thread which the contractor had not bothered to recess into the plaster. The line paralleled the ceiling, ran into the foyer, then dived down a corner and disappeared through the floor.

Now Dean remembered. Every phone line in the building led to a junction box in the basement, where it joined the main outside cable.

Dean snagged his gun from the nightstand and removed a box of bullets from the freezer. He'd gotten in the habit of keeping them separate many years ago, afraid his son, Patrick, would carry his fascination with weapons too far.

He slipped on a sweater, pants, and heavy wool socks. He unbolted the door and stepped onto the landing. The stairwell was freezing. Weak illumination from the streetlights fought through the scarred windows at every floor, the only relief in the shaft of darkness.

He descended the stairs two at a time, his silence calling attention to the noise the building made. How could it be so loud with everyone asleep? Plumbing rumbled. Water heaters shuddered. Wind hissed through hairline cracks in the walls.

He reached the lobby. Faces stared at him from the walls like a portrait gallery, campaign posters taped up by politically minded tenants. He checked the front door. It was secure. The mystery car was still there, slowly frosting with snow. The night was lifeless. Not a single light burned in the giant apartment complex across the street.

He turned reluctantly to the basement door. No light escaped from beneath it. He pressed his ear against it. Not a sound. As he reached for the doorknob, he stopped himself. If someone was down there, he'd probably jimmied the service door in the alley. He could go in that way, too, perhaps force the intruder into the lobby.

Outside, he ran to the car, the fresh snow soaking through his socks. He lifted the hood and disconnected the ignition coil wire.

He slipped it into his pocket, then edged into the alley next to his building. It loomed up gray and windowless. He heard the faint buzz of a radio, then Jimmy Swaggart's strutting Louisiana accent, followed by a Russian translation: a revival meeting, broadcast live from somewhere in Russia where it was already tomorrow afternoon.

He looked for telltale footprints but found none. The eaves sheltered the alley from snowfall. He descended the granite steps to the basement door and twisted the handle open.

The basement was a forest of shadows. The ancient oil-fired furnace grumbled, like some leftover from the Industrial Revolution. Laundry hung from a lattice of clotheslines, drying in the halo of the heater's warmth. Cross-country skis were stacked against each other, like muskets on a battlefield.

But no signs of an intruder. He inspected the junction box. A tangle of frayed phone lines, some wearing fresh splices. Had a monitoring device been attached to them? Or were they just the innocent handiwork of the Moscow Telephone Service?

He stood stock-still, waiting for the intruder to commit himself. Not even the shadows stirred.

Then Dean sensed a brush of cold air on his cheek; the prickle of snowflakes melting on his skin. Behind the furnace a tiny, street-level window was open a notch, allowing snow to flurry in. Dean rushed to the window. Old cartons had been stacked up like a staircase. Outside, footprints led across the snowy grass behind the building.

He left the basement and circled through the alley to the backyard, which had been converted to a playground. A swing set was silhouetted against the snow, bristling with icicles. A seesaw creaked in the breeze. Dean followed the footprints, which marched around the other side of the building, out to the street.

He permitted himself a gloating moment. The car was still there!

The street was silent . . . or did he hear fleeing footsteps, cocooned by the falling snow?

It didn't matter. A car was often a more plentiful source of information than a human being.

After several minutes dueling with a screwdriver, he managed to force open the wing vent on the driver's side. He opened the door, and made a brief inspection. Something small, black, and metallic was slipping beneath the front seat. Something the driver had forgotten . . . or tried to hide?

Dean didn't need to hold it up to the light. He didn't even need to see the whole object to recognize it immediately.

His chest twitched with fear, almost as if his heart were pumping needles through his veins. Then, strangely, he was enveloped by a warm billow of nostalgia.

These are sensations I'm intimate with, he mused. Welcome to old times: Alliances shift; friends become enemies; enemies become neutral; uncertainty becomes constant.

Tonight it had happened all at once.

He'd figured Richard Gardner for a pajama man, maybe sensible flannels with a clipper ship or some other masculine talisman embroidered on the pocket. Instead, he came to the door in a Spartak Moscow hockey jersey and long underwear. He swerved with drink; his face was gray from a lack of sleep.

"Dean, what are you doing here? Don't you know it's—" He darted a glance toward his wrist, but his watch was missing. "I don't know what the hell time it is. I think 'dawn' is the operative word."

"We have a problem, Richard."

He scoffed. "You sound like an astronaut." He cupped a hand over his mouth and slurred through a blur of static. "Houston, we have a problem."

"May I come in?"

"Barge on in. And don't bother being quiet. Everybody's already been rudely awakened."

Dean followed Gardner inside. Though dawn traced the sky, the curtains were still closed, and every light in the apartment was on. The living room showed the strains of a long night: paper work scattered over the floor; empty coffee cups; overturned glasses. Shattered Christmas tree ornaments had been ground into the carpet by angry feet; a display of Christmas cards had collapsed on the mantel. "What you see is a mental and emotional battlefield," Gardner said. He picked up an empty vodka bottle. "Looks like we forgot to bury the dead."

In the next room Dean heard hushed conversation, a masculine voice, authoritative and familiar.

Dean's first instinct had been to shatter Gardner's jaw with a nice right hook, but now he decided to listen, to let Gardner lead.

"Come in and join the wake." Gardner escorted Dean into the den.

Gardner's manly retreat looked as if it had been under siege. His Exercycle and weight machine were knocked over dead on the carpet. His historical map of Russia was shredded, clinging to the wall by a single thumbtack. Shattered picture frames glistened in the lemony light of a desk lamp. Dean spotted Gardner's CIA commission, an Annapolis diploma, a certificate of completion from the Military Occupation Police's Moscow operations section.

"My life in parchment and gothic print. Now just something else for the kids to cut their bare feet on."

"Don't be melodramatic, Richard." The commanding voice belonged to Taylor Willis, Gardner's attorney. He sat placidly on a leather couch, impeccable in a western riding outfit, dictating into a pocket tape recorder. "I've just been gathering some thoughts for our defense." He rose and poured Gardner a cup of coffee. "Here, the sun's up, for God's sake. Time to pump some sobriety into your veins." He turned to Dean. "Excuse the costume, Mr. Joplin. Richard paged me in the middle of my early-morning ride. I've an arrangement with the manager of the Hippodrome; he allows me a quick canter on one of their quarter horses before the morning workout."

"Not exactly the Painted Desert, is it?" Dean said.

"Homesickness does wonders for the imagination."

Gardner pushed aside the curtains and squinted into the harsh morning.

"They want to can me, Dean. How about them apples? Just as I'm making some headway in the Bukharin case."

"It's just temporary," Willis said. "I'm sure of it. There are several options we can employ to get you reinstated.

"It's really only a leave of absence," Willis explained to Dean. "A probationary period. Richard's been under a great deal of pressure, tremendously overworked if you ask me. I'm going to argue for job-induced stress, shift the blame to the MOPs so we can avoid blemishing Richard's exemplary record."

"Dean's not a word mincer, Taylor. He doesn't have much patience for legalese, do you, Dean? I've been given the ax. The sack. The old heave-ho."

"On what grounds?"

"First of all, the Nina Zinovieva arrest. The prosecutor's waffling; now he's starting to think the evidence is shaky. I know, I know, you warned me. You can give me a failing grade on that exercise. Secondly, there's this: The chief got hold of it around six this morning through a contact at the paper. He about hit the tip of the tallest onion dome on St. Basil's."

Gardner handed Dean a coffee-stained copy of *Pravda*'s morning edition. A banner headline read: MURDER SUSPECT DIES IN POLICE CUSTODY. The reporter attributed his scoop to an "informed source" close to the investigation.

"The 'informed source' called me this morning, too," Dean said.

Both Gardner and Willis seemed startled.

"Don't look so surprised, Richard. I'm sure you heard every word of our conversation."

"What are you talking about?"

Dean looked suspiciously at Willis.

"You can talk in front of Taylor. He knows about our relationship. He is my lawyer after all."

Dean was stunned.

"Who else knows?"

"No one, of course."

"Not your chief, not your fellow cops, not your secretary?"

"Not a soul. It would have been career suicide for me to admit I'd hired an outside detective—not that it makes any difference now."

Dean produced the black box from his overcoat and pressed it sharply into Gardner's palm.

"Then I presume you planted this yourself."

Willis, only mildly interested, glanced at the box. Gardner turned it around in his hand as though it were a precious gem and he were waiting for the perfect angle of light to illuminate its interior.

"Where'd you get this?"

"Bullshit, Richard, you know where it was, my basement junction box."

"Do you mind letting me in on your secret? What is that thing?" Willis asked.

"What's the matter, Mr. Willis? Don't they tap phones out west? This is a phone bug, a unique model designed specifically to be used by the Military Occupation Police on Soviet telephones."

Gardner sighed. Willis looked at him warily, perhaps expecting his client to burst out with a startling confession.

"Look, I don't know anything about this, I assure you."

"Come on, Richard. Who else would be behind it?"

"How would I know? And anyway, what would someone gain from monitoring your conversations?"

"I called you from the Raikin dacha to tell you I'd found the painting; that night I'm assaulted in my apartment. We've discussed Mintz on the phone, you or I may have let the address slip, we turn our backs for a second, and he's murdered. Someone inside the police department is following our progress on this case. The minute we uncover something important, they strike."

"They strike, they strike! Listen to yourself, Dean. They, not me! Why would I plant the bug? Why would I need to monitor my own case?"

"He makes a salient point, Mr. Joplin. If someone is indeed spying on you, I suggest you look to Richard's superiors in the department. The same men who are lobbying for his leave of absence, who accuse him of mishandling the investigation, might have stumbled across his relationship to you. They would certainly be served by a taped record of your conversations with Richard." Willis extended a manicured hand. "Why don't you let me have the device? I'll have it analyzed by independent experts. Let's just see if your suspicions are founded. You know, Richard, this might strengthen our case if we can establish unprovoked surveillance by your superiors."

Dean tightened his grip on the bug and backed away. Willis and Gardner were trying to outflank him, trying to muddy the waters.

"Honestly, Dean, your suspicions are understandable. But I didn't place that bug in your apartment. You want me to pull out the lie detector, I will."

"This is just a bullshit attempt to co-opt me."

"No one's co-opting anybody. I want us to continue working together. Look, the people back home are getting annoyed, they're tired of supporting the occupation troops, sick to death of reading about chaos and disorder in the republics. In two weeks there will be two hundred and forty-five members of the U.S. Congress in Moscow to observe our progress, and I intend to prove we're making some.

"I'm not going to let the MOPs shuffle me off like a bad poker hand to the Black Sea or some government resort in Scandinavia while the big boys are in town. We can crack this case together, and we can do it in front of the only audience that really counts."

Gardner closed in on Dean, his eyes pleading dots. Before Dean could answer, a thud, then a series of crashes echoed from somewhere in the apartment.

"That came from Jack's room!" Gardner exclaimed.

He wheeled out of the den, Willis and Dean following.

They found Jack on a rampage. Dressed in overcoat and hat, he swirled through his room, swinging a hockey stick at shelves of toys, toppling stacks of books. He turned to the model Soviet Air Force which dangled on fishlines from the ceiling. The hockey stick screamed through the air, shattering the models in flight. In red and silver shards, the Backfire bombers and MiG-29's dived to the floor.

Emily, her fur coat billowing heavily around her, chased Jack, trying to restrain him. Bryn crouched in the corner, eat-

250

ing a bowl of cereal, watching Jack's tirade with fascination, as though it were just another morning cartoon show.

Gardner waded in and wrested the hockey stick from his son. "What are you doing, son? What's gotten into you?"

Jack bent over, out of breath. Emily knelt, trying to calm him. He burrowed his red, violent face in her fur collar. Her coat began to shiver with his sobs.

"Emily?" asked Gardner, mystified.

"You've heard the phrase 'like father, like son'? You left the door open when you went on your little tirade in the den. Jack saw it all. I guess he just felt inspired." Emily gave her husband a withering look, then noticed Dean for the first time.

Her face was gorgeous in anger, each feature hot and accentuated. He felt an urge to lift her into his arms, to take the kids, one in each hand, and fade with them through the walls, like a quartet of ghosts.

"Why did you wreck everything, Dad?" Jack asked. He pulled away from his mother and tried gamely to pump himself up.

"I just got a little angry, son. I lost my temper, is all. Sometimes adults have trouble controlling their emotions, too."

"Don't call me son."

"Why not?"

"When you call me son, you sound official. You don't mean anything you say."

"Jack, please."

Jack turned his back and began to gather the wreckage of his planes.

Gardner zeroed in on Bryn, who wiped a fringe of milk from her lips. "Bryn, sweetheart, you're not cross with me, are you?"

She shook her head silently.

"Well, come on then, why don't you dance with your father? Let's do *Romeo and Juliet,* by Prokoviev." Capitalizing on the hint of delight he imagined in Bryn's eyes, Gardner led her through a series of clumsy ballet steps, singing in a thin falsetto. "It's amazing what kids can absorb . . . every note . . . every step. It's all stored in that little computer up there," he

251

said, tapping her forehead. "You see, Emily, Bryn's not angry with me. She's not frightened of me, are you?"

Emily pried Bryn away from Gardner. "Of course, she's not frightened of you. She probably doesn't even recognize you! Jack, Bryn, let's go."

Gardner froze, as he realized for the first time, that his family was dressed to go out.

"What is this? What do you mean, 'Let's go'?"

"Jack, come on." Emily furiously began to stuff plastic rudders, wings, and ailerons into her purse. "Your kids are taking a leave of absence from you, Rich. This household is starting to fall apart again, and I don't want them pinned underneath the rubble."

"Now just a goddamn minute!" Gardner raised a fist. Dean flinched, poised to intervene. The kids ducked behind the wall of Emily's fur coat. She faced her husband like a pillar, her rage manifested only by a gentle rippling on the surface of her skin. She was daring him to attack, but she seemed to know his threshold. He dropped his fist against his thigh with a dead flop.

"I'm not going to fight you, Amelia. I'm sure you counted on my surrender, didn't you?"

Gardner's use of Emily's Spanish name served as some sort of private signal between them, a plea of nolo contendere.

"I'll call this afternoon to explain the arrangements," she said.

Everyone stared at each other for an endless second.

Then, rather formally, Gardner's family left him.

He stood there in the vacuum, sniffing, staring at the red star on the vertical stabilizer of a plastic Soviet bomber. He dabbed at his eyes with a handkerchief and seemed surprised that they weren't moist with tears.

CHAPTER TWENTY

Dean took advantage of Gardner's motionless shock and let himself out. He didn't feel like pressing him on the issue of the phone bug, didn't make further mention of the phone call from the guard or the mysterious missing sketch. The case was twisting on him, and he needed time alone with it, time to decide if he should continue or should bail out while he still had a chance.

Dean and Natalie spent the morning tearing his office apart, hunting for bugs, and the afternoon reassembling it when they didn't find anything.

Every few minutes there was a frantic call from Gardner, begging Dean to stay on the case. Dean let the pleas pile up on the answering machine.

He and Natalie sat around the samovar as the sun set, sipping green tea, following their own thoughts. Natalie hummed as she mused, a melancholy dirge that matched the fading daylight.

"What's that tune, Natalie? It sounds familiar."

"I take that as a compliment. It's something I wrote myself."

"A composer, too? You're a wealth of hidden talent."

She plumped herself up and hummed a few more bars. "I've entered the new national anthem contest sponsored by *Pravda* and Capitol Records. They're going to unveil the winner on national television the night of the election. Can you imagine if the State Symphony Orchestra would play my song in the Hall of Columns?"

"Any lyrics?"

"Words are not permitted. The judges decided that the new national anthem should be free from the taint of politics. The safest lyrics are no lyrics at all."

"And the right opinion is no opinion," Dean taunted.

Natalie shrugged. "For the moment, yes. It may take years to know which opinions the Americans wish to hear."

Dean refilled their teacups and turned on the desk lamp.

"Maybe we're considering this from the wrong perspective," Natalie said. "This *tolkach* Gerasimov, the painter Anatoly Mintz, the prostitute Nina Zinovieva, even the victim Bukharin—they all have their private explanations for their presence in the Kosmos Hotel."

"In my experience, that's how these things usually work. Human behavior's confusing, varied. Everyone out for something else."

"Put aside your American experience for a minute. Try the Communist approach: everyone moving in lockstep, pulling together toward a common goal."

"You're suggesting that everyone gathered at the hotel that night for the same reason?"

"Perhaps. The painter Mintz claimed he saw various people call on Bukharin. We've always assumed they had their own reasons for tracking Bukharin to the hotel. What if the reverse were true? What if he summoned them? What if they all were there to conduct a single enterprise? One business transaction in which they all were involved?"

Dean looked at Natalie, her scratchy features laced with satisfaction. She had put a fresh slant on the case, he had to admit it.

"Unfortunately that means everyone I've interviewed so far has been lying. Mintz said he was after his painting; Gerasimov told this involved story about his efforts to scare up some black-market aviation fuel; Nina was just visiting her husband. They're all covering up the reasons they were really there."

"At least you still have your varied human behavior, Dean. Everyone's telling his own lie."

"And if that anonymous phone caller was right, there's another suspect we haven't even found yet. I can hardly wait to hear his lie."

Dean tried to digest this new theory, tried to crowd all the suspects under one umbrella.

The conclusion he reached was unsettling. "If everyone's lying, it's not because they're all guilty of murder. They're lying to protect the nature of this 'enterprise,' as you call it. This business, whatever the hell it is, is unfinished!"

He drove Natalie home. He didn't want her to take the metro after dark. He waited until she was inside the raucous safety of the White Palm before heading off. As he drove, he tried to get rid of the fear that was knotting inside him. He looked into the eyes of commuters stalled at traffic lights. The faces of Moscow had always been a comfort; now they looked harsh and suspicious.

She came at him from the darkness next to his door, her face crisscrossed by the shadows of the elevator cage. His nerves were at such a taut pitch he threw her roughly against the wall and pierced her eyes with a penlight.

"No wonder your marriage broke up," she said, "if this is the way you treat your women."

Dean backed off when he recognized her. "My wife didn't usually wait in ambush for me. What are you doing up here?"

"Waiting for you."

"Well, next time think of my heart and turn on the light." Dean reached for the switch, but she pressed her hand over his.

"I don't mind the dark."

Dean didn't speak for a moment, waiting for his pulse to slow its tempo.

"Come on in, it's freezing out here."

"Do you mind if we drive somewhere?"

"OK. Anyplace in mind?"

"Maybe head west toward Arkhangelskoye. The countryside's pretty out there."

Dean shrugged in agreement and switched off the penlight. Emily's face swam in darkness; its soft edges merged with the gloom. Her scent gilted the air; her breath lifted the hairs on his neck.

They didn't say a word until they'd passed the Moscow perimeter. At the checkpoint Emily was anxious, as though she were a disguised prison escapee, fearful of capture. Only after they left the lights of the city did she relax.

Dean drove west toward Arkhangelskoye, site of the former palace of Prince Yusupov, picking back roads.

"I'm sorry I startled you back there," Emily said.

"I overreacted. Once a paranoid spy, always a paranoid spy, I guess."

"I phoned, but there was no answer, so I just came over."

"Which proves you do lurk in doorways after all. Why didn't you want to come in?"

"You'll think I'm vindictive."

"I'll think you're vindictive, and I won't care."

"I didn't want to be anywhere Richard had been. I didn't want to sense him anywhere around me."

Dean didn't break the spell cast by the darkness and the singing tires to tell her that Richard had ridden in his car.

"How're the kids doing?"

"They're safely ensconced with a Russian friend on the fifteenth floor on an anonymous building in an anonymous neighborhood. Richard would need a divining rod to find them."

"Sometimes a separation is for the best, I guess."

"You don't need to console me, Dean. Or reassure me that I made the right decision. In the course of time I'll discover that for myself. Tonight I just want to live outside the pressure cooker for a few hours."

Dean concentrated on the curling road. A mist was falling,

swirling in the headlights like a dust storm. They were alone, canyons of pine and spruce walling them in. The car radio murmured in the background, liked hushed dinner conversation.

"There's a bottle of brandy in the glove compartment. That always helps reassure me."

As she reached for the bottle, the light of the glove compartment turned her vibrant bronze skin a queasy yellow. A red and black scar was scored across her neck, only partially disguised by a fresh bandage. A new drop of blood glistened against her collar.

"Christ, Emily, this is fresh. Where'd you get this?"

She sipped violently on the brandy. "And they say Latins have the temper."

"Richard? That son of a bitch. How did it happen?"

"The picture frames you saw shattered on the floor? One of them died on my neck."

"The asshole attacked you? What about Bryn and Jack?"

"He didn't touch them, thank God. And I don't think he meant to hit me. . . . Yes, he did. Oh, shit, I don't know."

Emily looked out the window at the blurring landscape. "Those stoic New Englanders. They're so good at holding it in, but when it finally explodes, you'd better get the hell out of the way."

"But what is it? What's he got inside him that could make him turn on you like that?"

She didn't answer. Headlights from an approaching truck lanced her eyes, but she didn't squint.

Her eyes are fantastic, Dean thought. Intense, curious. It would be difficult to keep a secret from those eyes.

The road dipped out of the forest, and snow-dusted fields billowed on both sides of the road. Along the knife-edged horizon, small collective farms were strung out in a row of beckoning lights.

Emily's hand found Dean's, and her fingers twined around his in a gesture that glowed with intimacy. "I don't want to talk about Richard for a while. It's too draining. Like—"

"Like war. You told me "

Dean downshifted, her hand still burning on his. He caught her at the edge of his vision, a beautiful contrast with the dead snowfields. It had been a long time since Dean had given himself over to instinct, but now, in a shouting rush, his inhibitions jumped ship.

He swerved into a turnout at the edge of a village. Before the skidding snow could settle, he'd reeled Emily into a tight, panting kiss.

At first it was more leisurely fun than anything else. Can you kiss and grin at the same time? he wondered. But seconds later they were both steaming and short of breath. Her mouth still brushing Dean's, Emily tore off her gloves finger by finger and hurled them into the back seat, like a stripper desperate to unveil herself. The hiss of her fingernails on his thigh was crisp and erotic; blood seemed to boil to the surface wherever she touched him.

Dean's emotions were in a storm, his guilt level rising with each kiss, then falling when Emily turned away. What the hell were they doing? What would Gardner do if he found out? Scarlet *A*'s sprang to life on their clothes as he imagined Gardner's New England puritanism scolding them in public. Gardner would not call this an "affair," a somehow forgiving word. He would call it "adultery," a biblical, archaic-sounding word that was unequivocal in its condemnation.

But moral shadings escaped him in the haze of his desire. Emily's Cuban roots and tropical veneer were powerfully appealing; her face, her hair, and her skin were a travelog for the senses. But it was her internal secrecy, her unknowable blood that magnetized him. Her life centered on closed doors and furtive disappearances, and Dean had always found it easy to love enigmas.

Emily pressed her palm against the chilled window, misted with their breath, and left her handprint on the glass. Then she slipped her hand between his shirt buttons onto his chest.

"I'm afraid we're turning your car into a sauna, Mr. Joplin."

"It always gets hot when the two of us are in a room together. What's the matter? Haven't you ever made love in a car before?"

"I made a brave attempt once. In the backseat of my father's government limo with a boyfriend he didn't much approve of, an aide to a congressman who was a little too pro-Castro."

Dean leered. "How could anyone be soft on Cuba?"

Emily groaned at his joke.

"If you continue through this village, then go left about thirteen kilometers, you'll come to a fantastic little inn that has cramped rooms, so-so cooking, a pitiful wine cellar, and a grouchy owner."

"Sounds perfect," Dean said.

"As much as my mind is enjoying this flashback to my youth, my body's beginning to show its age."

"I'll be the judge of that," Dean said.

Their lips met for another kiss. It was the most intense yet. Dean felt his head swirl with vertigo.

Dean unbuttoned her coat and began to trace the surface of her silk blouse, discovering her sculpture. Her kisses turned delicate and withdrawn, as though she were unsure whether to yield or attack.

"Dean, before we go any further, there's something we have to discuss."

"Don't tell me you're pregnant already?"

She gave him an obligatory smile. "I want to hire you."

He began to unbutton her blouse. "I'll be happy to disarm you for nothing."

"I mean, hire you as an investigator."

Dean's hands froze on her second button. He felt his breathing stop.

"Of course, I figured it out, Dean. Fifteen years of marriage to a spy have given me a nose for the truth . . . or lack of it."

His first reaction was embarrassment. His cover identity, the "coincidental" meeting outside the Moscow Disneyland, the conspiracy of gestures and secure phone lines—they must have been amusingly transparent to her.

"But why didn't you say anything?"

"I didn't want to destroy the myth Richard created for himself: the lone cop, cleaning up Moscow, restoring law and order. I thought if Richard could just get this one case behind him, it might save us."

"But?"

"Ever since the assignment landed on his desk, our lives have been hell."

"Because of this thing . . . this crisis that's been growing inside him?"

"I've got to know what it is. It's like a parasite or something, changing him cell by cell. It's filled our lives with secrets."

She pulled herself closer to Dean, her body trembling.

"The war is over, goddamn it," she said. "The CIA's a relic. There aren't supposed to be any more fucking secrets."

Dean was convinced that the key to the Bukharin case lay with Emily and Richard Gardner, not with the confusing march of suspects and contradictory clues. They were the starting point, the hub from which all the other lines of the case spoked. Perhaps the vanishing point as well, the dot over the horizon that everyone—Dean, Gardner, Nina, Viktor Gerasimov—was converging on. He recalled Natalie's words: "a single enterprise. One business transaction in which they all were involved."

The Centralnaya Inn was a battered two-story building perched on a bleak rise. Its interior had been redone in storybook Russian: stiff-backed, carved chairs, oiled wood tables set with Ukrainian embroidery, and a silver skyline of samovars. A buffet table bulged with solid Russian fare: sorrel and kidney soup, cucumbers in sour cream, duck in a thick brown gravy, cheese cakes, and plum jam. The excuse for this flagrant *pokazukha* was the American officer corps billeted at one of the phased-array antimissile radar sites four kilometers away. While the troops stayed on site, dismantling the radar system, the officers pulled rank and stuffed themselves at the Centralnaya, drank until they were deaf, then assaulted the inn's waitresses with obscene Russian lyrics they improvised to Motown classics.

The bedroom was tiny and neglected. Apparently the inn had run out of forced charm downstairs. The window was opened two inches. "For your healthy sleep," the innkeeper boasted, but in reality, it was broken. A sliver of wind rippled across their clothes as they fell onto the bed.

"Shouldn't we discuss business first?" Dean asked.

"This is business," she said. "The business of escape."

They faced each other, upright on their knees, undressing themselves to the waist. Their bodies were distant in the reflected gray of the snow outside. Emily's skin turned blue and arctic. Goose bumps pebbled her stomach and breasts.

"I want to see you in the light," she gasped.

She pulled a chain which drooped from the ceiling. In the harsh light, Dean felt that his body was all edges and bones, an overexposed Polaroid. But Emily was a sepia vision, black hair meandering to her shoulders like wet vines.

They rushed out of their pants, belt buckles and shoes slamming into the window. Dean turned off the light again, and they prowled for each other in the blue shadows. Emily kissed his chest, her saliva seeming to freeze on his skin as the wind picked up.

They snaked under the covers. As they made love, Dean felt his body had two sides: the one that fitted Emily's in a burst of skin on skin; the other that absorbed the weight of the cold room, forcing him closer and deeper into her.

Dean found himself drifting into love, wishing he could draw every pore of her skin into his mouth. He longed for a remote-control switch on the light, so he could make love to both flickering images at once: the golden, vibrant Cuban Amelia and the glacial, quiet Emily, who throughout the night remained strangely cold to his touch.

He awoke once as Emily's thigh caressed his cheek. She was kneeling, her elbows resting on the headboard like a tired drinker at a bar, gazing out the window above the bed. For several moments he watched her secretly as her expression veered from blank to tragic.

"You look like your life's passing before your eyes," he said. "I don't know whether to be flattered or insulted."

"I was just thinking how relieved I feel . . . how wonderfully irresponsible."

"I'm not even on the case yet."

"Says who?" She grinned. But it was a smile that struggled, like weak sunlight trying to burn off a cloud cover.

"If that's relief, I'd hate to see despair. C'mon, bring that beautiful body back down here before it turns into a block of ice."

"That doesn't sound so bad. You could lick me until I melted."

Dean was instantly excited by the idea, but he saw that to Emily for the moment they were just words. He propped himself up on an elbow and drifted his hand up and down her back, warming the cold knobs of her spine. Her eyes lingered outdoors, on the white, furrowed field that curved up to the sky like a bent piece of paper, the steely thread of a frozen creek, the windowless facade of what appeared to be a military installation, intruding gracelessly on the smooth horizon.

"We can talk about him now. I won't be insulted," Dean said.

"You can talk about her, too."

"Her?"

"Molly . . . Don't look so mystified, I haven't been prying into your past. I met her once, at a reception to celebrate Richard's graduation from Camp Peary. A willowy, unspoiled girl. She seemed very much in love with you."

"You caught us at a good time."

"The calm before the storm?" Emily asked.

"Molly was happy that summer. I was teaching nine to five; our lives were comfortable. We did a lot of local things. I wrote editorials for the local paper; Molly sat on the board of the local playhouse; we had box seats at the community symphony; Patrick played short on a Little League team sponsored by some corner hardware store."

Emily slid down from the headboard, trailing her breasts across his shoulders. "Sounds idyllic, but it doesn't sound like you."

"It wasn't. At the end of the summer we moved back to

Washington, and ambition sank its hooks in me. I threw everything into my climb up the espionage ladder.

"She followed in my wake for years, but by the time I finally landed the Moscow assignment, she'd had enough. 'Other men come home at night,' she'd say. 'Other men don't have code names for the dog and cat, for the doughnut shop in the mall. They don't tear out new wallpaper looking for bugs; they don't make their wives call them from phone booths.'

"Both Molly and I knew she wouldn't be coming to Moscow, but we couldn't confront the fact. We rented out the house, kidding ourselves we'd return to it as a family. We even sent our stuff ahead to Moscow. Molly took Russian at a local junior college. She and Patrick drove me to Dulles—just another family seeing its State Department breadwinner off on another routine mission. I booked seats for them on a Pan Am flight to Moscow a month later. We kissed good-bye at the gate, held each other as a family for the last time. It looked like a losing team's locker room, the players slapping each other on the back, spouting clichés about next season.

"I got to Moscow. Picked up the trunks, rented us an apartment, and went to work. A month later the divorce decree arrived at the embassy . . . in diplomatic code!"

Emily let an appropriate silence reign. Then she shrugged the soft points of her shoulders. "All men are ambitious. That doesn't make you the villain."

"But some men are fanatics. Like me. Like Richard."

Emily's face was veiled in the shadow of the headboard. She drew her knees up to her stomach. Dean tugged the blankets up to their necks and fitted their bodies together.

"If you want me to find out what's driving Richard, I need some hints. So far it sounds like a job for a psychologist, not a detective."

"I don't know what to tell you. He's always been ambitious, always had this need to prove himself."

"Maybe he's finally ready to step out of his father's shadow," Dean suggested.

Emily scoffed. "Psych one-A."

"Not everyone's complex, Emily."

"Anyone who'd marry me would have to be. Look, he's assisted on homicide cases before. They've never threatened us; they've never become obsessions. What makes this one different? That's what I want you to find out."

"That's what your visit to the Lubyanka was all about, wasn't it? The late-night phone calls, the disappearances. You've been investigating your own husband."

CHAPTER TWENTY-ONE

E mily wanted a life without secrets, yet the next morning dawned with her disappearance. The warmth of her body had departed, leaving behind a chill which awakened Dean.

There was no message from her at the front desk. The concierge was no help; courtesy was not in his job description. He even added a nasty remark about the "lady's sudden departure," which implied all sorts of things about Dean's performance in bed, a taunt he wisely left unchallenged.

She didn't take the car; there's no public transportation out here. She'll be back, Dean thought. She hired me; she went to bed with me. She's got to return for one thing or the other.

Clouds had assembled during the night and pressed down on the landscape, a gray, suffocating overcoat. There was no wind, no hint of sunshine. It was a weather system that would linger for weeks, pushing lower day by day, as if the ground were clawing at the clouds. Suicide weather, Dean thought. The annual foggy pall of Europe. It was weather that everyone complained about but that Dean always found invigorating.

Dean paid for the room. He wandered outside and scraped the frost off the Zhiguli's windshields. He started the car and watched it warm up, pumping thick white clouds into the cold air. Where was she? Had she been overcome by guilt and called for a taxi back to Moscow?

He saw her in the distance. She was walking away from him along the edge of the road that led to the horizon. She was the only thing that moved in the wintry landscape; she reminded him of a single letter, an *l* or a capital *I,* typed on a blank sheet of paper.

Dean got into the car and skidded through the rutted driveway into the road. He tried to keep an eye on Emily, as the road dipped behind hills or curved through thick stands of trees. Dean calculated the distance between them and figured she must have left the inn at least an hour ago. He couldn't imagine her destination; the surroundings were hibernating farmland, broken by the occasional outbuilding or workshed. Maybe she was just taking a walk, he thought, mulling over the night before and the complications it would bring.

Dean passed American officers, their jeep tilted at the side of the road as they struggled to repair a flat tire. The road dived into a patch of forest. The overcast pushed down to meet the treetops, imprisoning the car in a natural tunnel.

The road burst out of the woods, and the effect was like film running out of a projector, blinding a dark-adapted audience with the white-hot screen. It curved up a slight incline, steep enough to conceal Emily, whom Dean figured he'd catch on the other side. Near the crest of the horizon he passed the complex of buildings he'd seen out the bedroom window. They were two-story 1950's-era blocks, surrounded by neatly squared fields and trim hedges. A wrought-iron gate barred a meandering driveway, lending the place the subdued distinction of a country estate. But its tranquil impression was marred by the presence of two American MOPs, who stood in the driveway, rifles slung over their shoulders, sharing a cigarette. A faded sign dangled by a single screw from the gate. The Cyrillic lettering read: INSTITUTE OF PSYCHIATRY OF THE SOVIET ACADEMY OF SCIENCES, CLINIC 12.

A former mental hospital. It had once been a prison for dissidents, whose euphemistic, even surrealistic "crimes" had included, "sluggish schizophrenia," "mania for truth seeking," "insufficient self-criticism," and Dean's favorite, in the society that had produced Dostoyevsky and Tolstoy, "fruitless philosophizing."

The hospital blurred past as the Zhiguli coughed up the last hundred yards of the hill. The engine exhaled in relief as the road began to descend through a lazy series of switchbacks.

But there was no sign of Emily. No roadside café where she could have gone to warm up over a cup of tea. No buses ran along this road; there were no cars or trucks that could have picked her up.

A hollowness buckled Dean's stomach, like a hunger pang, as he realized Emily must have gone into the mental hospital.

The guards didn't give him any trouble. They were just kids in their early twenties, and the loneliness of their outpost combined with the drab procession of winter days made them desperate for conversation.

Though the hospital hummed at full bore, it seemed colder inside than out. There were the white coats of the doctors and nurses, the ice blue smocks of the patients strolling down cavernous ivory-colored corridors, the blanched skin of people who worked indoors, everything sere and ghostly, painted with fluorescent light.

A receptionist with a Brooklyn accent answered his questions without suspicion; she, too, seemed starved for company. Yes, the clinic had once been part of the psychiatric gulag, in which dissidents underwent treatment, but now it was under the authority of the Military Occupation Police. It was still a mental health facility, providing inpatient care for the American staff of the MOPs and their dependents. "As you can see, we're still redecorating."

An orderly walked past, arms piled high with official portraits of Lenin, which had been plucked from the walls. Would they be replaced with pictures of Freud?

Painters were at work in the corridors. The light walls were giving way to a rainbow paint scheme, which arched across the ceiling (presumably leading to the pot of gold of sanity), in a spectrum of phony good cheer, the upbeat "human" touch that the American government insisted on giving its public buildings.

Yes, a woman with dark hair had been there, and she'd been directed to the records section on the second floor. "The wife of one of our former patients, I believe."

The records section was not the cobwebbed cubbyhole staffed by Gogolesque clerks that Dean had expected. Instead, it was a well-lit room, humming with energy and the rhythmic tap of fingernails on computer keyboards.

Dean saw Emily at an empty desk in the corner, buried in a stack of folders and printouts. She looked up at him with distracted, then panicked eyes.

"What are you doing here?" Dean asked. Then, realizing his tone was spiteful, he bent down to give her a kiss. "If it was important, why didn't you wake me? I would've driven you."

"I didn't think it would take this long." She riffled through the papers, her expression confused as though she were reading a foreign language.

"Already keeping secrets from the boss?"

"I'm sorry. I wanted to spend some time alone here first."

"Last night you weren't just giving me random directions, were you? You steered us right to the Centralnaya. When you couldn't sleep, you were staring out the window at the clinic."

"I'm like a kid, I guess. I know the flame on the stove's going to burn, but I have to touch it anyway."

Exasperated, she dropped the files on the desk with a thwack, which caused several irritated faces to spin in their direction. "But I haven't learned a thing."

"Why don't you tell me what you're after? You hired me, remember?"

"I mentioned Richard had a nervous breakdown shortly after we moved to Moscow? Well, it was a little more serious than that."

"He was here?"

Emily nodded. As she shifted in her chair, she exposed the files in her lap; the name Richard Gardner appeared on each of them, in Russian and English. A young man in short-sleeve white shirt and overpressed slacks dipped into their conversation.

"Mrs. Gardner, your friend's gonna have to leave. Our patient files are confidential."

"Mr. Travers is one of my husband's private psychiatrists. I'll take full responsibility for him."

The young man wavered. He scouted the room for an unseen superior. "This is a military hospital, you understand."

"And we are at war after all," Emily scolded.

"You're just doing your job, young man," Dean said. "We understand. I'll just have a quick glance at the paper work. His insurance company requires I sign off on the diagnosis. Ten minutes?"

"Five? Please? You'll keep me out of trouble."

Dean agreed, and the man heeled off. Dean watched him cross the office, where he argued animatedly with someone obscured behind a partition.

"Asshole," Emily snorted. Dean grunted in agreement. But he felt a shiver on the back of his neck; there was something in the young man's concerned gaze that belied the image of an insecure bureaucrat. Dean glanced around the office, at the workers pecking away at their data processing, seemingly uninterested in them.

Why had this comfortable, cheery office taken on the unsettling decor of a trap?

". . . was diagnosed as 'andogynous depression.' Free-floating. In other words, anything could have caused it." Dean attempted to focus on what Emily was saying. "He became paralyzed. He couldn't work. He had anxiety attacks that would have him swinging from our prerevolutionary chandeliers. Next day he'd drop into a trough of depression that would confine him to bed. He'd lie there for hours, listening to those damned JKF tapes. The MOPs paid to have him committed here for intensive therapy. I'd visit him on the weekends and stay at the Centralnaya."

Dean glanced at Gardner's folder. It inventoried a pharmacy of drugs that had once been prescribed for him.

"He took Xanax and Ativan for anxiety, Vivactil and Elavil

for depression," Emily said. "Then the drug industry got smart; it came up with Limbitrol, which worked on both. For a while it seemed to help. His spirits improved; he was able to sleep. When I returned from Cuba with the kids, he was released."

She stopped abruptly, as though a black memory had carved its way into her mind. "That's when the real insanity began. The violence. The total lack of self-control one day, the obsessive confidence the next. Something happened here to change him, Dean. Something that wasn't a cure but was just the opposite."

Dean read the file with more care. The medical language and arcane jargon of psychiatry offered no clues.

"Could it be something as simple as an adverse reaction to all this medication? A misdiagnosis maybe, an improper dosage—"

"I checked with several doctors. They didn't blame the drugs. Maybe they wouldn't, who knows? So I got desperate. I replaced them all with placebos, Contac, Excedrin; there was no difference."

Dean read the same lines over and over, waiting for something to strike him as revealing. The young bureaucrat threw them a severe glance and tapped his watch.

Dean walked to the window, hoping a dose of natural light would reorder his thoughts. He looked down on the parking lot, a clutter of proletarian vehicles, so different from the BMWs and Mercedeses that filled the personalized parking spaces of American hospitals.

Then his hand tightened into a fist. Parked at the edge of the lot, its rear tires grooved into the snow, was the gray Volga, its radio antenna still bent from when Dean's attacker had grasped it for support. The man who'd stolen Anatoly Mintz's masterpiece here. Here, where Richard Gardner had retreated to restore his psyche. What was the connection between them?

Dean forced himself to concentrate on the files, sitting at an angle so he could keep one eye on the parking lot.

Over his shoulder Dean saw him for the first time, arguing with the bureaucrat. Dirty blond hair and lined skin the texture of suede. Definitely one of the men who'd waylaid him and Natalie, the one who'd escaped with his throat intact. Dean prodded Emily to her feet and led her toward the exit.

"What the hell is the hurry?" she complained as Dean force-marched her down the stairs, his adrenaline circulating like hot gas injected into a cylinder. He chattered out a brief explanation of the attack and the mysterious Volga.

Once in the lobby, Dean considered ambushing the blond man. Forcing him to talk. But what would he do with him afterward? Shoot him? Turn him in to the police? What if he worked for the police? And how could Dean be sure anything he said would be the truth? The most sensible tack would be to follow him. He'd seemed agitated, maybe even panicked. He was not the type of man to act decisively on his own. Dean had sensed that in his slow-moving eyes the night he'd been sprayed with his friend's blood. Blondie would report to his employer. He'd want orders, like all good Russian soldiers.

They double-timed across the parking lot to the Zhiguli. Dean chugged through the acre of frosted cars, then slowed at the gray Volga and read the sign on the reserved parking space: YULI GRINKOV.

At least now Blondie had a name.

"I don't understand what this has to do with Richard's stay in the hospital," Emily said. They were parked in a grove of trees just to the side of the road, about a kilometer from the clinic. From their vantage point they would be able to see Grinkov leave, and they were close enough to catch him if he took off in the other direction.

"You said something happened to him back there," Dean said.

"I'm certain of it."

"Maybe it was someone, not something. I think that during his stay here, for some reason, Richard became involved with Grinkov."

"Involved?"

"Connected. Allied. Either voluntarily or against his will. When did you say he was released?"

271

"Last spring. March. Look, I visited him frequently. So did the police chief and a couple of Russian lieutenants Richard had befriended. He would have mentioned Grinkov to one of us."

"But you were out of the country for much of his stay. He might have forgotten to tell you . . . or felt he couldn't."

Emily was silenced by Dean's logic. More secrets.

"March," Dean mused. "About seven months before the murder of Andrei Bukharin. Somehow this hospital and that crime are linked. You said Richard seemed relatively well adjusted after his release?"

"Until he became immersed in the Bukharin case. Then the desperation began all over again. More ferocious, more unpredictable than ever."

"So, we have a man committed to a hospital for depression. A man so paralyzed by stress he finds it impossible to work. He undergoes therapy for what? Three months? He comes out, is able to function again until snap, a homicide case sets him off again."

Dean stared at the black lace of switchbacks which led to the clinic gate. The clouds were solid and steely, poised to give a hammerblow to the limp, unprotesting landscape.

"What does all this give us?" Dean asked. He answered his question in the same breath: "Nothing. Nothing that makes the slightest bit of sense."

A few minutes later Grinkov's Volga veered out the hospital gates and sped toward them. Dean glimpsed Grinkov as he passed, bowed over the wheel with the intensity of a student driver.

Dean followed but kept a safe distance, afraid the empty road would make him conspicuous. But as the road switchbacked toward the valley floor, the countryside opened, and it was easy to keep Grinkov in sight, no matter how far ahead he was.

When they drew closer to Moscow, traffic began to appear, joining them from a network of side roads. As Dean had anticipated, Grinkov stopped at a filling station, a state-run business whose owner had hand-painted the proud message on each of

272

his pumps: COMING SOON. CHEVRON PRODUCTS! Grinkov hurried to a phone booth and made a brief call, which seemed to be harsh and argumentative. Less than two minutes later they were on the road again. But Grinkov held to a more leisurely pace, occasionally glancing at his watch. Dean assumed he'd made an appointment which he had plenty of time to keep.

On the outskirts of Moscow Grinkov turned off the main road and led them through a rutted web of alleys and access roads, which trembled with trucks and tankers. The snow here was brown with soot from the refineries and factories which clustered in this industrial suburb. Here and there, among the smokestacks, warehouses, and sagging tin roofs of Stalin-era assembly lines, were apartment blocks, smoke-stained towers whose thin walls and miserly windows didn't seem to offer much refuge to a worker trudging home from the factory in his front yard.

Grinkov parked in front of one of these buildings but didn't go in. Instead, he climbed out, lit a cigarette, and strolled down the access road, dodging trucks and workers milling toward their lunch breaks. The streets were so congested now the only way to tail him was on foot.

"Look, Emily, I'm going after him. No confrontations, I just want to see who he meets. Stay put, lock the doors."

Before she could protest, he'd vaulted out of the car. He ran to the street and slogged through the muddy shoulder after Grinkov.

They moved through a thicket of overcoats and exhaust, past factory workers pushing into rude cafés that specialized in cheap, fast lunches and cheaper ungraded vodka. Grinkov chain-smoked, a man who'd mastered the art of lighting a cigarette on the run.

Dean followed him along the road for at least a kilometer before he abruptly cut into an empty lot. There was no path. Instead, Grinkov walked where the snowfall was the lightest, picking his way through stacks of nameless industrial equipment. At the far edge of the field Dean spotted something so curious it looked like a mirage. The vacant lot ended at a chain-link fence. Behind the fence was a mammoth office building. Perched on top of the building, spinning like a lighthouse beacon against the frowning sky, was the gleaming five-pointed star of the Chrysler Corporation.

Dean followed Grinkov through an open gate onto the Chrysler grounds. Immediately he became aware of the presence of hundreds of people. He couldn't see or hear them, but he felt them, a hum of breath. He felt like a performer about to take the stage, a massive audience held in arrest just beyond the curtain.

Dean walked along the side of the building, past a fleet of empty auto transport trailers that reminded him of skeletons. Now he heard laughter and the dense throbbing of conversation. As he rounded the building, he was thrown into a jostling, excited crowd.

The building faced a curved driveway, which recalled the carriage approaches to Russian country estates. Stretched between two 1984ish pillars that supported the canopied entrance to the lobby was a billowing red banner embossed with the portrait of Lee Iacocca. Sequined, speedlined lettering announced that Iacocca himself would be speaking there in two weeks, to celebrate the opening of Moscow's first Chrysler showroom. Adjacent to the building was the showroom itself, a huge chrome-and-glass display case patterned after the Chrysler star. It was covered with construction workers, storming to complete the project in time for Iacocca's arrival.

But the crowd was not fixated by the showroom or the looming picture of Iacocca. It was the cars themselves that generated the panting gazes, the expert appraisals, and friendly elbow nudges. Dean had read about this scene in the papers: how the crowds began to assemble at dawn to await the first auto transport of the day, to cheer the freshly minted made-in-America Chryslers as they finished their overland odyssey from the Black Sea port of Odessa. All through the day, the transports boomed into the lot with their LeBarons, and New Yorkers, and Fifth Avenues, their Plymouth Reliants and Sundances, and the first American car designed specifically for the Russian market, the Barguzin, named for the sleek black sable that to a Russian embodies wealth and exclusivity.

People gathered to admire the new cars, read the sticker prices, and recalculate their household budgets. Down payments could be arranged with a temporary staff of salespeople inside the Chrysler building, and Dean noticed a steady flow of customers on the front steps.

He spotted Grinkov folded into the crowd, trading car talk with an enthusiastic teenage couple, all the while darting glances over his shoulder. Dean kept an eye on the driveway, waiting for a familiar face to arrive and huddle with Grinkov.

After about fifteen minutes the crowd thinned as people who'd spent their lunch hours car-gazing trudged back to work. Grinkov was still waiting for his rendezvous, his eyes anxious now, as they bounced over the crowd, then back to his watch.

Suddenly his face flared with recognition. But Dean saw a sheen of fear there, too. His appointment didn't come from the street or the crowd. Instead, he nipped confidently down the stairs from the Chrysler lobby, tucking a checkbook into the pocket of his overcoat. Grinkov scurried over to him, his shoulders cowering in subservience. He met the man half-way down the stairs and clung to him like a fan hounding a movie star for an autograph.

It wasn't whom Dean had expected.

It was Richard Gardner's attorney, Taylor Willis.

CHAPTER TWENTY-TWO

Dean watched the two men from behind a gleaming Chrysler New Yorker. Grinkov was a whirl of gestures; Willis was rigid and thoughtful. He strained to overhear them but could pick out only tones, a mixture of fractured English and Russian. Then a burst of luck. The slipstream of a passing truck carried a snatch of conversation over to Dean, and he picked out a word that Willis and Grinkov both repeated with emphasis: *Drovyanaya.* Rumbling engines blotted out the context, leaving Dean to wonder if the word had any significance at all. *Drovyanaya.* It sounded like a brand of cigarette.

Dean tried to worm into the lawyer's mind. What would he be most afraid of? That Dean had connected Gardner to Grinkov and would therefore suspect Gardner had a role in the attack and the stolen painting? Maybe. But Dean felt Willis's prime concern would be self-preservation. How to make certain that as a lawyer carving out a niche for himself in occupied Moscow, he was never linked to criminal activity. How to keep his schemes alive, whatever they were.

Grinkov listened patiently now, as Willis outlined a sequence of orders. He illustrated his speech by forming his hands into squares and triangles, the gestures of a confident prosecutor summing up before a jury.

Then they both climbed into a taxi, which lashed out of the driveway in a spray of mud.

Dean and Emily were parked in front of the building where she'd stashed Jack and Bryn. It was an apartment block in the Olympic Village, yellowed with age, water stains blackening the walls like smeared ink.

"You've already proved something to me, detective," she said.

"What's that?"

"I don't know what I want."

"You want what everyone in Russia wants: order restored."

"But is that enough to make people happy?"

"Ah. That's another question entirely."

Emily twined her fingers around his, which were still gripping the gearshift knob. Dean bent over and kissed her hand. "You always keep your hand there when we drive. Have you noticed?" he asked.

"Of course, I've noticed. One night together, and we're already developing an old couple's habits."

"You think we're made for each other?"

Emily balanced her head in her palm. She rolled down the window, perhaps hoping the answer would float in on a cloud of blowing snow.

"I could move into those empty bedrooms you're always complaining about. Maybe that'd help us find out."

"It's too dangerous, Emily. You're staying right here, and I'm staying with friends; I think I still have a couple left."

"May I just ask one thing? Whatever you feel for me, try to keep it separate from everything else." She realized the absurdity of her statement. "Right. And whatever you do, don't think of the color red."

Dean walked Emily to the lobby. They circled each other with their arms, unconcerned by eavesdroppers.

Streetlights came on. Windows turned blue in the glare of the evening news. Tonight was Dan Rather's first night as Moscow anchor, Dean remembered. Preelection coverage would drag on until midnight. The Russians would watch for a dutiful, curious hour, then probably switch to a hockey game.

"I've got to go after Richard," Dean said. "The sooner the better. Tonight even."

"What do you mean, 'go after him'?"

"I'm not sure. I want to get to him before Willis does. Find out the truth before it gets all fogged up in lies and legal maneuvering."

"Well, this is where the woman usually says, 'Be careful.'"

"And this is where the man says, 'Wait for me.'"

"I will," she answered.

"I will, too."

He tried not to expose his fear as he kissed her. But his mouth was dry and reluctant. She must have noticed, he thought, but she didn't say anything.

"Look, I don't want you to call Richard. Don't meet with him or tell him where you are. If he asks you for any favors, turn him down."

"You don't actually think I'm in danger?"

"This thing's gotten out of control. I don't think Richard has any better a grip on things than I do. He may not be able to protect you even if he wants to."

"If he wants to! He *is* my husband after all."

"He started this murder investigation as your husband .   "

He let the sentence hang, both for emphasis and because he didn't know how to complete it. Emily gripped him as if he were some sort of broken machine she was trying to force back to work.

"When you find out what he's become, you'll tell me."

"Right, boss."

"Then we'll know if there's a chance of getting him back to normal."

Dean looked at her skeptically.

"Even if we split up, I want the kids to have a father. A sane one. The one I married twenty years ago."

Dean held the door open for her. A humid warmth, heavy with frying onions, escaped from the lobby.

Her beauty disarmed him. He longed to follow her upstairs.

"We have to go to Cuba sometime, Dean. You'd love Havana. Café cubanos, black beans and rice. Streets crawling with '57 Chevies. All those Cuban show girls with feathered hats. We can finally have some fun. Fuck all this Russian seriousness."

Yes, Dean thought as he walked back to the car. Fuck all this. Fuck Gardner, and Willis, fuck the hospital and the Kosmos Hotel, fuck Anatoly Mintz and Viktor Gerasimov. Fuck this weather, and fuck this election.

Fuck Russia.

He idled past his apartment building. Unsure what he was looking for. Suspicious characters lurking in the lobby? Cigarettes smoldering in darkened cars? Shadows behind his curtains? He was waiting for a gut signal that the place was safe. He didn't get it and drove on.

He negotiated the rush-hour traffic to Dzerzhinsky Square and sliced through the crowds outside the Turgenevskaya metro station. He turned down an alley behind the Lubyanka and stopped across from MOP headquarters. Richard Gardner's window was dark; his parking spot, empty.

Dean headed for the Gardner apartment. At each stoplight he glanced down the streets that funneled toward Red Square. Its vast, haunted moodiness was scalded by floodlights as hundreds of workers rushed to erect bleachers for the election day festivities. Bunting was strung across the red-marbled Kremlin balcony, where occupation officials would view the parade. A polling place was being constructed in front of the GUM department store, where high-ranking Russian and American officials would cast the first ballots over nationwide television, then toast each other over caviar and Texas prime rib. David Wolper's crew supervised the painting of each cobblestone in Red Square, into a mosaic of red, white, and blue. Seen from the Goodyear blimp the night before the election, they would spell out the word "peace" and its Russian translation, *mir.*

The windows on the Gardners' third floor apartment were

black. Dean parked behind the building and walked to the front door. He rang the bell several times without an answer. Using Emily's key, he let himself in.

On the third-floor landing he marched directly to the door and let himself into the apartment with calm assurance, just another friend the Gardners trusted with their key.

He paused inside the door. There was no moon to cut the darkness, and the weak light of the gas lamps outside didn't reach the third floor. Dean groped to the kitchen, figuring light escaping from it wouldn't be visible in apartments across the street. He turned on the kitchen light. It played into the living room, fanned out into the hallway, and spilled through the open bedroom doors.

What was he looking for? He hadn't the slightest idea. He knew what he *hoped* for: a signed confession; a detailed description of every impossible facet of the case; a family tree connecting the players.

He searched the rooms one by one: Jack's bedroom, its floor still resembling an airline crash site; Bryn's room, with its pyramid of ballet slippers and tangled closet, where Emily had frantically snagged a handful of clothes; the kitchen, with its collection of dirty dishes and stained Russian cookbook, opened to a recipe for kulebiaka.

He entered the master bedroom. The bed was unmade; the tousled sheets suggested early-morning sex to Dean's jealous antenna.

In many marriages the bedroom takes on an exclusively feminine persona. The man abandons its decoration to his wife, who stuffs it with a canopied bed, gingham picture frames, sprays of potpourri in antique brass pots, an old doll house, and garage-sale teddy bears. But Gardner's bedroom seemed a continuation of his study, the walls hung with photos from his naval career. He was always pictured behind a desk, smiling stoically, while his eyes looked for adventure.

Emily's personality was totally absent, testimony to the behind-the-scenes role she played in the marriage.

A search of the dressers turned up the minutiae of daily life and several pairs of silk underwear Dean would have liked to see Emily in. But no secrets.

He entered Emily's collection room.

If her mind's this cluttered, she's in a lot of trouble, Dean observed. There seemed no method to her collecting. She accumulated everything: coins; hats; movie posters; onyx figurines; cuckoo clocks; *znachoki,* the commemorative pins that Russians traded with ferocity. Antique glassware was heaped on bookshelves; *matryoshka* dolls crowded the chairs; a desk struggled to survive beneath a suffocating layer of travel brochures and train schedules. Overlaying it all was the thick fragrance of Emily's clove cigarettes, testifying to the hours she spent in the room.

It wasn't a hobby, Dean realized. It was therapy. Therapy to divert her from an obsession. What was the obsession?

Dean didn't even begin to search the room.

He moved on to Gardner's office. He scurried through desk drawers, then attacked the filing cabinet. Bills, investments, medical and insurance records, tax returns, but nothing on his stay in the clinic.

Finally, in the bottom drawer, Dean found a bulging file marked "Legal." It held an agreement between Gardner and Taylor Willis, setting out the services the firm Weisman, Kaplan & Solomentsev, of New York and Moscow, was to render; the rough draft of a will; a letter drafted by Willis to an insurance company concerning damages in a recent auto accident. Nothing of real interest.

A subfile contained summaries of criminal investigations currently under way in Gardner's office. Not only were there notes on the homicide cases under Gardner's jurisdiction, but there were reports on robberies, fraud, illegal currency transactions, black-market smuggling—the entire gamut of Moscow crime. They were inferior copies, the kind made on cheap copy machines in libraries and supermarkets. Why hadn't Gardner simply copied the crime reports at work? Why were they filed under "Legal" with the rest of the Taylor Willis material??

As Dean was about to return the file, his eyes were drawn back to the will. The notes and calculations were in Willis's handwriting, and there was something familiar about the zeros. The way Willis closed them with a little circle at the top was as unique as a signature. Dean knew he'd seen it somewhere before.

He traced his way backward through the case, following the lines that connected the dots. Back to the Kosmos Hotel and the mysterious numbers in the envelopes. Now he was sure. One of them had been in Taylor Willis's handwriting!

Could Willis be the missing sketch? The fifth man to have visited Bukharin's room at the Kosmos? Was he just another witness . . . or had he killed Bukharin?

Dean was furious with himself, disgusted that he'd been so easily manipulated by Gardner, who'd withheld information and obscured facts, keeping the true nature of his relationship with Willis a secret. For the first time in several months Dean wanted his Tokarev 7.62. He'd bought the clunky, dependable Russian revolver on a morbid whim, from a gun collector. "This is the kind of gun that Carlos, the world's most famous terrorist, used to drill three French cops right between the eyes," the collector had boasted. It had taken Dean six months to realize why he'd bought it: It made him feel clean. The gun had been used so despicably that his use of it would seem heroic by contrast. It felt good in tense situations to hold a bit of indiscriminate death in your hands; it might mean you already held a piece of the enemy.

Dean switched off the kitchen light and opened the front door. He would go to the White Palm, marshal his resources, and let Gennady spoil him with drink.

Sometimes you expect enlightenment to be a searchlight, and it turns out to be a twenty-five watt bulb. It wasn't secret files or safety-deposit boxes that told Dean the truth with frightening clarity; it was the mail.

Three days' worth was scattered on a phone table next to the front door. Dean didn't know why the top envelope caught his eye. Perhaps it was the way it held the light spilling in from the stairwell. He'd already torn through Gardner's apartment; he had no reservations about opening his mail. He slit open the top envelope, a bank statement from the Carib Bank in the Cayman Islands. The Switzerland of the Caribbean, the islands conjured up images of banking secrecy, dummy corporations, shadowy holding companies. Gardner's quarterly statement listed three deposits of fifty thousand dollars paid through an affiliated bank in the Netherlands Antilles from a corporate account maintained by the law firm of Weisman, Kaplan & Solomentsev of New York and Moscow.

In Dean's experience, lawyers *charged* that kind of money; they didn't like to pay it out unless they got something dramatic in return.

He'd heard of the Carib Bank. Read about it in the papers, watched on the nightly news as government investigators from the United States and the Caymans pored over its books, interviewed its directors, sentenced three of them to a country-club prison for tax evasion, and, reluctantly, gave the bank a clean bill of health. With all the evidence that the FBI and the President's Commission on Organized Crime had amassed against the bank, Dean remembered thinking that it must have magicians for lawyers. The United States Department of Justice was never able to prove what witnesses and informants had been claiming for years: that the Carib Bank was owned and operated by a West Coast branch of the Mafia. Specifically, by the Tucson, Arizona, branch of the Bonnano family, number fourteen and climbing in *Fortune* magazine's ranking of America's most powerful Mafia organizations.

Arizona. Taylor Willis's home state.

Dean sat in his darkened office, the reassuring weight of the Tokarev folded in his hand, staring at the green eye of the fax machine.

While he waited, he played back his messages. Creditors. Natalie, wondering where he was. Finally, Sergei Borodin, who called twice to say he'd uncovered some interesting information about Vladimir Raikin, his voice tinged with accomplishment and anxiety.

Dean thought about his friend working the fax machine at the other end, in the fluorescent hothouse of the FBI's computer room. One of the few old acquaintances in government he kept in touch with. A wild man by bureau standards, he refused the regulation gray suit and impenetrable Ray-Ban shades, opting for dark pinstripes and a J. Edgar Hoover-style fedora. Dean could hear him complaining about the weather: twenty degrees, the Potomac frozen, traffic snarled, government offices shutting down early. Dean laughed. After three years in Moscow, a D.C. winter would seem balmy.

The fax machine whined to life. This'd better be worthwhile, Dean thought as he sifted through the slick incoming paper. At the rates charged by Moscow Bell, this could turn into the most expensive part of the investigation.

Neither his friend nor his hunches let him down. Internal FBI documents listed Taylor Willis as one of the directors of the Carib Bank. Dean was curiously relieved. At least now he knew who the enemy was.

The mob in Russia.

Some things in life are inevitable.

Moscow seemed like a different city to Dean as he cruised through the night, a city unaware of what was about to hit it. Was Taylor Willis the advance guard, a seed that the mob had sown in Moscow, hoping he'd grow to power, like the redwood saplings the state of California had planted along Gogol Boulevard as a gesture of friendship? Or was he a general, supervising troops that had already infiltrated the city?

Dean was grateful that the White Palm was empty. He was exhausted and in no mood for conversation with strangers. Wordlessly he drained three tumblers of vodka.

For two years he and Gennady had played a drinking game: after each shot they'd toast each other with the name of a bar they one day hoped to open. The Siberian Express, Gennady's Gulag, and the Bomb Shelter had been their favorites.

"Here's to my latest: Lenin's Tomb," Gennady said.

When Dean didn't jump in, Gennady knew things were serious. Natalie joined them, and Dean sketched out the events of the last few days.

"And if you've got another padlock, use it," Dean said as Gennady closed for the night. He looked into the mirror above the bar. His reflection appeared small and bent; a shadow seemed to gather around him.

"We have to assume they know I'm on to them. At least about the Mafia connection. I don't think they'll find me here, but if they do . . ." Natalie followed Dean's gaze to the Tokarev, jutting out of his belt in a flash of black metal. Her features didn't flinch. Her jaw tightened into a grim smile, and she thudded her son's machine gun on the countertop.

"Don't tell me you've never seen a bartender with a Kalashnikov before." With the indifference of a waitress who has just brought her customer the check, Natalie turned her attention away from the weapon to a dishcloth and a row of dripping glasses. With a quiet gesture Natalie had declared her loyalty. Dean felt grateful, sentimental, melancholy, all at the same time. Maybe he'd become more Russian than he knew.

"Are you going to the police?" Gennady asked.

"Who in the police? The cop on the beat? The chief of homicide? How do we know who's on Willis's payroll and who's not?"

A gloved fist pounded on the front door.

Gennady switched off the light. Natalie's hand curled around the Kalashnikov. They stood in the darkness, watching a figure grapple with the lock, then press against the glass, framing his face with his hands.

Dean stalked toward the door, feeling the reassuring heft of the Tokarev in his palm.

Then he heard his name barked in a Russian accent. The figure moved back from the door, and the streetlight brushed his features. Dean relaxed as he recognized Sergei Borodin.

"It's OK. I told him to meet me here."

They let Borodin in and offered him a drink. He was out of breath, his face red and constricted. He perched on a barstool, and his stomach flapped as he gasped for air.

"My wife's right. I should exercise. Limit my intake of alcohol. This detective work's a healthy man's game. . . ."

"What is, Sergei? You've found something on Vladimir Raikin?"

He nodded and slammed a schoolboy's old-fashioned satchel onto the bar. He noticed the Kalashnikov and stifled his breath.

"Things have gotten a little more serious since I talked to you last," Dean said.

"Fuck your mother, what happened?"

"Later. First, Raikin."

"Just like old times." Borodin winked at Gennady. "All business. Me, I could've had an appointment to trade for the complete plans for the MX missile, and I would've canceled it if Spartak Moscow had a hockey match the same day. I had a satellite dish on the consulate roof, you know, I could—"

"Sergei!"

Borodin fanned out a sheaf of documents on the counter. "The first week I turned up nothing on Vladimir Raikin. I couldn't find anything in print; worst of all, I couldn't find anyone who owed me any favors. All those Committee and GRU secretaries I used to take to those long lunches at Kropotkinskaya Thirty-six? Those voluptuous receptionists at the Defense Ministry whom I used to bring Chanel and copies of *Playgirl* from the States? All married or moved."

Dean looked impatiently over Borodin's shoulder. To his surprise, the documents were in English.

"The KGB data bank's in bits and pieces. I work with it every day, and I'm still lost. Then I had a brainstorm. We had destroyed our own files, but yours were intact. I linked up our computers with the CIA computers at Langley . . . and this turned up."

Dean was amazed. The dossier his old pals at the Company had assembled on Vladimir Raikin was much more extensive than the usual biographical sketches and psychological profiles they kept on their Soviet counterparts.

"Let's start with his life story," Borodin said. "Born Stalingrad, 1941. A city whose name has been sponged off the map. It seems he was made for the world of espionage. Fair grades in school. A real joiner: Children of October, Young Pioneers; a brief flirtation with the arts as an actor in a local theater group. I remember this play: *Return Address.* A big hit—officially sanctioned, melodramatic pap. Secretary to his Komsomol chapter. My guess is he licked enough ass there to swing admission to the Moscow State Institute for International Relations, not an easy school to get into. Of course, as you see, he soon flunked out of there and wound up in the Committee in a less . . . specialized capacity."

"Job description: bully."

"Basically. Attached to the Ministry of Culture as a watchdog over the arts. In his own thuggish way he'd let them know when they were getting a little too abstract. I know his type. Because he'd acted in a play or two, he considered himself an expert."

Dean sifted through the papers. The collection of personal detail was astonishing. Raikin had a penchant for short women, found ankle hair erotic, wore blue-tinted contact lenses, and plucked his heavy eyebrows in an attempt to appear more ethnically Russian. He loved Italian food and Bombay gin martinis and was tone-deaf.

"How the hell did we know all this stuff?" Dean wondered. "It's like we had a camera up this guy's ass for years. You don't get this intimate with someone unless—"

Dean paused. He supposed it was possible. Information had been jealously compartmentalized. He wouldn't necessarily have known the name of every Soviet they'd turned. "This almost makes me think we recruited him," Dean said.

Borodin laughed. "The left hand never knows who the right hand is jerking off. You recruited the next best thing, Raikin's chauffeur."

He thumbed through the printouts until he came to a list of names with the handwritten heading "Action Agents."

"On the thirtieth of July, 1986, his chauffeur appeared at your embassy, volunteering his services as a spy for the United States of America. As proof of his sincerity, he offered a copy of Vladimir Raikin's schedule for the next three weeks. As a gesture of patriotism, he recited the names of your National League's most valuable players of the last ten years." Borodin squinted at a squiggle of his own handwriting. "He also knew the Cy Young Award winners, but his case officer stopped him."

Dean read the name of the chauffeur-turned-spy letter by letter, as if he were watching a videotape advance frame by frame: VIKTOR GERASIMOV. He brushed over his shock and kept going, barraging Borodin with questions. Gerasimov had been added to the agency payroll in 1986, and when Dean scanned the pay sheets, he saw that his salary had escalated dramatically a year later.

"Those cheap bastards don't hand out a raise like this unless they feel they're on to something lucrative," Dean said.

He battled Borodin for the pages, whipped on by a rushing pulse and a thrill of curiosity. This was one of those moments when danger subsided and was replaced by movement, as goals that had seemed impossible were suddenly within reach.

"Sergei, you are a master craftsman, and information is your raw material," Dean gushed. Even Gennady and Natalie were caught up in the quest and rushed from behind the bar to peer over Dean's shoulder.

"Transfer papers!" Dean exclaimed. "At some point in late 1987 Raikin left his post with the Ministry of Culture and was reassigned. His staff—*including* his chauffeur and his family—stayed with him. Obviously he was kicked upstairs, or Gerasimov wouldn't have earned himself a raise for reporting on his activities."

Borodin permitted himself a gloating nod and poured another shot of vodka. Like a trainer taunting his dog into learning a new trick, he dangled a scrap of paper in Dean's face. "I'd say a transfer to the Strategic Rocket Forces counts as a promotion, wouldn't you?"

Dean was stunned. The Strategic Rocket Forces were the branch of the Soviet military which had controlled the country's ICBMs: the first line of defense, the last line of offense. The men in charge of the missiles were the committed elite of the Soviet Union, the men whose fingers really were on the button. Yet Dean knew they had never been trusted completely by their superiors and had been forced to accept KGB "advisers" and "technical assistants," who reported regularly to the supreme high command on their political reliability and mental preparedness. Assignment to an ICBM launch site must have been a major coup in Raikin's career; the fact that the CIA's man went along for the ride would have popped champagne corks all over Virginia.

"And that's where Raikin was when the war broke out?" Dean asked.

Borodin nodded, still reading. "At an SS-eleven site. I can give you missile throw-weights, maximum ranges, and launch modes if you want."

Dean coughed impatiently. "Just tell me where the hell he was, Sergei."

Borodin scratched his head, as he made another effort to decipher his handwriting. "A depressing little outpost east of Lake Baikal. I've heard of it, a real piece of nowhere called Drovyanaya."

CHAPTER TWENTY-THREE

Drovyanaya—the same mellifluous name Dean had heard Taylor Willis whisper on the wind.

They found it on a map, one of the new Rand McNallys which corrected the deliberate distortions Soviet geographers had made in the name of state secrecy. Drovyanaya was about 275 miles east of Lake Baikal, a village of fewer than ten thousand inhabitants on the Ingoda River. The nearest cities were Ulan-Ude and Irkutsk. To the south was Mongolia; to the north and east were China and the white-sheeted emptiness of Siberia. A collective dread descended on the bar as everyone's eyes were drawn to the black border which circled the Lake Baikal region, including the village of Drovyanaya.

"Fuck your mother!" Borodin exclaimed. "It's inside the Baikal NUCDET zone!"

The imagination could only abstractly picture the megatonnage that the cross-targeted American missiles had dropped on the Baikal zone. Irkutsk was a natural bull's-eye, near a nuclear bomber base and the center of the Siberian oil-refining industry and now, it turned out, downwind from an ICBM base.

"But the entire region's sealed, quarantined. No one's ever escaped from there." Natalie said.

"Vladimir Raikin did," Dean answered.

"How can you be certain of that?" Gennady asked.

"It's an educated guess. As a high-ranking KGB officer Raikin would've had access to top secret road maps of the area. He'd know the locations of airfields, railyards. And he'd know how to use his authority to get whatever information he didn't have. Plus he died of leukemia. He was riddled with every type of cancer you can imagine. His body was so polluted with radioactive isotopes he was like a human nuclear proving ground."

"Then why isn't Gerasimov dying, too?"

"He must've gotten out before the war. Maybe he was called back to Moscow," Dean suggested.

No one felt like talking any further. The air itself seemed transformed—gray, heavy, and obscure—as the ghastly memories of the war, never far off on a good day, pressed down on the bar. It was as though they all suddenly realized they were at a funeral and had been shirking their duty to mourn. Gennady opened a bottle of Jubilee vodka and began the somber toasts that lasted until well past midnight.

Dean was grateful for the stone wall the vodka built in his head. In the last twenty-four hours revelation had followed revelation with such punching intensity that his mind couldn't absorb them. Better not to try.

Sometime toward early morning Borodin let himself out, and Gennady fixed up a cot for Dean in the upstairs hall. Dean collapsed, longing for oblivion. But the vodka began acting up, spawning mischievous visions. Dean had a sudden picture of the Bukharin case as an octopus, and the leads he'd investigated were tentacles, reaching out from the inky center—the Kosmos Hotel. Dean began to laugh as he imagined the octopus climbing the stairs to get him, tentacle over tentacle, its suckers creaking against the sagging floorboards.

He didn't know if he'd slept. It seemed like only five minutes later that the vodka headache began to pound. Then it started talking. Shouting even. Why wouldn't his eyes open?

291

They were open. Who was talking? Why were they holding a conversation in the darkness? Why were some shouting, some whispering.

A flashlight beam danced in front of him. He was reminded of black-and-white movies of the London blitz.

Someone was shaking his shoulders. "Dean, Dean, wake up. Quickly, please!"

Dean pressed himself up onto his elbows, swung his feet to the floor. Natalie knelt by the cot in her nightgown and began to knot his shoelaces.

"The MOPs are here. They have an arrest warrant for you."

"What?"

"They are dispersed up and down the street. Gennady's downstairs arguing with them, trying to convince them you're gone."

Dean slapped his face. As he wobbled to his feet, he kicked something. It began to roll toward the stairs with a ferocious roar. A vodka tumbler.

Natalie dived after it, like an American football player throwing a tackle. Her fingers curled around the tumbler, but it skittered away and clattered down the stairs.

They both froze. The echo of metal against wood seemed deafening in the narrow hall. A sudden burst of light strafed the darkness at the top of the stairs. Dean heard arguing voices: Gennady's; then an American's, a backwoods Alabama accent.

"Who the hell you got up there, sir?"

"I have told you. No one."

"That didn't sound like no one."

"Mr. Joplin has left. I sent him home."

"Then what's his car doing outside?"

Dean flinched. There was a deathly pause.

"Mr. Joplin was drunk. I could not allow him to drive. If you leave now, you might still catch him."

"But you don't mind if we check upstairs for ourselves?"

"You are required to have a permission."

"I guess you're talking search warrant. Well, when you opened that front door for us, you opened the whole can of worms. Don't need a warrant now."

"May I ask what Mr. Joplin is accused of?"

"Nothing that I know of. The good folks down at Dzerzhinsky Square would like to have a chat with him, that's all."

"At this hour? It's five in the morning."

"Just one of the advantages of American occupation, sir. Twenty-four-hour service."

Dean had sufficiently recovered from sleep and his vodka haze to know the MOPs wanted to do more than chat. After what he'd learned about Willis and his connection to Gardner, he was certain that Mintz's death in police custody had been arranged. He wasn't going to wait for the same thing to happen to him.

He whispered frantically to Natalie, "Is there a back door up here? Outside stairs or something?"

She shook her head helplessly. Downstairs the argument was heating up. Determined footsteps grew louder, closer. Dean ran to the window at the end of the hall. It looked down three stories to a cobblestoned alley. No New York-style fire escapes, not even a rusting drainpipe. Just bare wall, and a jump that would break both his legs.

He pushed into the bathroom. No window.

Into the bedroom, which faced the back of the building. A large window beckoned from above the bed. As Dean crawled across the covers, he was dimly aware that the walls were alive with icons and candles, paintings of St. Vladimir and St. Michael the Archangel. He'd never known Natalie was religious.

He forced open the window, bowed from dampness, muffling the creaking hinge with his sleeve. Below was a cramped backyard of patchy snow and the frozen stalks of a forgotten summer garden. Beyond the garden was the bare facade of another apartment building.

Could he jump to the opposite roof, which looked a meter lower than the window? Too far. If he missed, he'd crash-land in a pile of bricks and be carried to jail on a stretcher.

Behind him, the Alabama accent was growing more demanding. Natalie appeared at the bedroom door. She glanced

293

wildly at him, then—was he only imagining it?—turned an imploring face to the gallery of saints.

"I'm sorry, Dean," she said, her eyes aligned with St. Vladimir's.

"What are you talking about?"

"We shouldn't have let them in; it was habit."

"No one's blaming you," Dean said. He hopped onto the windowsill, still hunting for an escape. He noticed heavy footprints in the snow. They were fresh.

"We're still Russians. When we hear the police, we hate them, but we're afraid. It doesn't enter our minds to defy them."

Fresh footprints. Had the police already checked back here for a possible escape route and satisfied themselves it was impossible? If he could just find a way down the building.

"I assure you no one's here. You have no right—"

Gennady and the MOPs were in the upstairs hallway now, and Dean heard doors thrown open as they began a methodical search. His mind raced to the edge of insanity . . . the Tokarev . . . he'd shoot his way out. No, in the apartment's tight quarters someone would die, the wrong people probably.

The vodka came back, wrenching his head, twisting his neck, burning his eyes. He felt as if he were about to fall.

Seconds later he knew he could make it. He'd never been so grateful to shoddy Soviet construction in his life.

"Hold them back, Natalie."

"What?"

"Delay them. Any way you can."

He waved at her, a gesture he hoped conveyed gratitude along with his fear. He crawled onto the narrow ledge outside the window. He focused on the net which hung below the neighbor's window. It was strung between two pipes, which extended from the wall. Like an outstretched palm, it was there to catch the bricks which tumbled loose on a daily basis from the sloppily assembled building.

Dean probed into the darkness with his left foot, until he found the edge of the net. He hugged the building like a fly, his left foot sliding over the slippery frame of the neighbor's window. He inched his way over to the pipe and eased into a crouch on the edge of the net.

Inside, he heard the crash of a breaking bottle. Natalie shouted a barrage of Russian obscenities, her words choppy and tongue-tied.

"It's my wife, you see," Gennady improvised. "I'm afraid she's had too much to drink again."

Gripping the pipe with both hands, Dean did a reverse chin-up, lowering himself to the net directly below him.

His feet wouldn't reach. He hung there, like an amateur gymnast.

He let go with one hand. Like a sky diver's as his parachute opens, his body jerked. His foot collided roughly with the net. Already bulging with bricks, it ripped, dumping its load into the alley with a crash, which the cold air amplified. A light blinked on behind Dean.

His head throbbing, he closed his eyes and jumped backward.

His legs collapsed when he hit the ground, spilling him forward into the snow. He got up and listened. Arguing voices and the squawk of a police radio came from his left. He cut to his right, climbed a wooden fence to another backyard. He ducked beneath a row of apple trees, their dormant branches swatting his shoulders.

He emerged onto the street and stopped. It was broad and empty, laced over with tram wire. Dawn was still an hour away. At one end a traffic light flashed a lonely red message; at the other corner Dean saw a sedan wearing the new MOP color scheme. Two officers were talking with their superior, who was giving them orders from the warmth of the back seat. Then the door opened, and a tall California blond lieutenant got out. He had a Hollywood face, square and tan, and for a Moscow winter, he looked outrageously healthy. He disappeared around the corner with his men, heading for the White Palm.

Dean took off in the opposite direction. Tram wire, trimmed with icicles, sputtered with electricity. As Dean walked, he was joined by haggard, resigned workers, bundled against the 5:30 A.M. cold. They trickled out of dim doorways and nodded at him grimly, as if to say, "We're all in this together."

Moscow was suddenly a foreign city, and he felt lost.

He ran to a phone booth. He thought of Vera, of Emily, of Richard Gardner. He fed in two kopecks and dialed Sergei Borodin.

He expected a sluggish voice, frayed with sleep. Instead, Borodin seemed wired and impatient.

"Yes?"

"Sergei, it's me."

"Ah. Yes. Of course."

"Did you notice anyone following you last night?"

"No. No one was evident to me."

There was something odd about his voice. "Did you stop by my place at all?"

"Yes, yes, that's a certainty."

That explained it. The police had been staking out his apartment and had followed Borodin to the White Palm.

"Listen, I need a car, maybe some money. Can you meet me?"

"I don't think I would recommend that course of action."

"Goddamn it, Sergei, this is a Mayday!"

"The seriousness of the situation is prominent in your voice; however, I must decline."

"Are the police there with you?"

"That's affirmative."

Dean slammed down the receiver. He smashed angrily out of the phone booth and confronted the night, waiting for an internal compass to settle, to provide guidance, if not inspiration. A siren echoed off the sullen walls of the boulevard's apartment blocks, which seemed inhospitable and out of bounds only to him. Breakfast lights winked on in innocent kitchens. He suddenly wished a perfect stranger would ask him in for coffee. But the siren came closer, and he darted into an alley as the red and blue lights of a squad car painted the neighborhood like a demented sunrise.

Everything was happening so quickly, but he couldn't hold on to any of it.

He felt like a spectator at an obscure play performed in a foreign language. While everyone around him applauded and laughed hysterically, he sat in the dark, waiting for a translation.

He needed sleep. He found a decaying tourist hotel near the Kursk train station, the lobby milling with peasants who'd come from the countryside's empty stores to shop in Moscow's brimming food markets. Dean checked into the last single room. He drifted off to sleep on a pillow fragrant with garlic, the case spinning endlessly in his head.

Afternoon sun brightened the room and the booming exhaust of commerce jolted Dean awake. He looked out the window at the freight trains, the trucks and cars, the passengers streaming into the railroad station with apparent purpose. He imagined them all rushing toward the same destination, spinning down a funnel, fighting for space.

The image triggered a thought. Nearly an explanation. A theory began to form in his mind.

At the nearest telephone office Dean made a series of calls.

Viktor Gerasimov's father confirmed what Dean had expected: His son had left that morning in a rush and hadn't said where he was going.

He called Psychiatric Clinic 12 and asked for Yuli Grinkov. Naturally he wasn't there either, and his boss was steaming. Did Dean know where that *podonki* was? One more day showing up late with a hangover, and he'd be out of a job.

Taylor Willis wouldn't be in that afternoon, a blasé-sounding secretary at Weisman, Kaplan & Solomentsev told Dean. No, she didn't know when to expect Mr. Willis, or where he could be reached.

Dean played his hunch and called the Central Military Prison, identifying himself as a friend of the prisoner Nina Zinovieva. He was told to wait. He heard arguing Russian voices and the hunt-and-peck typing of tired office workers. A flat voice returned to the phone, and told him Zinovieva, Nina Ivanovna, had arranged bail and had been released in the company of Taylor Willis, her American attorney!

His mind spinning in anxious speculation, he dialed the

apartment Nina Zinovieva shared along with Andrei Bukharin's mother. After some animated discussion among the other tenants, Mrs. Bukharina came on the line. "Yes, who is this, please?"

"Mrs. Bukharina, I was—I am a friend of your son's—"

She hung up instantly. Dean glared at the phone as though it had acted on its own and cut him off. He redialed.

"Yes?" This time the voice was a sigh, not a challenge.

"Please don't hang up, Mrs. Bukharina. I'm a private investigator trying to solve your son's murder."

"That whore he married killed him. If you were actually involved in the case as you claim, you would know that."

"The police think Nina killed him. I don't."

"Who is it that you work for?"

"If you have an interest in learning the truth, then let's just say I'm working for you. I need to find Nina."

"My son made a bad marriage. He circulated with hooligans, kept despicable company. If Nina didn't kill him, does it matter who did? The truth won't return him to me."

There seemed no way to cut through her bitterness, no softness to which he could appeal.

"If you find another killer," she continued, "he'll just find another lawyer. Is that what we can expect from your American laws? Even the KGB was not so sloppy."

How had she learned about Nina's release?

"Please hear me out, Mrs. Bukharina. I've been following your son's case for a long time. I'm not some sleazy detective who's dropped into your life because he smells money. I was even at your son's funeral—"

"I don't believe you."

"He was buried in the Second Old Believers Cathedral in Fili-Mazilovo. The service was held at ten-thirty at night. You and Nina had a brief argument with the priest over the prayer sheet before he reluctantly gave it to you. Now please, once again, where can I find Nina? If I'm able to move fast, there's a chance we can save her life."

She snorted with hatred. "Please, do not run to her rescue for my benefit."

She was a brick wall of contempt. How to break through it? Pressure? Lies? He settled on the most obvious, the most Russian approach.

"What about for the child's benefit?" Dean asked. "I can't believe you're willing to abandon it."

He heard an exhausted hiss of breath, like air escaping from a tire.

"I'm certain that whoever killed your son is coming after Nina. She was at the center of some business deal that fell apart. I think she's trying to revive it. If you give a damn about your grandchild—"

There was an emptiness on the other end as Mrs. Bukharina seemed to back away from the phone.

"I want the mother to survive, so the child can survive, that's all," she answered at last. She spoke with the frank brutality of the purges and pogroms, prepared to slaughter the contemporary generation in order to spoil and dote on the next.

"With any luck, they'll both live through this," Dean said. "Now please, Mrs. Bukharina."

"She's in Zhukovka. She came by two days ago after her release from jail. I was afraid she might go into labor at any moment. I tried to get her to go to a hospital, but she refused. She struck me and took Andrei Pavlovich's old rifle "

"His rifle?"

"She said she was going hunting."

CHAPTER TWENTY-FOUR

It took hours for Dean to rent a car for the drive to Zhukovka. The congressional delegation and the camp followers in the press corps had reserved everything at Hertz and Avis, forcing Dean into a battered Czechoslovakian Tatra 613-3, which seemed to chip away into flakes of rust with each kilometer. A long drive would wear the car down to nothing, he calculated. A self-tour cassette provided a running commentary on the landmarks of Moscow, despite Dean's attempts to shut it off: "The Lenin Mausoleum remains intact, undisturbed by the occupation, continuing to draw thousands daily, who file enthralled past the final resting place of one of history's most influential thinkers. The scaffolding you see to the left of the mausoleum entrance hides a beehive of activity, as work continues on the Soviet-American monument to the Third World War's Unknown Soldier, a powerful reminder of duty and sacrifice to be administered by the National Park Service."

He crossed the Moscow perimeter at sunset, choosing a remote border station. The guard was so happy to have some business that he waved Dean through after a brief discussion of the election. "Who do you think I should vote for as deputy republic president?" the guard asked. Dean told him he should vote his conscience, make up his own mind. This baffled the guard, who could only ask, "But who do you think the authorities want us to vote for?"

Dean passed Solzhenitsyn's revival camp. Its nighttime appearance was torchlit and gothic, a grand outdoor cathedral in the snow. A centuries-old haze seemed to have settled over the camp. Visions that were both medieval and Oriental summoned up Ivan the Terrible, Boris Godunov, all the czars and their compact with Christianity. A banner urged followers to boycott the election and cast their votes within themselves for Christ. The crowds had grown since last time. Solzhenitsyn's message, the relinquishing of self-authority, had always been a popular one in Russia. If the Rodina party ever ran a candidate of its own, Dean suspected it would do very well.

He passed the turnoff to the Raikin dacha but drove a kilometer farther. He burrowed the Tatra behind a grove of spruce, then used a hubcap to shovel a coating of snow onto it until it seemed reasonably hidden from the main road.

He took a fix on the dying sunlight and crunched through the snow toward the dacha. Whenever he came within sight of the road or another house, he angled back into the woods.

He would begin as an observer, unannounced until he could understand what was happening, until he could size up the odds. He wasn't sure whom Nina Zinovieva was "hunting," but it had the ring of violent finality, the sense of things closing in on themselves.

He caught a glimpse of the Moskva River to his left, flat, totally frozen now, trapping the blackening sunset like a lens. Perhaps that augmented his feelings of conclusion. They all would have the river at their backs; it loomed like a cliff that closed off compromise or escape.

White doves appeared against a field of green, the decorated shutters of Raikin's dacha. Dean stopped behind a lace of bare branches and surveyed the setting. The main house was boarded up, placarded with NO TRESPASSING signs of the Occupation Soviet Assets Division. The shed which housed

Raikin's model railroad was also sealed; shards of vandal-shattered glass angled out of the snow like a row of teeth.

Absolute quiet. Wonderful isolation. A perfect site for a summer home. Ideal for a writer, wasted on a KGB agent. There were no cars in the driveway yet. Nothing moved, no animals or insects. The trees were still; the evening was crisp and windless.

He sat on a tree stump that had once been used to chop wood and waited. An hour passed. Darkness fell, bringing a cutting cold with it. Traffic hissed on a distant road, then faded, blending into absolute silence.

He heard an irregular scraping sound coming from the direction of the river, almost like a saw cutting through a knotty piece of wood. A few seconds later he heard someone breathing heavily, then a pounding noise, and overlaying it all, a woman crying. Dean approached the sound, the sobbing so loud and intense it masked the crunch of his boots through the snow.

It was like following a trail of smoke. The night was deceiving. Occasionally the crying would evaporate, and he would have to stand motionless and wait for the sound to pick up again. He crossed his own footprints more than once.

The full-bore crying stopped. Now and then there was a whimper, an afterthought, like a leaky faucet that drips all night. He realized he was lost. He'd tried to keep the crying off to his left, against the river, but now the sound wasn't steady enough to home in on.

Something burning. A campfire? He sniffed the air. No, this was different, but also familiar. Strangely it reminded him of a church. . . . It was candle wax. He walked toward the smell, and it grew overpowering, as though a million candles had been set ablaze.

Then he saw a yellow flickering between the trees. He pushed through a last stand of fir until he came to the edge of the river.

The scene that confronted him was one of haunted lyricism, Russian folk art, invaded by ghosts. At the center was a woman's figure bent over some chore, like a peasant woman doing her laundry. She moved her arms vigorously up and down, producing the sawing noises Dean had heard. She shuddered as she worked, convulsed by silent tears. Beside her was a dark bundle, which she occasionally caressed. She sat between two parallel rows of votive candles, which stretched twenty or thirty feet across the ice, like a runway at night. At the end of each line of candles were two more rows, one leading left, the other leading right like outstretched arms.

The pattern resembled a giant *T,* and Dean's first thought was that the candles had been arranged as some sort of signal for an airplane or helicopter. But when he moved closer and his perspective shifted, he realized they'd been set up in the shape of a giant crucifix. Each candle created its own curl of smoke and shaft of yellow light, which probed weakly at the ice, trying to illuminate the current below.

Wherever Dean looked, at the clouded sky, the coal black brushstrokes of the opposite shore, or the polished desert of ice, his vision was drawn back to the cross, a frame around the forlorn woman and her private ritual. The rifle was a dark scrawl on the ice at her feet.

He didn't want to interrupt the ceremony, but he needed time with her, time to plan for the confrontation he knew was coming. He edged onto the ice, skidding on the worn tread of his boots.

"Nina?"

She looked up, her face taut and startled. Her cheeks were swollen and battered; her eyes ringed with bruises.

"Jesus Christ, what happened?"

Her answer was to reach for the rifle.

"Listen, I'm not the enemy anymore. Who did this to you? Was it Willis?"

She nodded. "He got me out of jail. But when I wouldn't give him what he wanted, he tried to take it. He attacked me. Or rather, his bodyguard attacked me. A Russian employee, naturally; the American was too squeamish to handle a physical confrontation himself."

"This bodyguard? A tall man, dirty blond hair, rough skin?"

303

Nina's anger momentarily stalled as Dean described Yuli Grinkov.

"Nina, you have to believe me. It's not too late for me to help you out of this."

"Your help has always been too late. Why should it be different now?"

"I know. I didn't get Vladimir out of the camp in time. But I tried, damn it. He died before we could reach him. I don't know how much we could have done for him anyway."

"He could've died in a Moscow hospital. I could've been at his bed." She cocked the rifle, nearly an explosion in the frozen air. "I grew up around men like you. Collective farm managers. They sit on their asses all season, drinking vodka and brandy. They forget to order seed, forget to pay Gosplan for the tractors. They wake up from their drunkenness in time to notice that the crops have died. Then they put on a show; they wring their hands and slap our backs and shout, 'I want to help. What can I do to help?'"

"I'm here now, Nina. And I'm not wringing my hands, waiting for inspiration. Whatever happens tonight, I can protect you."

"Protect me?" The words came out in a guttural laugh. "Why are you such a bad joke?"

"They want me, too, if it's any consolation."

She continued to scowl with suspicion.

"Look, my motives are as selfish as they are charitable. I want to stay alive. Does that make me seem more real to you?"

"Why do they want to kill you?"

"Because they think I know what this is all about."

"Is that the truth? You know?"

"Maybe half. I'm hoping you know the rest."

Her grip on the gun tightened as Dean moved closer.

"I'm not interested in facts or confessions," she said. "I don't care what I know or don't know. I don't care about life anymore."

The rifle began to chatter in Nina's hands. Dean caught her eye as it sighted down the barrel, then darted to the small black bundle. He glimpsed something white and red-speckled beneath the tattered blankets.

Dean realized Nina had lost her child when Grinkov attacked her. He was intruding on a funeral.

He moved closer. She seemed welded to the gun. Even as the grief rippled through her, she continued to aim at some point on the river, focusing her sadness on the bullet's imaginary path.

She was right. His help had always been too late. He'd made a habit out of being in the wrong place at the wrong time. While he thought and puzzled, people died. He arrived in time to offer his condolences, then moved on to the next victim. Soon there would be no one left to save, and then he could rest.

"There's nothing I could say that you'd respect . . . or even believe. But I have two strong hands. . . ."

Her body loosened, and she lowered the rifle away from her face.

"Don't ask me questions about it yet, all right?"

Dean nodded, relieved as Nina set down the gun. Still unable to master the vibrato sobbing, she knelt next to her baby and began pawing at a hole in the ice. Dean stood over her, like an apprentice at a construction site.

She gave him an authoritative nod. "Use that."

Dean picked up an auger, a giant steel corkscrew used by fishermen to bore through river ice. A mental image of Bukharin's cut throat flamed, then died. The blade of the auger was too broad for the murder weapon, and it had no serrations.

He broke through the ice with a thud, and Nina's gloved hands scooped away the shavings. He started on a second hole next to the first, then a third and a fourth, trying to compete with Nina's intensity, trying in some small way to share her burden. They worked feverishly side by side for twenty minutes, like greedy miners clawing for gold. Finally the ice was perforated enough so that one smash of the auger caused it to collapse, tiny icebergs tumbling into the black river.

Nina rested, hands on her knees, panting. "They would have taken her, you know," Nina said. "Even after she was dead."

"Who?"

"The police. The Nuclear Recovery Authority maybe. A bounty hunter could have sold her to a laboratory. He could have earned a month's salary for a baby."

Dean recalled the terrifying episode in the squatters' camps, when the Georgian long lifer had dropped out of the sky like a falcon to try to seize that helpless teenager. A contaminant, he realized, not a criminal. A potential guinea pig for the radiation laboratories that had sprung up around the world in the wake of the first nuclear exchange. Anyone who survived the nuclear strikes and had emigrated from the NUCDET zones before the quarantine was established was both a target and a pariah. Sociologists called it the Hiroshima syndrome, after the survivors of the atomic attack, who had wandered Japan as outcasts, unable to find work or marry, for fear that their mutated genes would contaminate the future.

But the Third World War had added a brutal technological twist: The same outcasts were in demand by researchers, both private and governmental, who were studying the effects of nuclear radiation on the human body. A child from an irradiated father like Raikin and a clean mother would have been a valuable specimen.

Dean tried to keep his eyes off the pathetic bundle. But he was drawn to it, like an audience at a carnival, waiting for the freak show. Nina sensed his guilt.

"Are you afraid of her?"

"Afraid? No . . ."

"Some people believe she's contagious, that she can spread radiation poisoning."

"People like to believe myths."

"They're curious, too. Would you like to see her?"

Dean suddenly despised Nina for appealing to his morbidity. But he supposed it was her right.

"Would you like to see if her head is misshapen? If there is webbing between her toes, if her spine is twisted like a root? Maybe you expect her to have wings, instead of arms, claws

306

instead of fingers. Would you like to see her, detective? You, who live to uncover secrets, who make your living from listening to bodies tell you how they died. You're a collector of corpses, aren't you, detective? A connoisseur of the strange and bestial ways people die. But you've never seen anything like this, you're telling yourself. I should see this, you think. It would be instructive."

She reached for the blanket, provoking him. "Come on, you want a look, detective?"

"Stop the fucking charade, Nina."

"Oh, my audience is getting impatient. Time to raise the curtain."

Nina tugged furiously at the blankets, like a Russian shopper who'd found a scarce item on the shelves. Dean lunged, trying to stop her. She pulled the bundle away, knocking over a group of candles. The flames died on the ice with a sizzle, darkening the night by inches. Nina unwrapped the last of the blankets and displayed her child.

The baby was normal.

A girl, her body curled and pink, her eyes closed, her thumb in her mouth—an innocent image of nap time. Dried blood flecked her cheeks and upper back. Nina dipped a handkerchief through the ice in the river, and scrubbed away the last of the bloodstains.

"She's beautiful, don't you think?"

Nina held the baby above her, examining it from all sides. Though she'd been crying earlier, she now seemed detached, a shopper critiquing a porcelain figurine in an antique store. "Are you disappointed, detective? I didn't expect her to be normal either. But we can only see the outside. Who knows what she's like on the inside? Maybe she's altered somehow. A hybrid."

"Stop torturing yourself. Let's just get this over with."

"By all means. We mustn't make the investigator uncomfortable."

Nina wrapped the baby again, lashing the blankets around her with a length of twine. She lifted the baby's eyelids open and stared into blankness. "I wonder what color her eyes would have been." She pressed a kiss onto her forehead, then shrouded the face in the last foot of cloth. She whispered a few words in Russian to the baby, lilting and cadenced, maybe a prayer or a stanza of poetry.

Nina lowered the baby through the hole in the ice. She clung to the ankles, unable to let go. She couldn't watch, Dean realized. She looked across the river at nothing and opened her hands. As the shroud vanished beneath the ice, it seemed to pull the strength out of Nina's body. She wilted to her thighs, cushioning her fall with her palms.

The baby became a shadow when it hit the water. The current took it, and it passed beneath the thin ice at Dean's feet, like a fast-moving cloud. Nina gazed along the curve of the river, as though trying to imagine the baby's path.

"An hour and she will be in Moscow," Nina said.

"Did you name her?"

"A name would have made me love her more. I couldn't stand that."

Dean backed off, leaving Nina to her reverie. He quietly extinguished the candles. Several suspended minutes passed. With the candles out, his sense of perspective vanished. Ice, sky, and shoreline blended into one horizon. He watched for approaching lights through the trees, listened for sounds.

"When will they be here, Nina?"

She looked at him as if he'd asked the distance to the stars.

"Gerasimov, Taylor Willis, Richard Gardner. You know, the survivors of this little deal you've been running."

"The deal, as you term it, is over."

"Not quite. I think you told all the original players to meet you here tonight. Whatever wasn't settled that night in the Kosmos Hotel, you intend to finish right here."

"You are like the police!" she shouted. "Worse, like a KGB thug. Because they watched us through binoculars, tapped our phone calls, they thought they knew what we were thinking. They considered themselves mind readers; that gave them their arrogance. But they never really knew. Neither do you."

"Then tell me. Help me sort it out." He grabbed her shoulders. She was stiff and resistant. "What do they want? Can we trust any of them?"

"Of course not. How long have you been in Russia?"

"Who killed Andrei Bukharin? Was it Willis? Gerasimov? Richard Gardner? Or was it someone who hasn't stepped on the stage yet?" Dean cradled the Tokarev in his palm, waiting until Nina's gaze fell on him. "Or was it you?"

She turned her back. She kicked over the candles and stalked across the ice to the shore. Dean snatched up her rifle and followed. He caught her at the edge of the trees which fringed the dacha's backyard.

"Damn it, Nina. You were in the hotel that night. You saw what happened!"

Nina's eyes quivered as they noticed Dean holding her rifle. She bit down on her lip until it bled.

In that instant Dean saw madness in her face, a bright burst that lit her up like a flashbulb, then faded.

"I didn't see anything."

"A witness saw you in the room. He remembered your face!"

"I was there earlier maybe. To discuss something with Andrei Pavlovich. But not during."

"Bukharin was selling something, wasn't he?"

"Maybe a few things."

"Gold?"

She shrugged.

"That's why you carry a gold lighter; that's why Andrei Pavolovich died wearing forty-karat cuff links."

"Sure, Vladimir had some gold."

"Radioactive gold? Siberia's laced with gold mines, Nina. Did Vladimir bring gold with him from Drovyanaya?" Dean's suspicions were slamming into focus. The sound that the Kosmos Hotel guests had presumed was diligent late-night typing was instead the clicking of Geiger counters as cautious buyers tested Raikin's gold for radioactivity.

"Vladimir had some with him . . . not a lot . . . I don't know how much."

"What else? Paintings? Sculpture Vladimir twisted away from dissident artists he arrested?"

"Everything," Nina shouted. "We were trying to sell it all!"

Dean continued to press. "Vladimir couldn't leave the

309

camps, so he made a deal with Andrei Pavlovich to sell his possessions. That's why the dacha was looted, wasn't it? To raise cash for Vladimir. In return, Andrei Pavlovich got to live like a king. He got Vladimir's car, the Italian suits, the French cognac, all the symbols he'd missed out on his whole life. He even got you. The plan was to raise enough money to get Vladimir out of the camps. You needed bribes, forged identity papers, a *propiska.* And you had to get out fast because you knew he was dying!"

Nina shut her eyes, numbed by memory.

"But you realized these piecemeal sales weren't going quickly enough," Dean pressed. "Selling a painting to a pawn-shop here, a bit of sculpture to a collector there . . . you couldn't raise the money in time. So you settled on one final sale. Discreet, secretive. Shrouded in elegance so the buyers would be intrigued. Andrei Pavlovich moved into the Kosmos to complete the facade. My guess is you decided to sell some-thing you'd been holding back, the grand finale, something that would raise all the cash you needed in one night."

Nina nodded bitterly, her gaze still on the rifle. Her face had shed its youth; her wispy blond hair seemed to be dying, strand by strand. Only her eyes pulsed, a livid, frightening blue.

"What was it?"

She nodded a petulant no.

"If it's all over like you say, what harm can there be in tell-ing me?"

Nearby, tires crackled on the icy road. Headlights from a slow-moving car swung through the trees, then died.

"Tell me what they're after, damn it!"

"Hand me the rifle first," Nina said, her voice rising, sharp and wild. She picked up a handful of snow and rubbed it vio-lently on her face.

"You're not so fucking devastated at all, are you? Everything still has its price, doesn't it?"

"Yes, yes! Everything. Please, the rifle." Her body appeared to vibrate, like a drug addict shivering for a needle.

A car door slammed. Boots crunched through snow. A second door creaked open, and another pair of boots joined the first. A flashlight beam fluttered through the trees.

"Come, detective, hand me the gun. There will be two of us then. Or do you think you can stop them on your own?"

It was spinning out of control. Dean no longer knew if he was in the middle of an investigation, a business deal, or a battlefield. Why was Nina so desperate for the rifle? Was she going to use it on him? Or was she his only remaining ally?

Approaching voices propelled him to a snap decision. He double-checked the action on his Tokarev and at the same time tossed her the rifle.

For a second her eyes warmed with gratitude. Then she vanished into the forest.

It was the last thing he'd expected. He opened his mouth to shout after her but realized it would pinpoint his location to whoever was out there. From the deliberate pace of their boot steps they didn't seem to be in much of a hurry. They probably think they have the upper hand, Dean mused. Perhaps he could use their confidence to his advantage.

He ducked behind the shed, pressing himself against the ice-glazed wood. He had an unobstructed view of the dacha, the yard, and the narrow path that led to the street. The night was moonless; the snow, barely distinguishable from the black wall of the woods.

The flashlight beam moved into the yard, followed by two figures: the hospital orderly, Yuli Grinkov, next to him, Taylor Willis.

The flashlight beam froze. They'd heard the same thing he had: hushed footsteps somewhere in the night. Nina on her furtive mission. The beam snapped off, and Grinkov and Willis traded hoarse whispers. Grinkov called out in Russian, acting on Willis's orders.

"Nina, is that you?" No answer. "It's Willis, Nina. Let's proceed with our arrangement." The only answer was the drone of a small plane, probing through the overcast for an airport.

Willis and Gardner conversed again.

"We've got the money. More than that *tolkach* Gerasimov could raise, even with all his connections."

The reply was distinct, ominous: the clink of a shell dropping into a rifle chamber, followed by the rasp of the bolt. Grinkov swore in Russian, and Dean heard Willis attempting to settle him down. The same smooth, modulated tone of voice he'd used with Gardner. Willis is an ice block, Dean thought. Calm and in full self-possession, even while facing a hidden sniper.

Grinkov's voice wobbled in fear. "Who's out there, fuck your mother? Come on, Nina, don't play like this, or I'll finish what I started."

"You're right to ignore him, Nina," Willis said, taking over. Dean wasn't surprised to hear him speak in Russian. It was simple language-book grammar, but the pronunciation was precise. It was the kind of lawyerly preparation Dean expected from a man like Willis. "I admit it was a mistake to force the confrontation on the street. It was callous, impetuous. I apologize. Let's conclude our business and put all that violence behind us."

"Mother of God," Grinkov shouted. "Just show yourself and we can get this over with!"

Grinkov lapsed into inarticulate frustration until Willis cut him off.

"You called us, Nina. You wanted to continue the auction. I can assure you my bid was the highest that night at the Kosmos. . . . I'm prepared to double it right now. A hundred and fifty thousand occupation rubles, cash!" Willis paused, letting the number 150,000 drift through the cold air, where it seemed to echo off the trees.

An auction! The numbers in the sealed envelopes had been bids, delivered by hand from the hopeful buyers to Andrei Bukharin, one by one.

Again, Willis was confronted by silence. "This isn't some exercise in showmanship, Nina. It's not bluff; I wouldn't know how. I can accommodate you in other ways, too—passports, plane tickets, a new identity. I'm not a man of limited resources."

An unruffled ruthlessness that held no room for survivors, Dean thought. He saw Willis's arm disappear into his overcoat and emerge cradling an angular shadow, an automatic weapon of some kind.

Willis split away from Grinkov and, using his speech as a distraction, edged along a low stone wall that flanked the dacha's dormant vegetable garden. Now Dean understood what Mrs. Bukharina had meant when she'd said Nina had gone hunting. She was going to kill Grinkov and Willis, maybe Viktor Gerasimov, too. She'd never intended to conclude the auction at all; it had merely been a way to lure the victims into her rifle sight. The death of her child had smashed her dreams of escape, erased her instinct for self-preservation, leaving only a surpassing drive for revenge.

"I suppose you've got your mind fixed on some romantic Russian gesture of vengeance. You feel yourself impelled toward a tragic end. Is that a fair assessment, Nina? May I make a simple point? Let's presume you got off a lucky shot, and Yuli goes down. You've taken care of one of us. But I've done enough hunting back home to recognize that's a bolt-action rifle you've got out there. Maybe they were great for buffalo hunters, but they're a little slow by today's standards, aren't they? And in the time it takes you to reload, my Kalashnikov will pour a hundred rounds in the direction of your muzzle flash. You'll have taken cover behind the stand of trees, so it will be an interesting clash of national symbols—the Russian machine gun against the Russian silver birch. In this case, my vote is against nature."

Willis snapped on the flashlight again. The beam tracked across the snow, stopping on a stack of firewood. Willis whispered back to Grinkov, who crouched on the porch steps. Something flew through the darkness and landed against the firewood, haloed by the flashlight. A bundle of money.

"That's twenty-five thousand rubles, Nina," Willis shouted. "Look through your rifle scope if you don't believe me. I've got five more just like it."

The bank notes glowed against the snow. Then Willis switched off the flashlight. They all waited in the dark, like chessmen. Dean's breath quickened; anxiety spread through him like a rash. He had to make a move, had to save Nina from the explosion of violence that seemed inevitable. But he was outgunned, outnumbered, and Nina was only an invisible presence somewhere behind him.

Willis switched on the flashlight again, and Grinkov pitched a second wad of money through the air, landing it a few feet from the first. Dean traced the beam back to Willis's hand. He tried to line up a shot, but Willis had cannily hidden himself behind a stone wall.

"That's fifty thousand. Be practical for once. Don't be victimized by your emotions." Nina didn't take the bait, and Grinkov tossed out the rest of the money, four distinct plops in the snow.

"A hundred and fifty thousand. Spend it; exchange it for dollars; use it to buy your way out of Russia. I can't believe you're not tempted."

Dean heard a rustle in the snow. Nina, shifting her position, moving closer. Was she actually considering Willis's bargain?

"I can't threaten you, I can't bribe you, but that doesn't mean I'm discouraged," Willis shouted. "Are you listening out there? I'm not going to shrug this off and drive back to Moscow. I strike bargains for a living, and in my experience there's no such thing as an unworkable deal. If we just exercise a little imagination here, I'm sure we can come to terms.

"Let's see. I'm just thinking out loud, of course, but considering the rifle you're undoubtedly pointing at my voice, your obvious lack of interest in money, the injuries you've endured in the clumsy hands of Yuli here—"

"Taylor, no!" gasped Grinkov, lurching to his feet. He began to spit obscenities at Willis, his voice laced with terror.

"It's revenge you're after, isn't it? Well, here, goddamn it, here's your chance. Take it!"

Grinkov dropped a hand into his jacket for his gun, but Willis was faster. He flicked on the flashlight and swung the beam across the night like a skyrocket. It sliced across the snow, across the shed, lanced over Dean's waist, cutting him in half with light, and landed on Grinkov.

Grinkov's eyes screamed, his mouth yawned, but nothing came out. His hand froze in his pocket, nailed dead by the flashlight beam. Light crackled in the forest, and Nina's hunting rifle exploded with a flat, echoless detonation. Grinkov reeled backward in a movement that was strangely sedate, as if he'd been slapped by an indignant woman.

The next few seconds jerked by like slides on a living-room screen, as flashes of light froze, then released the action. Willis reacted instantly to Nina's rifle burst, homing in on her muzzle flash, spraying fire into the trees with a ghastly aura of calm. Stray bullets gnawed into the shed, and the window blew apart, raining razor flakes of glass. Dean felt as if his movements were not his own. He saw his arm rise, then watched as his finger curled around the Tokarev's trigger and fired at Willis.

His first shot missed. Before he could line up another, Willis had emptied the AK-47's clip. He finally lowered the exhausted muzzle, and in the halo of the flashlight Dean saw him wipe his forehead with a handkerchief and administer his eyedrops, as though he were simply tired from reading in dim light. He glanced at Grinkov's splayed form, assumed he was dead, then walked to the firewood. He retrieved the money and stuffed it haphazardly into his overcoat, as trivial to him as a soiled handkerchief.

Dean briefly considered confronting Willis but rejected the idea. He's too comfortable with death, Dean thought. And he'd never reveal anything important anyway. He had to beat Willis to the evidence, whatever it was, then get back to the car.

Dean crashed into the woods, zeroing in on the spot where he'd seen Nina's rifle flash, slogging through the thick snow that the trees protected from the sun. His mind outpaced his droning heart and heaving lungs; for the first time he felt as if he had a chance to get ahead, to seize the upper hand.

The darkness of the forest brightened as the silver river appeared between the trees. A sudden wind blistered against his cheek, a signal that the weather would worsen during the night.

Nina lay beneath a crosshatch of branches cut down by machine-gun fire and a dusting of snow the shock waves had knocked loose from the trees. She was surrounded by a barrier of absolute silence. Dean felt a sudden urge to embrace her, to carry her to the river and bury her beneath the ice with her child. He wanted to hurl himself into the snow, to apologize telepathically. He imagined the two of them frozen in a block of ice, looking up at Willis like surgery patients under a glaze of anesthesia, while he searched for clues, secure because Dean had the power of revival.

Cut out the emotional nonsense, Dean ordered himself. Willis doesn't give a shit if you have time to mourn.

He tore away the branches and began to search Nina, careful to avoid looking into her face.

Her clothes were sticky with blood; her skin was lacerated with metal. In her pockets were a handful of coins, occupation rubles and Soviet kopecks, a Spanish-Russian phrase book, a tattered photo of Nina as a teenager, smiling in front of some mass-produced monument to the Great Patriotic War, a gift certificate for a Carl's junior caviar burger, Vladimir Raikin's KBG identity card. Her pockets held tragedy, too: a list of baby names, male and female, Joaquin and Carmela circled in ink.

But nothing worth killing for. Certainly nothing worth dying for.

Perhaps she hadn't brought it, whatever *it* was. Hadn't felt she needed to give the buyers a glimpse of the goods. Perhaps it was buried in the backyard or hidden in the plaster mountains of Raikin's model railroad or behind a secret panel in the dacha. His imagination began to babble: bank account numbers written on her skin in invisible ink; directions to a buried treasure tattooed on her scalp; freckles patterned into Morse code.

Willis's unhurried footsteps approached. Dean turned Nina's body over, looking for hidden pockets.

Beneath her back, pressed into the snow slowly puddling with blood, was a handprint! Next to it a bootprint, too large to be hers. Someone had already searched her. Despite a rushed attempt to cover it, a trail of bootprints led away from the body toward the river.

Dean hurtled after the bootprints, trying to make sense of it

How had someone gotten to the body before him? If the body had been searched, it would have been a frantic, sloppy effort, lasting no longer than the two minutes it took Dean to reach Nina after the gun battle. Why were there no signs of a search? No ripped clothes, opened buttons, turned-out pockets?

He reached the river, opposite the site of the funeral. He heard the coughing backfire of an engine and remembered that the river ice was often strong enough to support a car.

Then he spotted it, the silhouette of a motorcycle clipping away from him toward Moscow. The rider didn't risk the ice for long, cutting into the trees at the first sign of a road, carrying Nina's secret into the night.

CHAPTER TWENTY-FIVE

Dean knew the gunfire would attract the police. Willis knew it, too; from his vantage point Dean saw Willis stab the night with his flashlight as he conducted a hasty search of Nina's body, then retreated through the forest to his car. Dean did the same, sticking to the ice until he sensed he was opposite the turnoff where he'd hidden the Tatra.

By the time he heard the whooping of a MOP siren, he was on the road back to Moscow, the snow he'd heaped onto the car swirling behind him like a bridal veil. The self-tour cassette continued its annoying narration, despite a savage blow from Dean's bootheel.

Dean tried to fit the motorcycle rider into the action back at the dacha. What had he taken from the body? Had Nina given him something voluntarily? Or had he taken nothing, as thwarted in his search as Dean and Willis had been?

Suddenly speculation seemed useless. What would the truth accomplish now? Nothing in human terms. So many lives had flamed out already that a full understanding would be academic at best. To search any longer for the truth seemed a supreme act of cruelty, the satisfaction of his curiosity an inhuman exercise. He felt like a general who orders his troops into a fusillade of enemy fire, then demands a full explanation of the slaughter in triplicate on his desk by the next morning.

He joined the sparse traffic on the Moskovskaya Kolcevaya, the freeway that ringed Moscow several miles from the city center. It was an asphalt desert, light-years removed from human activity. It was perfect. Dean could drive until his gas ran out, circling the city time after time, cut off from light and people.

Toward midnight he turned into the city center. To his surprise he found himself in a traffic jam. Horns blared furiously; the sidewalks were clogged with Russians carrying presents and GIs waving vodka bottles. A gangly man in a Grandfather Frost suit staggered out of an alley, pushing a wheelbarrow brimming with champagne bottles. Dean realized he'd been on a different schedule from the rest of the city, immune to its rhythms and rituals; he'd completely forgotten it was New Year's Eve.

Tomorrow would be the first day of an election year.

The tour cassette droned to a finish and ejected in a brown tangle. Dean stared at the cassette as if it were a telegram he'd been expecting for weeks. His mind was torn back to his first visit to the dacha, to the Young Pioneer compass, and the glossy red road map of the Soviet Union that lay on top of the spinning Japanese cassette player. He combined this memory with others he'd collected over the last several weeks, he sorted through the faces and the lies, and then he knew what Nina had been up to. He knew what had been stolen from her body, and most haunting of all, he knew where it would lead.

Life is a merciless cheat, he thought, a pathological liar with a sadistic sense of humor. Just when you decide to hide from the truth, the truth finds you.

The graves were in a tranquil corner of the Rogoshsky Cemetery, a neatly divided square of land just north of the Moskvich Stadium. As the caretaker guided him through the neatly edged footpaths, the excited shouts of a soccer game brought a bit of life to the grim surroundings. The caretaker, a young, well-tended Russian who prided himself on his intimacy with the cemetery's geography, pointed out the three matching headstones and fussily cleaned dirt from the grooves of the engraved inscriptions.

"You're certain no one's buried here?" Dean asked.

"I keep perfect records. There was no funeral. No burial. No gravediggers engaged at their usual wage. I accepted payment in cash for the headstones, then arranged for the work to be done by our monument maker. He takes great care with detail, wouldn't you say?"

Dean nodded, agreeing that the work was a cut above the usual Moscow headstone.

"And the flowers?" Dean asked.

"They arrive once a week via FTD. From a store in Beverly Hills, California."

"Hell of an indulgence."

The caretaker blinked in puzzlement.

"Expensive," Dean explained.

The caretaker nodded in enthusiastic agreement and dusted snow off the peaked roof that covered the fresh flowers adorning the grave. "He insists on California poppies. I think he loved America."

"It doesn't bother you to tend an empty grave?"

"He pays me well, I must do a good job. And for me, tending them these three years, they're not really empty anymore."

The shouting from the soccer game grew louder. Four stocky players, nipping from a bottle of brandy, dressed in shorts despite the cold, charged through the cemetery gates, seeking a shortcut to the Moskva II railroad station. The caretaker growled indignantly at the players, ordering them to lower their voices.

"He's lucky to have you," Dean said. "Not everyone would be so conscientious."

"I don't mind the work. Fresh air, time to think. And the extra money helps." The caretaker knelt and began to pluck loose pine needles from the poppy petals. "Would you have a grave here needing attention? A relative maybe? A loved one killed in the war?"

"Sorry, I'm afraid not."

"No," he said. A statement, not a question. "You're lucky."

"One last question. When he visited the graves, what kind of car did he drive?"

"I never saw him with a car," the caretaker replied. "He always came on a motorcycle."

Dean gazed over the caretaker's shoulder to the annex, a sloping plain of assembly-line headstones, one of several military cemeteries financed out of guilt by NATO. Crows dueled in the gray skies, their grinding cries reminding Dean of the whistle of incoming missiles. To complete the metaphor, the crows dived to the ground, their eyes focused on invisible prey.

"They're after the mice," observed the caretaker. "I must caution our visitors against leaving food as offerings."

"You're right," Dean said, his eyes resting on the three graves and their simultaneous death dates. "I'm lucky."

"C Novim Godom," the caretaker answered. "Happy New Year."

Dean called Emily from a travel agency in the new Holiday Inn on Gorky Street. The lobby was standing room only, as journalists from around the world and the occasional famous television face jousted for the few remaining rooms that offered a view of the election day parade. A knapsack rested at his feet, stuffed with supplies he'd bought that morning: propane stove; ice ax; crampons; flares; emergency tent, and rations—a complete winter survival kit.

When he told her Richard had followed the killer to the Baikal NUCDET zone, her voice collapsed into tearful Spanish.

"I'm booked on a flight out of Sheremetyevo this afternoon. I think I have a good shot at finding him."

He waited while Emily collected herself. It seemed to take an hour. A travel agency employee gestured irately at Dean, tapping his watch.

"But surely . . . they won't let him cross into the zone."

"I don't think anyone's ever tried it."

"They won't let the killer in either, will they?"

"It'd be suicide. And that's not what the killer has in mind. The farthest thing from it."

"Is that the truth, or are you just trying to reassure me?"

"I'm trying to reassure myself. Look, there was that Academy of Sciences study which suggested that the mutation rates may have been exaggerated, and there've been a couple of government commissions that've concluded the radiation levels may drop to livable tolerances soon. . . ."

"I don't believe those studies, and neither do you, Dean. The only person I've ever met who believed his government is Richard . . . poor, gullible Richard. . . ." Her voice trailed off into memories.

A line had formed at the phone, headed by a man waving a *Rolling Stone* press pass, his face flaming with annoyance.

"Look, Emily, I've got to go."

"Why can't you call someone? The MOPs, the regional police?"

"Send in a posse? The cavalry? That'll just drive them both deeper underground."

"Who are you really doing this for?" she asked.

Dean felt a force pulling him into the phone, disassembling his resolve. I'm doing it for you, damn it, he wanted to shout. I'm going to save your husband from himself, then return him to you in a gift-wrapped box, so you can stand us in a lineup, naked, each of us clutching our résumés in his hand, and you can finally choose between us.

But he didn't say anything. He didn't know how to answer her. As Emily repeated her question, he dropped the receiver, got his ticket from the travel agent, and fled the hotel.

The Texas Air logo marched across the fuselage of the Il-yushin Il-62 jet in bold, fresh paint, but the tail still bore the blue insignia of Aeroflot.

More unfinished business, Dean thought as the airline bus clattered across the tarmac to his plane.

The stewardesses did their best to relax the passengers. Pillows were fluffed, blankets distributed, tea was served, even before the engines spooled up, all in an effort to paint their trip as just another routine flight, their destination just another city.

But they couldn't change the name on the destination board, New Irkutsk, or hide the chill that spread through the terminal when the flight was announced. And the captain's cheery recitation of the flight path couldn't lighten the faces that surrounded Dean. There was none of the bustle, laughter, and petty arguing that usually accompany a boarding flight. The passengers stowed their luggage and fitted themselves into their seats in dispirited silence, as though they all were bound for the same funeral.

Dean dug through the knapsack at his feet and felt for the small but reassuring bulk of the radiation dosimeter. He double-checked to make sure it was *zeroed.*

"First trip to the Baikal zone?" asked the man next to him, a stocky Russian with a face of deeply carved laugh lines and probing blue eyes, who introduced himself as Boris. Already the ashtray on his armrest overflowed with cigarette butts. It was going to be a long seven hours.

"That's right."

"Let me give you a little advice. The minute we're in the air, get drunk and stay drunk. Bribe the stewardess for extra vodka if you have to."

"Why?"

"They use the oldest planes and the youngest pilots on this route. The maintenance is a joke because they can't get decent mechanics to work in New Irkutsk, even though it's theoretically outside the contamination zone. Texas Air doesn't want to fly this route at all, but the occupation makes it a condition. They don't fly Radgrad; they don't fly Paris to Moscow either. I think they're praying for a crash—a good excuse to abandon the route."

Dean peered out the window. Two airport workers exited the baggage compartment and pulled away the conveyor belt. Both wore orange anticontamination suits, goggles, and respirators. Dean's seatmate spotted the suits and chuckled.

"These Moscow assholes. They think the plane's radioactive. As if those suits would do a damn thing against gamma radiation. Wait till you get to the NUCDET zone. Half the border guards wear them, Baikal tuxedoes."

"You an engineer?"

"Don't insult me. It's the fucking engineers that created this plague. I'm self-educated, you could say. I have a brother in Irkutsk, an usher at the planetarium. He's got cancer now and can't work. They closed the planetarium. Who gives a shit about the stars anymore?

"I make this trip once a month. Bring him fresh fruit and vegetables, frozen meat, the latest bullshit miracle drugs. We spend an hour in the viewing stands, talking on phones that don't work, separated by glass that hasn't been cleaned since it was installed. By the way, I hope you got a reservation at the viewing stands. Looks like it's going to be packed."

"I was hoping to make a reservation at the airport in New Irkutsk."

The man appraised him with skepticism, mingled with disgust at Dean's naiveté. "I guess no one filled you in on the situation out there. Maybe I shouldn't paint it so grimly. You'll see for yourself." He looked up the aisle as a stewardess pulled the forward door shut. "Too late to turn back now, anyway; we're finally rolling. As usual, one late passenger holds up the entire plane."

As the plane pushed back from the gate, Dean stiffened in shock. The late passenger was Emily. Her back was to Dean as a stewardess roughly escorted her to a bulkhead seat.

The takeoff was frightening. The NO SMOKING sign never illuminated, and the passengers continued to puff blithely away as they accelerated down the runway. The nosewheel shuddered from side to side, the left wing dipped ominously, and the jet crawled into the sky at such a steep angle that Dean feared a stall. The passengers gasped collectively as their bodies told them something was not right, then sighed collectively as the captain finally lowered the nose.

Dean squeezed up the aisle to Emily. The passengers pressed against the windows and watched the consoling landmarks of Moscow flicker beneath a wispy cloud cover. Everyone continued to stare down long after the jet was shrouded in a thick overcast and rain beaded on the windows. No one wanted to let go of the familiar, to confront the dim terrors that lay seven hours in front of them.

"What are you doing here? The client checking on her employee?"

"There's something you have to know about us."

"Us?"

"Richard and me."

"You couldn't have told me over the phone?"

"No."

She looked around the plane as though she were afraid of eavesdroppers. But people had fallen into their own oppressive thoughts. Some sought sleep. Others, like the old woman next to Emily, wafted in and out of prayer.

"I need to be there when you find him. I'm the only one he'll listen to."

"No way. It's ten below out there. Christ knows what kinds of guns they're carrying."

"I survived five Boston winters, Dean. And who do you think it was who helped Richard polish his shooting those nights he came home from your operations course clutching a blank target sheet?"

Dean eyed her skeptically.

"That's right. My father used to be deputy police chief of Camagüey. He felt his daughter should familiarize herself with the tools of his trade."

Dean urged Emily to her feet and led her to a pair of empty seats at the back of the plane.

"OK, I capitulate. You've got warm blood, and you're an ace with a target pistol. But what makes you so damn sure he'll listen to you?"

"He's doing it for me. This whole insane little crusade, this suicide mission: He's doing it for me. He thinks I need him to be a hero."

She curled her right hand around his thigh, mimicking the way they'd held each other on the drive to the inn.

"I'm not much of a shrink, so I don't know if there's a

325

clinical name for it. But Richard has always suffered from what I call a mentor complex."

"Not this obvious shit about him living in his father's shadow?"

"That's the point. He's always lived in someone's shadow. Not because he was forced to but because he chose to. He couldn't exist any other way. His older brother, Tom—the youngest vice-president ever in the mergers and acquisitions department at First Boston—was Richard's first mentor. He guided him through hockey, high school, and girls. Coached him every step of the way. Until he went off to Harvard on a scholarship and left Richard in a vacuum. He always talks about that first summer away from his brother, how terrified he was of making a move on his own.

"At that instant I think he had a chance to become his own man. Instead, he transferred his allegiance to his father. Hero worship is the only way to describe it. He clawed his way through sailing school to impress his father, even though he had no aptitude for it. One thing about Richard, he's bull-headed enough to make people respect his failings. Then came Annapolis, again with his father pulling the strings—"

"Then the old warrior died, and Richard was out in the cold again," Dean said.

"His mother took on the role of mentor for a few months. She handled the funeral arrangements, put the house on the market, moved them to a smaller place. Made a few calls to her husband's old friends, trying to scour up a commission for Richard. The woman never faltered, never broke down. A real Rock of Gibraltar."

"Yeah, perfect. I hate women like that," Dean said.

The plane shuddered through an abrupt downdraft, throwing Emily closer to Dean. He decided to take Boris's advice and he ordered them each a double vodka.

"She was so perfect she had no understanding of her own son. She couldn't begin to comprehend the pressure Richard was under to perform, to outshine his father and brother. But I did." As she pronounced these last words, a hardness set in her face. For the first time Dean sensed she was capable of brutality, not physical threats but mental intimidation.

"That first night at the Czech Embassy most people only saw a timid junior intelligence officer. Helpless, groping his way in the dark. A straitlaced nice guy with few prospects. But I sensed a lot more. As my father used to tell me, I always did have a talent for spotting the dangerous rocks hidden beneath the waves. I saw a driven man. He gripped a champagne glass like he wanted to crack the stem; his eyes prowled the room like loaded guns. As we talked—party chitchat mostly—I realized here was a man who wanted the world but was afraid to go after it on his own."

"So you decided to help him get it."

"You make it sound like a contract. We were in love, and I wanted things to happen for him. I grew up in those teak-paneled State Department suites that Richard needed access to, as a girl I played on the same embassy row Persian carpets he desperately patrolled with a cocktail glass. My father, the illustrious Cuban émigré, was a man everyone wanted to meet. The same people wanted to meet his daughter, and pretty soon they wanted to meet her husband, too."

Emily portrayed Gardner as an eager apprentice, led on a leash to the offices of important people. She was the trainer, molding him into a savvy political player.

Dean was fascinated by this manipulative Svengali-like aspect of Emily. He wondered what she would have made out of him had they met under different circumstances.

"You see, Richard's father was an order giver and an order taker. His life was marked out, literally, by rank. He never really taught his son how to improvise, how to—"

"Scheme?"

Emily forced out a tepid smile. "Let's say 'how to handle people.' On the other hand, I'm sure the first sentence I heard as a child was some sort of intrigue my father was plotting against an enemy . . . or a friend, for that matter. I was raised on conspiracy, so it was only natural that I teach Richard what I know. I showed him how to pit egos against one another, how to exploit weakness and vanity, how to win promotions. How to appear interested when you're bored and, more important, how to appear bored when you're really interested.

"I guided his career, advised him on which jobs to take,

which to turn down. He didn't make a move on a case without me. He was dedicated, but a slow learner. Those damn Puritans just don't have much instinct for duplicity, so I force-fed him mine."

She finished her drink and pulled away from Dean. But she took care to keep their hands linked as she pressed her face against the cool window. Ice crystals had formed on the glass, creating sharp-edged patterns that reminded Dean of cities seen from the air.

Dean realized Richard had been her life's work, her masterpiece. But there was one mentor she didn't know about, the Mafia lawyer Taylor Willis, who had recruited Richard at his low point in the psychiatric clinic and had promised him— what? Money? There was that $150,000 in the Carib Bank. There had probably been more. Power? Advance knowledge of throwaway criminal activities so that Richard would stand out in the police department? Maybe all of it. What had Taylor Willis gotten in return? Organized crime's most treasured possession, a cop on the payroll. Dean thought of the Willis files in Gardner's apartment. Gardner had fed Willis a steady diet of information about MOP criminal investigations, information that would become more valuable as the scope of Willis's Moscow operations expanded.

Richard had been seduced by Willis, and Emily's influence had waned. Perhaps that explained her mania for time-filling hobbies, her compulsion to uncover Richard's secrets.

She was Lady Macbeth, forced into early retirement.

"You see, he has to solve this case on his own or die trying," she continued. "It's like an offering to me, the final proof that my faith in him hasn't been misplaced. He thinks I demand it of him, but I don't. I just want him sane . . . and alive."

Sunset flared off the wing tip. The plane banked, speeding toward darkness. Dean watched Emily, entranced as her features receded into dusk. She's equally beautiful in sun or shade, he thought.

"In a way"—she sighed—"I guess you could say I created Richard Gardner the spy."

CHAPTER TWENTY-SIX

The plane scored a silver line through the night, and the rhythms of the passengers shut down. Emily slept, her head resting in Dean's lap, while his imagination raced ahead, trying to anticipate Gardner's moves.

But it was like trying to plan a vacation to an unmapped country. He knew little about the NUCDET zone because the occupation kept it shrouded in obscurity. It was a wound on Russia, a permanent cast. It was a reminder of war, of human failure, of Soviet and American aggression. An inconvenience to the new government trying to lift 280 million people out of defeat and depression with the spectacle of free elections.

Dean studied the map in the weak overhead light. American MX and Minuteman missiles had struck several locations in the Soviet Union, but only three were quarantined, only three earned the militaryspeak name NUCDET zone, and only one, the Baikal zone, encompassed a substantial population. Its borders enclosed the cities of Irkutsk and Ulan-Ude, a portion of Lake Baikal, the deepest freshwater lake in the world, and thousands of square miles of desolate taiga.

Escape was considered impossible. Irkutsk was circled by a

deadly quilt of guard towers, cement walls, and electrified fences. The border traversed the southern tip of Lake Baikal, running west to east, its poisoned waters laced with mines and sensors, its skies patrolled by helicopter. The zone's southern frontier was Mongolia, impregnably fortified by thousands of Chinese troops who reclaimed the former Soviet client state in the closing days of the war. To the east the border was less definite. The roads were sealed, the bridges demolished, effectively choking off the movements of large groups of people. But the trackless taiga—in winter a moonscape of ice and temperatures that defied belief, in summer a maze of mud and marshland—lured the solo daredevils who gambled they could elude the foot patrols without getting lost. Dean assumed that an occasional hunter or woodsman intimate with the area slogged his way out, but for the average person, an attempt to escape across the taiga was really a drawn-out death sentence.

The inhabitants of Radgrad, as it was dubbed by the New York *Post,* a nickname that instantly entered the language of the occupied USSR, condemned by the outside world to isolation, ironically depended on it for their survival. Their rivers and lakes were irradiated, the soil so polluted with radioactive isotopes it could only produce a fraction of its prewar harvest, and even that was not entirely safe. They survived on charity: daily airdrops of drugs and grain; weekly food trains. Television and radio programming instructed the citizens in techniques for decontaminating soil, in building dikes to contain melting radioactive snow, in animal husbandry, in radiation measurement, and in hospital management (radiation had weakened their immune systems, and thousands died from flu, pneumonia, and other nonfatal diseases). Via satellite, Moscow psychologists beamed advice on coping with catastrophe and its attendant depression into Radgrad living rooms.

But the citizens of Radgrad lived for the one thing the occupation would never grant them, permission to rejoin society. The occupation hoped that ultimately the NUCDET zones would become self-sufficient, autonomous entities, that the population would settle into routine and resignation. Genera-

330

tions of East Berliners had grown used to walls and guard towers, so why couldn't Siberians?

Dean felt the engines reduce power, as the Ilyushin began its descent to New Irkutsk. Stewardesses rudely slammed shut the window shades raised by reviving passengers. They dimmed the lights and announced a "brief, instructional film detailing for our cherished guests customs formalities and visiting procedures at the New Irkutsk border station." But the film broke during the titles, and unprepared and anxious, the passengers bumped through the cloud cover.

The landing jolted Emily awake. She stared out the window, beyond the rough runway and prefab terminal, at the forest, deceptively soft and inviting. Somewhere out there her husband was timed to explode.

The stewardess threw open the forward door, and blinding light and cold poured in. There was no rush for the exit as on most flights. The passengers seemed suspended, afraid to confront their destination.

Dean and Emily were the first out the door. Their eyes began to water as the cold hit them like a curtain of dry ice. The thermometer Texas Air had thoughtfully bolted to the mobile stairs read minus sixteen—mild by Siberian standards. They tightened their overcoats and turned up their fur collars.

The airport had the feel of a military camp at the end of a long, losing war. The soldiers' faces were slack with apathy, their minds counting the days until they'd be recycled to Moscow.

The terminal was an airless bunker. Its triple-thick windows kept out the cold but weakened the incoming light so that everyone moved about in perpetual dusk.

The passengers filed past a plywood counter, where a rail-thin sergeant of the Occupation Forces Guard Division conducted a cursory search of their baggage.

"What are you looking for, Sergeant? Afraid I'm gonna smuggle in a helicopter bolt by bolt?" Dean joked.

"I find something like that on you, I'm using it myself. Anything to get outa here."

"How safe is New Irkutsk?" Emily asked.

"Radiation levels have subsided to levels recognized by the U.S. government as tolerable, ma'am." He winked. "Otherwise we wouldn't be here."

Dean presented a shield identifying himself as Richard Gardner, deputy homicide inspector, Moscow, and showed the sergeant a picture of Gardner. "Have you seen this man, Sergeant? He would've come in on yesterday's plane. Maybe the day before."

"Looks like an old CO of mine. Sad case. Wife left him, he drew a six-month tour in Vladi, turned into an alkie. MOPs caught him one night breaking into an Air Force weather station, trying to drain alcohol out of a thermometer. Mercury freezes out here, you know. Sorry, ain't seen him. Been on duty all week. Who's he supposed to have killed?"

"Calm down, Sergeant. He's just wanted for questioning."

"Kinda drastic coming out here to get out of a couple questions. You sure he's not a killer?"

"Sorry."

"Too bad. The men get kinda bottled up here. A Saturday night manhunt sounds like it'd do a world of good."

"One other thing—I'll need a map."

The sergeant looked at Dean in amusement. "Map? Map of what?"

"Of New Irkutsk. Maybe a top map, too: rivers; backcountry trails."

"New Irkutsk is one airport, which you already seen. A couple of viewing centers, one hotel, the top three floors still under construction, one bar, one restaurant just this side of poisonous, five thousand bottles of Bud, not counting empties, and two thousand bored, horny, terrified GIs. Except for the soldiers, you'll find it all on one little street."

The sergeant pressed a blurred stamp onto their internal travel passes and beneath it scrawled the words "Approved to Perimeter."

"Present your travel passes if asked to do so by forces personnel. No pictures of the perimeter allowed, no tape recordings or videotapes—"

"Without the express written consent of major-league baseball," Dean shot back.

"You got it." The sergeant laughed. "You'll find rental cameras at the viewing stands if you want to take snapshots of friends and relatives in the zone. And I wouldn't plan on any nature walks. You'll only be disappointed."

He handed Dean his backpack.

"Hope you find your man."

Unnerved by the sergeant's obvious boredom and the shabby banality of the airport, Emily and Dean jostled through the crowd to the exit. But they both hesitated, their minds suddenly unwilling to pull their bodies forward.

"I feel guilty all of a sudden," Emily said. "Like this is something we shouldn't see. Like we're kids, vandalizing a graveyard."

"That's exactly what we are—vandals." Dean threw open the door.

The first thing they noticed was that the forest had died.

Three American Minuteman III missiles, each with three 170-kiloton warheads had struck Irkutsk Air Base and the nearby oil-refining center of Angarsk. One and a half megatons, 120 times the explosive power of the Hiroshima bomb. The air base, the refineries, and every man-made structure within six to seven miles of ground zero had been instantly disintegrated by the blast waves. Then the gamma rays had gone to work, killing invisibly, saturating the forests with fatal doses of radiation in the thousands of rads. Fallout, carried by capricious winds and freak rainstorms, settled on the taiga, beta particles burning the life out of millions of pines, birches, and larches.

Dean and Emily faced a tortured horizon, an endless jumble of brown, knotted sticks that could no longer reasonably be called trees. The word "taiga" would soon vanish from the local vocabulary. We've stabbed Russia right in the heart, Dean thought.

A crude asphalt road, buckled by permafrost, paralleled the dead forest. Ranks of American troops trudged past, some in full radiation suits, others in fatigues and ski jackets, their faces polished with Coppertone. Half-tracks, bulldozers, personnel carriers dueled in clouds of exhaust.

Above the din they heard the roar of bullhorns. Three

333

stocky Buryats, their features more Mongolian than Russian, held color-coded signs in the air and attempted to divide the newly arrived visitors into three groups of red, blue, and yellow.

Boris pushed past Dean, his face shining in exhilaration.

"I'm red this time," he shouted. "That means I'm in the first group."

Dean and Emily fell into step behind Boris's group. Their Buryat guide, his brisk regimentation and warehouse of statistics a testimony to his Intourist training, led them at a furious pace. Every hundred yards or so, like emergency call boxes along a Los Angeles freeway, Dean spotted remote radiation war meters, their needles hovering in the low millirems end of the scale, the exposure level deemed safe by the government. Had they been tampered with to reassure visitors, or were they there to warn the GIs to get the hell out if the radiation level inexplicably jumped? Dean checked his own dosimeter. The accumulated exposure was rising, but still tolerable.

They passed the gray edifice of the half-finished hotel. It was typical Siberian construction, cement slabs slapped on top of one another like square pancakes. Rusting reinforcement wires shot out of the cement, whipping in a rising wind.

"*Sarma,*" warned the guide. "Northwest wind. Very cold. I suggest we hurry."

The group shrank together, seeking warmth, and began to jog. The road dipped toward a wide valley, but the view was blotted out by a convoy of trucks piled high with cement pillars and barbed wire reinforcements for the perimeter wall.

With the convoy finally past, the group drew to an abrupt stop, a single machine whose power had been cut off. Some gasped in awe; others yawned indifferently; one old woman collapsed in prayer. Emily grabbed Dean's thigh, her nails piercing his skin like a sharp pair of incisors.

The trees had been cleared for miles around, creating a vast no-man's-land that gave them their first view of Irkutsk, capital of the Baikal NUCDET zone.

CHAPTER TWENTY-SEVEN

The missiles had rearranged the Irkutsk skyline. The massive high rises that walled in most Soviet cities had been destroyed, absorbing the brunt of the blast wave. The center of the city had been spared, its churches and museums and government buildings defiantly intact, though many were scorched black, like match heads. Roads leading into the city had been chopped into pieces and were only now being repaired. From a distance of several kilometers the city seemed deserted, the buildings just stage flats, the inhabitants just ashes, blown away by the wind.

The red group pushed on to the viewing stands. There were two, one on the other side of the perimeter, in Radgrad, and the second in the noncontaminated zone. They were water-stained bunkers, more than a city block long, perched on stilts. They faced each other across no-man's land, separated by a distance Dean estimated to be 250 feet. Dean and Emily climbed a flight of stairs with the red group, buffeted by the shoving, expectant crowd.

Inside was a scene of deafening chaos. The entire front wall of the viewing stand was triple-thick glass, looking out on the identical viewing stand on the other side of the border. Flimsy partitions, defaced with drawings and hastily scrawled notes, had been erected every five feet along the window, in an attempt to provide a sliver of privacy. Within these makeshift booths, people bunched against the glass, waving to their friends and relatives vaguely visible in the other viewing stand, shouting tearfully into plastic telephones. Each booth was equipped with a bulky telescope, the kind you'd find at Niagara Falls or the observation deck of the Empire State Building. People focused on the magnified images of their loved ones, like submarine commanders manning their periscopes. Buryat vendors slammed through the crush, renting cameras and telephoto lenses for five occupation rubles a minute. Flashbulbs popped relentlessly, ricocheting off the smeared glass.

A siren blared, announcing a shift change. The current visitors were roughly shouldered aside by the red group.

"It's like being inside some grotesque aquarium," Emily observed.

They split up, working their way toward the exit. They showed Gardner's photo to every Buryat vendor and GI security guard they saw but each time were met with an indifferent shrug or a discouraging no.

Dean grabbed a free telescope. The faces he saw on the other end of the lens swam behind layers of dirty glass, their eyes wide and gaping at freedom. The rest of their features were sanded away by resignation. Some faces appeared healthy; others, anemic, diseased, victimized by shedding hair or milky cataracts.

Some people held up handwritten messages to the glass; others wrote on the window itself. Newborn babies were displayed to relatives who would never hold them; a choir dressed in tattered folk dance costumes sang into a phone; a beautiful young woman attempted to transmit a violin solo, the receiver balanced delicately on her shoulder.

Dean swung the telescope away from the viewing stand toward the treeless panorama behind it. Now he could see that the roads leading to Irkutsk were flooded with people, dense columns like armies on the march, filing to and from the viewing stands. The fields were junkyards of abandoned automobiles and trucks. The destruction of the refineries meant gasoline shortages, and those citizens wealthy or influential enough to have afforded a car were forced to throw them away like broken toys.

He focused on the city itself. The distance and the wind-stirred snow cut the visibility, adding to the eeriness of a large city without traffic. There were no trucks. Baggage moved by horse-drawn carriage and handcart. An occasional bus slogged through the swirling dots of pedestrians, but for the most part Irkutsk, once a modern, energetic industrial city, looked like a rambling, incomplete frontier town, anxiously awaiting the arrival of civilization.

A hand tapped Dean on the shoulder. He turned to face a distantly smiling Buryat, his wrist clenched in Emily's grip. He was bizarrely dressed in a Squaw Valley ski parka, mirrored sunglasses, and high-top red tennis shoes.

"This is Richard's watch," Emily said, waving the man's wrist.

"Where the hell'd you get this?" Dean asked.

"In trade."

"Trade for what."

A pair of exhausted GIs edged past, fixing stares of distaste on the Buryat.

He lowered his voice "Could we conduct our talk outside? I'm not appreciated here; your soldiers have been complaining about the quality of my homemade vodka. I tell them they are welcome to stick with their Budweiser—"

The Buryat led them out of the viewing stand, to a secluded spot behind a truck piled with used anticontamination suits. Dean sniffed the air. Normally crisp and pure, it was polluted with the stink of *plan,* cheap marijuana from Samarkand.

He glanced into the cab of the truck. Two American sergeants were attempting to coax themselves into oblivion, marijuana smoke curling thickly behind their antiradiation goggles and vented out through their respirators

337

"This Richard . . . is he a criminal? Or worse still, a contaminant?"

"This Richard is my husband. Now how did you get hold of his watch?"

"He was sent to me by my brother, currently the bartender at the hotel, formerly the second-best guide in Irkutsk."

"You being the first," Dean said. "He gave you the watch to lead him someplace. Where?"

"The same place I took the other criminal . . . or, worse still, contaminant."

Dean felt his throat constrict. Emily leaned against the truck, the cold steel invading her hands through her gloves.

"What's the name of this place?"

"It doesn't have a name. It's not really a place," answered the guide.

"What is it then?"

He shrugged. "A rock, a group of larches. A creek favored by fishermen for its *omul.* Frozen now."

"You didn't see any village? Maybe a military base?"

"Nothing. It's a spot near the perimeter of the Baikal zone. That's why I thought these two were criminals, perhaps fleeing to the only place they know the police will not pursue them. Or contaminants. One who has already been contaminated would have little to lose by entering the zone."

"This first man you guided . . ." Dean sketched a brief description of Viktor Gerasimov, and the guide nodded. "How did he know where he wanted to go?"

"He had a map"—the Buryat paused, searching for words—"a map that was not a map."

Emily rolled her eyes in frustration. But Dean felt his nerves firing, his blood pulsing as his hunches began to pay off. This is like guessing the hidden card in the magician's hand, he thought, and being rewarded with your life. Now he was sure Nina had transcribed the map onto a cassette tape, either to disguise it or to make it more portable; she'd probably gotten the idea while listening to her Spanish lesson. She must have been wearing her Walkman, which contained the map/cas' sette, during the shoot-out at the dacha, and that's what Gerasimov had taken from her body.

He thought of poor Anatoly Mintz. Because he'd wanted his masterpiece so desperately Dean had figured it was central to the case. So had Willis, presuming the map was somehow disguised in the canvas. Mintz was dead because he'd inadvertently got in the way; his "Moscow Straitjacket," in shreds because people had wanted it to be more than just a painting. Maybe an art historian could restore the original on the gulag wall; maybe someday Mintz would bask in a little posthumous glory.

The Buryat rubbed his palms together, trying to explain himself. "Not a map, but a . . . I don't know the word in English—"

"A cassette tape?" Dean asked.

"A cassette tape, yes."

The hike to "the place that was not a place" took three and a half hours. They'd tried to hire the guide on a cash basis, but he'd turned them down: "Money is useless when there is nothing to buy." Instead, he demanded Emily's earrings as payment. He opened his Squaw Valley ski jacket to reveal a sweater glittering with earrings, which had somehow become collector's items among the locals.

The *sarma* had blown away the cloud cover, then subsided, its work done. The afternoon was the clearest Dean had ever experienced, the piercing white of the snow a reminder of the lost purity of Siberia. They trekked over softly curved hills, forded frozen streams, walked single file between canyons of dead trees.

Dean looked up at the untainted blue sky and tried to picture it on that day three years ago: the blinding flashes of the nuclear warheads, the roiling fireball of the thermal pulse, the monstrous storm clouds of fallout obliterating the sun, then settling on the landscape like a slowly closing coffin lid.

The guide left them at "the larches, the rock, and the creek." He'd marked the trail clearly so they could return on their own, but he advised them to leave well before dark. Like many isolated, rural people, he didn't exhibit an ounce of curiosity about the Americans' bizarre wilderness expedition. He quietly pinned Emily's earrings to his sweater, then turned and vanished into the forest.

"Now what?" Emily asked, pacing the narrow clearing. "We just wait for Richard to materialize out of thin air?"

"Vladimir Raikin was stationed at a missile site in Drovyanaya, on the other side of the zone, but he couldn't get out in that direction. He escaped this way. That means this spot has got to be on his map, the first landmark outside the NUCDET zone. Gerasimov's following the map; Richard's following Gerasimov."

"It could take days."

"I don't think so. If my sense of geography is accurate, the perimeter's just over there, not more than a kilometer."

They sat on a flat rock, and Dean boiled tea on his Primus stove. As they greedily sipped the scalding liquid, they became aware of an oppressive buzzing, an integral part of the forest that had always been there but now, in the muffled isolation, seemed clamorous. They scanned the sky, their city instincts telling them to expect an airplane or a helicopter.

Dean shuddered as he realized what it was.

"Insects," he said. "Radiation has probably killed most of the birds, and the insects have multiplied." He spotted a cloud of locusts, staining the blue sky. "By summer every entomologist in America will probably have found his way here: Siberia, kingdom of the bugs."

They drank cup after cup of tea, trying to warm themselves as the temperature dropped. The sun crept across the sky, the shadows of the irradiated trees lengthened, like crosses in a cemetery.

Finally Emily bolted to her feet and splashed her tea into the snow. "I can't deal with this another second. We've got to go in after him. Gerasimov's a murderer—how do we know he hasn't killed Richard? How do we know they're not both dead and we're just waiting here for nothing?"

"Emily, we're so close. Let's not blow it by tearing off in a panic."

"Panic's the only thing that's going to save him! Patience, logic . . . they're useless where Richard's concerned. It's a suicide mission, I've told you. We can't rationally predict what he's going to do." Her face was stark with determination. She held out a demanding palm. "Give me the compass. I'm going to the perimeter."

Dean knew he'd lost Emily—if he'd ever really had her to begin with. She'd never turn this desperate for me, he thought. She'd never risk her life, jump through fire, succumb to panic over me. He'd always assumed her love for her husband had been fading when in reality, it had merely been frozen. I helped thaw it out, he told himself. The heat of Gardner's impending death had brought it back to life.

"Emily, if we find him—make that when we find him . . ."

He refused to complete the sentence.

"I'm taking him back to the States. In a carry-on bag stowed under my airplane seat if I have to."

"And if I try to stop you at the airport?"

"You can try to stop me right here. You can smash the compass, refuse to help me find the perimeter. Force me at gunpoint back to New Irkutsk."

Dean threw his head back and laughed bitterly. It was laughter that threatened to become uncontrollable. It forced tears out of his eyes and sucked his mouth dry. He backed against a tree for support and felt the stubby branches needling his back.

"I was just thinking what a strange feeling it is to hold all the cards. I don't think I've ever had so much power over someone in my life."

"I presume you're enjoying it."

Dean gathered himself and wiped his damp face with the back of his glove. "That's where you're wrong. I hate it."

"Well?"

Dean pulled the compass from his rucksack and held it in the palm of his shaking hand. He clamped his other hand around his wrist, willing the needle to settle. Dean nodded to the east.

"This way," he said flatly.

Dean marked their location by arranging a row of stones in

a crude *A* on the frozen creek bed, then led Emily into the dense forest.

They followed the creek for a half hour, as it descended through a rocky gully. Dean felt Emily's eyes on his back, but he knew they were looking through him, scanning the trail up ahead for her husband.

The creek disappeared underground. The trees thinned, and they came to a bare swatch of no-man's-land that surrounded the NUCDET perimeter. The border here was sloppy and improvised, a fence of pine logs topped by a braid of barbed wire and a single wooden guard tower, like a snowbound Fort Apache. As Dean's eyes grew accustomed to the brilliant blanket of snow, he realized the wooden fence obscured another barrier of twisted steel and scorched concrete. Through the binoculars he recognized the wreckage of a Soviet air base.

It looked like the moon, rained on by model airplanes. Two enormous craters, gouged out by Minuteman warheads, overflowed with the remains of Soviet Bison, Bear, and Backfire bombers. The Air Force appeared to have been reduced to silver candle wax, melted by the intense nuclear heat into shapes that were aesthetic and soft, weapons transmuted into art. The hangars and warehouses, the barracks and control towers were gone, just heaps of rubble, littered with pins and needles of metal that had once constituted radar antennas and satellite dishes.

Dean and Emily inspected their surroundings. Snow, piled high and apparently impenetrable. They looked for footprints, for litter or the traces of a campfire, but the early-morning wind had blown away all signs of life.

"Another dead end," Emily said.

Dean nodded in agreement. "They must not have come this way. The area's too exposed, no natural cover at all; you've got a guard tower right over there. And I can't believe the escape route would be right in the middle of an Air Force base."

Dean continued to scour the area, relief that they might not find Gardner replaced by guilt and challenge. He struck off to his left, staying within the shelter of the treeline, hunting for anything out of the ordinary.

He'd covered about four hundred meters when he spotted them.

Emily had missed them, perhaps assuming they were animal tracks or some freakish, windblown grooves in the snow.

"Right here," Dean shouted. "This is where they went in!"

Serrated tooth marks formed a path through the snow, evenly spaced and identical, as if some metallic animal had bitten down on the ice. It was a pattern Dean had committed to memory, a pattern identical to the throat wounds on Andrei Bukharin.

This is it, Dean thought. The trail that began in room 1365 of the Kosmos Hotel ends right here.

A nearly forgotten sensation gripped him. Like light pouring into dark rooms; like waking up energetic from a dizzying, drugged sleep; like replacing the embalming fluid in his veins with fresh, untainted blood. He'd felt that way when he'd married Molly, when Patrick had been born, when he'd aced his first field assignment, but it had been a long time. . . .

He held on to the rush and led Emily down the narrow footpath the killer had carved into the snow.

It jogged deeper into the forest, slicing through shrubbery and snowdrifts, seemingly at random, chunks of snow pushed away like blocks of marble. The path veered downward, in a series of roughhewn steps, like those a mountain climber might hack with an ice ax. White walls reared up on both sides. Now lumps of dirt were mixed with the snow, as the trail bored into the ground itself.

Dean felt as if they were descending toward some ancient buried tomb, on a mission to loot the graves. Finally the path dead-ended at a featureless concrete wall that Dean estimated was at least ten feet below ground level.

At the center of the wall was a massive iron door, partially opened.

A hand, half frozen, half chewed away by insects, protruded from beneath the door.

Dean veiled his shock behind action. Using his entire

weight, he managed to shoulder the door open wide enough to permit entry.

The single human hand had not prepared him for what he found inside.

He felt as if someone were strangling him. His teeth seized together, and he forced himself to breathe through his nose in painful, staccato gasps. Emily suddenly grabbed his shoulder, and an image flashed through his mind of the disembodied hand returning to life.

He knew it would be useless to try to keep her out. She wasn't a woman who needed to be protected from gruesome sights or led away whimpering from the spectacle of death. And she would want to know if her husband were down here.

But this . . .

They forced the door open wider, spilling a sheet of light into the grotesque corridor.

"Madre de Dios." Emily pressed herself against Dean. It felt as if her body had grown a hundred hearts, all beating uncontrollably.

Dean's premonition of a burial chamber had not been far off. A trio of parched skulls lay in the corner, their steel dental work melted into curiously satisfied grins. Bone fragments were heaped against the walls, like the leftovers of an archaeological dig. Strewn among the bones were shards of fused metal—perhaps the remains of belt buckles or revolvers or wedding rings. Bizarrely intact in the center of a twisted rib cage was a medal, Hero of the Soviet Union, the highest honor that could be bestowed on a Russian soldier.

Several frozen human hands clutched with outstretched fingers at the door. But they were connected only to ashes or, more accurately, to dust. Dean looked down at his shoes, lightly powdered in white and wondered how many dead soldiers were mingled there.

He moved forward cautiously, trying to avoid trampling the ashes, but it was impossible. They lay thick under his feet, as fine as sand on the whitest beach. He clambered over more bones, the burned sculpture of a bicycle, the black, knotted threads of automatic weapons, unidentified metallic globs, emergency supplies grabbed by the soldiers in their doomed efforts to escape. He looked for an end to the horror but saw none. The heaped ashes extended beyond the limits of the sunlight, into infinite darkness.

"What was it, a bomb shelter?" Emily asked.

"I think the shelter itself is farther down there. This was probably some sort of escape tunnel for the officers at the Air Force base, for the party bigwigs, the KGB personnel. They must have known a missile strike was inevitable and panicked, not trusting their blast shelters. But the tunnel wasn't dug deep enough. When the missiles hit, this whole place became one giant crematorium."

"It's incomprehensible," Emily said, staring at a severed hand dangling from a bank of switches. "But somehow I'm not even repulsed. It's all just dust; it's like they're not even people, and never were."

Dean didn't answer.

He was suddenly back in his childhood, back in his suburban hardware store-outfitted bomb shelter. He and his friends Frankie and Steve were playing Atomic Bomb.

Frankie charged screaming through the shelter, throwing handfuls of C&H powdered sugar into the air.

"Fallout, fallout! Put on your gas masks."

His thick glasses coated with sugar, Frankie dived under a cot. Steve, wearing a radiation suit his mother had sewn out of a Man from U.N.C.L.E. *shower curtain, patrolled ominously, using a clicking kitchen timer as a Geiger counter.*

"I'm the neighborhood civil defense man, and there's about a half million things of radiation in here. You're all dead."

"We are not!" protested Frankie.

"Come off it, you are so."

"Am not. And if I am, you are, too."

"You lose, buckwheat. . . . I got my suit on. I survived. I'm the President of the United States now!"

Suddenly Dean ambushed them from the top bunk where he'd been hiding, brandishing a toy machine gun.

"Prepare to die, Yankee dogs. I'm Boris, the Russian spy, and you stupid Americans left the bomb shelter door open."

Steve looked at Frankie in disgust. "Smooth move, Ex-Lax. Now we're really dead."

I've been prepared for this, Dean thought. This is nothing. It's just a diorama of war brought to sixth-grade show and tell. A book report on World War Three. Duck and cover during recess.

Kids playing atomic bomb.

Emily pointed down the corridor. Two flashlight beams crisscrossed in the darkness. Approaching footsteps stirred up clouds of ashes.

"Richard!" shouted Emily. "Rich, it's me."

At the sound of her voice the flashlights clicked off.

"Come on," Dean whispered. "We're like targets in a shooting gallery in here." They reversed course and ran for the exit, recklessly kicking their way through the bones and ashes.

Outside, they scrambled over a ledge of rock and slogged through the snow to a barrier of trees, careful to keep the tunnel entrance in sight. The stifling compactness of the tunnel had warmed them; the cold came as a stinging shock.

Emily shivered, hugging herself. Dean drew his Tokarev. The trigger was frozen. He breathed on it, slipped off his gloves, and rubbed the frigid metal with his hands.

"I don't understand it . . . where the hell is Richard?" asked Emily.

Dean didn't voice his suspicions. Gardner was probably already dead, the victim of some offstage subterranean duel. The winner was about to surface into the sunlight.

A cloud of breath appeared at the tunnel entrance, like steam escaping from a boiler. A tiny hand clasped the edge of the door; a pair of children's rain boots appeared. A young girl of five or six emerged, wearing a fur hat and parka. Her eyes were troubled and deep-set, her eyebrows wisps of light contrasted with her dark, straight hair. She lugged a teddy bear under one arm, a butane lantern under the other.

She was followed by an older girl of nine or ten, with a long, slender nose and wafer-thin lips, her back bowed beneath a mountaineer's rucksack. Though her hair was straw-colored, she was obviously a sister; Dean saw the same world of experience in her eyes. Her face brightened as it lapped up the sun, and her cheeks flushed.

The mother was next. She was lanky and blond, her hair curled luxuriously, as though she'd had it done just for the escape. She wore hiking boots and puffy mountaineering pants, a jacket that identified her as a Ford mechanic named Eddie. When she turned her blue eyes to the sky, Dean saw them drip with tears.

She enveloped her daughters in a bear hug. They jumped up and down, kissing each other, screaming hysterically. The younger daughter pulled away and battered the others with snowballs. Their laughter was infectious and raucous, soaring through the dead forest.

When Viktor Gerasimov walked out of the tunnel, straining under the weight of two battered suitcases, his smile was already wide and joyous. His single gold tooth glittered like a bolt of lightning.

He wore a pair of headphones on his ears. A Walkman cassette player was tucked into his pocket: Vladimir Raikin's escape map. The map Bukharin had tried to auction at the Kosmos Hotel; the two-faced map that had killed three people, only to turn around and save three others.

Dean whispered to Emily: "The mother is Marina, born 1955; the older daughter is Yelena, born 1979; the young one's name is Rosa, born 1982."

As Rosa looked up at her whispered name, a hoarse voice split the air. "Viktor Gerasimov, you're under arrest for violating Section One-eight-seven of the Occupation Penal Code. Please step away from your family, lower your suitcases to the ground, and turn your palms outward."

Richard Gardner descended the ice steps, pistol extended in a shooter's stance, the detective shield on his pocket catching the sunlight.

Gardner seemed to have aged ten years. His features were slack and washed out, one half of his face dotted with shaving cuts, the other black with a three-day growth of beard. Bags drooped under his eyes, which were red and shifty with exhaustion.

"Richard Gardner, deputy homicide chief, Moscow, northern division. You're charged with the premeditated murder of Andrei Pavlovich Bukharin on November fourth of last year."

"Don't be childish," Gerasimov said. "Do you think I'm going to surrender to you now? Here?"

Gerasimov's wife and daughters were still laughing with one another. Perhaps they didn't speak English, or perhaps they simply didn't believe their newfound freedom could be snatched away so quickly. But Viktor Gerasimov understood perfectly. He didn't move. He didn't lower his suitcases, and he didn't turn out his palms.

"I'm authorized to offer you the services of a military attorney. If you can't afford one, an attorney will be appointed to your defense."

"Your sense of protocol is impressive. I congratulate you."

"I've filed a copy of the arrest warrant at the headquarters of the Military Occupation Police, and it will be available for public inspection next Monday—"

"My God, he's gone crazy," Emily gasped.

Dean and Emily skirted the treeline, avoiding sudden or loud movements. Gardner seemed on autopilot, as he continued to follow the minutiae of arrest procedure, his voice amplified by the cold, dense air.

"My office hours are nine to twelve and three to five, Monday through Thursday. On Fridays—"

"We're at the edge of the world, Mr. Gardner. Your protocol, your devotion to duty—they don't matter out here."

"I have a national mandate. The law is the law, even in Siberia."

"And I must be 'shown the error of my ways,' isn't that the phrase?" asked Gerasimov. Rosa began to cry; his wife and other daughter merely stared with hatred. "Every American seems to be obsessed with his own little moral crusade. But they're harmless; they're temporary. Nothing more than hobbies, really. You Americans have no patience anymore, no real energy left. Which is why you'll eventually give up on Russia. If I stand here motionless for an hour, you'll give up on me, too."

"I could be provoked into shooting you. Quite legally, too."

"You won't shoot me either. Not if I stand here with my eyes open. Your will has gone the way of your patience, it's ridden off into the sunset with John Wayne."

"Nonsense. It's stronger than ever. Russian-American cooperation has strengthened it."

Gerasimov laughed. "You see, you can't even form an original thought anymore. You've just inherited a load of Communist bullshit and slapped an American accent on it."

Gardner began to shiver with indignation. "This is a philosophical question that I think the elections will answer quite nicely. If you like, we can discuss it all on the plane back to Moscow."

Gardner moved forward, gun wobbling, right hand sifting through pockets for handcuffs. "Your family will be provided for, and I personally can assure you that you will receive— that you are owed, I want you to mark that word, owed a fair hearing. Now let's go."

Gerasimov slipped out of the protective circle of his family. "I'm not going to permit myself to be arrested. Surely you can see that. So let's try an experiment, Mr. Gardner. Let's see if you can learn the brutal efficiency it's going to take to run Russia. Go ahead. Shoot me. 'Bring 'em back dead or alive.' Unless you kill me right here, in front of my family, I'm turning around and walking away."

Gerasimov raised his arms, like a bird about to take flight, offering himself as a target.

"Marina, take the girls and walk up the steps to the treeline . . . slowly," Gerasimov ordered his wife.

"Viktor, no," she protested.

"Do it! He won't shoot."

The family crunched carefully across the snow, their eyes darting between Gerasimov's encouraging nods and Gardner's gun.

"I've always loved American cops," Gerasimov said. "But

349

you're a hell of a disappointment—just a propaganda poster with a gun."

Gardner kept his attention focused on Gerasimov, his face webbed with determination. Dean knew he would never let Gerasimov stroll to freedom. But Gerasimov was CIA-trained. Probably someone Dean knew, some instructor right down the hall, had taught Gerasimov gamesmanship, psychological warfare, the art of concealed weapons. He would be a match for anything Gardner tried.

Like hostages released from a hijacked jetliner, Gerasimov's family edged past Gardner, their clothes brushing in a hiss of nylon.

Dean led Emily cautiously toward her husband. No ambush, no surprise attack, Dean thought. Handle Gardner calmly and with care; defuse him one wire at a time.

Gardner spotted Dean and Emily and blinked uncomprehendingly.

Emily paled as she saw her husband in close-up. He was a man stretched out to the limit, a man operating according to a nerveless, internal motor that had taken over when his strength gave out.

"Emily, Dean, what in God's name are you doing here?"

"Trying to prevent a tragedy."

"How on earth did you find me?"

"Frankly, you were never one of my best students at shaking a tail."

"I'm not your student anymore, Dean. I'm not anybody's student. That's been my mistake all along. Relying on teachers, looking to authority for all the answers . . ."

"So you've declared independence. That doesn't mean you can't be rational. Come on, just put down the gun. Let's negotiate our way out of this one."

"No room for negotiations. This man is a killer."

Dean and Emily stepped closer.

Gerasimov began to follow his family.

"Rich, please. Listen to Dean."

"I'm through listening to him."

"You hired me, Richard. Remember."

"Another mistake. I should never have hidden behind you."

"I'm still on the payroll. So why not get your money's worth? Let me help work out a deal, one that'll let everyone walk away in one piece."

"Why would I compromise when I have the gun? Unless—" Gardner suddenly seemed injected with intuition.

He sees it in my eyes, Dean thought. He knows I don't respect him.

"You bastard. You don't think I can handle him myself!"

"Let him go, Rich!" Emily screamed. "Let him win. Let them *all* win. I don't care anymore. Let's go back to Moscow, grab the kids, and keep going. Let's go home. Let's go somewhere else and make it home."

"Soon as I'm finished, honey, soon as I've earned it."

"Rich, please!" Emily rushed toward her husband; Gerasimov charged after his youngest daughter, spun her around, and tore open the flap of her rucksack.

Dean saw it before Gardner did. He raised his Tokarev. It felt bulky and useless in his gloved hand. He tried to take aim at Gerasimov, but his line of fire was blocked by Marina and the children.

When Gardner spotted Dean's gun, his face exploded with disbelief, his eyes a glaze of betrayal.

"You fucking bastard, Joplin!" Gardner swung his own gun toward Dean.

"Not me, Richard!" Dean shouted. "Behind you!"

Dean's legs pumped, but they seemed like imaginary stalks, swimming through air. His boots skidded on the ice, and he tacked over like a sailboat, righting himself with a burning palm . . . and hurled himself at Gerasimov.

From the folds of a Disneyland sweatshirt Gerasimov grabbed a gun, an American police Python. With a speed and brutal accuracy he'd probably honed in a basement shooting range at the American Embassy, he fired at Gardner.

The children screamed. Marina attempted to cover their faces. The butane lantern fell to the ground and shattered.

Gunsmoke coiled to the sky like the dying breath of a camp

fire. The explosions echoed briefly, then fell dead. Insects took over the silence, announcing their survival.

Gardner collapsed against the ice steps. With his stubbled beard and ravaged face, he looked like a bum who'd fallen asleep drunk on the steps of a public building. Emily knelt next to him, holding his wrist in her hand, as a stream of blood soaked into the ice.

Dean felt for a pulse, though he knew it was hopeless. He tore off his gloves to bandage the bleeding, though he knew it was too late.

Empty gestures, but words would be worse.

He looked behind him. The Gerasimov family had scrambled up the ice walls and were slogging away through deep snow.

He went after them.

It was a sloshing, tripping chase in slow motion. Gerasimov led the pack, Rosa perched on his shoulders, followed by Marina and Yelena, holding hands tightly as though they were wading across a stream.

Everyone fell. They picked themselves up and carried on. Dean felt energy draining from him with every step. The snow was deep and soft; it seemed to demand incredible strength just to put one foot in front of the other. When he fell the second time, the cold white ground seemed as warm as a pillow fluffed by a Grand Hotel maid.

I think I'll just sleep here, he thought. He suddenly knew what it was like to be a swimmer carried out to sea by a riptide, arms and legs limp and useless, a curtain dropped over the mind. He'd read somewhere that it was supposed to be euphoric to surrender to nature.

Duty, memory, ambition pricked his brain. I've lost my first client, he thought. Literally lost him. He deserves the maximum, doesn't he? How much should he charge a dead client? What were his daily expenses? Where should he have Natalie send the bill?

He picked up the pursuit, a snail inching across the landscape. But his second fall had revived him, while the Gerasimovs were slowing. Viktor was weaving under the added weight of his daughter. By the time Dean caught him, he was barely moving; Rosa, who'd saved him before, was his downfall now. Before Viktor could set his daughter down and reach for his gun, Dean's Tokarev was pressed roughly into his back.

"Powell and Geary," Dean said, choking for air.

Gerasimov looked at him fiercely. With hatred? With respect?

"Don't insult me. San Francisco."

Marina turned pleading eyes on Dean. "Please, don't arrest us. They'll send us back."

The smell of Gardner's blood was still fresh in Dean's nostrils. "You'll survive. That's a Russian specialty, isn't it?"

Dean backed away from the family so he could cover them all. They were drained—from the chase, from the grisly path of their escape, from the sudden detonation of violence.

"Look, what'll you accomplish by busting us?" Gerasimov asked. "Who'll know? Who'll care?"

"I'll care. The wife of the man you just shot will care."

"He was an unavoidable casualty," Gerasimov answered. "If he'd just let us go in the first place . . ."

"Don't rationalize to me. Don't try to stack one life against another. You began this whole violent spectacle, back when you killed Bukharin!"

"There was no other way. Maybe you'd have liked me to call a travel agency. I'd like three tickets out of the NUCDET zone, please? Smoking or nonsmoking, sir? Window or aisle seat?"

"You were a valuable asset to the CIA. The only agent they'd ever placed inside an ICBM base. You could have gone to your old buddies, they'd have helped you get your family out."

"You don't think I didn't try? Look, I was lucky. I was in Moscow for a debriefing when the war broke out. So for three months after the armistice I presumed my family was dead. Did my 'old buddies' try to find out the truth? Send out a search party, pull strings? They didn't give a rat's ass. The war

353

was won; they were all trying to outhustle each other to hang on to their jobs.

"Finally, when the phone service was restored, I got a call from Marina herself. They'd been out of the city during the attack. On some cultural visit to the Barguzin sable farms. I contacted the MOPs, the occupation secretary, the reunification director. I explained how valuable I'd been. I showed them copies of the notes I'd assembled on the Soviet *nachalstvo.* Sorry, they said, it's a whole new ball game now. They had no idea who I was! They couldn't find my file. My contacts at the embassy had all been replaced, the information I'd risked my life to gather fed into some computer somewhere and forgotten. We can't let you into the NUCDET zone, they said. It's against the law. As if I hadn't broken every law in the book for them.

"America crumbled into dust for me at that moment. I realized you have no memory, while we Russians have nothing but memories."

Rosa and Yelena recovered their energy. They began to chase each other through the snow, perhaps assuming their parents were playing some obscure, boring adult game.

Viktor looked up at the sky. The thin streak of a contrail followed a passenger jet, heading north.

"Texas Air," Viktor said. "New polar route: Peking to New York. You're even buying up our sky."

"You don't know what it's like in there," Marina said. "People die from common colds; they hang themselves from chandeliers in hotel lobbies. The concert halls are hospitals; the museums are cancer wards. An entire city waiting to die. I'll drown my children before I'll send them back."

Again, like so much in Russia, it all came down to children. They were the ultimate bargaining chip. The deals that could have been struck at Geneva, Dean mused, if our negotiators had slapped a single, squealing, swaddled Russian baby on the table and demanded disarmament as the price for sparing his life.

"How did the Company lure you into its net?" Dean asked. "What in God's name did they promise you back then to set this whole thing in motion?"

"They promised to make me an American."

The Angara River wound into the invisible north like a frozen superhighway. Marina Gerasimova knelt by her children, buttoning buttons and turning up collars. Viktor peered through binoculars, hunting for the glint of an approaching truck.

Dean stood off to the side, trying to imagine all the outrageous promises the CIA must have fed Viktor: His family would be spirited out of the Soviet Union on false passports, they'd have bank accounts at Chase Manhattan and brokerage accounts at PaineWebber. An apartment on the Upper West Side would be waiting for them, the refrigerator stocked with T-bone steaks for their arrival. They'd have front-row seats for every Broadway show in town; they'd dine at the Tavern on the Green with the casts. Viktor would sip scotch during a tête-à-tête with the President, Marina would have tea with the First Lady. They'd meet Michael Jackson and Frank Sinatra, Clint Eastwood and Meryl Streep, David Rockefeller and Donald Trump. They'd spend weekends ballooning with Malcolm Forbes; they'd have lifetime first class passes on American Airlines. They could pick and choose the careers of their choice: Did Marina want to write romance novels? Here's Jacqueline Onassis, your editor. Did Viktor want to become a nationally syndicated talk-show host? Say hello to Phil Donahue. Did the kids want to appear on *Sesame Street*? Big Bird's waiting downstairs with the limo.

Just give us another couple of months, Viktor, and it's all yours. Just stick with Vladimir Raikin when he moves to the SS-11 base in Drovyanaya, and tell us what it's like. Move your family out there, too; we'll spring for it. We're all just family men here, right, Viktor? Just a few more photographs, Viktor, and try to sharpen up the focus on the next batch, OK? Just a couple more transmissions, a telex or two, maybe a tape recording of secured phone conversations between Drovyanaya and Moscow. Just give us a little bit more, Viktor. You know the American sayings by now: Give us that extra edge, give us 110 percent, go that extra mile. . .

"Can I ask you a professional question, Viktor? One ex-spy to another?"

Gerasimov nodded, binoculars glued to his face.

"How the hell did you get out of the hotel room without attracting any attention?"

"I relied on the Russian fear of authority, A well-dressed businessman leaving a hotel suite with a briefcase is unlikely to be questioned."

It was so simple. So obvious. The item Dean had always sensed was missing from Bukharin's possessions, his briefcase.

"You wore one of Bukharin's suits," Dean said. "Carried Bukharin's briefcase with your bloodstained clothes and the murder weapon inside."

"Call it a self-defense weapon. A glaciologist's saw. They use it to cut snow samples. I figured I'd need it out here. When Bukharin realized I wasn't going to let him sell the map to anyone else, even if the bid was higher, he freaked. He had a gun, some old Russian thing, tucked under his pillow, like a sad little gangster. The saw was the only thing I could think of."

"And the phone tap in my basement. That was yours, too, wasn't it? How did you scare that up— Why am I even asking the best *tolkach* in Moscow?"

"There's quite a supply of used spy equipment kicking around Moscow these days. Used spies, too, I hear. Jealous wives have never had it so good; I predict that the secret affair is a thing of the past."

He lowered the binoculars and looked at Dean. It's those eyes, Dean realized. The deal maker's eyes. They look right through your defenses, cut away the facade of politeness. They penetrate the gift wrapping directly to the price tag. But when it came to America, they'd been blinded.

"Now I have a question for you. Why are you really letting us walk? Is it to apologize for the missiles before the memory fades?"

Dean didn't answer. A truck approached with a rumble of backfires. The ice seemed to vibrate. The Gerasimovs leaped into the air, whirling their arms and shouting. The truck stopped in a spray of ice. Viktor scowled. It was loaded with Coca-Cola.

Dean identified himself to the Russian driver as Deputy Homicide Police Chief Richard Gardner. He introduced the Gerasimovs as a war-torn family reunited through the selfless, dedicated cooperation of American police and the Russian Re-unification Authority. The driver agreed to carry the family as far north as they wished and helped Marina and the children into the cab.

Viktor looked up at his waiting family, as they each accepted a Coke from the driver. "I feel like Dostoyevsky," he said. "Pardoned from a firing squad at the last moment by the czar."

"Dostoyevsky ended up exiled to Siberia," Dean pointed out.

Gerasimov extended his arm to the horizon. "So will we. We'll find some little town where the trees are still alive and set up shop. As far away from government . . . all government, as possible."

Gerasimov loaded his gear onto the back of the truck and climbed into the flatbed.

"You still haven't answered my question."

"I don't intend to. Now get the fuck out of here before I change my mind about letting a murderer go free."

"You still consider me a murderer?" Gerasimov asked in disbelief. "After all I've told you?"

"A motive isn't an excuse. It wasn't under communism; it isn't now.'"

Dean nodded to the truck driver, who wrenched the gearshift forward.

"Then why?"

Dean thought of his own family, splintered, acrimonious, isolated from one another by time and geography. Then he thought of the Gardners, of the pain, the impossible decisions and the blank days that lay in their future. He looked at the Gerasimov girls and Marina, already swigging on their second Cokes, pointing excitedly up the river toward a green fringe of living trees on the crest of a hill.

"You expressed it quite eloquently yourself. What the hell good would it do?"

Gerasimov stared at Dean, perplexed. He's trying to see through me, Dean thought. He knows it's not that superficial. But he has the common sense . . . and the grace not to press. As the truck lumbered off, he staggered forward between the shuddering cargo. Dean watched him wave to his family through the cab window; then the truck turned, and Gerasimov was hidden behind a caramel-colored forest of Coke bottles

Emily claimed she understood, claimed she'd be able to forgive.

But not yet, she said, and Dean wasn't about to argue.

They lit a fire, and she waited by her husband's body while Dean trekked back to New Irkutsk to arrange for a military helicopter. It was nearly midnight by the time the chopper lifted off with the body, now encased in a government-issue aluminum coffin. Dean looked down at the diminishing landscape, and in the glare of the strobing anticollision lights, he saw a team of Army engineers welding the escape tunnel door shut. His hand closed on the tape of the escape map in his pocket. Viktor Gerasimov had given it to him, asking only that he share its secrets judiciously. Was it still worth anything, now that the escape route was plugged? Or was it just a morbid plastic souvenir?

In the New Irkutsk Guard Division headquarters, there were questions and forms and tears. Though the death of a Moscow homicide inspector was a major event on their watch, the night shift officers went easy on the grieving widow, relying on Dean to recount the night's events. He told them he was a private investigator hired to help Emily's husband in his pursuit of a dangerous felon. He'd obviously failed. The husband was dead; the killer had vanished into the taiga. The soldiers were skeptical, but Emily numbly corroborated Dean's lies.

Dean sat in the dingy offices for three hours, as the soldiers filled out papers, showering Emily with concern, shooting Dean glances that bristled with their contempt for his perceived incompetence. Toward dawn the soldiers considered waking their superior officer but decided against it. The choice was theirs: Either believe Dean and Emily, or stir up a maelstrom of bureaucratic activity, which could very well lead to their freezing their asses off, digging through the forest for clues. Ultimately, on the frontier of a half-dead city, Richard Gardner was just another inconvenient victim.

The flight back to Moscow was interminable. Dean sat in the back, unable to sleep or eat. Behind a first class curtain at the front of the plane, Emily sat next to the coffin. The comparisons were inevitable: Jackie Kennedy flying back to Washington with the murdered President. Dean thought of Richard Gardner's obsession with JFK and smiled.

The military commander from New Irkutsk had notified Moscow. Dean and Emily were met at the airport by a red carpet of official mourning and separated by MOP authorities. Emily rode with the body in a Lincoln limousine to the Kremlin Polyclinic on Kalinin Prospekt, where Gardner would undergo an official autopsy in an environment once reserved for the Soviet elite. Dean was driven to MOP headquarters, where he endured seven hours of debriefing.

He told them what they wanted to hear. He'd been helping Gardner on the Kosmos Hotel case. Yes, he knew, it was a violation of his series 000 charter. He'd gone with Gardner to New Irkutsk in pursuit of a suspect. Gardner had been shot by said suspect. Dean had tried to save him but had screwed it up. The suspect had fled into the NUCDET zone Kind of tough to put out a warrant for him.

Of course, Gardner was responsible for the key breakthroughs in the investigation. A hell of a detective; a credit to your MOP training. I was just his backup; little more than a sounding board really.

Oh, yes, we remember you, Mr. Joplin. We had to let you go right after the armistice. Still haven't gotten yourself back on course, we see. Well, a word of advice: Stick to peeking through keyholes and leave police work to the professionals. Occupied Moscow is no place for meddlers, no matter how well meaning.

Dean left shortly after midnight, Moscow time. There'd be further hearings at which his attendance would be mandatory, but with Emily backing him up, he didn't expect serious trouble.

At first he was surprised that he'd emerged from the interrogation with his detective license intact. But then he realized it wasn't strange at all. The police considered him a fuck-up. They liked anybody who made them look good.

He never mentioned a word about Gardner's connection to the Mafia and its ambassador at large, Taylor Willis.

He was determined to see that Gardner remained unblemished in official eyes and, as far as it was possible, in Emily's eyes, too.

Then he went home and slept.

Three weeks later he was back at Sheremetyevo Airport.

They sat in a burgundy Naugahyde booth, sipping see-through coffee and picking at plates of sticky apple pie. The flags of the fifty states adorned the walls; the entrées were named after American Presidents. The remains of three Roosevelt burgers and a U.S. Grant taco salad littered the table, ignored by indifferent waitresses. It was the first Denny's coffee shop in Russia.

"It's kind of like a decompression chamber in here," said Dean. "Easing you back into America."

"I don't think I'll have any trouble making the adjustment at all. It'll be tough on the kids at first." Emily nodded toward Jack and Bryn, who stood on the observation deck, watching the ground crew fuel their Washington-bound Delta 767.

"They've always got their 'perfect' grandmother," Dean said.

"I think Jack's inherited that role. He's been great, hasn't he? The way he's taken care of Bryn."

"I love his explanation: 'Only Dad's skin has died; the rest of him still lives with us.'"

"She'll grow into the real explanation soon enough."

"Provided you keep her out of the hands of well-meaning child psychologists."

Dean saw the silver flash of Gardner's coffin gliding up the ramp into the cargo bay and tried to distract Emily by loudly adding up the check.

"Do you believe this? Seventeen rubles! You haven't even left the ground yet, and they're already charging American prices."

She suddenly seized Dean's hand and pulled their bodies together. Her breath on his neck was hot and smelled of cinnamon. Her voice cracked, like a drama student delivering a speech she hasn't had time to rehearse.

"Listen, Dean. I haven't slept for nights thinking about this. Why don't you come with us? The kids adore you, we love each other in a way—"

He raised his hands in protest.

"Just hear me out. We wouldn't have to dive off the deep end all at once. We wouldn't even have to live together at first. But we'd be there for each other. You'd have a family ready to step into when you felt the time was right. We'd go to Havana on vacations; we'd get drunk on rum and console each other when the subject of Richard came up."

"Emily, please."

Emily sipped her cold coffee with a grimace. "I could get a job at State, and you'd—"

"I'd what?"

"Well, you could open another detective agency. They still have crime and infidelity in America, you know."

"Hold it, hold it. I can't picture myself as good old Uncle Dean, the pathetic little guy in the plaid pants with his own business, who hangs around the widow until a decent interval has passed, then proposes marriage. If I were going to start a family again, I said if, I'd want to start one from scratch."

"You don't want one that's slightly used but could run like new in a few months?"

"You'll always be his, Emily. I'll never get past that. You need someone who comes to you fresh, who doesn't know your history. I'm a guy who can get very hung up on history."

Emily nodded and began to trace patterns in her ketchup with a toothpick. "You're right, you son of a bitch. I knew what you'd say. But I wanted to do the polite thing and ask."

She tried to pull away, but Dean held on tightly.

"Will you ever come back to the good old USA?" Emily asked.

"I don't think so. Look, Emily, I don't feel Russian, and I don't feel American." He tapped the menu, and read the description of Denny's combo number five aloud: "'A half pound of Texas beef, fresh from the wide-open spaces, broiled to perfection, then lightly flamed in a shot of *zubrovka* vodka.' You see, this is where I belong."

They sat silently for another half hour, thigh to thigh, and Dean was reminded of their drive through the back roads, and the night they'd spent together. He hoped she was daydreaming of it, too.

A Delta chaplain appeared, fawning and impersonal, and asked if Emily and the kids would like to spend a few "reflective moments in the chapel before embarking." She rolled her eyes at Dean and blew the stray hairs off her forehead, the challenging, skeptical expression that had captivated him when they first met.

"No, thank you," she said curtly. Then she looked at Dean and gave him a searing kiss. "We'll be fine."

She walked out of the coffee shop, scooped up the kids, and marched toward the plane.

As Dean paid the check, he spotted something glinting beneath her coffee-stained saucer. He picked it up, and examined it curiously, walking it across his fingers like a magician's coin. It was the Military Occupation Police's Medal of Valor, given for "conspicuous gallantry and sacrifice in the service of the United Peoples of the Occupied Soviet Union."

Awarded to Richard W. Gardner posthumously.

Emily had left it as a tip.

Baryshnikov danced Twyla Tharp on a float donated by the New York City Ballet. The Red Army chorus sang Stephen Foster; the Pointer Sisters sang Vladimir Vysotsky.

Spartak Moscow played the Philadelphia Flyers on a mobile hockey rink; the New York Yankees played pepper on a patch of infield towed by a VAZ station wagon

The Kremlin wall viewing stand thundered for the first time with the pitter-patter of little feet. Children from all fifty states and all fifteen Soviet republics were boosted up on risers, so they could wave to the audience massed in Red Square.

Military hardware was nowhere in sight. Veterans' groups had protested; the Pentagon was furious. But it was David Wolper's show all the way, and he felt a display of weaponry and marching soldiers would contradict the "feel-good feeling" of the first election day parade.

Heated VIP bleachers stretched in front of Lenin's tomb. They were bunched with the obligatory dignitaries: MOP officers, the American Vice President and the speaker of the House, the Joint Chiefs of Staff, the deposed general secretary of the Communist Party, and several ex-members of the ex-Politburo. They were joined by a surrealistic collection of invited guests: Walter Cronkite, Lee Iacocca, Coretta King, George Steinbrenner, Gary Kasparov, John McEnroe, Mariel and Margaux Hemingway, Bruce Springsteen and Russian rock star Boris Grebenshchikov. Aleksandr Solzhenitsyn had stubbornly refused to attend, but returning exiles Natan Sharansky, Arkady Shevchenko, Joseph Brodsky, and Rudolf Nureyev made up for his absence.

Behind the bleachers were four flagpoles, each flying a banner emblazoned with a single letter. The acronym for the experimental society whipped in the cold wind, still more a taunt than a political reality: U.S.S.A., the United Soviet States of America.

Dean had wangled passes to the VIP standing section, and he and Vera Polivanova stood in the shadows of the CNN cameras, nipping on a bottle of cognac for warmth.

Vera's experiment with aimlessness had finally failed. She'd realized life was unendurable without some sort of order or discipline. The men she'd met while living at the airport Sheraton had been transients; though they'd given her their phone numbers in the cities they came from, she knew that once they'd walked through the passport control at Sheremetyevo, she would never see them again.

She'd awakened Dean early the morning of the election and insisted they attend the parade.

Was it curiosity or fear that dictated to Vera now? If American democracy would truly be calling the shots from now on, maybe she'd feel safer committed to a democractic American lover. Did she want a political alliance that was separate from a romantic relationship? It seemed that Vera's external and internal lives, like those of many Russians, would never blend. It was a schizophrenia Dean was used to and had even begun to appreciate.

The crowd turned to a giant Mitsubishi color television screen which hung from the facade of the GUM department store. Nightmarish, unrecognizable shadows of Dan Rather and Vladimir Posner jousted across the screen in a vapor of electronic dots and lines, before finally forming into clear side-by-side images.

They began to announce the election results, occasionally consulting their colleagues draped across Russia for exit poll analysis. The initial results were discouraging. Not for any particular candidate but for the process as a whole. It seemed that Russian voters were not streaming to the polls as hoped; instead, they were waiting around their televisions and their dinner tables. Perhaps hoping for a trend, perhaps hoping for orders. Was change permanent, or was it just cosmetic? Better to wait and see. Better to fall asleep, better to let tomorrow decide today. As always, a Russian proverb sprang to mind. He'd heard it his first day in Moscow as he'd unpacked his books in his office and looked out on the gray-toothed skyline with its scattered crowns of bloodred stars: "Morning is more clever than night."

There was an impatient bustle in the crowd to Dean's left. An overcoated VIP was making an early exit. Dean recognized him by his ostrichskin Tony Lama boots, Taylor Willis. Dean slipped through the crowd until he blocked Willis's path.

The attorney stroked his aluminum hair and examined Dean disdainfully, like a boss who has unexpectedly encountered a dismissed employee.

"Well, Mr. Joplin," he said, in his polished Bronx accent,

"it's good to see you out here on such an auspicious day. We can all use a little optimism in our lives . . . especially considering the tragedy we've both been associated with."

Willis looked over his shoulder. Hovering nearby, part bodyguard, part valet, was the tanned, eager police lieutenant with the Hollywood face who had supervised the raid on the White Palm.

"How's your new boy in the police department working out?" Dean asked.

"Much less trouble than your Mr. Gardner. I don't expect Lieutenant Myers there to develop any sudden pangs of conscience, any unexpected need for independence." He looked up at the podium, where the Vice President and the former general secretary were toasting each other.

"It's a shame about the map, though." He sighed. "I'd always imagined it would be like owning a private road through the Berlin Wall. Think of all the good we could have done."

"Not to mention the money you could have made."

The election results paraded across the giant TV screen. The crowd shifted and ebbed restlessly; the applause and cheers were subdued, tentative. The numbers coming out of the precincts were confirming a shockingly meager voter turnout.

They don't care, Dean thought. We've given them nothing to care about.

"It would have been spectacular from a financial standpoint, yes. And I had hoped that Richard Gardner would be the man to profit from it with us."

"But there'll always be other cops for sale, right?" Dean said.

"And there'll always be other ways to make money in Russia. Democracy will see to that."

Dean stared at Willis. His eyes were so clear. His shoulders so confident. The scarf that neatly ringed his neck was so damned white.

He looked so . . . forgiven.

"I hear the mob's a great believer in democratic institutions."

Willis was still unruffled. He reached for his habitual eyedrops, drawing out the gesture to underline his lack of concern.

"That horseshit again. I drove three Arizona newspapers into Chapter Eleven when they started reporting unsubstantiated allegations against me. And they had three-hundred-dollar-an-hour lawyers on their side." He smiled indulgently at Dean. "They were never able to link me to any crime, let alone organized crime. How far do you honestly think you'll get with your imaginary little charges?"

"As far as my 'imaginary evidence' will take me."

Willis sighed wearily. "What am I accused of this time? Income tax evasion? Jury tampering? Whom do I make out the check to?"

"Oh, I'm not in this for the money. And the charge this time will be murder."

"Whose?"

"Anatoly Mintz's . . . Nina Zinovieva's . . ."

Willis's pockets bulged as his fists clenched inside them— the only outward sign that he was surprised by the extent of Dean's knowledge.

"How do you intend to prove it?"

"The guard you paid to look the other way while you killed Mintz is out there somewhere. With a guilty conscience that's only going to get guiltier. I'll find him."

"His word against mine. I'm a prominent attorney; he's just a disgruntled former policeman. There's no proof there."

"I've got a touchingly loyal secretary who'll testify that Yuli Grinkov attempted to kill her. With a little homework I can connect Grinkov to you."

"And with a little more homework, I can make those connections seem very dubious," Willis retorted.

"I'll do some ballistics work, match Nina's wounds to your gun. . . ."

"That, of course, presumes you can trace the gun to me, that I bought the gun under my own name from a legitimate dealer. For God's sake, why put yourself through this? What are two more Russian deaths after all we've done to them?"

"Three, but who's counting?"

"I'm not, and you shouldn't be either. Sentimentality looks ridiculous on an ex-CIA agent."

"An ex-CIA agent with a lot of time on his hands. I've cleared off my desk, Mr. Willis. You're my only assignment. The Bukharin case was just practice. Spring training. Honing the skills I'd let deteriorate. I'm at the top of my game now, and you're just the kind of project I need to sink my teeth into. I'm making you my crusade. My private experiment in democracy. I'll prove you're guilty of murder, and I'll get the military courts to indict you."

"Courts don't indict on the basis of an experiment . . . not even in Russia."

"But they might indict on the basis of a recording," Dean said.

"Recording of what?"

"Of you committing a murder."

Dean watched Willis's skin tighten as his legal mind rewound through the last two months, searching for flaws, for mistakes, trying to determine if Dean was a serious adversary or just bluffing.

"You seem to have an unlimited capacity for self-delusion, Mr. Joplin. Who would have made a tape like that?"

"Your victim."

Dean reached into his pocket and flipped the playback switch on the cassette recorder. Not loud enough to attract attention, just loud enough for the two of them to hear. Nina Zinovieva's voice crackled through the tiny speaker, describing the escape route from the NUCDET zone.

Willis leaned closer, his eyes suddenly flecked with anxiety.

Dean fast-forwarded. There was a blur of static, followed by Taylor Willis's voice, cold and commanding: "I admit it was a mistake to force the confrontation on the street. It was callous, impetuous."

Willis was magnetized, his anxiety shading toward disbelief. Dean advanced the tape. Willis's voice continued: "And in the time it takes you to reload, my Kalashnikov will pour a hundred rounds in the direction of your muzzle flash."

"Where the hell did you get that?" Willis growled.

Dean ignored him and turned up the volume as the tape spun to its conclusion, the gruesome, seemingly endless chatter of Willis's Kalashnikov.

"Maybe it was part of her plan . . . or maybe she accidentally hit the record button," Dean said. "In any event Nina Zinovieva recorded her own death." Dean patted his pocket. "You've got to appreciate the irony, Mr. Willis. "The same tape you've been searching for is going to plant your ass in jail."

The veins on Willis's desert-tanned neck stood out like snakes. His confident facade began to flake.

The gunfire on the tape still echoed in Dean's mind, drowning out the loudspeakers, the marching bands, the balalaika orchestras, the deadly platitudes from the podium.

"You fucking son of a bitch." Willis lunged toward Dean.

Come on, Dean thought. Just give me an excuse. Dean's hand jumped from the cassette player to his pocketknife. He wanted to slit open Willis's stomach right there; he wanted the world that watched CNN to watch his amoral blood drip onto the cobblestones of Red Square.

But then Willis stopped. A fierce dignity flashed across his features. Lieutenant Myers spotted his boss and tried to thrash through the crowd toward him. Willis waved him off.

"I'm not a street brawler, Mr. Joplin. We'll settle this another time, in another place."

"Count on it," Dean answered.

Willis's eyes appraised Dean from head to foot, trying to worm inside him. But Dean gazed back with bland confidence, and for the first time he saw fear collect in Willis's face. Willis backed away, straightening his tie, inflating his shoulders, trying to restore his aura of superiority.

He can't do it, Dean thought. He can't shake his fear. Perfect. His fear is my retainer. His doubts, his apprehensions, the over-the-shoulder life that I'll force him to lead will be my hundred and fifty rubles a day, plus expenses.

I've done a good day's work.

The crowd ebbed and jostled, in impatient waves. The scene on the television screen shifted from the depressing voter turnout to the production trailer behind the Kremlin walls. David Wolper gave the signal, and a hundred thousand balloons were set free from hidden positions behind the onion domes of St. Basil's Cathedral. Emblazoned with the words "peace" and *mir,* they disappeared into the low overcast above Red Square like champagne bubbles.

Dean turned and pushed through a wall of people, his hand searching for Vera's. When he found it, he grabbed it so tightly she gasped in pain.

He didn't relax his grip until he'd freed them from the crowd and they were hurrying down a snow-dusted gray alley, their only pursuers a trio of red, white, and blue balloons.